Tempt Me Twice

PRAISE FOR BARBARA DAWSON SMITH
AND HER NOVELS

Countess Confidential

"Smith outdoes herself with a romantic suspense that not only keeps you turning the pages, but . . . turns the tables on you until you're breathless for the truth to surface . . . A major craftsman of the genre."

—*RT BOOKclub Magazine* Top Pick

"In her latest elegantly written and subtly sexy Regency, Smith neatly untangles a complex plot composed of equal measures of desire and danger."

—*Booklist*

"Tremendous . . . exhilarating story line . . . Claire is a delight."

—*Midwest Book Review*

"A delightful fast-paced story with charming characters, great dialogue, and plenty of sexual tension."

—*Rendezvous*

The Duchess Diaries

"With a strong mystery as the backdrop and sizzling sexual tension throughout, Dawson's enthralling tale of murder and passion will keep you up all night."

—*RT BOOKclub Magazine*

"A wonderfully captivating tale . . . the mystery is well-crafted and will keep readers guessing to the very end."

—*Romance Reviews Today*

"Smith has penned a charming, easy-to-read novel . . . fans will find this a treasure."

—*Huntress Reviews*

More . . .

The Rogue Report

~

Barbara Dawson Smith

ST. MARTIN'S PAPERBACKS

THE ROGUE REPORT

Copyright © 2006 by Barbara Dawson Smith.

ISBN: 0-312-93240-5
EAN: 9780312-93240-4

Printed in the United States of America

St. Martin's Paperbacks edition / June 2006

St. Martin's Paperbacks are published by St. Martin's Press, 175 Fifth Avenue, New York, NY 10010.

10 9 8 7 6 5 4 3 2 1

The
Rogue
Report

Jack William Mansfield, the Earl of Rutledge, was leaning over the billiards table, lining up a difficult shot, when he learned that his fiancée had called off the wedding.

"Evelyn found out about your party," Gresham announced. "She says you've humilated her for the last time."

A trim man with clean-cut features and sandy-brown hair, George Gresham was Evelyn's cousin. He had been observing the match between Jack and Whistler for the past ten minutes, bouncing back and forth on his heels, clearly waiting for the opportune moment to unload his shattering news.

No wonder. Gresham had staked ten guineas on Whistler.

Jack concentrated on the layout of the table. With the leather tip of the cue, he sent the ivory ball careening across the green baize to strike the edge and change direction, knocking Whistler's ball out of play and his own into the corner pocket, where it landed with a *thunk*.

Gresham and Whistler groaned in unison. "The devil's own luck," said Albert, Viscount Whistler, in his usual gloomy manner.

"Not luck," Jack said. "Geometry."

When both men gazed blankly, Whistler with his shaggy black hair and slumped shoulders beside finely groomed Gresham, Jack decided against explaining the practical application of scalene and isosceles triangles. He oughtn't have blurted out such a revealing remark, anyway. Better to foster the myth of his pact with the devil—and to display his legendary coolness in the face of financial crisis.

Yet the prospect of losing Evelyn left him reeling. *Who had told her?* It couldn't have been Gresham; he wouldn't want his cousin to find out that he'd also attended the party. Nor would any of the other gentlemen have tattled lest their wives and mothers and sisters rake them over the coals of disapproval.

In a show of insouciance, Jack strolled to the other side of the table and contemplated his next shot. A pair of oil lamps cast a soft yellow glow over the table. A faint haze of tobacco smoke emanated from the cheroot that dangled between Gresham's fingers.

Gresham planted his hands on the rosewood edge of the table and glowered at Jack. "Good God, man! Is that *all* you have to say?"

"No." Jack gazed pointedly at the cheroot. "Let me add, if any ash falls onto my table we'll be meeting at Hampstead Heath tomorrow at dawn."

Gresham hastily retreated a step. Tipping the column of ash into an empty brandy glass, he barked, "Blast it, old chap, what about Evelyn? You've lost her—and the creditors will be swarming like vultures on your carcass."

"Just think of that dowry," Whistler added, driving another nail into Jack's coffin. "Ain't a richer heiress in all of London."

Or a more vain, self-important one, either. Jack didn't fool himself that Evelyn would be heartsick with grief. Along with her money, she had inherited a deplorably pragmatic side from a merchant grandfather. She and Jack had made a bargain; she would pay off his debts in exchange for becoming a countess and, someday, a duchess, for he was heir to the Duke of Wycliffe. But she had also stipulated that any further losses at gambling would put an end to their betrothal.

He clenched his jaw. Hell, why was he worried? For all her practicality, Evelyn was young and beautiful—and she desired him. He'd yet to meet a woman he couldn't charm.

Cue stick in hand, he leaned over the table. "So she heard a rumor. I'll convince her it was false."

"Not this time." Gresham reached inside his tailored green coat and drew out a folded document, which he flung onto the table. "My uncle is out for your blood—and so's Evelyn. Have a look."

Unfolding the paper, Jack anchored it in place with the tip of his cue. He cursed under his breath. *The Rogue Report* was the scourge of every scapegrace in the *ton*. For the past few years, the printed broadsheet had been delivered once a fortnight to the unmarried ladies of society. It was slipped under their front doors at night, and no one knew the identity of its author.

Thus far, Jack had escaped with only a few minor skewerings. He had laughed at acquaintances whose profiles in the scandal sheet had caused them grief with their families. After all, he didn't have any female relatives to plague him—and his own father and grandfather had been featured in *The Rogue Report* themselves.

But Jack wasn't laughing now. Lips thinned, he

scanned the detailed description of the party at his town house.

> *By day, the drawing room of the Earl of R. is a tasteful haven decorated in blue and gold. By night, it is a cesspit of profligate activities. Last week, the Infamous Earl hosted a private party where lightskirts entertained the gentlemen and vast sums were wagered on the turn of a card. It is said that the Earl himself lost an enormous amount . . .*

The story went on, uncannily accurate, right down to the hookah pipe in the sitting room, the horde of whores, and the thousand guineas he'd lost at cards that night.

Money he didn't have. Money he'd signed vowels to repay as soon as he and Evelyn walked down the aisle at St. George's next month.

But if there was one thing Evelyn valued above all else, it was her spotless reputation. She would never forgive him for this public humiliation.

The truth hammered him. *There would be no wedding.*

Whistler craned to see past Jack's shoulder. "My name ain't mentioned, is it? Mama nearly took the whip to me when she read that story last spring about the fire in the whorehouse."

"Next time," Jack quipped, "remember to grab your clothes on the way out."

"Enough of your jests," Gresham spluttered. "My father's been like a bear with a sore tooth ever since he fell ill. He's cut off my allowance, and I'm short of funds. I could use that hundred guineas you owe me."

"Righto," Whistler added, drawing himself up to his full, rangy height. "There's your sixty to me, too."

Jack shrugged. "You'll have your funds, gentlemen. Starting with me winning this game."

But as he lined up his next shot, he felt caught in a real-life version of the nightmare he had from time to time. He was chained in a deep black pit, slowly suffocating, a dense weight pressing down on him. He would wake up gasping, struggling to suck air into his lungs.

Now, he felt the dampness of sweat beneath his coat. It wasn't merely the loss of money that troubled him. Not even his friends knew that he'd wanted this marriage for more complicated reasons. Reasons Jack didn't entirely understand himself. Reasons that had to do with the gnawing discontent inside him, a feeling that had begun after he'd nearly killed a man in a duel eight years ago.

Imprisoning the memory, he refolded the scandal sheet and tucked it into an inner pocket of his coat. He had no one to blame but himself for losing Evelyn. Nevertheless, for the first time in his misbegotten life, Jack Mansfield had a mission.

He wanted revenge.

A scapegrace will not hesitate to tell falsehoods when it suits his purposes. One such man is Lord N.C., who continually lies to his creditors by promising payment on his bills . . .
—*The Rogue Report*

Chapter One

Two weeks later

As the gray-bearded old man shuffled out of her office, Lady Julia Corwyn still hadn't made a decision.

She felt hot and sticky and out of sorts. Late afternoon sunlight slanted across the pristine mahogany desk with its tidy stack of papers. If only the solution to her dilemma could be so neat, Julia thought. She'd spent a long, tiresome day interviewing a parade of applicants for the position of mathematics instructor at the Corwyn Academy.

And not one of them was perfect for the job.

To make matters worse, the weather was unseasonably warm for early September. She had the mad urge to strip down to her chemise, stand in front of the open window, and catch what little breeze riffled the tall green draperies. Wouldn't *that* shock the neighbors and confirm their ill opinion of her? She would only add fuel to the fire of their attempts to oust her school from this respectable area of London.

Resigned, she plucked the lacy fichu from her bodice and used it to vigorously fan her face. Little corkscrew curls sprang free from her bun and plastered themselves to her damp neck. Under any other circumstances, she would have repinned the irksome devils—curly hair was truly a curse—but today she didn't bother. The hour was late, and there were no more appointments left in her schedule book.

She forced her attention to the notes from today's final round of interviews. The autumn term had been in session for only a week when Miss Dewhurst, the mathematics instructress, had been called away to her sick mother's bedside in Lancashire. Julia needed a replacement, and quickly. The trouble was, the best teachers had already found positions at other schools. And none of the dozen or so men who had answered her advertisement met her high standards.

Which one was she to hire?

Not old Mr. Blatts; he barely spoke above a whisper, a detriment to controlling a class of spirited children.

Not young Mr. Knightly; he had fidgeted and blushed—while stealing glances at her bosom.

Certainly not pompous Mr. Grimshaw; he had gazed down his sharp nose at her as if disdaining to speak to a fallen woman.

Julia had dismissed him at once. She had long ago vowed to ignore those who judged her. It was far better to expend her energies on worthwhile tasks than to rage at small-minded bigots.

Picking up a quill, she dipped the nib into the ink pot and crossed through those three names. Then another and another, until she threw down the pen in disgust. Either the candidates resented having to seek employment from a lady with a checkered past, or they disliked the notion of teaching the illegitimate offspring of servants.

Blast them all!

And blast the scorching temperature. It made her irritated and indecisive.

On impulse, Julia scooted back the chair, kicked off her shoes, and removed her garters and silk stockings, leaving them in a damp heap beneath the desk. Still fretful, she sprang up to pace the spacious office with its shelves of textbooks and her collection of figurines. The floorboards, at least, felt blessedly cool beneath her bare feet. With its ivory striped chaise, marble mantelpiece, and tall windows, the office was usually a soothing retreat. Yet today, the trill of childish laughter that drifted from the small garden served as a reminder of her dilemma.

By the heavens, if she weren't a complete dunce at sums, she'd teach the class herself!

Swiping at a trickle of perspiration on the side of her neck, she had a sudden vision of herself lying submerged in a cool bath. But the flood of blissful longing met the dam of common sense. The staff had enough to do, preparing supper for forty-eight hungry children, without the headmistress of the school making selfish demands.

Unless she pumped the water herself and hauled the cans upstairs. *Yes.* Half an hour of hard labor would make the end result all the more heavenly. If she had to ponder the dilemma of finding a mathematics instructor, she might as well do it in comfort.

Performing an about-face, Julia started toward the door. She could only imagine what her parents would say to the notion of a Corwyn doing the work of a servant . . . Mama, who considered a trip to the shops exhausting; Papa, who grumbled if he had to get up from his chair in the library to pour himself a brandy. But of course, they knew nothing of her daily life; they had washed their hands of Julia—and their grandson—seven years ago. A deep-seated bitterness stirred in her, but she buried it beneath wry amusement. At least *she* need never complain of idleness or boredom.

As she reached for the knob, the door swung abruptly inward, forcing her to step back. Agnes poked her head into the office. The young maidservant's blue eyes sparkled beneath a white mobcap, and her cheeks glowed with excitement. That flirtatious look put Julia on instant alert.

"Ye've a gennelman caller, m'lady," Agnes said, her Cockney accent more pronounced than ever. She glanced over her shoulder, then added in a reverent whisper, "A right fine one fer a perfessor."

Another applicant?

Julia remembered her shoes and stockings, lying behind the desk. And her lovely bath. "It's past five o'clock. Kindly inform him that I'm no longer taking interviews."

But Agnes—impetuous, silly Agnes, who tended to forget all propriety in the presence of the opposite gender—was already moving back to admit the visitor.

A tall, broad-shouldered man stepped into the office. Julia forgot her good manners and stared. No hunched old scholar this time. Despite her own better-than-average height, she had to tilt back her head to gaze at him.

He had hair the rich dark brown of coffee, slightly long and brushing the back of his collar. His clothing had seen better days. The forest-green coat, frayed at the cuffs, was cut a bit short for his long arms and powerful torso. The plain white cravat called attention to the strong line of his jaw. Tan breeches hugged his legs like a second skin.

Her bare toes curled against the wood floor. He was a man in his prime, around thirty years of age, and so strikingly handsome that she distrusted him on principle. Despite his ill-fitting garb, he exuded an air of panache. If he weren't here seeking a temporary post, she might have mistaken him for an indolent aristocrat—and she'd certainly encountered enough of *them* in her brief stint as a debutante.

The stranger absorbed the tidy surroundings at a glance, then focused his attention on Julia. Her insides lurched and shifted in a way she hadn't felt in eight years—or perhaps ever.

Those eyes.

Framed by dark lashes, they were the same forest green as his coat. Surely it was a sin against nature for a man to possess such beautiful eyes. The boldness of his gaze made her feel an unmistakable echo of the blithe, frivolous, foolish girl she'd once been.

He bowed, then held out his hand. "Good afternoon," he said, his voice deep and mellow with well-bred enunciation. "William Jackman. I'm here to interview for the teaching position. And you must be"—he paused, those marvelous eyes flicking over her dishabille—"Lady Julia Corwyn."

No hint of impropriety colored his tone. Yet with her low bodice, mussed hair, and the bare legs beneath her skirts, she felt at a distinct disadvantage. Mr. Jackman had a frankly sensual air about him and the easy confidence of a man who knows his effect on women.

Most women, anyway. Julia had more sense than to fall prey to a handsome charmer. For the better part of a decade, she had devoted herself to educating her pupils. They—and her son, Theo—were the center of her universe. Nothing could distract her from that purpose.

Especially not a man who looked as if he'd be more at home in a ballroom than in a classroom teaching children.

Ignoring his outstretched hand, she thumbed open the gold watch that was pinned to her bodice. "It's five-eighteen, Mr. Jackman. I'm afraid you've neglected to schedule an appointment during the appropriate hours."

He lowered his arm and gave her an apologetic look. "Forgive me, my lady. I'm new to town, and I only just saw the advertisement. I'd hoped perhaps it wasn't too late for consideration."

Julia parted her lips to voice a polite rebuff. But the thought of all those crossed-out names gave her pause. Was she being too judgmental? Mr. Jackman appeared to be well mannered, at least. What if he also had excellent credentials? Didn't she owe it to her students to interview every possible candidate?

She fought a brief battle with her selfish desire for respite, then inclined her head in a stiff nod. "I shall make an exception, then. Pray be seated."

Turning, she retraced the path to her desk. Sensing those eyes following her progress, she felt as stiff and awkward as a puppet on strings. At least her abandoned shoes and stockings were hidden from his sight. With luck, he wouldn't notice her toes peeking out from beneath her hem.

Then her gaze fixed on her desk. Atop the litter of papers, her fichu lay like a discarded undergarment.

Instantly, she scolded herself. There was no reason to feel so . . . *exposed*. The length of lace was hardly a corset or a chemise.

Reaching the desk, she casually picked up the fichu. And dropped it, for Mr. Jackman loomed at her side.

Her heart skittered madly. He had moved with the swiftness and stealth of a wolf.

"Sir, what are you doing?"

"Assisting you with your chair, my lady." All chivalrous politeness, Mr. Jackman crouched down and scooped the fichu from the floor. "I didn't mean to startle you."

The sight of his long, masculine fingers on the white lace unsettled her . . . as did a whiff of his dark, spicy scent. Her reply came out sharp and shrewish. "I assure you, I'm perfectly capable of seating myself."

"As you wish." He glanced down at the fichu, rubbing it between his fingers as if contemplating the fact that it had so recently lain against her breasts. "How beautiful."

His gaze lifted to hers, and the air seemed to sizzle. She had the distinct impression that his comment had been directed at her rather than at the lace. A giddy burn of pleasure threatened to melt the years of hard-won prudence.

"This lace," he went on after a pause, "is it Belgian?"

She snatched the fichu from him. "Yes."

Seemingly unperturbed by her snappishness, Mr. Jackman remained standing respectfully until she resumed her seat behind the desk. Only then did he settle onto the straight-backed chair opposite her. Despite the sluggish heat, he appeared cool and at ease.

And far more collected than Julia.

Determined to regain her usual efficiency of command, she opened a drawer at random and dropped the fichu inside. She doused the fire in her cheeks with the salt of common sense. He was here to apply for a job. It must be the high temperature that had addled her senses.

That, and the fact that she'd never conducted an interview without shoes and stockings. But she could hardly pull them on while he sat watching with those unsettling eyes.

Taking a deep breath, she launched into her prepared speech. "As stated in the advertisement, I'm in need of an instructor who is well versed in all aspects of mathematics, from simple arithmetic to geometry and algebra. The position involves teaching a wide range of ages, including a class for those just learning their numbers."

Did he blanch ever so slightly? Several of the other candidates had balked at working with very young children.

But Mr. Jackman merely nodded, so she went on. "I

would also point out that my pupils are not the typical boarding-school students. All of them have come from an impoverished background. To put it more bluntly, they are the illegitimate offspring of women from the streets."

He showed no sign of distaste or superiority, only keen interest. "A charity school. Is it funded by you, my lady?"

"I prefer to use the term *academy*," she corrected. "And it is funded by those who have an interest in educating the less fortunate."

Namely, herself.

Julia refused to feel guilty for misleading Mr. Jackman. He was a stranger, after all. He needn't know that a substantial inheritance from her grandmother provided the sole financing for the school.

Men, after all, had a habit of taking advantage of heiresses.

"I see," he said.

Did he? Julia felt the need to impress upon him the importance of her mission. "It is my strict belief that no child should be judged by the circumstances of his birth," she said. "Consequently, my students must be treated with the same respect one would afford the privileged children of the gentry. If you've any objection to that philosophy, Mr. Jackman, then there is no point in further discussion."

"I've only admiration for your work, my lady. Pray, go on."

Sitting relaxed in the chair opposite her, he looked both alluringly handsome and incongruously earnest. Flustered by his compliment, Julia picked up the quill, dipped it in the inkwell, and added his name to the bottom of the list of candidates. *Mr. William Jackman.*

In the next instant, she had to subdue the dreamy, schoolgirlish urge to doodle *Julia Jackman* on the paper, as well.

She laid down the pen at once. Her cheeks were burning again, her body overheated beyond the effects of the sultry day. What was wrong with her? She was no longer a flighty debutante who fell in love with every attractive man who tossed her a compliment. Harsh reality had scoured her life of all romantic inclinations. Maturity had awakened her to the value of devoting her life to a worthy cause. Now, she had a school to operate and a position to fill.

Besides, for all she knew, William Jackman already had a wife and half a dozen children. Her gaze stole to his hands. They looked elegant, proficient, masculine. He wore no gold ring, but that didn't necessarily mean anything.

Annoyed with herself, she continued crisply, "What is your experience in teaching, Mr. Jackman? I should like to know the names of the schools at which you have been on staff."

"I'm afraid the answer is none."

He flashed a winsome smile, and Julia found herself paying undue heed to the dimples that bracketed his mouth. "None?"

"Quite so. You see, I've spent the past ten years as a tutor for a family in Devonshire. The last son has gone off to attend Eton, so I'm in search of new employment."

She seized on the deficiency. "Then you've never been in charge of a classroom of students."

"I beg to differ. The Ballingers have a dozen energetic children who required my firm guidance."

Julia had to admit Mr. Jackman looked eminently capable of handling high-spirited students. She couldn't say the same about the other candidates she'd interviewed.

"Firm guidance?" she questioned. "Under no circumstances would you be permitted to use physical force in my school as a means of discipline. I am not an advocate of corporal punishment."

"Nor am I. As the saying goes, one can catch more flies with honey than with vinegar."

Was that a comment on her acid tone? The thought stung, but she could read only geniality in his expression.

Irked nonetheless, she picked up the quill again. "Why would you not seek another position as a tutor? It would certainly be less strenuous."

He leaned forward, resting his forearms on his knees. "I've grown disenchanted with tending the coddled youth of the wealthy, my lady. I've a wish to teach children who crave learning in order to better their lot in life. Poor students who have been denied the advantages of a proper education."

He radiated sincerity. And he expressed himself with a fervor that was ideal for a teacher. So why did she feel a compulsion to find fault with him? Why did she wonder if he voiced platitudes designed to win him the post?

Perhaps simply because . . . he was a man.

Men had caused nothing but trouble in her life. For that reason, she had employed only female teachers until now, when circumstances had denied her that leisure.

"I trust you have the proper credentials," she said. "Along with a letter of reference."

"Indeed, I do." Mr. Jackman reached into an inner pocket of his coat and withdrew a folded paper, which he handed across the desk. Their fingers brushed, transmitting a flash of lightning. Instantly, her bosom felt swollen, heavy with heat.

Resisting the urge to fan herself, Julia broke the red wax seal with her thumb, unfolded the paper, and scanned the letter. A Mr. Oscar Ballinger enumerated the excellent qualities of his children's tutor, William Jackman, praising his skill at settling disputes, his organizational abilities, his superb grasp of mathematics.

She looked at Mr. Jackman. "I'm not familiar with the Ballingers."

"Landed gentry. A number of tenant farmers provide much of the family income."

Was that a hint of inbred arrogance in his voice? "You speak like the nobility yourself."

His eyes narrowed slightly, masking his thoughts, adding to the mystery of William Jackman. He chuckled, his dimples giving him a disarming aspect. "Hardly," he said. "My father was the vicar of a small church in Devonshire. He provided me with an exceptional education. So you see, my background is quite humble."

Humble was not a word Julia would have used to describe Mr. Jackman. He was charming, smooth, polished. Yet he appeared to have all the intelligence and dedication she required in a teacher. Like rich cream, he had risen to the top of the other applicants.

So why did she hesitate?

Those dazzling eyes made it difficult to think. It certainly couldn't be because she doubted her ability to resist him.

She afforded him a cool nod. "That will be all, Mr. Jackman. If you'll tell me your address, I'll send a note when I make my decision."

Although she sat with quill poised, he did not provide the information. Instead, he regarded her with a frown, as if struggling with an inner demon. "You'll award the position very soon, I hope. It pains me to admit this, my lady, but my nest egg has been stolen. I'm in dire need of employment."

Julia blinked. "What happened?"

"On my way to London, I was set upon by brigands. You see, in order to save the price of a room at the inn, I'd camped outdoors. A gang of thieves came upon me while I slept. I fought back"—as if to assuage a bruise, he absently rubbed his ribs—"but there were four of them and they'd caught me off guard. They overturned my satchel and found my money . . ." Mr. Jackman smiled sheepishly. "But never mind. You'll think I'm playing on your sympathies."

"Oh, no! Certainly not." But the thought *had* occurred to her, and she felt lower than a worm for always assuming the worst of a man.

Her mind revisited a worrisome incident that had happened the previous week. After checking on an ill child one night, Julia had been returning to her bedchamber when she'd heard a muffled crash downstairs. Wondering if a student was up to mischief, she had gone to investigate, only to startle an intruder in her darkened office. The man fled through an open window, leaving the drawers of her desk pulled out, the contents strewn over the floor. Now, a lingering sense of horror and violation clamped like a vise around her rib cage.

Luckily, the villain had stolen nothing. She kept only papers in this office along with a collection of figurines that held more sentimental than material value. But Mr. Jackman had not been so blessed.

"I'm afraid I can't give you a permanent address," he went on. "If it isn't inconvenient, may I call on you tomorrow to find out your decision?"

No address?

Aghast, Julia realized he must be homeless. Did he have no money at all, not even a few shillings with which to secure a roof over his head?

The thought threatened to breach the gate of her resistance. Her lips parted, though she had no idea what to say. She was saved from responding by the patter of footsteps in the corridor.

A young boy dashed into the office and barreled straight toward her. The sight of his perpetually tousled russet hair and liberally freckled face made her heart clutch with a powerful mix of emotions: love, exasperation, protectiveness.

"Mummy, Mummy, I have a riddle for you!"

"Not now, Theo," she said, jumping up to hasten around the desk. "You mustn't intrude when I've a visitor."

Ever polite, William Jackman rose, as well.

Brown eyes wide with curiosity, Theo craned his neck to look up at him. "Who are you?"

"Mr. Jackman. I'm here to apply for the post of maths instructor."

"You can't," Theo said bluntly. "Only ladies are teachers."

His naïve logic underscored the fact that at seven, he had seldom experienced the male-dominated world outside the walls of this school. A familiar worry niggled at Julia. Not for the first time, she wondered if she'd been wrong to insulate him here.

She placed her hand on his shoulder. He felt wiry and warm, boyishly sturdy. "This is Theodore Corwyn. My somewhat outspoken son."

A hint of speculation in his eyes, Mr. Jackman gazed straight at her.

She stared coolly back. *He knew*. He had heard of the scandal. Had Agnes blurted it out? She must have.

But he couldn't possibly know everything. Only a handful of people were privy to the truth. Julia had made certain of that.

He bent down to shake the boy's hand. "It's a pleasure to meet you, Theo. I promise you, I'm as skilled at mathematics as any lady."

"Oh, not all ladies," Theo confided. "Mummy isn't very quick at sums. That's why I make up riddles for her."

"Theo!"

Mr. Jackman gave Julia a teasing look. "Never mind. I'm sure your mother has other, equally important talents."

A flush suffused Julia. Was there a hidden meaning to his words? Or was she reading layers into a casual remark because of her own wayward desires?

He addressed her son. "What is your riddle? Let's see if she can solve it."

Theo's eyes took on a crafty light. "How many feet are in a yard?"

"Three," Julia said promptly, although she suspected there was a catch.

Sure enough, Theo giggled. "No. The answer depends on how many *children* are *playing* in the yard!"

Mr. Jackman chuckled with what appeared to be genuine amusement. "I'll do you one better. Why was the arithmatic book unhappy?"

"Why?"

"Because it had so many problems."

Theo shouted with laughter. "Oh, oh, that's funny! Wait till everyone hears it!" He started toward the door, then paused. "May I tell it, sir? It's *your* riddle."

"Go ahead," Mr. Jackman said with a wave of his hand. "I've plenty more—including some true mathematical puzzles."

"You do?" Theo's freckled face revealed avid interest. "What are they, sir?"

"They'll have to wait for another time, I'm afraid. I don't want to take up any more of your mother's time."

The boy dashed to Julia and tugged on her gown. "Mummy, will you hire Mr. Jackman? Please, you must."

The exuberance of his request overwhelmed her misgivings. Her resistance lay in shambles, anyway, after hearing Mr. Jackman's story about being waylaid by brigands and then watching him trade silly jests with her son.

With uncanny accuracy, he had penetrated the very center of her vulnerability. Theo adored numerical puzzles, and she often felt woefully inadequate in satisfying his craving for them.

Another thought nagged at her, too. Perhaps Theo needed a man's influence in his life . . .

She looked at Mr. Jackman. "I have indeed decided to offer you the post. Provided you're willing to start at once."

Something flashed in Mr. Jackman's eyes. Triumph? "I accept with great pleasure, my lady."

His mouth curved in a warm smile that brought to mind other pleasures. How she wanted to trace those dimples with her fingertips, to feel the raspiness of his cheek against hers. Until this moment, Julia hadn't realized how much she had missed being close to a man.

The dangerous awareness triggered caution in her. She must take especial care to hide her combustive reaction to him. It would be unethical to indulge in a personal attachment with a staff member. As headmistress of the Corwyn Academy, she had trained herself to be aloof, self-possessed, professional.

"Mummy, why aren't you wearing your shoes?"

She looked down to see her bare toes visible beneath her hem. Mr. Jackman looked down, too, and she hastily readjusted her skirt. "It's a hot day," she said by way of explanation. "Run along now and tell your riddle. Then you and the other children should wash. It will be suppertime soon."

Theo dashed out of the office, leaving her alone with Mr. Jackman. The trace of a smirk curled his lips, making her wonder if he was pondering the unstockinged state of her legs. Embarrassed, she threw out a distraction. "The position includes room and board."

"Indeed? The advertisement said nothing of it."

Julia battled a blush. Although the other four teachers lived under her roof, she'd had no intention of offering that same privilege to a man. But she could hardly let him sleep in a doorway somewhere. "The carriage house is unoccupied. It's yours if you would like. In fact, if you'd care to move in straightaway, you may certainly do so."

"That's very kind of you. I'll need to fetch a few belongings. You may expect my return at eight o'clock."

He bowed, then started toward the door. His commanding manner ought to have annoyed Julia. But the rare prospect of an attractive man on the premises filled her with treacherous anticipation.

Unable to stop herself, she called out, "Mr. Jackman. Will you be bringing your family?"

Looking back, he gave her an inscrutable stare. "I've no attachments, my lady. No children . . . and no wife."

Take care, young ladies, to avoid drunkards, for they are devoted to the bottle rather than to their families. To view the shameful ruin of a life, pray turn your eyes to the Duke of W. . . .
—The Rogue Report

Chapter Two

"Wycliffe." Jack gave his grandfather's broad shoulder a shake. "Wake up."

The Duke of Wycliffe sprawled facedown on a chaise in the dim-lit library. A stocky man, he wore an old-fashioned powdered wig. His dark gold dressing gown was crumpled and stained, and his big toe protruded from a hole in his brown stockings. One arm trailed down to the empty bottle of cheap gin lying on the Turkish carpet.

The sight wrenched Jack as it always did. It was just past seven in the evening, and already his grandfather had drunk enough to float an armada.

"Wake up," he commanded again. "I need to speak to you." When the old man didn't respond, Jack uncorked a vial of hartshorn and waved it under that hawk nose.

His grandfather came back to life with a choking cough. Flailing his arm, he aimed for the small, foul-smelling bottle in Jack's hand.

"Go 'way," he slurred.

"As a matter of fact, that's why I'm here," Jack said, capping the vial and thrusting it back into his pocket. "To tell you that I'm going away for a while."

He'd be working as a mathematics instructor—and wouldn't his friends be aghast at the notion of his laboring for a living, even if only for a short time. But no one would know. He wouldn't confide his plans to anyone, not even to his grandfather. Not until he found proof that Lady Julia Corwyn was the author of *The Rogue Report*.

He had spent the past fortnight researching old scandals and pinpointing her as the most likely suspect. Several other ladies had been disgraced over the years, but one had moved to Italy, another to Yorkshire, and yet another was now married with a brood of children.

Lady Julia Corwyn was the only one still living in London.

With her dark curly hair and smoky blue eyes, she had been a delicious surprise. Although they both hailed from high society, Jack had never before had occasion to meet her. Not only did he pay little heed to debutantes—virgins were too much trouble—he had been abroad during her first and only season eight years ago, and she had not set foot in a ballroom since then.

But he had heard plenty of gossip. An outrageous flirt, Lady Julia had been the talk of the *ton*. For three glorious months, she had reigned as crown princess in a court comprised of admiring gentlemen. Then she had vanished from the social scene, borne a child out of wedlock some nine months later, and had steadfastly refused to name her seducer.

Her parents, Lord and Lady Brookville, had washed their hands of her; the scandalmongers whispered that she'd brought her troubles onto herself. Jack had prepared himself to charm a woman worn down by life, an embittered virago who used her newsletter to achieve revenge

on all scoundrels. He had not expected her to be poised
and confident, yet vulnerable in her love for her son.

Or so beautiful she'd stolen his breath away.

"Bloody hell." Wycliffe struggled into a sitting position on the chaise. His wig hung askew, and his rheumy
hazel eyes appeared unfocused. "Wha's it now, Charles?
If 'tis money, I haven't tuppence t' rub together."

Jack's attention returned with a jolt to the shadowed library. Charles was his father, and he'd died the previous
year. Too often of late, Wycliffe had been prone to
episodes of forgetfulness. His once-sharp mind had been
dulled by the ravages of age and the years of drinking.
His fortune having been lost long ago to the gaming tables, the duke lived alone in a modest town house with
only a skeleton staff in residence.

Angered by his inability to improve matters, Jack
grimly vowed to take those lazy servants to task. By God,
before he left here, he'd make certain the cook was
preparing nourishing meals, and he'd drill the valet about
the slovenly state of his grandfather's garb.

He pulled over a hassock and sat down. Summoning a
wry grin, he reached out and rubbed the old man's sinewy
forearm. "Grandpapa, it's me, Jack. It seems I'll have to
buy you a pair of spectacles."

Wycliffe blinked. The confusion in his eyes slowly
cleared, and his cheeks went ruddy with embarrassment.
"Jack, m' boy! 'Course 'tis you. Must've been dreaming."

"I'm sorry to awaken you. But you need to know that
I'm leaving town for a while."

"Wha's a matter? You ain't killed somebody in a duel,
have you?"

Jack concealed a wince. "No, no, it's nothing of the
sort. I'll be with a woman. But I didn't want you to think
I'd fallen off the face of the earth."

"Sowin' your wild oats, eh?" Wycliffe loosed a deep

belly laugh that reminded Jack of the jovial man who had taken him fishing as a boy and to a high-class bawdy house on his sixteenth birthday. "Ah, t' be young again. Tell me, is she pretty?"

"Very. Quite possibly the most dazzling woman I've ever met." Lord, *that* at least was the truth. And now that he'd met Julia Corwyn, seduction was a definite part of his plan for her.

His grandfather leaned forward, bringing with him the stale odor of gin. "Never fear, your secret's safe with me. I won't breathe a word to Miss Gresham."

That troubled twist of the gut assailed Jack again. He had informed Wycliffe a few days ago about the broken betrothal. Rather than cause the old man discomfort, he repeated the news. "I'm afraid Evelyn has called off the wedding."

"The devil you say! She's mad for you. Why, th' time you brought her t' dinner, she wouldn't leave your side."

"Things change," Jack said curtly. There was no need to go into Evelyn's attempts to guard her fiancé against the influence of his wicked grandfather. Or the fact that Jack had had to cajole her into visiting the old reprobate. "She found out I've been gambling."

"Wha's that t' do with it? There's naught wrong with a little wagerin'."

"I lost a thousand guineas. After I'd promised her I would stop."

A deep sense of shame accompanied the admission. He didn't know what had induced him to play so deeply. At the time, he had known it was disastrously foolish, but the need had been like a fever in his blood, a desperation to prove . . . what? That he could keep up with his friends who had unlimited pockets? Or that no woman had the right to dictate his actions?

Mumbling curses, Wycliffe pushed to his feet and

swayed like a mighty oak about to topple. Then he started on a stumbling track to the arched doorway.

Jack sprang up to catch him by the arm. "Where are you going?"

"T' get dressed, b'gad. I'll call on that tightfisted chit. Who's she t' make rules for my grandson?"

"She's the one with the money."

His grandfather ignored Jack's attempt at ironic flippancy. He shook his fist in the air. "Bah, you'll be Wycliffe one day. Who th' devil was *her* grandsire? A common tradesman!"

"Be that as it may, there was a story about me in *The Rogue Report*. Evelyn couldn't abide the public humiliation."

"That rag! Just tell her 'twas lies. All lies."

"It's useless. She won't have me. It's over."

Lord, it had been mortifying to be refused admittance to Evelyn's house. He had gone there in the hopes of smoothing things over, but a footman had barred his entry. Jack might have shoved his way inside had not Evelyn returned home from a shopping expedition at that very moment. When she and her mother had emerged from the carriage, it had been Mrs. Gresham who had curtsied and spoken to him, albeit with a nervous glance at her daughter. Evelyn herself had ignored him, her cold blue eyes sweeping past him as if he didn't exist. The silver-tongued apology had died in his throat. In her pale pink gown and fine straw bonnet, she had resembled a porcelain doll.

Unlike Lady Julia Corwyn in all her untidy glory.

In a rush of hot blood, Jack reflected on that generous mouth, the bare feet beneath her prim blue gown, the skin of her face and throat dewy with perspiration, as if she'd just experienced the pleasures of the bedchamber. Lady

Julia had a lush sensuality at odds with her role as head of a charity school.

And it *was* a charity school, no matter what fancy name she had chosen for it. He just couldn't get a grasp on why she'd opened it. Although her parents had renounced her, she had inherited a sizable fortune from her late grandmother. She could be living a life of leisure instead of caring for the discarded offspring of commoners. Was she punishing herself for her fall from grace? Did she think to atone for the sin of bearing a son out of wedlock by taking in children off the street?

Hell, her reasons didn't signify. All that mattered was that she had swallowed his lies. Hook, line, and sinker.

Wycliffe clutched at Jack's arm. His bewildered frown had returned, enhancing the wrinkles on his ruddy features. "You . . . you told me about Miss Gresham a few days ago. Didn't you?"

Jack considered lying. But the stark look on his grandfather's face pleaded for the truth. "I may have mentioned it," he said, steering the old man back to the chaise. "It doesn't matter. Have you eaten your dinner yet?"

Sinking heavily to the seat, Wycliffe ignored Jack's question and passed a hand over his face. "M' God, boy. Am I losing my wits?"

Jack picked up the empty gin bottle. "Here's your problem," he said lightly. "This cheap brew would rot anyone's brain. Now stay put, I'm going to see about your dinner."

After a brief squeeze of his grandfather's shoulder, Jack headed through the arched doorway in search of a servant. He was running late, but before he left for the Corwyn Academy, he had to make certain Wycliffe was settled in for the night.

The need for revenge burned in him. Nobody knew it,

but he'd been determined to marry Evelyn as much for Wycliffe's sake as his own. He had hoped to give the old man a better life, to have the money to improve these dilapidated surroundings, to present him with great-grandchildren before his mind slipped deeper into senility.

But Lady Julia Corwyn had robbed Jack of that chance. She had exposed all of his faults and mistakes at the worst possible time. She had ruined his plan to pull himself up out of the quagmire of debt and debauchery.

And by God, he intended to make her pay.

From the doorway, Julia surveyed the bustle of activity in the dining chamber. It was a spacious room with pale green walls and a mantelpiece fashioned of cream marble from the mansion's previous life as the residence of a wealthy cloth merchant. The pure light of early morning streamed through the tall windows.

The delicious scents of breakfast wafted through the air, as did the happy chatter of children. They stood in line to get their food before finding a place to sit at one of the benches on either side of the long table. Toward the back of the queue, Theo's russet hair shone in the midst of a group of boys. Nearby, four teachers occupied a smaller table with two empty chairs.

One for her—and one for Mr. Jackman.

Frowning, she considered asking them if they had seen him this morning. But Elfrida Littlefield, the literature instructor, and Dorcas Snyder, who taught music, had been less than happy at the prospect of a man joining the staff. Even now, Elfrida's sallow features looked sour and disapproving, and Dorcas's mouth resembled one of the prunes that lay beside the dish of porridge on her plate. Julia had no wish to draw attention to Mr. Jackman's lack of punctuality.

Especially since they hadn't even met him yet.

She veered in the other direction, wending past the line, pausing now and then to straighten a collar, to separate two boys who were pushing each other, and to hug one of the smaller children who didn't mind a display of public affection. At length, she reached the group of maids who served the students their boiled eggs, toast, and ham.

Keeping her voice low, she asked, "Has anyone seen Mr. Jackman this morning?"

Morag, a middle-aged woman with plain, placid features, lifted her broad shoulders in a shrug. "Dunno."

"Mayhap he overslept." Her blue eyes alight, Agnes let the ladle sink back into the pot of porridge while she wiped her hands on her apron. "Do ye wish me t' run out t' the carriage house, m'lady? I don't mind."

Julia could only imagine the folly of allowing the flirtatious young maid anywhere near Mr. Jackman's sleeping quarters. She held up her palm. "Finish your work. I'll handle the matter."

Heaving a sigh, Agnes returned to the task of filling bowls. But she aimed a dreamy glance at the door as if expecting the only man on the premises to stride inside at any moment.

The four teachers kept watch, too, though more discreetly. A palpable aura of tension enveloped their table. Elfrida and Dorcas seemed to be doing most of the talking, no doubt venting their displeasure about the new male teacher to Faith Rigby, the dreamy-eyed art instructor, while old Margaret Pringle, the history teacher, played her usual role of peacemaker.

A sinking sensation assailed Julia. Oh, why hadn't she introduced William Jackman immediately upon hiring him? At least it would have broken the ice. But the thought simply hadn't occurred to her until shortly after he'd walked out of her office with a promise to return at eight. So she had made up for the oversight by gathering the staff in the library to greet him at the appointed time. When he'd finally arrived over an hour late—with a glib excuse about having lost his way through the unfamiliar streets of London—she had been the only one still waiting, the other teachers having retired for the night. Hiding her displeasure behind a brisk manner, she had given him his schedule for the following day, handed him an oil lamp, and then pointed him in the direction of his new quarters.

Now, her misgivings clamored louder than her empty stomach. She surreptitiously flicked open the gold watch that was pinned to her bodice. Seven forty-one. Mr. Jackman was eleven minutes late already. If tardiness was his failing, she must see to it that he mended his ways.

Once all the students were seated, Julia proceeded to the head of the table. She clapped her hands and the dull roar of conversation died down at once. The only sound was a faint *clank* as Agnes settled the lid over the empty pot of porridge. "Good morning, children."

The chime of young voices rang out in unison. "Good morning, Lady Julia."

The sight of them, freshly scrubbed, clad in uniform— the girls in white pinafores over marine-blue gowns, the boys in dark breeches with pale blue shirts—gave Julia a much-needed sense of calm. All that mattered was providing them with the best possible chance of a secure future. Not petty quarrels among the staff or one late teacher.

"I've only one announcement today," she said. "I'm happy to say that we have a new mathematics instructor. His name is Mr. Jackman. He will be with us indefinitely." At least until the winter term, if Miss Dewhurst could return from her mother's sickbed by then.

The children exchanged glances that ranged from eager to apprehensive, but no one looked surprised. Evidently, Theo had already accomplished the task of informing everyone. Her son sat grinning from ear to ear, his excitement a ladle that stirred up the stew of tension inside her. By the heavens, she would do everything in her power to ensure that Mr. Jackman wouldn't disappoint Theo or the other children.

"Unfortunately," she went on, "Mr. Jackman has been delayed slightly. But you should all have a chance to meet him in class today. Now, if you'll excuse me, Miss Pringle will lead the blessing."

The elfin, white-haired history teacher rose to perform the task. As everyone bowed their heads and prayed, Julia slipped quietly from the dining chamber.

She headed toward the rear of the house, the click of her footsteps echoing in the marble corridor. To either side, the formal chambers had been converted into classrooms. The huge drawing room had been divided into areas for spelling recitation and literature study. A sitting room now housed the art center with its tidy rows of easels and boxes of paints. Even the grand ballroom served a purpose by providing a place for the children to stage theatricals during inclement weather.

Cutting through the music room with its pianoforte, harp, and violins, Julia opened a door and emerged onto the veranda that bordered the narrow garden. She marched down the pebbled pathway to the rear of the property, where the empty stable and the carriage house sat nestled side by side.

The red-brick building appeared deserted. The window of Mr. Jackman's tiny upstairs chamber stood open to the cool morning breeze, and sunlight reflected off the glass panes. On the roof, the sticks of a bird's abandoned nest protruded from the slats of the cupola.

Julia saw no need to keep horses and a carriage when a sufficient array of shops lay within walking distance. On the rare occasions that she ventured beyond that radius, it was a simple matter to hire equipage from a nearby ostler. Consequently, there had been no activity in the yard to awaken Mr. Jackman. Nor did the children play outside until later in the morning.

She thinned her lips. Blast it, she wouldn't make excuses for him.

A tangle of ivy framed the doorway to the carriage house. Julia rapped hard on the plain wood panel. She waited a few moments, impatiently shifting from one foot to the other, but heard no sound of movement inside the building. She knocked again, then stepped back to frown up at the open window. Mr. Jackman had to be in there; her own chamber faced the garden, and before climbing into bed precisely at ten the previous evening, she had seen the hazy yellow light of the lamp still burning in his room. Had he risen early and gone somewhere?

Anxiety penetrated the armor of her anger. Or what if he'd fallen and grievously hurt himself? What if he'd been set upon by robbers during the night?

Ridiculous. No thief would think to find anything to steal in a carriage house. Especially not with so many fine residences in the area. Yet prickles of alarm touched the back of her neck. Only a week ago, that midnight intruder had invaded her office . . .

"Mr. Jackman!" she called out. "Mr. Jackman, answer me!"

The cool morning breeze tugged a few corkscrew tendrils from the tidy brown twist at the back of her head, and Julia distractedly tucked them behind her ears. The cloudless sky promised another scorching day. Narrowing her eyes against the sunlight, she strained to detect some sign of life beyond the open square of the window. Raising her voice, she repeated, *"Mr. Jackman!"*

A minute crept past at the pace of a snail. She counted the seconds in her head in an effort to hold apprehension at bay. Upon reaching sixty, she opened the door and stepped into the shadowy interior of the carriage house.

The odors of dust and neglect pervaded the large, empty room. A wide rear door, kept closed for years, gave access to the mews that ran between the rows of houses. To her right lay the smaller rooms that had once contained tools and harness. To her left, a narrow staircase led to the attic chamber that had housed a coachman long ago.

Julia hastened to the base of the steps. "Mr. Jackman?"

Only the faint chirp of a bird outside answered her.

Worry swamping her scruples, she lifted the hem of her skirt and went up the wooden stairs. She made her approach as loud as possible, continuing to call his name along the way.

The door at the small landing was closed. She knocked, so hard her knuckles stung. Then she pressed her ear to the wood. No groan of pain or faint plea for help issued from within. A horrible vision of her new mathematics instructor lying dead in a pool of blood made her dizzy.

Julia inhaled a ragged breath. On the exhale, she forced herself to open the door and step inside.

Her gaze widened at the untidy surroundings. After Agnes had given the room a thorough scrubbing late yesterday, Julia had inspected the chamber to ensure that it met her exacting standards. There had not been so much as a speck of dust on the plain oak furnishings.

Now the place was a jumble of clutter.

A shabby leather valise sat open on the floor, with arti-

cles of clothing strewn all around it. Shaving utensils and
assorted bottles littered the top of the bureau. The class
instructions that she had given to Mr. Jackman no longer
rested in a neat stack; the breeze had blown the papers all
over the desk and onto the threadbare brown rug.

Then her gaze flashed to the narrow cot against one
wall. Her insides tangled into a suffocating knot.

William Jackman lay sprawled on his back. His eyes
were closed, his dark hair rumpled, a lock falling onto his
brow. The coverlet stopped halfway up his bare chest, and
a shaft of morning light illuminated the sculpted muscles
of his shoulders.

He lay so still Julia feared he was dead. In the next instant, she noted the slow rise and fall of his chest, and her
legs went weak with relief. Thank the Lord, he hadn't
been murdered. He was merely asleep.

The slugabed was *asleep*.

Her hands on her hips, she ventured closer, stepping
past a pile of starched shirts on the floor. "Mr. Jackman,
get up this instant!"

When he didn't stir, she was struck by a sinister
thought. Had he been *drinking* last night? Had he smuggled spirits onto school property? All the while she'd
been worried, had he been sleeping off the effects of a
binge?

Her gaze alighted on a small silver flask amid the clutter on the bureau. She uncorked it and sniffed, wrinkling
her nose at the pungent aroma of brandy.

All her hard-won discipline melted in a blaze of
anger. She stormed to the bed and overturned the flask
onto his head.

He jerked himself upright, sputtering, backhanding
the liquid from his eyes. "What the devil! Marlon, I'll
kill you—"

His gaze met hers and he froze, one hand in the midst

of wiping his brow. The moment stretched out into tortured eternity. He looked as shocked to see her there as she felt at her own recklessness.

Who was Marlon? And why, oh why, hadn't Julia considered the impropriety of entering this bedchamber?

Her heart fluttered wildly. When he'd sat up, the sheet had slipped down to ride the crest of his lean hips . . . his naked hips. As she watched, a droplet of brandy rolled down his neck and over the muscles of his chest. She had the mad urge to halt its descent with her lips, and to press herself to the chiseled perfection of his body.

The feeling was so powerful, so seductive, she actually had to stop herself from taking a step forward.

Furious at herself as much as at him, Julia reverted to the stern headmistress. She snapped open her watch and checked the time. "You're late, Mr. Jackman. Twenty-eight minutes already."

"Sorry," he said, his gaze wary. "I must have overslept."

"Because you were drinking *this* last night?" She brandished the empty flask. "For shame! I will not tolerate a drunkard for a teacher."

Raw anger flared in his eyes. "I am not a drunkard," he stated coldly. "I keep brandy for medicinal purposes, nothing more."

"I make judgments based on evidence, sir."

"Then explain why that flask was nearly full. You surely can't believe I fell into a stupor after a few sips."

Julia couldn't deny the logic of that. In the throes of temper, she hadn't been thinking. But his very possession of liquor enhanced her mistrust of him.

Walking to the bureau, she set down the flask. "Perhaps you've brought other bottles. They may be hidden away somewhere in this mess. Shall I look for them?"

A muscle tightened in his jaw. He ran his fingers through his damp, sticky hair, then grimaced. "Good

God, woman. Do you have a habit of searching the bed-chambers of your male teachers?"

She felt herself flush. How dared he make her feel defensive for protecting her students from evil influences? "I have no other male teachers. And it seems, Mr. Jackman, I was mistaken in hiring *you*."

Her movements stiff, she stalked to the door. The school would have to manage without a mathematics teacher for a few more days, she fumed. It was better than having a man on staff who flouted her rules.

"Wait," he said in a conciliatory manner.

She ignored the rustle of bedcovers and the pad of footsteps. "My decision is made. I see no point to further discussion."

"Hear me out." He had a commanding voice, until it softened into liquid silk. "Please, my lady."

Her fingers gripping the door handle, Julia stopped and stole a glance over her shoulder. It was a colossal mistake. Mr. Jackman stood only a foot away, the bed-sheets like a toga draping his legs and torso, emphasizing the breadth of his shoulders. A warm ache pulsated inside of her. With his tousled dark hair and green eyes, he looked like Apollo offering her nectar and ambrosia.

Or, as it turned out, an explanation.

"I'm a firm believer in sobriety," he began. "If you'll allow me to tell you why, then perhaps you'll realize I couldn't possibly have committed such a despicable act—"

"I'm not interested in a soliloquy of excuses, Mr. Jackman. If you've something specific to say, then say it."

A dull flush spread up his neck and into his face. No hint of charm curved his mouth. His dimples were a mere suggestion against the unshaven stubble of his cheeks. "My grandfather drinks to excess," he said bluntly. "I grew up seeing him drunk every hour of every day. Morning, noon, or night he'd stagger home, slurring his words, falling asleep in the middle of a conversation. Or I'd find him passed out somewhere in the house with a bottle beside him." He glanced away, then regarded her with stoic intensity. "He's sixty-eight and I've no doubt he'll drink until the day he dies."

His grating tone conveyed a world of harsh memories. The glimpse into the purgatory of his childhood touched a place deep inside Julia. She felt herself softening, and shored up her defenses. Whatever his personal problems, she had to think first of her students. "I do not permit intoxicants on the grounds of this school."

"I didn't know. You have my word that it won't happen again."

She shouldn't be swayed. But she desperately needed a mathematics teacher. And William Jackman had a way of looking at her that wiped all rational thought from her mind.

Stepping out onto the tiny landing, she shot him a cool stare. "You may consider yourself on probation, Mr. Jackman. Your first test is this: you'll join me downstairs, dressed and ready, in ten minutes."

Those men who gamble to excess pursue their reckless vice without cease.
Recently, Lord E.M. missed the birthday celebration of his dear mother be-
cause he was desperately trying to win back his losses . . .
— *The Rogue Report*

Chapter Three

A short while later, Jack emerged from the carriage house
and squinted as his eyes adjusted to the bright morning
light. His head hurt like the very devil. Accustomed to
late nights playing billiards or attending parties, he had
stayed up into the wee hours, devising number puzzles in
order to ease the boredom of being stuck alone in a chamber smaller than his dressing room back home.

Then this morning, he'd had the monster of rude
awakenings.

His jaundiced gaze sought out his nemesis. Lady Julia
Corwyn stood across the small garden, reaching down to
pick up something lying behind a scraggly bush. The
pounding in his temples subsided somewhat, lulled by the
tonic of a beautiful woman. Not even that prim gray gown
could disguise the shapeliness of her figure. The sunshine
coaxed fire from her dark brown hair, and several twisting
curls had found freedom from the prison of her bun.

He vastly preferred this view of Lady Julia to the one

that had startled him out of a sound sleep. When he'd opened his eyes—his stinging, doused-with-brandy eyes—she had been standing over him like an avenging angel come to banish him to hell. And for the first time in his adult life, he had been naked in bed without a chance of cajoling his female companion into joining him.

Now, however, she looked soft and approachable. She might have been the lady of the house tending to her garden.

He reflected that *garden* was a relative term. A few spindly roses straggled up the stone fence, and a large oak provided the only shade. The barren earth in the flower beds had long since been trampled by the feet of countless children. He didn't want even to imagine forty-some little hooligans set loose in this confined space.

By God, they'd better behave themselves in his class-room.

When Lady Julia straightened, she held a length of rope, the ends dangling from her hand. He knew the instant she spied him. Her posture stiffened. Her shoulders squared with military precision. She marched straight toward him, and her grim expression made him wonder if she was thinking about strangling him with a little girl's skipping rope.

Her critical gaze scanned him from head to toe. Jack could only imagine what Miss Perfect thought of the shoddy black coat and brown breeches. In order to look the part of the poor tutor, he had traded several of his expensive coats to his valet in exchange for a couple of cheap, too-small versions. Marlon had been gleeful, but Jack hadn't realized until now just how much he himself valued fine tailoring. He wasn't accustomed to the tightness across his shoulders or the shortness of the cuffs that no amount of tugging would ever restore to the proper length. He sorely missed his perfectly starched cravat, his gleaming black Hessians, his fine buckskin breeches.

As he bowed, the fabric of his coat strained against his back. "My lady."

She flicked open the gold watch pinned to her bodice. "You're two minutes late."

Jack was beginning to despise that damned timepiece. Little did she know, he wasn't accustomed to living by a schedule. Under normal circumstances, he went to bed when he pleased, rose at whatever hour suited him— often past noon when he'd come home at dawn. He had the leisure to take his time over shaving, instead of wielding the razor in such haste he could now feel the sting of a cut along his jaw.

"Pray forgive me," he said in a pleasant tone. "I was delayed by the need to wash the brandy out of my hair."

She glanced up at his still-damp hair and flushed, much to his satisfaction. Then she surprised him by saying, "I owe you an apology for that. When I knocked on your door and you didn't answer—"

"You assumed I was drunk."

"Not at first. I called your name, loud enough to wake the dead, but you didn't respond. Not even when I came upstairs to check on you."

Biting her lip, Lady Julia started down the graveled path to the house, and he fell into step beside her. An astounding thought struck him. "You were worried? That I was *dead*?"

She flashed him a scornful, defensive look. "What else was I to think? It's natural for people to wake up when their name is shouted right in their ears."

The last person he could remember being concerned about his welfare was his mother, who had died when he was ten. "I'm an exceptionally sound sleeper. It's an unfortunate family trait."

His father had been that way, and his grandfather, too—though perhaps the latter's shortcoming was due more to drink than heredity.

The thought of Wycliffe made his chest tighten. Jack regretted having to spill that truth to Lady Julia. It wasn't that he was ashamed of his grandfather; rather, he scorned her pity. He didn't want her to know anything at all about his real life. But there had been no other way to avert the disaster of being sacked before he'd had the chance to search for proof that she published *The Rogue Report*.

Upon reaching the porch, Lady Julia dropped the skipping rope into a bin filled with bats and balls and other childish paraphernalia. She dusted off her hands and fixed him with a prudish stare. He wondered if she knew the gray gown turned her eyes a striking shade of smoky blue. "I will not abide any further tardiness," she stated. "If you require a wall clock, I shall provide you with one."

"I'll take care of the matter myself."

"See to it that you do, Mr. Jackman. No one is permitted to disrupt the daily schedule. Our curriculum requires your prompt arrival at half-past seven in the dining—"

"Jack," he corrected.

"Pardon?"

"Since we're to be colleagues now," he said in a disarming tone designed to halt her tirade, "I'd hoped we could be less formal."

"I thought your name was . . . William."

"My friends call me Jack. You know, short for Jackman. I'd consider it an honor if you did so, too."

"I hardly think it's appropriate—"

"Please, my lady." He flashed his most dazzling smile and shoveled a load of horse manure. "We've started off badly, and I'd like to rectify matters. You see, it's my hope to foster a sense of camaraderie with you and every-

one else here. I would like to become a true member of
the extended family at the Corwyn Academy. If I've offended you, I sincerely apologize."

The breeze blew, tugging another curl loose from her
tightly wound hair. She imprisoned it behind her ear. "I
suppose your request isn't unreasonable ... Jack." Although her voice was cool, a trace of pink colored her
cheeks. "I'll show you to your classroom."

As he followed her inside the house, he noted that she
didn't offer him the same privilege. But in his mind he
took it. *Julia.* He imagined himself whispering her name
while he kissed the scented hollow of her neck, while he
undid the buttons at the back of her gown, while he
cupped her breasts in his hands . . .

"Who is Marlon?"

Jolted, he stared at Julia as they proceeded down a
wide marble corridor. "Pardon?"

She looked defensive again, as if she regretted blurting
out the question. "You spoke the name Marlon when I
awakened you."

"He's an old friend," Jack lied. "He knew I was a sound
sleeper, so if he wanted me to go fishing early in the morning, he'd come into my chamber and toss a pitcher of water
at me."

The truth was, Marlon enjoyed using that trick to roust
Jack out of bed whenever he had an early visitor, invari-
ably a dun collector. One of these days, he was going to
sack the cussed old bastard. And never mind that the valet
had a limp that would likely keep him unemployed, or
that one of Jack's first memories was of Marlon teaching
him to ride a pony.

Julia wore a frown that foretold another lecture about
oversleeping. But she merely said, "All the classrooms
are located along this passageway with the exception of
the library, which is on the south corridor near the ball-

room. I had planned to introduce you to the students and teachers at breakfast. However, that will have to wait until the noon hour since school has already begun."

Although most of the doors were closed, he could hear the chatter of youthful voices in the chambers to either side, and the firm voice of a teacher calling her students to order. He could also smell the delicious aroma of ham emanating from somewhere ahead. "About breakfast—"

"I'm afraid you've missed the morning meal," Julia said without a trace of sympathy. "Classes begin promptly at eight-fifteen. There are no exceptions to that rule."

His temples throbbed again. He craved a cup of strong coffee. But he wouldn't admit that to Miss Tyrant. "You certainly run a tight ship."

"Perhaps in your days as a tutor to children of privilege you could afford to be more lax. However, my students need the advantage of an excellent education in order to better their lot in life." Her steps brisk, she led him toward a door near the end of the corridor. "Here is your classroom now. Your first group includes ages five through seven. You should have no trouble following the lesson plans left by Miss Dewhurst. You did study them, didn't you?"

"Certainly."

He had given the notes a cursory glance and left them in his chamber. Surely he wouldn't need them. How much trouble could it be to teach an assembly of youngsters to add and subtract?

Eyeing Julia's trim figure, he followed her into the classroom. She wore shoes today; he glimpsed the thin black leather beneath the swish of her skirt. He wondered if her stockings were plain, or if she indulged herself with the finest silk beneath that plain gown. Probably the former, but that didn't keep his imagination from tracking up slender legs to frilly garters and the satiny skin of her—

"Mr. Jackman, this is Miss Elfrida Littlefield."

At the front of the classroom, he found himself staring at a battle-axe face with sharp brown eyes beneath a helmet of iron-gray curls. Miss Littlefield's mouth formed a tight slit without any trace of lips. Jack knew the type. She was one of those sour old maids whose female parts had shriveled from lack of use.

"Welcome to the Corwyn Academy," she said, her hostile tone conveying the opposite sentiment. To Julia, she added huffily, "Since the younger ones cannot fend for themselves, I took it upon myself to leave my own upper-form class reading *Beowulf*."

Jack glanced out at the sea of small faces, girls on one side of the room, boys on the other. Like little soldiers, they sat in regimental form at their desks, slates held ready, chalk grasped in tiny hands.

On impulse, he swept an exaggerated bow. "Miss Littlefield, you are indeed the dearest, kindest woman in all the world." Then he grasped that wrinkled hand and lifted it to his lips, landing an audible smack on the back of it.

His silliness had a gratifying effect. Giggles swept through the class. Toward the rear of the room, Theo sat with the bigger boys, and a grin swooped across his freckled face.

Yanking back her hand, Miss Littlefield scowled without a shred of appreciation for his famous charm. "Well, sir! I cannot think what you mean by such a ridiculous display."

"I'm sure Mr. Jackman means that it was very good of you to help out here," Julia said, taking the older woman by the arm and steering her toward the door. "Now it's time for him to get started teaching his class."

She glanced back at Jack. Despite her efficiency of manner, her eyes danced with merriment. The look caught him like a punch to his gut. So she had a sense of humor, after all. For reasons he couldn't explain, he would have rather not known that.

As the door shut behind them, Jack found himself thinking of a thousand things he'd rather do than be left alone with some fifteen children under the age of eight. Eat a leisurely breakfast. Go for a gallop in the park. Coax Julia into bed with him.

Unaccustomed to postponing his pleasures, he surveyed the spacious chamber. It was fancier than any schoolroom he'd ever had the misfortune to occupy. The mantelpiece of cream marble might have graced the finest home in Mayfair. Pale blue draperies framed the open windows. The multiplication tables and a list of numbers in large type looked incongruous against the silver and blue striped wallpaper.

He seated himself on the edge of the teacher's desk. The moment of levity gone, the students sat staring up at him with goggle-eyed wariness. His mouth went dry. Good God, they were young. For some of them, their feet didn't even touch the floor. Their faces showed the sort of trusting innocence that made him want to turn tail and run.

Devil take it. If he could trade shots on a dueling field, he surely could survive a few days as a maths instructor.

He cleared his throat. "All right, then. You know me but I don't know you. So first off, I'd like for all of you to write your names on your slates and then turn them around for me to see."

Immediately, the scratching of chalk filled the air as the pupils bent over their work. A minute later, all the slates were facing him.

All but one, he amended. A tiny blond girl in the front row sat with her head bowed, hugging her slate to her white pinafore. She sneaked a glance at Jack, and her blue eyes welled with tears that rolled down her pale cheeks.

The sight kicked his heart. Good God. What had he

done? More to the point, what should he do? Go on with the class?

But how could he ignore her obvious misery?

Reluctantly, he walked to the girl and crouched down. "Er . . . is something wrong?"

She sobbed harder, her eyes streaming and her nose running. If anything, he'd made matters worse. Accustomed to the crocodile tears that women used to get their way, he felt helpless to unravel the mystery of a little girl's unhappiness.

Jack glanced at her neighbors. Several girls gazed on in scornful silence. Beside her, a pint-sized brunette with *Anne* printed crookedly on her slate appeared on the verge of sympathy tears.

He didn't need another wailing child. In desperation, he addressed the class. "Does anyone know what's the matter?"

At the back of the room, Theo thrust his hand in the air. "Mr. Jackman, Mr. Jackman, I do."

"What is it?"

"Kitty can't write her name. She hasn't learned all her letters yet."

One of the boys loosed a piteous meow—someone in the rear whom Jack couldn't see while hunkered down. A titter rippled through the room, and Kitty huddled deeper in her seat.

"Silence," Jack roared. "The next one who misbehaves will return here at the end of the day for extra work."

Instantly, he cursed himself. What the hell was he thinking? He'd have to sit here on guard duty. But thankfully, the room went quiet, allowing him to return his attention to Kitty.

He dug into an inner pocket of his coat and produced a handkerchief, which he unfolded and handed to the girl.

"There now, dry your eyes. Would you like me to write your name for you?"

Sniffling, she nodded cautiously and gave him her slate. He took the chalk and wrote *Kitty* with a fancy flourish. "Look," he said, "you have the prettiest name of anyone here."

A wobbly smile broke through her tears. It was a relief to discover that like any female, little girls were susceptible to flattery. Kitty scrubbed her face with the handkerchief, then pushed the crumpled mess across the desk to him. Jack tried not to cringe as he shoved the damp linen back into his pocket.

He rose to his feet, grateful to have weathered the crisis. Surely the remainder of the class would proceed better. Unless Kitty—and the other younger ones—didn't yet know their numbers.

The thought undermined him. He had a horrible inkling that he ought to have studied those lesson plans more closely. How the devil was he to teach basic numbers to the youngest, addition and subtraction to the middle ones, and multiplication and division to the oldest, all at the same time?

"I'm sure that all of you are on different levels of learning," he said, thinking out loud. "I cannot imagine that Miss Dewhurst taught everyone the same lesson. So perhaps she divided you into groups based upon your level of skill . . ."

His gaze sharpened on Theo and a black-haired boy seated side by side in the back row. The furtive movement of their arms alerted Jack that they were passing something back and forth.

He stalked to the rear of the room. Theo gave him a nervous glance and shrank down in his seat. Jack knew exactly how he felt. At one time, he would have been the one in trouble. He often had been bored by classwork and looking for any diversion.

But now he was beginning to understand a teacher's need to maintain authority.

He held out his hand. "Give it over."

Shamefaced, Theo slowly extended his arm and dropped a plain glass marble into Jack's palm. "I—I'm sorry, sir. Will you tell Mummy?"

The other boy, a large, rough-looking lad with the name *Clifford* laboriously written on his slate, muttered, "Mummy's pet."

Jack suspected he'd found the one who'd meowed. But he didn't have time to pursue the thought because Theo swung out his fist.

"Am not!"

"Are, too!"

Before a brawl could erupt, Jack seized the boys by the scruffs of their necks and separated them. And in the do-ing, he had a mad inspiration about teaching this class.

"Turn out your pockets, both of you," he said grimly. "I'm confiscating all your marbles."

A man is known by the company he keeps. Thusly, Mr. G.G., Viscount W., and Lord R. are all scoundrels of the worst ilk . . .
    —*The Rogue Report*

Chapter Four

The raucous screech of violins warred with the banging of keys on the pianoforte. Trying not to cringe, Julia reminded herself that this was the start of the school year, and the beginner class would vastly improve by the time of their first recital in November. But for now, until this heat wave ended, she had to do something about the open windows.

She wended her way past frowning Sadie and tow-headed Georgie, both dutifully—if badly—sawing away on their violins. Angelically fair Lorna was, as always, the only one practicing her scales in perfect pitch.

Julia gave them all an encouraging smile and continued toward Dorcas Snyder, who sat on the bench of the pianoforte, instructing Lucy Wilkerson, a solemn nine-year-old whose plunking notes showed that her musical talents had yet to flourish.

"Miss Snyder," Julia said over the noise. "If I might have a word."

With a long-suffering sigh, Dorcas rose from the bench and followed Julia out into the corridor. She was a plump, middle-aged woman with an apple face and graying brown hair topped by a white spinster's cap. "What is it?" she asked, wringing her sausage fingers. "Are my students disturbing the other classes? I know they aren't playing well yet, but I promise you, they will improve."

"Actually, it isn't the other classes, it's the neighbors again. We've had a complaint from Captain Perkins next door."

Julia had been hard at work in her office, trying to devise the budget for the school year, when the retired naval captain had called on her in a huff. "A man deserves to have peace in his own home," he'd ranted. "How am I to complete my memoirs with such caterwauling blasting at my ears?"

Julia suspected it was his afternoon nap that had been interrupted. But she could hardly ignore him, for the neighbors were already up in arms about a charity school operating in the midst of their respectable homes. She didn't need any more trouble.

"I suppose I shall have to close the windows," Dorcas said, heaving another sigh. With a handkerchief, she dabbed at her perspiring brow. "But never mind. We shall swelter for the sake of our musical arts."

Julia was tempted to mime playing a sympathy song on the world's tiniest violin. If Elfrida Littlefield was a grouch, then Dorcas was a martyr, and Julia didn't know which was worse.

"I'm not asking you to close the windows. Rather, I'd like for you to move your class temporarily to the ballroom and away from Captain Perkins's house."

"The ballroom! How am I to manage *that*? The violins, of course, are easy to transport. But what about the pianoforte—and the harp? They're far too heavy for me, what with my poor, aching back."

Julia prayed for patience. "Could you not cancel those particular lessons for a day or two until the weather cools?"

Dorcas looked horrified. "Cancel? Why, these childen need their practice time. There is not a moment to lose!"

"Then have your students move the violins. I'll see if Mr. Jackman can help me with the other instruments."

As a frown deepened the lines on Dorcas's face, Julia turned on her heel and walked away. She had no wish to foster the antipathy that Dorcas and Elfrida Littlefield harbored against William Jackman.

Jack.

Her heart skipped a beat. Lord help her, she oughtn't have agreed to the informal address. But now that she had, she couldn't seem to think of him any other way. *Jack.* The nickname perfectly fit his charming nature.

During the noon meal, he had been the quintessential gentleman, holding the chairs for her and the other teachers, soliciting their opinions of various students, and paying particular heed to Dorcas and Elfrida as if he sensed their dislike and was determined to win their good will. Occasionally, he had aimed a special smile at Julia, one that hinted they shared a secret no one else knew. And each time, she had felt a lurch of attraction deep inside, in a place where no man had stirred her in many years.

Or perhaps forever. Had her younger, naïve self ever experienced the true depth of attraction between a man and a woman? Back then, she had been caught up in playing the heady role of society's darling. She'd had scores of suitors and had shamelessly flirted with all of them. Her life had been centered around deciding which viscount or earl would be allowed to escort her to the park,

which heir to a duke or a marquess would be permitted
more than one dance at a ball.

Now, however, she had the maturity to judge a man by
his character instead of his noble birth. Curious, how
she'd changed in eight years. She would far rather be
loved by a poor scholar like Jack—

Julia stopped in the middle of the marble corridor. She
felt overly warm and in need of her fan. What was she
thinking? She had no time or inclination for romance.
And especially not with an employee!

Drilling herself with that despicable thought, she
turned the corner and approached Jack's classroom. She
could hear his deep voice, followed by a burst of childish
laughter.

Laughter?

This morning, Theo and the other first-period students
had been abuzz with conversation about Jack. She had
overheard his name bandied about in tones of excitement.
But upon her appoach, the children had fallen silent, and
even talkative Theo would only volunteer that they all
liked the new mathematics teacher. The others had given
vigorous nods of agreement.

Her curiosity piqued, Julia had intended to sit in on
one of his classes, but other tasks, including the geography class she herself taught, had kept her busy. In this final session of the day, Jack had a small group of older
students.

Curling her fingers around the handle, she considered
knocking. But at another rush of muffled laughter, she
opened the door. Her eyes widened and she froze in
place.

Instead of neat rows of hardworking pupils, the desks
had been rearranged into tables, facing each other. Instead of solving problems on their slates, the students
were . . . playing *cards*?

Jack was bending down to offer advice. "Hold on to your seven," he told Clive Spratt, a skinny fifteen-year-old with a thatch of dusty brown hair. "See if you can pick up a four to bring your hand to twenty-one."

"Aye, sir. Er . . . what are the odds?"

"That's for you to calculate."

A fist of rage sent Julia marching into the classroom. As her heels clicked on the marble floor, the cacophony of voices died to a hush. Six pairs of eyes fastened on her in guilty silence. The seventh pair, a gorgeous shade of green, held a flare of annoyance that vanished into inscrutable coolness.

She hardly trusted herself to speak to Jack, so she addressed the class. "I need a word with Mr. Jackman. As you don't seem to be doing anything of importance and it's nearly time for the bell, you are all dismissed early."

She had never seen a classroom empty so swiftly. With a screeching of chair legs and a clattering of books and slates, the youngsters fled, a few of them sneaking sympathetic glances at Jack.

Seemingly oblivious to her anger, he wore a pleasant smile as he watched them depart, nodding to several, slapping one hulking boy on the back and offering congratulations for a game well played. But when Jack turned to her, Julia saw her mistake.

Irritation blazed in his eyes. The instant they were alone, he said, "We were in the midst of a lesson."

"A lesson?" Too angry to stand still, Julia paced to one of the desks, snatched up a pile of cards, and shook them. "Do you expect me to believe this is part of your curriculum?"

"It's a practical way to teach them how to work out odds and percentages."

"By *gambling*?"

His mouth tightened. "Gambling involves the wagering of money or other valuables. That didn't happen here."

"But they'll be tempted later in life to use the lesson you taught them today," she said, flinging the cards back onto the desk so that several fluttered to the floor. "Someday, they'll have to labor for a living, as you do. Do you truly wish for them to squander their hard-earned coin on foolish wagers?"

"That wasn't my intention. Rather, by learning to calculate the odds, they'll realize just how difficult it is to win a game of chance."

"That is the most absurd logic I've ever—"

"I thought it rather brilliant myself. But of course, coming from high society, you undoubtedly have a very different perspective than a mere churchman's son." Settling himself on the edge of the desk, Jack gave her an enigmatic stare. "You must have known quite a few men who gambled."

Julia opened her mouth to rant that she *still* knew of many a gentleman who wasted his fortune on a roll of the dice—and that she despised the notion of unwary young ladies falling prey to their promises. Yet by going off on that tangent, she risked exposing a part of her life best kept hidden.

"Yes, I've certainly seen men behave like fools. But we aren't speaking of them, we're speaking of my students. I will not allow children to be exposed to such evils."

Giving her a conciliatory smile, Jack spread his hands wide. "I'm not trying to corrupt young minds, my lady. Rather, games keep their interest high. I realize it isn't a conventional approach, but if it can persuade them to work harder, then why not use it? Why not give them a way to understand the practical applications of a boring lesson?"

His glib logic stirred doubt in her. Was he right? She

certainly understood what he meant about holding the interest of her pupils. She had a sudden memory of herself as a child, staring out the window of the schoolroom and wishing she were running free outdoors.

But . . . *cards*?

Recalling the secretiveness of Theo and his friends, she asked coldly, "Did you allow the younger ones to play cards as well?"

"Certainly not. They used marbles."

"Marbles!"

"It's an effective method for teaching children their sums. You have five marbles, and you shoot three to your partner. How many do you have left?" His mouth curled in an engaging grin. "I challenge you to find one of those youngsters who doesn't know that five minus three equals two."

A bubble of humor caught Julia unawares, and she frowned to keep herself from laughing. Why was it that she was so easily swayed by him? Hadn't she learned her lesson about falling under the spell of handsome, charming men? Or believing their persuasive nonsense?

"I'll allow the marbles this once," she said coolly. "But there will be no more card-playing. Now, follow me. I've a task for you."

Jack sprawled on the narrow cot in the carriage house and wondered how he'd ever survive another day as a teacher.

The shouting and laughter of boisterous children in the garden penetrated the open window of his bedchamber. The attic room was stifling, and he'd stripped off his coat, cravat, and shirt in a futile effort to find relief from the late afternoon heat. He hadn't felt so exhausted since he'd raced his curricle to Brighton and won against Sir Harry Masterson by a hair. At least back then, he'd had the thrill of success and a sack of gold guineas to invigorate him.

Today, his reward for a day in hell was the lash of Julia's scolding.

He had actually been feeling a certain sense of pride in seeing his students grasp a concept. Granted, he'd encountered difficulties all day long—a little girl had been struck in the arm by a marble, several boys had nearly come to blows over a disputed card, another lad had been sick all over the floor and had to be sent upstairs to bed. But all in all, Jack had to admit that teaching wasn't as tedious as he'd envisioned. Rather, it was a demanding task, and he'd been pleased by his ingenuity in holding the interest of the pupils.

Not that Julia appreciated his efforts. After issuing another of her lectures, she'd assigned him to moving musical instruments to the ballroom in order to ward off complaints from the neighbors. It was a nonsensical task since the ache in his thigh foretold rain.

Absently, Jack rubbed the scar where he'd taken a bullet in a long-ago duel. He had warned Julia they'd have rain by morning—without revealing the source of the old injury—but Miss Slave Mistress had scorned his weather prediction. Then she had insisted upon helping him, never mind his chivalrous protests. Together, they had managed to wrestle the heavy pianoforte onto a flat cart for transport to the ballroom.

Oddly enough, the incongruous sight of a lady doing manual labor had whetted his appetite for her. Jack usually liked his women to be soft and feminine and seductive. But now he found himself remembering the dewy glow of Julia's skin, the way she had strained to lift her side of the pianoforte, the pursing of her full lips as she'd blown a silken brown curl out of her eyes.

And he wondered what villain had seduced and abandoned her.

None of the gossip he'd heard had pinpointed the

identity of Theo's father. Eight years ago, Julia had had scores of suitors and as many marriage proposals. She had flirted with droves of gentlemen, seeming never to favor anyone in particular.

Yet one of them had taken her maidenhood. Who? Had she given herself freely in the heat of the moment? If so, why hadn't she insisted upon marriage?

Or had she been forced?

Realizing he was clenching his fist around the bed-sheets, Jack obliged himself to relax. For all he knew, she could have romped with a footman. Her past was none of his concern. She wasn't the first woman to have been burned while playing with fire—and she certainly wouldn't be the last.

But as a result of her folly, she had set out to punish all scoundrels by illuminating their sins in *The Rogue Report*. She had wrecked Jack's marriage plans even though he'd had nothing whatsoever to do with her fall from grace. Because of her, he had lost Evelyn and his one chance to pull himself up out of the mire of debt.

So in return he would expose Julia's secret authorship to the world. That would put a swift end to her scandal sheet. The grandes dames of society would never allow their innocent young daughters to take advice from a ruined woman.

Staring at the sloped ceiling, Jack mulled over the problem of finding proof. He had deemed it unwise to search her office on his first night here. But now he itched to put his plan into motion. The children went to bed at half past eight, and if he waited until the house was dark—

Tap, tap, tap.

In instant reflex, he scrambled to a sitting position. Julia? It had to be her at the door. And he was half naked, stripped to the waist.

Jack swung his legs off the mattress, then stopped.

Hell, why throw on his shirt and coat? It might prove amusing to wrest another blush from Miss Priss. Then maybe she'd learn to steer clear of his chamber.

He lay back down on the cot, settling into a pose of indolence, his arms stretched up to cradle his head. "Come in."

The door inched open. Instead of Julia's beautiful face, however, he found himself gazing at the freckled features of her son.

"Hullo."

"Theo." Jack struggled not to show his disappointment and annoyance. Apparently, there was no sanctuary from children anywhere in this blasted school. He was sorely tempted to send the boy away, but a certain anxiety in those brown eyes stopped him. "Step inside. You needn't cower out there on the landing."

Theo opened the door wider and trudged to the middle of the threadbare rug. A typical little boy, he had a dirt smudge on one cheek, and the back of his pale blue shirt hung out of his breeches. He dipped his chin to his small chest and stared at Jack in bed.

"Are you ill, sir?"

"What? No, I'm just resting." The noise of the play yard filled the long silence between them. Jack prompted, "Did you come up here for any reason in particular?"

Theo lifted a shoulder. "Just to see if . . . if you told. About the marble."

"Your mother knows that the class played marbles as part of our lesson. As to the other, it's unsporting for a man to tattle."

Theo's eyes widened with relief. "Oh."

Jack expected the boy to dash back downstairs, but instead he tiptoed around the tiny bedchamber, peering at the tumbled belongings, in particular the shaving equipment on the washstand. Jack wondered if he had even met any other men.

Probably not. Julia had been renounced by her family, so Theo had had no affiliation with a grandfather or uncles. And what was it the boy had said on their first meeting? *Only ladies are teachers.* Jack must be the first male instructor in the history of the school. Not even a groom or footman had a place on the staff. He wondered if Julia realized that her grudge against men had left a void in her son's life.

A pucker still marred Theo's brow, as if something else weighed on his mind. Jack took a shot in the dark. "This Clifford chap, the one who sits next to you in my class. Is he your friend?"

"Yes, sir." For a moment, Theo's expression shone with hero worship, then his face fell. "But mostly he plays with the older boys."

Judging by his bigger size, Clifford must have failed and been held back with the younger children. "He strikes me as a troublemaker."

"Oh . . . er . . ."

"Never mind. I won't ask you to snitch on him. But don't forget, you're known by the company you keep. If he's always getting into scrapes, he'll pull you down with him."

Lord, if his friends could hear him now. They would hoot at the irony of the infamous Earl of Rutledge dispensing advice on proper behavior to a child.

"Yes, sir," Theo mumbled. He kicked the rug with the toe of his sturdy brown shoe. "Anyhow, he wouldn't let me be a pirate on his ship just now. He told me to go play hide-and-seek with the girls."

No wonder he was dejected. Jack hid a smile. It wouldn't do to tell Theo that someday, when he was grown, he'd enjoy playing with the fairer sex. "Do you want to solve a puzzle?"

The boy's face lit up. "Oh, yes, sir."

Jack waved his hand toward the desk. "Go find a piece of paper and a quill."

"Miss Dewhurst only lets us write on a slate."

"Then it's a good thing Miss Dewhurst isn't here. Go on now. Tell me when you're ready."

Theo scampered to the desk beneath the open window, and Jack heard the rustling of paper, the scrape of chair legs. Glancing over, he saw Theo poke the quill into the inkpot, drip on the paper, then scrub at the mess with his fingertip. He glanced guiltily at Jack. "Ready."

"Write these numbers. 1 plus 9 plus 1 plus 9 plus 1. Got it?"

Theo nodded vigorously.

"Now, figure out how you can combine those numbers to equal fifteen. You may use whatever operation you like, division or multiplication included." Jack closed his eyes. "And no questions or hints allowed. If you can't reach fifteen, then take the paper back to your own chamber and work on it."

There, that should keep the pesky little tyke busy for a while. And when he couldn't determine the correct answer, he'd be obliged to leave, and Jack could go back to contemplating his revenge—

"I know," Theo shouted. "I know!"

Jack opened his eyes and frowned at the boy. "Impossible."

"You just turn the paper upside down. See? Then it reads 1 plus 6 plus 1 plus 6 plus 1, which adds to fifteen."

"Clever lad," Jack said with a slow grin. "How did you figure that out so fast?"

"I dunno." Theo wriggled on the desk chair. "Will you give me another one? *Please?*"

All that youthful enthusiasm tugged at Jack. As a child, he'd learned to hide his own interest in numbers. His father had scorned academics, declaring that a gentleman needed only enough brains to succeed at the card table, enough vigor to please the ladies in the bedchamber, and enough speed to elude his creditors. To this day, Jack didn't let any of his acquaintances know his guilty secret, that he often devised mathematical conundrums for his own entertainment. He'd be laughed out of White's Club if anyone found out.

But a mathematics teacher suffered no such restrictions. Here at the Corwyn Academy, it would be nothing out of the ordinary for him to give number puzzles to a student. The thought boosted Jack's spirits—and inspired the solution to a nagging problem.

"I'll make you a trade," he told Theo. "I'll give you your fill of riddles. But in return you'll have to do something for me."

Ladies, guard yourselves from the rogue who would lure you into a deserted chamber. A scapegrace like Lord P. will not hesitate to ruin your good name . . .
   —*The Rogue Report*

Chapter Five

The whoosh of the wind awakened Julia. Huddled in bed, she came to a slow awareness of the darkened bedchamber. A chilly gust riffled the draperies and stirred a flurry of gooseflesh over her skin. After five days of intolerable heat, it was vaguely startling to have to grope for the covers. The smell of dampness foretold a storm, the warning punctuated by the distant growl of thunder.

Half-asleep, she realized that Jack had been right. He had advised against moving the pianoforte, but she had scoffed at his ability to predict the weather. At the time, the sky had been clear blue, the air unceasingly oppressive. Now they would have to move the instruments back to the music room in the morning.

Which meant she owed him yet another apology. How he would enjoy it, smiling in that dashing way of his, the dimples grooved deeply on either side of his mouth and a devilish gleam in his eyes. He had the most intriguing smile, full of mystery and knowledge, as if he were privy to a fascinating secret.

Come closer, it seemed to say. *Kiss me and you'll know, too.*

She snuggled deeper into the pillows, her drowsy mind allowing her imagination to run free with the thought of kissing Jack. His cheeks would have a delicious roughness, his lips would be firm and demanding, his hands caressing as he clasped her tightly . . .

The wind whistled for attention. Through the gloom came the fluttering of papers being blown off the desk near the window. Her notes for her geography class tomorrow. She had been working on them right before bedtime.

Nestled in fantasy, she resisted the notion of leaving the four-poster bed. But a nagging sense of duty overruled the luxury of selfishness. She needed to close the windows throughout the upstairs, including the large, dormitory-style chambers where her pupils slept.

Reluctantly sliding out of bed, Julia padded across the plush carpet, feeling her way unerringly through the darkness. Though she lived the life of a commoner, she relished her creature comforts. Her chamber held dainty rosewood furnishings, draperies of brocade and silk, and a thick Axminster rug to cushion her bare feet. No one knew that beneath the plain gowns suited to a headmistress, she wore the finest undergarments, lace and silk and diaphanous linen. Indulging herself with hidden finery was a guilty pleasure, the only remnant she allowed of her old life.

As she neared the window, another cold gust cut straight through her gauzy white nightdress and made her shiver. She wrestled with the sticky window sash until it slid downward and thumped shut. Then she hastened to the other window and did likewise. Immediately, the air felt warmer.

Pressing her face to the glass, she peered into the night. Clouds had blotted out the moon and stars. In the garden, the branches of the oak swayed back and forth like the dancing of mischievous sprites. Aided by the distant flash of lightning, she could discern the black shape of the carriage house. A candle had shone in the window when she'd retired, but now it had been extinguished.

Jack must be asleep. Her insides quivered at the memory of him sprawled in bed that morning, the sculpted muscles of his chest bare to her scrutiny. Would the soundness of his slumber prevent him from hearing the approach of the storm? The spray of rain through the open window would drench his belongings. She could hurry over there and close it, and he'd likely never awaken—

Julia halted the reckless thought. He was a grown man. He could take care of himself. Her only concern was the children in this house.

Groping her way to the foot of the bed, she found her blue silk dressing gown and donned it, tying the sash at the waist. Then she ventured out into the passageway and picked up the small oil lamp kept burning outside her door for those times when she had to tend a sick child during the night.

Moving quietly through the girls' dormitory, she shut all the windows. Amazingly, no one stirred in the rows of narrow beds, and she envied the children their ability to sleep without fear or worries, secure and happy.

In the boys' dormitory, she completed the chore, then paused by Theo's bed. When he was five, he had rebelled against remaining in the spacious nursery with his own governess and had begged to live with the other children. With some misgivings, she had granted his wish, reasoning that it was better not to show him preferential treatment. Ever since then, he'd had the best of both worlds, and she was fiercely determined to see that he grew up cherished, innocent for as long as possible of the prejudice against the circumstances of his birth.

The golden light of the lamp bathed his small, freckled face, the closed eyes with the fringe of russet lashes. A tender ache squeezed her heart. She bent down to draw up the coverlet that had half fallen to the floor, tucking it around his small form. He sighed and turned over, his breathing slow and steady.

Her son. What a precious gift he was. In so many ways, he made her life complete.

It shamed her to remember that at one time, she had feared to raise him alone. The notion of relinquishing her comfortable place in the world had been horrifying to contemplate. After his birth, her parents had decided—without consulting her—to send him far away for adoption. No one need know of the family disgrace, they'd said, and she'd been tempted to accept that easy solution. But somehow she'd found the courage to take Theo during the night and flee to London. She had come straight to her grandmother, the one person in her family willing to accept her decision.

Yet not even Grandmama had been able to forestall the gossips, and the news of Julia's disgrace had spread like wildfire. Her reputation had been ruined forever.

And good riddance, she thought with maternal ferocity. Theo *was* a Corwyn, whether her parents and society accepted him or not. The sacrifices she'd made had been well worth the price.

Bending, Julia gave him a light kiss on the brow, relishing his little-boy scent. Then she left the dormitory, quietly closing the door behind her. As she headed to her bedchamber at the opposite end of the corridor, her mind crept onto a path of doubt.

Was she giving Theo the best possible upbringing?

Should she have married so that he could have a father, perhaps brothers and sisters? Maybe she ought not banish the occasional gentleman who came courting, lured by the prospect of her wealth and willing to overlook her status of pariah.

The thought disturbed her. The last complication she needed was a debt-ridden fortune hunter who would squander Theo's inheritance. Hadn't she dedicated her life to saving other women from—

A muffled thump emanated from somewhere beneath her.

Julia froze at the head of the staircase. She held up the lamp, but the light failed to penetrate the great pit of darkness below.

It couldn't have been the wind knocking something over inside the house. Ever since an intruder had broken into her office over a week ago, she had locked all the doors and windows on the ground floor each night, even during the heat of the past few days.

Had a thief broken a window? Was he downstairs, creeping around, looking for something to steal?

Fear squeezed her rib cage, but she took a deep breath as a countermeasure. It couldn't be the same man. Why would a burglar return to a school when there were far richer targets in the immediate neighborhood? And to experience another random intrusion in so short a time span would be extremely unlikely.

There had to be another explanation for the noise. Perhaps one of the teachers couldn't sleep and had gone down to the library. Perhaps Faith Rigby, the art instructor, had taken to walking in her sleep again. Or perhaps it really had been the blustery weather that had thrown a branch or a piece of debris against the exterior of the house.

Listening, Julia gripped the newel post. The only sound was the crying of the wind, a harbinger of the storm. She should return to bed. But the sense of uneasiness lingered and she knew she wouldn't sleep until satisfying herself that no stranger lurked in the house, plotting to harm one of her students.

Julia made a swift detour to her bedchamber to fetch the iron poker from beside the fireplace. Then she descended the stairs, holding the lantern in one hand and the poker in the other. Her palms felt damp, her muscles stiff with tension. She wished fervently for a robust manservant to call on for help.

Or Jack. Broad, strong Jack who looked less like a scholar of mathematics than a gentleman who honed his boxing skills at a gymnasium. Unfortunately, if she went out to the carriage house, she'd likely have to jab him awake with the poker.

She briefly considered one of the other teachers. But why disturb them when she needed only to pacify her irksome imagination? All she needed to do was to check the downstairs rooms.

In the gloom of the foyer, the tall casement clock ticked quietly. A table against the wall held a vase of orange and yellow chrysanthemums that she'd purchased on impulse from Covent Garden. The air here was still warm and stale, the marble floor cool against her bare feet.

Gripping the iron poker, Julia stepped into the drawing room, where rows of empty desks sat forlornly waiting for the next influx of literature students. She forced herself to shine the light into every deep crevice of shadow, behind every table and chair. She checked each window to make sure it was secure.

The art room was next, the easels taking on the form of trolls crouching in the darkness. The odors of paint and

turpentine tainted the air. Assuring herself that no inter-
loper lurked unseen in the corners, she turned her attention across the corridor to her office.

Except for the small sphere of radiance cast by her
lamp, an impenetrable darkness swallowed the passageway. Shadows shrouded the doorway. Her steps faltered
as images flashed through her mind.

*Papers strewn everywhere. The dark form of a man
bending over the drawers of her desk. His mad scramble
through the open window.*

A pulsebeat of fear thrummed inside her. With effort,
Julia mastered herself, stepped inside the office, and
raised the lamp.

She slowly blew out a breath. The desk was pristine,
the shelves of books and figurines untouched, the windows tightly shut against the buffeting of the wind. The
distant bonging of the clock in the foyer heralded the
hour of midnight.

The familiar, lonely sound seemed to mock her. No
brigand threatened the safety of her students; she was a
victim of her own vivid imaginings. Why had she thought
a burglar would return when he'd found no jewelry or
valuables, anyway? She didn't entertain, so there wasn't
even any fine silver to steal from the butler's pantry.

Dread drained away, leaving in its place a bone-deep
weariness. Before returning to bed, she'd take a quick
glance at the rest of the rooms, but this time she didn't expect to find anything amiss. Yawning, she retraced her
steps out of the office.

And bumped into a man.

His solid form took half a second to register. Terror
flashed like lightning. By reflex, she swung the poker in
an arc. It met the solidity of flesh. Her lips parted, but his
voice rang out first.

"Argh—blast it, Julia!"

Her mind registered a familiar deep tone. Her scream emerged as a horrified gasp. "Jack!"

She lifted the lamp to see him vigorously rubbing his upper arm. Clad in only breeches and shirt, he had a disgruntled expression on his unshaven face. "What the devil was that for?"

"I thought you were . . . Oh, heavens. I'm so sorry. If I'd known it was you . . ." A rush of relief made her legs wobble, and she wilted against the doorjamb.

Jack took hold of her arm, his grip firm in spite of the injury she'd dealt him. "You look like you're about to swoon," he said, guiding her to the ivory striped chaise in her office and making her sit. He placed her lamp on a side table, along with the deck of cards she hadn't noticed in his hand until that moment. "I'd offer you a brandy, but I rather doubt you have any—and my own supply is sadly depleted."

His wry grin failed to calm the disturbance roiling inside Julia. Her heart was still pounding. She didn't want to think it was due to his proximity or the rich spicy scent of man.

"You need to sit more than I do," she said. "I'll have a look at your arm."

"Never mind, it's only a bruise." He uncurled her fingers from the poker and propped it alongside the empty hearth. "For a lady, you've quite a swing."

His teasing words only made her defensive. "You gave me a terrible fright, appearing from out of nowhere. What are you doing here in the middle of the night?"

"I couldn't sleep, so I came to fetch that deck of cards from my classroom. As I was leaving, I spied a ghost gliding into your office." His mouth curved lazily, creating dimples nestled in dark stubble. "But it seems I was mistaken, my lady. You're very much flesh and blood."

Julia's insides contracted. Was he flirting with her? Or was she reading too much into a casual comment?

Before she could decide, Jack walked to the window and opened it a crack, allowing a welcome trickle of fresh air. The sight of his tall, masculine form stirred a hunger that she resented for its disruption of her ordered life. With the lamp creating a soft glow against the darkness and the storm gathering strength outside, the spacious office was no longer her sacrosanct retreat. It had been changed by his invasion, shrunk to intimate proportions.

"What is this thing?" he asked.

A rounded lump squatted in his palm. He held one of the figurines from her shelves, and despite the uncertain light, she recognized it as one of the more disquieting of the collection. Like the others, it was fashioned of stone and had been painted in exquisite detail, right down to the sly grin on its broad face.

"It's a gnome," she said tersely.

"You collect little sculptures of make-believe creatures, fairies and unicorns and dragons." Jack strolled to another shelf, saying over his shoulder, "They all appear to have been created by the same artist. Miss Rigby?"

Julia tensed. For reasons of her own, it was not a topic she would allow him to pursue. Not even the other teachers knew about Bella. "No, and I wish to know how you managed to get inside tonight. I locked every door and window myself."

He returned the little gnome to its place on the shelf. "The door to the music room came open when I jiggled the handle."

A shiver enveloped her. Had it really been so easy to gain entry?

From the shadows, he was looking at her quizzically, so Julia felt compelled to explain her jumpiness. "One night last week, a thief broke into the school. I startled him here in my office."

Jack strode forward to give her his full, frowning attention. "He threatened you?"

"No, the moment he saw me, he ran off. He didn't steal anything, either, though he made a mess of all my papers. Luckily, I don't keep any valuables in my desk."

"What did he look like?"

She lifted a shoulder. "It was too dark to see. But when I heard a noise tonight, I thought he might have returned."

Muttering what sounded like a curse, Jack raked his fingers through his hair, mussing the dark strands. "So you came down here alone. With only a poker to defend yourself."

"I had no choice. I've children upstairs to protect."

"Next time, awaken one of the other teachers to accompany you. Better yet, hire—" He bit off the words, as if realizing the folly of barking orders to his employer.

"Hire a footman to stand guard?" Despite her antipathy, Julia privately admitted she was touched by Jack's protectiveness. But she was determined not to overreact to a random event, either. The neighborhood had always been safe. "This is a school, Mr. Jackman, not a prison. And *you* were the only intruder tonight."

Massaging his arm again, he regarded her with narrowed eyes. "Believe me, I'm grateful your aim wasn't better."

Then somehow, the air seemed charged with tension. The undercurrent of aggressiveness in his expression made her conscious of all the things she didn't know about him. And very aware that she wore only a thin nightdress and robe. Reflexively, she reached up to check her watch. But of course it wasn't pinned to her bodice; it lay upstairs on her dressing table. "You'd best leave before the storm hits."

"I'm afraid it's already too late."

He was right. With dramatic fanfare, the heavens opened with a deluge of drumming rain. Lightning put on a radiant show, while thunder clapped its approval and the wind keened its chorus.

"It appears I'm stranded for the moment," Jack added.

Gazing up at him, Julia felt seared by a bolt of attraction. "If you left now, you might be struck by lightning," she agreed.

And if you stay, the danger is mine.

"You needn't feel obliged to wait up with me," he said. "I can let myself out."

"I'll have to lock the door after you."

He frowned. "There won't be any thieves out on a night like this. Go on, now. You should be upstairs in case the storm awakens your son or one of the other children."

"A teacher sleeps in each dormitory. The children will go to them first."

Rain sluiced down the darkened windows. In the lamplight, Jack looked perturbed, his lips thinned. It reassured her to know he was chivalrous enough not to seize the opportunity to seduce her.

"Sit," she said, patting the cushion of the chaise. "Since you have your deck of cards, we'll pass the time playing vingt-et-un."

He sank down, one eyebrow cocked. "Surely you aren't asking me to succumb to the evils of gambling, my lady."

She threw his own words back at him. "Gambling involves money, or so I've heard."

"There are other sorts of wagers."

His gaze dipped to her mouth, and Julia felt a dizzying rush of pleasure. He *was* flirting. He wanted to play for kisses. And so, heaven forbid, did she. Would he actually suggest it?

As his employer, she mustn't allow him. Desperate to distract him—and herself—she blurted out, "We'll wager information."

Giving her an inscrutable stare, he reached for the deck and shuffled it. His fingers were long and nimble, languid in a way that made her think about them roving over her body. "What sort of information?"

"If I win the hand, I have to tell you something about myself that you don't know. And if you win, you tell me something about *your*self." The rules were safe. She could admit that peas were her least favorite vegetable or that she had a weakness for lavender-scented soap.

"Too easy," Jack said, denying her the ploy. "We'll turn the tables. The winner gets to ask a question, which the loser has to answer truthfully."

Julia's fingers gripped the silk of her robe. She didn't want to bare her life for his inspection. He might probe too close to her secrets. "We'll each have the power to veto the question."

"One veto allowed, no more." Setting the deck on the chaise, he nudged the pile of pasteboard cards toward her. "Ladies deal first."

She cut the cards, then dealt three to him and three to herself, facedown on the cushion between them. He waved his hand to proceed, so she turned over her first card and squinted to see it in the dim light. An ace.

He did likewise, for a four.

She had a queen next, and decided to stop lest the next one put her over the limit of twenty-one. "Hold."

He turned over a seven, and her heart pounded as she anticipated the face card that would mark him the winner. But his third card was an eight. "You win, my lady. Ask away."

Flush with victory, Julia studied him in the soft glow of the lamp. There was so much about William Jackman that she wanted to know, she hardly knew where to begin. "Will you tell me about your family?"

Though he didn't move, she sensed an instant tension in him. He gave her a brooding stare. "The question is far too broad."

"Then allow me to rephrase it. Who among your family did you admire the most while growing up?"

Jack glanced away into the shadows of the office. His fingers riffled the cards, the sound almost inaudible against the wild rhythm of the rain. "My mother, I suppose. She insisted upon proper behavior, made me abide by rules, and expected excellence in the schoolroom. But no matter how strict she could be, she was always there whenever I grazed my knee or fell ill from eating too many jam tarts."

"Was?"

"She died when I was ten," he said in a clipped tone. "From then on, I was raised in a bachelor household with my father and grandfather. Now, I believe it's time for another hand."

He shuffled and dealt, and Julia felt somehow cheated. He'd revealed a tiny slice of his childhood and it had whetted her appetite to find out more. But he won the next hand, and she had to submit to his question.

"You teach a class in geography," he said. "If you could live anywhere else in the world, where would it be?"

Home. She and Theo would go home to Claverton Court in Hampshire, where her parents still lived, back to the ivy-covered brick manor house with its mullioned windows and hidden passageways, the gentle hills and cool valleys, the twisting stream where she had gone on rambling walks. The memories made her heart ache. She would take Bella with her so they could all live together as a family again . . .

Julia drew a deep breath. "A silly question," she said with forced lightness. "I have obligations here."

"Silly or not, you have to answer honestly. Unless you wish to use your only veto."

She didn't. Turning her gaze to the rain-swept window, she considered the matter. Would she live in India, with its maharajahs and golden palaces? Italy, with the canals of Venice and the ancient monuments of Rome? Egypt, with its pyramids and exotic bazaars?

But Jack had asked for the truth, so she settled on a version of it. "The country," she said. "I'd stay in England, but I'd live in the country, somewhere with hills and fresh air and grazing sheep."

Stretching his arm across the back of the chaise, he watched her closely. "So why don't you? Move your school, that is. Leave the city for good."

Because she needed to stay close to society for a reason he couldn't begin to imagine. A reason known only to a handful of people who had been sworn to secrecy. "That's another question. And it's my turn to deal."

Julia dallied over the cards to buy herself a little time. He was going to pursue the issue, she thought. He would ask why she felt compelled to stay in the city when the country was a far better place to raise children. Should she tell a little white lie or use her veto? Perhaps she could talk around the topic, voice a viable reason, a truth that was not the whole truth.

He won with a two, a nine, and appropriately, the jack of spades. He leaned back on the chaise, his eyes a dark green in the wavering light. Julia braced herself, but he jolted her with a very different inquiry. "Do you miss being a member of society?"

Her mouth went dry. Why had he brought up the topic of her fall from grace? Was he merely curious about life in exalted circles? Or was he wondering about the facts behind her expulsion? Did he want to know the identity of Theo's father?

It would do him no good to probe. She didn't know the answer.

Burying the dead weight of the past, she decided to take the question at face value. "Sometimes I do miss it, but only in the sense of looking back on a golden memory, the ballrooms glittering with the light of a hundred candles, or the pleasure of gliding across the dance floor. It's easy to forget how tedious it could be to inch your way through a receiving line or how your feet would ache after a long night of dancing."

There had also been the sting of gossip and the petty jealousies from other girls. It still puzzled Julia as to why so many gentlemen had been drawn to her. Her hair was too curly, she was too outspoken, and her fortune was moderate in comparison to other debutantes. Seeing Jack watching her curiously, she added, "And in case you're wondering if, given the chance, I'd ever go back there, I'll save you the trouble of asking. The answer is no. Never."

He lifted an eyebrow at her steely tone. A dark, enigmatic expression hid his thoughts. It made her wild to understand him, to learn his likes and dislikes, to uncover his hopes and dreams, to know the feel of his naked flesh against hers. The gnawing hunger shocked her with its intensity.

He leaned closer. "I'm curious about your family," he said. "Are you still in contact with them? Do you have any siblings?"

"No!" Her palms damp, she reminded herself not to let him rattle her, and amended quickly, "What I mean is, we haven't played our hand, so you don't get another question."

"Quite so." Then he dealt the cards again, and for the third time in a row, he won.

Jack shifted his arm across the back of the chaise so

that his fingers brushed her shoulder. He looked like a man about to kiss her. Her heart lurched into an unsteady gait, and the pulsebeat of desire alarmed her. It had been a mistake to play this game with him, to invite confidences, to sit so near that she could smell the zest of man along with the dampness of the rain.

His mouth curled into a half-smile. "It seems to be my lucky night, wouldn't you say?"

Despite his respectable upbringing, William Jackman had an innate seductiveness worthy of a seasoned rake. But Julia knew how to fight temptation and win. At eighteen, she had juggled a score of besotted gentlemen; at twenty-six, she could certainly handle one overly charming mathematics instructor.

"Is that your question, then?" she said coolly. "The answer is, unfortunately for me, yes."

He stared at her, then laughed. "You can't mean to cheat me out of my question."

"You devised the rules, and I *did* answer you." Summoning a businesslike manner, she gathered up the cards into a neat stack and handed them to him. "Now, the storm appears to be passing. That means our game is over."

He frowned at the darkened window. The lightning flashes had subsided, the thunder had died to a grumble, and the rain had slowed to a monotonous drizzle that promised to continue through the night.

To her relief and regret, Jack didn't object. He helped Julia to her feet, but grasped her hand for a moment longer than necessary. The weight of his fingers caused a shiver of wanting. The feeling was intensified by the stroke of his thumb across the back of her hand.

"You're mistaken, my lady," he said. "The game isn't over. We'll finish it later."

A noble title is no guarantee of noble behavior in a gentleman. Recently, Viscount H. lured his young chambermaid into a wicked act of depravity.
—*The Rogue Report*

Chapter Six

As the comely maidservant walked past his prison cell, Jack liberated the pile of mail from her hand.

Her squeal of surprise echoed in the empty classroom behind him. At once, her cheeks gleamed pink and her blue eyes brightened. "Sir! Those aren't fer ye."

"Then I'll save you the trouble of delivering them."

She ducked her chin and batted her lashes in the universal way of a temptress. "'Tis me job. I wouldn't want t' be botherin' ye."

The language of her body spoke otherwise. She—Agnes?—had made her availability obvious from the moment he'd first set foot in the Corwyn Academy to interview for the post of mathematics instructor. It was faintly disturbing for Jack to realize that he felt no interest in her other than a connoisseur's appreciation for a lush, willing female.

"I'm on my way to confer with the other teachers. So it's no trouble at all." He grinned, giving Agnes a light slap on the rump to ease the sting of rejection. "Go on now, tend to your other chores."

"Aye, sir." Clearly disappointed, the maidservant flounced away and disappeared around the corner.

Jack retreated into the classroom and glanced through the packet of letters that had come in the afternoon post. The children played outside at recess, which meant he had half an hour of freedom. He intended to make the most of it.

In the two days that had passed since the storm, when Julia had interrupted his search of the ground floor, he had been unable to find anything to connect her to *The Rogue Report*. Not even when he'd stolen into her office the following night and examined the contents of her desk, which had consisted of ledgers, records, and forms pertaining to the school.

That meant she must keep her private papers stashed in her bedchamber. Unfortunately, the house teemed with students and staff members, and no opportunity to slip upstairs unseen had presented itself. Therefore, to gain entry he would have to seduce Julia.

It was a pleasurable prospect he'd been contemplating anyway. Far too much. He went to bed alone each night, thinking about hidden places he wanted to discover and explore, the secrets of her he craved to claim for his own. If he didn't know himself to be impervious to the appeal of bluestockings, he'd say she was becoming an obsession.

Frustration gnawed at him. Ever since their card game, she had kept him at arm's length by reverting to the role of stern headmistress. She had avoided his attempts to get her alone, addressed him with the aloofness of a lady speaking to a servant, as if he were as insignificant as one of those odd figurines that littered the shelves in her office. Her brisk manner revealed not a trace of the desire he'd seen in her eyes that night, the lust he needed to nurture into full blossom.

In his other life—his *real* life—he would have acted on that desire already. He would have wooed her with his mouth and hands, with soft persuasive whispers, until she'd lain down with him on the chaise, their moans blending with the crash of thunder and the pulse of the rain.

Jack cursed under his breath. It was pure hell having to proceed cautiously, to watch his every step. One false move and he'd be sacked. He'd be barred from the school, robbed of the chance to shut down Julia's scandal sheet once and for all.

He glanced out into the empty corridor, then closed the door. He could well imagine her reaction if she were to discover the mathematics instructor reading her private correspondence.

There were three letters. The first two belonged to other teachers. But the last one had Julia's name and address penned in precise, spidery script.

He extracted a small, sheathed knife from his pocket and crouched by the hearth to warm the blade in the embers. Thank God the weather had turned chilly enough to require a fire. He slid the hot blade beneath the red seal on Julia's letter.

The wax softened and gave way without breaking. Subduing a twinge of long-buried conscience, he unfolded the missive.

The writing was small and cramped and filled every millimeter of space, even up the sides when the sender had run out of space. Apparently, it had been written by someone to whom paper was a dear commodity. He glanced down at the signature.

Eliza.

No surname, so she must be someone well known to Julia. He scanned the letter, reading fast, aware that he had only a short time before the next batch of students arrived.

Bella has suffered from a nasty cold that has kept her abed for three days, but you mustn't worry for she is much improved now . . . we took a long walk down by the stream, and the spindle-berries have not yet split open to show their orange seeds . . . Bella wept when she found a butterfly lying dead beneath the yew hedge; we had to stop and give the poor little creature a proper burial . . .

On and on the letter went with descriptions of the countryside, a story about a neighboring farmer who had broken an arm in a fall from a hayloft, and numerous references to Bella—clearly a young child—and her mundane activities.

Jack slowly refolded the letter. Its tone held an aching intimacy that disturbed him in some unfathomable way. He certainly had no wish to lead such a dull existence. He despised rural life, had gladly left it all behind when his mother died. Well, perhaps not gladly at first, but at the age of ten he'd quickly discovered the advantages of living without someone reminding him not to wear muddy shoes in the house and to go to bed at eight every night.

He stared down at the letter. Who the devil was Bella? And Eliza? Julia had told him she had no siblings. Were Bella and Eliza her cousins? Or close friends?

He killed his curiosity. It didn't matter. He'd been hoping to discover a link to *The Rogue Report,* that was all. He needed to know how Julia gathered her information. Because she didn't travel in social circles anymore, she had to have spies, old friends who fed her slander about the misdeeds of ne'er-do-wells.

He heated the blade again, softened the wax, and carefully reapplied the seal, pressing down hard until it was firmly affixed. He'd root out her sources and her secrets. It was only a matter of time.

Julia sat on the ivory-striped chaise in her office, in the same spot where she and Jack had wagered questions two nights ago. Gazing at the man currently seated beside her, she felt none of that dangerous, heart-tripping attraction.

The Honorable Mr. Ambrose Trotter had arrived a few moments ago, ushered in by Agnes, who blithely refused to learn the art of checking to see if Julia was receiving visitors. But that wasn't Mr. Trotter's fault, so she pasted on a polite smile.

A ruddy-faced gentleman of perhaps thirty, he came from good English stock, a decent, solid citizen with no skeletons in the closet. If he had any history of rakish behavior, Julia had not heard so much as a whisper of it. But she almost wished he *was* a scoundrel. It would have been that much easier to toss him out on his ear.

"It's very good of you to call," she said, her hands folded neatly in her lap. "Especially as you haven't seen fit to do so in eight years."

Ambrose Trotter squirmed on the chaise, his fingers drumming his knee in a nervous tic. A rather bashful man, he had been one of her most persistent suitors, presenting her with a steady stream of flowers and lovesick stares. Today, he had brought a large bouquet of pale pink dahlias that sat in a silver vase on her desk. "I've thought of you often, my lady. Please know that I would have done everything in my power to help you had I but known before . . . er . . . before . . ."

"Before the birth of my son?" Julia spoke plainly, without the artifice she had once excelled in. She would not hide Theo as if he were a dirty secret. Her son had as rightful a place in the world as any well-born aristocrat.

"By the by, his name is Theo, short for Theodore. In Greek, it means God's gift."

Mr. Trotter's smile faltered. "Er, yes. I'm sure he's a fine boy. Fine, indeed."

The muffled sound of children playing outside the closed window filled the silence. There were two types of gentlemen who visited Julia from time to time, those who viewed her as a potential mistress, and those who wanted to marry her in order to gain control of her fortune.

She was guessing Mr. Trotter fit into the second category. The cuffs of his brown coat showed signs of fraying; the leather of his shoes appeared dull and worn. As a younger son, he would have few prospects other than the military or the church. He would need a wealthy wife in order to live in the manner expected by society. She couldn't entirely fault him; marrying well was the way of his world.

Julia was tempted to send him packing, as she had all the others. But ever since she had witnessed Theo's hero-worship of Jack, she had been nagged by the thought that her son needed a father. Since a romance with Jack was off-limits, perhaps she ought to open herself to other possibilities.

Resolutely, she focused on Mr. Trotter. He was prudent and predictable, with all the qualities of a steadfast husband. "How are your brothers?" she asked, taking pity on his tongue-tied silence. "Have they married yet?"

Apparently relieved to turn the conversation to a safe topic, he launched enthusiastically into a recital of his family news, giving the names and descriptions of his sisters-in-law, even the ages of his young nieces and nephews. Julia nodded and smiled and tried to imagine him playing catch with Theo or reading him a story at night. The image wouldn't come, but at least he did seem to like children.

However, that didn't mean he approved of her school. A gentleman would likely forbid his wife to teach the baseborn children of servants. But she wouldn't allow that. No man would control all aspects of her life, nor would she ever hand over to him her entire fortune, Theo's future inheritance.

Her stomach crawled at the thought. If she *did* marry, there would have to be an ironclad set of provisions drawn up by a solicitor—

". . . if you'll agree to it," Mr. Trotter said.

She snapped out of her reverie. "Sorry?"

He leaned toward her, groping for her hand, his face earnest. "I was asking if you might allow me to . . . to visit you from time to time."

Stiffening, Julia eluded his touch by folding her arms. Had she been wrong about him? In her iciest tone, she said, "If you're suggesting a liaison, you'd do well to leave here at once."

"Oh, no, my lady! You mistake me!" His widened brown eyes reminded her of a wounded puppy. "I assure you, my intentions are completely honorable. Perhaps my courtship seems odd after all these years, and if you don't wish it . . ."

She forced herself to relax. "It appears I've drawn the wrong conclusion, Mr. Trotter. Shall I order tea?"

Holding the three letters, Jack paused outside the art room and glanced across the corridor at Julia's office. Her door was partially shut, and he imagined her inside at her desk, working on papers, her face framed by silky brown corkscrew curls that had escaped the captivity of her bun. In a moment, he would have his opportunity to see her. But first, he would deliver the other two letters.

The murmur of voices emanated from within the art room, and a faint whiff of oil paint wafted out into the passageway. All at once, the familiar smell of his child-hood pulled him into the past.

He was back at Willowford Hall, where he sat in the morning room with its flood of strong light. He was trying not to wriggle in his chair while Mama painted his por-trait and entreated him to sit still. "Pretend you're a statue, darling, just for a little bit." The minutes dragged into forever. Gazing out the window, he longed to be climbing the oak near the stables, checking for tadpoles in the pond by the woods, stalking lambs as if they were lions on an African savannah. Then at last his mother re-lented, though delaying his escape by scooping him up in a hug. As always, she smelled of oil paint and flowers . . .

Gad, he hadn't thought about that in years. It wasn't like him to dwell on long-forgotten sentiments. Reading that purloined letter from the unknown Eliza must have sent his mind tripping down memory lane.

Jack stepped through the doorway of the art room. Two rows of easels dominated the chamber. A long table held pots of paints, boxes of pencils and brushes, and reams of paper. Dozens of drawings by students had been tacked to the walls.

By the window stood Faith Rigby, a young, board-thin brunette in a gauzy, paint-spattered gown. Her pencil moved in rapid strokes over her sketchbook. Not surpris-ingly, she was oblivious to his entry—and to the other three teachers who sat drinking tea at a small table near the hearth.

Except for the art instructor, all eyes turned toward him. Two resentful pairs out of three meant he wasn't even half welcome. But Jack liked a challenge, so he swept the women a courtly bow. "Ladies," he said. "What a delight it is to have all of you to myself."

Wearing a crow-black gown made uglier by the sour expression above it, Elfrida Littlefield harumphed under her breath. Her minion, pudgy Dorcas Snyder with the mournful hazel eyes, allowed him a wary smile that died a quick death when she glanced at Elfrida.

In stark contrast, Margaret Pringle's bright brown eyes sparkled in her elfin face. She beckoned to him with a delicate, age-spotted hand. "Mr. Jackman, do come and join us. We've a spare cup and the most delicious plum cake. I made it myself."

"That's very kind of you. But at the moment, I'm playing postman." With a flourish, he presented her with a letter. "And you are one of the lucky recipients."

"Why, thank you." The history teacher graced him with a beatific smile, then ran her fingertips over the letter as if savoring its arrival into the dreariness of her life. "It's from Thomas. I wonder if Hester has had her baby."

Jack couldn't fathom her excitement. He'd gathered that her only grandson, a prosperous banker in Leeds, let his widowed grandmother labor as a teacher rather than invite her to live in his fine home. Jack had a suspicion it was due to her utter lack of sophistication. She had been raised in the country, she'd told him at dinner one evening, and it showed in her coarse gray frocks and her plain speaking.

There were no letters for the two nags of the group, and they leaned in unison toward Mrs. Pringle. "Will you read it now?" Elfrida asked. "Pray don't let us stop you."

Dorcas heaved a heavy sigh. "You're so fortunate to have a family, Margaret. I myself never had the opportunity to marry."

And praise the lucky fellow who'd escaped her whining clutches.

But Jack couldn't resist the chance to win her over. "Your family is right here, Miss Snyder. How else would the children learn to play such beautiful music?"

Leaving Dorcas blushing with pleasure and Elfrida

scowling, he turned away and approached Faith Rigby by the window. Oblivious to him, she gazed at the drawing taking shape under her slender fingers, a whimsical scene of gamboling angels no doubt inspired by the children playing outside the window. At last she paused and he pushed the letter at her. It was a single folded sheet, cheap and thin, sealed by a wafer.

She cast him a startled look, her eyes as blue as the sea and as dreamy as his grandfather's—although for a different reason. "Oh! Thank you . . ."

"Jack," he supplied. "William Jackman."

"Ah, yes. Mr. Jackman. Mathematics, isn't it?"

At Jack's nod, she gave him a vague smile, tucked the letter inside the sketchpad without even looking at it, and returned to her work.

Jack wondered briefly what her story was, how she had ended up in this school for misfits. Not that it mattered. By his estimation, he had perhaps ten minutes before the start of his next class. It was time to give Julia her letter from the mysterious Eliza.

He said goodbye to the women, snagged a slice of plum cake—much to Elfrida's pinch-mouthed disapproval—and wolfed it down on his way out the door. The prospect of seeing Julia energized him. Even in a brief encounter, desire could be honed, double meanings bandied, small touches exchanged. Two days was long enough to allow her coolness to go on. The moment had come to remind her of the attraction between them.

The door to her office was ajar, so he didn't bother knocking. But she wasn't at her desk. The pristine surface held a neat stack of papers, a silver inkpot, and an extravagant bouquet of pink flowers.

Flowers?

He spotted Julia sitting on the chaise, conversing with a burly young gentleman. She was smiling politely, her face winsome and pretty, her attention engaged by whatever her visitor was saying.

A side view of her companion showed placid, ruddy features that looked vaguely familiar. The archetypal beefy Englishman, he was a study in brown, from his receding hair down to his tailored coat, breeches, and shoes.

Recognition grabbed Jack by the throat. Ambrose Trotter. One of Viscount Hungerford's numerous younger sons. The entire family made a virtue of penny-pinching. If Trotter had brought the flowers, he'd probably plucked them from some stranger's garden on the way here.

Why the hell was he visiting Julia? Was the leech *courting* her? Didn't she realize he was after her money?

Or had he come to proposition her?

Jack's fingers clenched into a fist. He was contemplating violence when another unpleasant jolt struck.

If Trotter spied him here, the masquerade was over.

A movement in the doorway caught Julia's eye. Her heart tripped over a beat. Her inactive senses, lulled by lackluster conversation, sprang to vibrant life.

Jack.

Tall and arresting, he stared first at Mr. Trotter, then at her. Those hypnotic eyes held hers for a moment, conveying the allure of a mystery that seemed to beckon to her. Then he turned on his heel and melted back into the corridor.

She found herself rising to her feet. "Excuse me."

"My lady—?"

"I—I'm sorry, I've just remembered an appointment. If you wouldn't mind seeing yourself out . . ."

Standing up, Mr. Trotter looked more bewildered than offended, and Julia knew she was being rude. It was madness to rush out the door, absurd to go chasing after Jack when she could find out later what he'd wanted. But the beguiling intensity of his eyes had made her wild with a curiosity that laid waste to her better judgment.

With swift, sure strides, he headed down the marble corridor. She hurried in pursuit. Her voice low, she called out, "Jack?"

He glanced over his shoulder. Rather than turn and meet her halfway, he disappeared around the corner. She found him waiting in the doorway of his classroom, his arms folded over his broad chest, the fabric of his form-fitting gray coat straining at the shoulders.

Like Mr. Trotter, he couldn't afford expensive tailors. Unlike Mr. Trotter, he caused heated tremors inside her, upsetting the balance of her composure.

Careful. Everything about this man intrigues you far too much.

She took a steadying breath. "Did you need to speak to me?"

"I don't wish to interrupt your . . . meeting." He glanced over her shoulder, unusually watchful, perhaps wondering why a strange gentleman had been in her office.

She had no intention of telling him.

"It's quite all right. Mr. Trotter was on his way out." From Jack's keen stare, Julia realized just how odd her dash after him must seem, and color burned her cheeks. She smoothed her skirts and gathered her aplomb. "As headmistress, I'm always available to my teachers. If there's a problem, I should like to know of it."

"I wanted to give you this." Jack reached inside his coat and produced a letter, which he handed to her.

Their fingers brushed, raising gooseflesh all over her body. In confusion, she glanced down at the sealed paper and, with a jolt, recognized Eliza's penmanship. She lifted her wary gaze to him. "Why would you have my correspondence? Agnes distributes the mail."

His mouth eased into a charming smile that flaunted his dimples. "I needed to speak to you, so I offered to drop it off."

"Speak to me?"

"Yes." With that peculiar alertness, he glanced out into the corridor. "It concerns your son. Shall we go inside?"

Without waiting for her assent, he ushered her into the classroom and closed the door. She didn't protest his high-handedness. Anxiety had wiped her mind of all thoughts but Theo. What could be so important that Jack didn't want anyone else to overhear?

"Has Theo been misbehaving? Miss Dewhurst mentioned that sometimes he and Clifford pass notes. I'm not trying to excuse my son, but—"

"It isn't Clifford." Jack settled himself on the edge of the desk and regarded her. "In fact, if Theo misbehaves at all, it's entirely due to boredom. He's mastered every concept in the beginner class—and then some. Not only can he divide and multiply large numbers, he can do so in his head without even using a slate."

Amazed, Julia sank down beside him on the desk. "He can? How do you know that?"

"I've been testing him outside of class. He's exceedingly sharp, my lady. It's my opinion he should be promoted to an upper-form class."

Shaking her head, she tried to absorb the news. She couldn't believe that in a few short days, Jack knew a vital fact about Theo that she didn't. "I don't like the idea of him being placed with older students. He's small for his age."

"He'll adjust. He can sit in the front so his view isn't blocked."

"It isn't that." Her stomach contracted with a mixture of pride and worry. How could she explain that Theo was her baby and she didn't want him to grow up any faster?

Or that he might suffer teasing from those who were not so bright, boys like Clifford? "If he switches one class, it will wreak havoc with the rest of his daily schedule."

The excuse sounded paltry even to her own ears, so she wasn't surprised when Jack smiled indulgently.

His hand settled over hers on the desk. It was a friendly touch, yet the classroom seemed to fall away, leaving only the two of them alone in the world. "You can arrange matters," he said. "I trust you'll at least consider it."

She bit her lip. Of course she would consider all angles; she always did when it came to her son. "Yes. I'll let you know what I decide."

"Excellent."

Jack's gaze strayed down to her mouth, and his fingers remained warm and heavy over hers. The deep green of his eyes watched her with the lazy intensity of a tomcat contemplating a sparrow. His manner had shifted smoothly into seductiveness, and the sudden sharp ache of need held her immobile. If she moved, she was afraid it would be toward him, rather than away.

Unfortunately, that one giddy, foolish act would have far-reaching consequences. It would cause irreparable complications to her position as headmistress.

With a coolness that went only skin-deep, Julia extracted her hand and stood up. She consulted the watch pinned to her bodice. "It's nearly time for your next class," she said. "If that's all . . ."

Jack rose, too, one hand pushing back his coat and resting on his lean hip. A smile played at the corners of his mouth. "It isn't all. We've unfinished business, you and I."

Though her heart jumped, she fixed him with a cool stare. "I can't imagine what you mean."

"Come now, my lady. Haven't you been curious about my question?"

"Question?"

"That night in your office. When you cheated me out of an answer."

"I did *not* cheat. It's your own fault you used an unfortunate choice of words." *It seems to be my lucky night, wouldn't you say?*

He chuckled. "Nevertheless, you owe me an answer. One true answer to any question of my choice."

Jack was flirting again, and she ought to put a firm stop to it at once. Never mind that the rejuvenated coquette inside her clamored to enjoy the game. Yet of its own accord, her mouth curved into a smile. "That's hardly fair. You've had two days to come up with a question."

"All's fair," he countered. "However, to keep the stakes even, I'll grant you the right to a question for me, as well. And I'll even allow you to go first."

In spite of all good sense, Julia was intrigued by his offer. Curiosity about him crowded her mind. *What was it like growing up in a vicarage? Do you have any brothers or sisters? If you're truly a respectable man, where did you learn to wield such remarkable charm?*

Would you like to kiss me?

She fought a giddy blush. "All right, then. But I'll need time to think—"

The hollow echo of a distant gong signaled the end of recess. Jack's mouth twisted in a wry grimace, and his eyes held a devilish twinkle.

Leaning forward, he dispelled any last illusion that he might only be interested in friendship. Tracing her lips with his thumb, he murmured, "Saved by the bell, my lady. It seems we've both been granted a reprieve."

Chapter Seven

"Early riser now, are ye? Never thought I'd live to see the day." Marlon limped over to Jack with a pile of starched cravats in his gnarled hands. Tall and hunched, the valet had sharp features that appeared hewn by a careless ax. He wore one of the coats Jack had traded to him, and the dull gold hue gave him a debonair look at odds with his uncouth manners. "'Course I never thought ye'd make it through the week, neither. Up at the crack o' dawn, facin' a pack o' little devils, havin' t' work like us common folk. An' here you are, still alive t' tell the tale."

"And kicking. Now, hand me that cravat. I'm in a hurry."

Jack set to work tying the starched linen at his throat. It was half past ten o'clock in the morning, and he had come home to change into garb more suitable to his club. If he was late, he'd miss the one person he wanted to see.

It was Saturday, thank God, and he had been granted half a day off from drudgery. Accompanied by Julia and

Miss Rigby, the younger children had gone to the park on a leaf-hunting expedition, while the older ones remained at school to practice for a play to be presented later in the term. He'd promised to return by three o'clock.

Clad in buckskins and a fine linen shirt, Jack hardly recognized himself in the gilt-trimmed pier glass. He was the Earl of Rutledge again. Odd how quickly he'd become accustomed to being plain William Jackman. He'd been at the school for a mere four days, as opposed to standing in this same spot more than a thousand times to tie his cravat.

Or maybe it was just odd to be ensconced in his own dressing room again, inhaling the scents of boot blacking and expensive cologne, surrounded by wardrobes and clothes presses, with the deep pile of the rug beneath his stocking feet. After fending for himself in that cramped chamber in the carriage house, he had almost forgotten the luxury of hot shaving water, clothes that fit him properly, and a valet to clean up his untidiness.

Not that he had time to enjoy any of it.

"In a rush, are ye?" Marlon went on, as always sticking his blade of a nose where it wasn't wanted. "Off to add another thousand quid t' yer mountain o' gamin' debts?"

"With luck, I'll whittle it down by a thousand."

"Huh." Marlon's sarcastic snort told his opinion of gambling. "If her ladyship knew how ye were spendin' yer free day, she'd toss ye out on yer ear."

"She won't know. She believes me to be a penniless scholar."

"Penniless. She has that part a-right."

Jack thinned his lips and ignored the comment. Over the past few days, he'd given little thought to his debts. He had slipped into another life, a life without creditors knocking on his door at all hours of the day. There had been a certain freedom in not having those worries constantly hanging over his head.

Of course, he would have achieved the same objective by marrying Evelyn. But his plan to pull himself up out of penury had been ruined by *The Rogue Report*. Or rather, by Lady Julia Corwyn.

As he put the finishing touches on his cravat, his thoughts strayed to the silken feel of her lips beneath his thumb. He had taken a calculated risk in revealing that his interest in her was carnal. She could have dismissed him on the spot. But the gamble had paid off. Those smoky blue eyes had shown shock, interest, desire.

And mystery. Julia had an enigmatic allure that fascinated him, something that went deeper than beauty. It was little wonder she had been the star of her one and only season. She possessed that indefinable *something,* the hint of secrets that a man craved to comprehend. Perhaps it was the sparkle of her fine eyes, or her dedication to her students, or the strength of will that made her a challenging conquest.

But conquer her he would. The keen thrill of anticipation gripped him. Soon . . . perhaps tonight.

Marlon brought over a pair of black Hessians gleaming with polish. "Her ladyship sounds like an angel, takin' them poor little ones into her school, teachin' 'em how t' read and cipher." He gave Jack an intimidating stare. "She ain't like yer other women."

Sitting down on a stool, Jack worked his right foot into the tight boot, tugging at the top while Marlon knelt down to push at the heel. He already regretted describing Julia to Marlon in vivid detail, right down to the blasted pocket watch she kept pinned to her bodice.

"She's hardly an angel," he said testily. "She's a fallen woman."

"She's a mother with a young son," Marlon shot back. "So tell me about the little tyke. You ain't mentioned him a'tall."

"His name is Theo, and he's seven years old." As Jack pulled on the left boot, his mind dwelled a moment on the boy. Jack would need to take extreme caution to keep his affair with Julia a secret. Otherwise, Theo might suffer jeering from the other children. Though the boy faced a cold future due to his bastardy, Jack didn't want to be the one to wipe the innocence from that small, freckled, trusting face. "He has a gift for mathematics."

The valet whistled. "Well, well. Just like ye at that age. Have ye given him any o' yer puzzles?"

"As a matter of fact, yes." Marlon was the only one who knew Jack's secret pastime, and Jack allowed him a grin. "We've made a bargain, Theo and I. Every morning, he gets a list of five puzzles in exchange for waking me up in time for breakfast."

Marlon loosed a raspy chuckle. "How's he manage that?"

"He bounces on the end of the bed. If that doesn't work, he tickles my ear with a feather." Jack stood up and donned the forest-green coat that Marlon handed him. He tried not to wince when the movement hurt the bruise on his upper arm, inflicted by Julia and her poker on the night of the storm. "He thinks it great fun when I swat at him."

"I'll have t' try that trick meself," the valet said, helping with the other sleeve of the form-fitting coat. "Mayhap the dun collectors would appreciate it. Especially after ye beggar yerself at White's today."

Jack ignored the veiled rebuke. If Marlon only knew . . .

Leaving the bedchamber in a hurry, Jack nearly knocked over a chambermaid in the corridor. The pile of folded linens in her arms tumbled to the floor. As she scrambled to pick them up, he bent to help her.

"M'lord! Ye mustn't. 'Twas me own clumsiness."

She was a short, drab, dark-haired creature in a voluminous white cap and aproned gown, with a hairy mole sprouting from her pale cheek. Jack paid little attention to his staff so long as the household ran smoothly. But now he found himself wondering about her life, if she was happy in her job, if she had a family to love. Gad! Teaching the bastard children of females like her was having an irksome effect on him.

"It was my mistake," he said curtly. "Not yours."

Leaving her mutely staring with blue saucer eyes, he strode toward the staircase, the brief encounter already forgotten. He was going to his club, but it wasn't to gamble, as he'd led Marlon to believe.

Today he had another purpose in mind.

Rubbing her arms, Julia paced her office and tried to absorb the horrifying news that had been delivered a moment ago. "Why in heaven's name didn't she tell me her father had returned to London?"

"She didn't tell any of us," Margaret Pringle said, tears swimming in her brown eyes. "She received a letter from him yesterday afternoon. It was lying right there on her bed. I only wish I'd gone into her chamber sooner."

Seated with her on the chaise, Elfrida and Dorcas murmured in sympathy. "It's hardly your fault," Elfrida said heavily. "Any one of us should have noticed Faith had gone missing."

Sometime after luncheon, Faith Rigby had disappeared from the school. Julia remembered the art teacher being unusually quiet during the noon meal, barely picking at her roast beef and potatoes. But she was often off in a dream world, and this once, so had been Julia.

She had been consumed by thoughts of Jack, remembering how he had touched her lips the previous afternoon. That one small act had made plain his interest in her, and ever since, she had been strung taut with anticipation of his next move. Would he catch her in her office? Or in a deserted classroom? Would he kiss her?

She must *not* allow him. Yet when he'd approached her at breakfast, his smile so charming, she'd found herself hoping he meant to maneuver her into being alone with him. But he'd merely asked leave to attend to some errands, promising to return in a few hours.

Those hours had flown by, and now she had a far more important crisis on her hands than his tardiness.

"I paid Horace Rigby a considerable sum to go away for good," Julia said. Dogged by dread, she walked back and forth in front of her desk, her blue skirt swishing with her agitated steps. "He departed for the West Indies three years ago. I saw him to the ship myself. Our agreement was for him never to set foot on English soil again."

"Men." Elfrida spoke the word like a curse. "I've yet to meet one who can be trusted."

For once, Margaret didn't defend the male of the species. She shivered within the black shawl that wrapped her tiny form. "I can't imagine why the poor, dear girl allowed him to coax her back home."

Nor could Julia. The last time Rigby had seen Faith, he'd beaten her bloody. "She can't have been gone long. A few hours at the most. I'll go after her, bring her back here."

Dorcas gasped. "You daren't! Only remember what a brute Mr. Rigby is. He threatened you harm!"

"We should send for the watchman," Elfrida said.

"The law won't get involved unless a crime has been committed," Julia said bitterly. "And it's no crime for a daughter to visit her prodigal father."

Not even if his violence had caused her injury in the past.

"It isn't safe for you to go alone," Margaret said, drying her eyes and creakily rising to her feet. "I'll accompany you."

Elfrida stood up, too. Beside tiny Margaret, she looked like an Amazon warrior—or at least the grandmother of one. "Don't be absurd, Margaret. You couldn't harm a flea. I'll go in your stead."

Dorcas sat wringing her plump fingers. "I—I'll go, too. If—if you like, my lady."

"Someone needs to stay with the children," Julia said. "I'm sure Elfrida and I can talk sense into Mr. Rigby."

And, God willing, bring Faith back here to the safety of the school.

The moment Jack stepped into White's Club on St. James's Street, he felt the familiar surroundings envelop him in luxury. The graceful, curving staircase with its iron railing dominated the central section of the foyer. The air held the smells of wealth: beeswax, rich foodstuffs, and an indefinable spice that belonged to these exclusive walls. Since the hour was not yet noon, the place was quiet and peaceful compared to the comings and goings of the afternoons and evenings.

That suited Jack's purpose. There was only one man he wanted to see, a man who had a habit of being here at this time every day.

But as Jack stepped briskly across the foyer, he had the ill luck to be spotted by George Gresham, leaving the wash closet in the opulent corridor that led to the card room.

Gresham's sandy-brown hair was mussed, his cravat had come undone, and his brown eyes were underscored by dark circles.

"Rather early for you, isn't it?" Jack asked.

"Rather late, you mean. Played through the night with Argyle and Sefton. Whistler's down fourteen thousand, and I've lost nearly twenty, but never fear, we'll win it back."

"I thought your father had cut off all your funds."

"Worse, he's disinherited me. But I'll convince the old miser to relent before he goes to the grave." Looking entirely too cheerful for a man in his dire straits, Gresham slapped Jack on the arm. "Wycliffe says you've been holed up with a female. She must've been quite the temptress to keep you from the tables all week, eh?"

Jack lifted a lazy eyebrow. If only Gresham knew he'd spent the past four days living like a monk. "Quite."

"Well, never mind, keep your secrets." Gresham rubbed his hands. "You should have been here yesterday to witness the new entry in the Betting Book. I've wagered Whistler fifty guineas that he can't find himself a leg shackle by Christmas."

Jack grinned. "He likes his women too much to be tied to one. Does he have any prospects in mind?"

"He has a notion to court Evelyn, but I doubt my cousin will let him in the door." Gresham cast a sly look at Jack. "Does that displease you, old chap? Whistler going after your former bride?"

It shook Jack to the core, but he held tight to his smile. God, Whistler must be drowning in river Tick if he too needed to wed an heiress. "I wish him luck."

"That's the sport. Say, will you join our game of hazard?"

The siren call of the cards pulled at Jack. For a moment, he considered sitting down with his cronies, betting on the next draw and letting the white-hot fever envelop him, the bright lure of hope that good fortune lay just around the corner. He craved the anticipation of riches to come. The cards held a brilliance of possibilities; anything could happen, even the chance of winning a king's ransom . . .

But not today. He drew a deep breath to clear his mind. He'd come to the club for a different purpose. And afterward, he intended to visit his grandfather at Wycliffe House before returning to the school.

"Perhaps another time."

Gresham gave him an envious look. "She's that good, is she? Well, I'm off to win back my twenty thousand— and more!"

The moment Gresham bounded out of sight, Jack headed in the opposite direction and hoped he wasn't too late. He entered an antechamber with tall white pillars and the portraits of past chairmen decorating the walls. A selection of comfortable chairs were grouped around the hearth, and it was a relief to see the man sitting in one of them.

"Ah, Trotter," he said, inclining his head in a nod.

The Honorable Ambrose Trotter looked up from his newspaper. His ruddy face bore an expression of startlement. "Rutledge, is it?"

Remaining on his feet as if he were waiting for someone, Jack withdrew a small container of snuff from his pocket. "Care for a pinch?"

Trotter cautiously shook his head. He must be trying to work out why a gamester had sought out his tedious company, Jack thought.

Jack inhaled a small amount of snuff, relishing the tingling rush of tobacco. Leaning an elbow on the mantelpiece, he gazed at his erstwhile companion. "So, Trotter, how are you faring these days?"

They had attended Eton at the same time, but no two boys could have been more different. Trotter had kept his nose in a textbook, obeying all rules to the letter. Jack had been the one to sneak out at night to visit the lightskirts in nearby Windsor, to pass playing cards under the pews during chapel. He'd thrived on his reputation for never cracking open a single book and for sleeping through examinations. He had finished at the bottom of his form, much to his father's amusement, while Trotter had placed somewhere in the middle—despite his diligent study— proving himself average to a fault.

A befuddled expression on his jowled face, Trotter looked up from his newspaper again. "Faring? Why d'you ask?"

Jack pocketed the enamel snuff box. "Curiosity, old chap. Have you married?"

"No." Trotter rattled the newspaper as if to remind Jack that he'd been interrupted. His lip curled in disapproval, he added, "As I recall, *you* were to marry. Quite a scandal, that."

Jack didn't want to talk about Lady Evelyn—or think about that huge dowry being courted by Whistler. Rather, he felt driven to ascertain Trotter's intentions toward Julia.

To gain the man's confidence, Jack strove for a commiserating tone. "A low point in my life, to be sure. When a man reaches thirty, he starts to think about setting up his nursery. Wouldn't you agree?"

"Perhaps."

"Then you must be looking at prospects, too. Have you any particular lady in mind?"

For a moment, Trotter had the air of a lovesick puppy. "No one you would know."

"Ah, so there is someone, a mystery woman. Is she a member of society?"

"She's someone I've long admired," Trotter admitted.

"So she isn't in society, then." Moving in for the kill, Jack came to stand over Trotter's chair. "Since you need to marry wealth as much as I do, I'm guessing she must be rich. Does she know you're after her money?"

From the mottling of Trotter's cheeks, he looked about to explode. "I'm nothing like you, Rutledge. And I will not tolerate your disparaging of the lady. She is far too good for the likes of you."

"Who is this paragon of virtue?"

"She's none of your concern." A clock bonged in the distance, and right on cue, Trotter snapped his folded newpaper down onto the table beside him. "Pray excuse me now. I must join my brothers for luncheon."

Reluctantly, Jack stepped aside and watched him leave. Trotter seemed sincere in his desire to marry Julia and earnest in his enumerating of her good qualities. But somehow, his defense of her only stoked resentment in Jack. He would far rather have cause to plant his fist in that ruddy face.

Dammit, Julia was too spirited and opinionated to find happiness with such a dull dog. So why the devil hadn't she tossed Trotter out on his arse?

Unless his courtship was a ruse.

A suspicion Jack had been mulling came to the fore of his mind. Was that bastard feeding information to her for *The Rogue Report*?

Mr. L.F. was spied whipping his hound last week. Ladies, beware the man with a foul temper. If he strikes out at his servants or his animals, he may well strike out at you, too.

—*The Rogue Report*

Chapter Eight

The house looked no different from the other residences along the quiet street on the outskirts of Mayfair. Built of soot-darkened gray stone and situated halfway down the row of town houses, it had no yard, only a few steps leading up to a plain white door with brass fittings. Here, sweet, gentle Faith had grown up under the thumb of her tyrannical father.

At the corner, Julia gave the hackney driver half a crown and bade him to await their return. Grinning at the excessive fare, he tipped his porkpie hat and settled down for a nap in his seat. Then she joined Elfrida beneath the gloom of a tree for a final, whispered conference on their plan.

"Keep Rigby talking," she reminded Elfrida. "Ask him about his plans for Faith, implore him for mercy, tell him how much we need her at the school, anything to distract his attention. But pray, don't make him angry. I won't have you harmed."

The gray cloak and plain black bonnet made Elfrida look grimmer than ever. Her lips were flattened, her homely features sharp with resolve. "Never worry, my lady. I've handled many a difficult gent in my time."

Julia knew that to be true. Having once worked in a brothel, Elfrida had trod a rocky path before joining the school. "All right, then. Listen for the signal."

"A shout from the cabbie," Elfrida said with a crisp nod. "It'll mean you're both waiting out front. Now, do be careful, my lady. You've the more difficult task of the two of us."

Julia felt a rush of affection for Elfrida, who hid a softer side beneath a gruff, no-nonsense manner. "Pray grant me five minutes to get into position before you knock on the front door."

At Elfrida's encouraging nod, Julia set off for the mews.

The opening between the two rows of houses was barely wide enough for a carriage, and the hard-packed earth had deep ruts left from countless wheels. To either side, twilight draped shadows over the tiny walled gardens. The stink of horse droppings and rubbish made her lift a gloved hand to her nose. Glancing up, she counted down to the fifth house and then opened the gate at the back of the property.

She paused a moment to get her bearings. To her relief, no grooms loitered outside the small stable. The leaves of a spreading plane tree whispered in a breath of wind, and through the branches, she could see the faint glow of a candle in an upstairs window.

Was Faith up there? Was she unharmed?

Julia shivered, partly from the cold, partly from dread. But she forged ahead, picking her way through an overgrown garden until she reached the back of the house. She wouldn't allow herself to dwell on the jittery feelings that urged her to turn and run.

Toward the right side, a thin pencil of light shone past the drawn draperies. She went instead to a door at the left, so dark and nondescript it had to be used by the staff. With any luck, it was situated near the servants' staircase.

Had five minutes passed? She felt through her cloak for her watch, but it would do no good to check the time. Instead, she counted silently to one hundred, then tried the door handle.

Locked. Now what?

The darkened windows were too high for her to reach, let alone wrest open and clamber inside. Having no other recourse, she approached the lighted room at the other end of the house, to try the door there.

Moving cautiously, she peered through the crack in the curtains. The room was a library, well lit from a branch of candles on the table, and hazy with smoke. In the next moment she saw why. A stout man sat smoking a cigar in a chair near the hearth.

Horace Rigby.

Though dressed in the garb of a gentleman, his deeply tanned, distinguished features were marred by a thin, cruel mouth. His brown hair, thinning on top, was neatly combed. As she watched, he bent down to scratch the ears of the black mastiff lying beside his chair.

Her stomach twisted. When had Rigby acquired a dog? Was the animal as vicious as its master?

Three years ago, from the rail of the ship, Rigby had cursed Julia bitterly, even as he'd pocketed her gold and promised never to return. She should have guessed that a man of his brutal nature wouldn't keep his vow. She should never have been so complacent . . .

But self-recriminations accomplished nothing. Better she should study the situation and decide what to do. Why was he still sitting there? Had their plan gone horribly awry? Had he already refused to admit Elfrida to the house?

Abruptly, the dog swung its massive head toward the doorway, as did Rigby. Craning her neck, Julia spied a squirrelly-faced footman gesturing toward the front of the house.

Elfrida. Praise God, Elfrida had arrived.

His face annoyed, Rigby spoke a few muffled words, which the footman answered with cringing insistence. Then Rigby clambered to his feet and stalked out of the library, the huge mastiff trotting at his heels.

Julia waited half a minute before trying the handle. To her relief, the glass door swung open on well-oiled hinges. She brushed aside the draperies and slipped into the chamber. The air was acrid with the smoke of tobacco, and dust coated the furnishings. Apparently, Rigby had an indifferent housekeeper—or perhaps none at all if he'd only just returned from abroad.

Her heart thudding, she crept to the door where Rigby and the dog had disappeared. Listening, she heard distant voices in the foyer, Elfrida's low, wheedling tone, then an irritated response from Rigby.

The plan had been simple. Elfrida would distract him while Julia spirited Faith out through the garden.

But now the way was fraught with peril. She prayed to God the mastiff wouldn't sense an intruder.

Julia's palms felt damp inside the kid gloves. Clenching her teeth to keep them from chattering, she slipped soundlessly into the corridor. No outburst of barking greeted her, but she did hear a growl and then a sharp command to hush from Rigby. With any luck, he'd maintain a firm grip on the mastiff's collar to keep the animal from lunging at Elfrida.

She kept to the rear of the house and searched for a

staircase reserved for the servants. Spying a door hidden in the paneling, she eased it open and entered a narrow, wooden shaft with steps leading up into the darkness. Should she encounter any servant, she intended to speak with authority, say that she was a friend of Miss Rigby's, and had come by her invitation.

But her luck held. The staircase was empty, as was the upstairs passageway. A shabby carpet runner muffled her footfalls. The house smelled of dust and disuse, for it must have been shut up these past three years. Spying light under a closed door, she headed straight to it and tried the handle.

Locked again!

As the hackney cab let him off in front of the Corwyn Academy, a brisk evening wind whipped around Jack. Deep shadows lurked on the front porch with its stately pillars. Along the splendid front of the mansion, the glow of lamplight shone from several windows.

It was late. Everyone would be at supper. He was supposed to have returned hours ago.

But not even that thought could mar his jubilant spirits. Lady Luck had smiled on him today; he had won two thousand pounds at hazard.

He hadn't intended to play, but the encounter with Ambrose Trotter had left Jack angry and unsettled. Needing an outlet for his frustration, he had gone back to the card room for the sole purpose of trading a few jests with his friends. He'd been sucked into the game within minutes, and the time had flown on the swift wings of a winning streak.

Two thousand pounds.

The amount was a mere drop in the deep well of his debts. But it was enough to hold his creditors at bay.

Enough to pay back his markers to Gresham and Whistler and a few other friends. Enough to clear his grandfather's household expenses until the quarterly revenues from Willowford Hall came in.

Jack bounded up the wide front steps. He'd meant to call on Wycliffe, but the game had enveloped him in a radiant glow that had blotted out all but the wager at hand. It was only when the needs of nature had forced him to take a break that he'd snapped to his senses and realized the lateness of the hour.

Devil take it. It wasn't as if his grandfather had been expecting him. Besides, Wycliffe understood the call of the cards. He'd be delighted to know that Jack had won a small windfall. Their celebration could wait until Jack had accomplished his purpose here at the Corwyn Academy.

Until he'd ended Julia's campaign to drag his name and the names of his friends through the mud of public opinion.

She reported only the truth, his conscience whispered. *You deserved to lose Evelyn. After all, you'd broken your promise not to gamble.*

Jack shoved away the thought. He'd intended to quit gambling *after* the wedding, not before. And as revenge for Julia's interference in his plans, he would put her scandal sheet out of business once and for all.

Tonight, while his luck was still running high, he would steal into her bedchamber. He'd coax Julia into shedding her inhibitions along with her prim clothing. Then, when they'd both slaked their needs and she'd fallen asleep from exhaustion, he'd search for the proof.

The spice of lust enhanced his euphoria. How he would enjoy taming her, melting that cool manner of hers, transforming the stern headmistress into his partner in passion. Maybe he'd even delay exposing her secret and stay at the school for a time, until he'd had his fill of her . . .

As he reached the porch, the front door opened and Margaret Pringle scurried outside. Her white hair shone in the darkness, and a black shawl draped her diminutive form. He had the mad impulse to grasp that tiny waist and spin her around in a circle—although he didn't dare tell her the reason he felt as if he'd conquered the world.

"Mr. Jackman! Praise heaven you're back."

Guessing the reason for her agitation, he winked. "Is her ladyship angry at me for being tardy? Just leave her to me."

"It isn't that." Her birdlike fingers clutched at his sleeve. "Oh, the most dreadful event has happened."

His elation fading, Jack placed his hands on her small shoulders to support her. "What is it?"

"Faith has disappeared. And her father has returned from the West Indies. I fear she's gone back to him."

"I see," Jack said, though he didn't. "So the school is without an art teacher."

"No, no, it's far more than that. You see, Lady Julia rescued Faith from the hospital three years ago. The poor girl had been thrashed to within an inch of her life, punished for daring to draw pictures instead of cleaning the house."

Icy fingers descended his spine. "By her father."

Tears splashing down her cheeks, Mrs. Pringle nodded. "Lady Julia paid him to go away for good. He was furious at her for interfering. He threatened to . . . to . . ."

"To what?"

"He threatened to kill Lady Julia if ever he saw her again. But she's gone after Faith anyway. Please, you must help before it's too late."

* * *

Standing in the empty corridor, Julia pressed her mouth to the crack of the door. "Faith," she whispered as loudly as she dared. "It's Lady Julia. Are you in there?"

No answer.

Was she hurt—or dying?

Was she even in there? She had to be. *She had to be*.

Holding panic at bay, Julia jiggled the handle of the door. If only she had the strength to knock down the wooden panel. If only she had a file, she might be able to pick the lock—

Glancing down, she uttered a breathless sound of surprise. How foolish of her! There, half-hidden in the gloom, a large iron key rested handily in the keyhole.

Quickly, she twisted it and opened the door.

The bedchamber was small and spartan, with drab brown draperies on the windows, a plain washstand and a chest against the bare walls. The narrow bed was empty, and beside it, a single candle flickered on a table.

Keen anxiety stabbed Julia. Then, as she stepped fully into the bedchamber, she spied a woman seated in a straight-backed chair behind the door. A blessed wave of relief eddied through her.

It was Faith. Her head was bowed, and a cascade of thick brown hair had fallen free of her bun, spilling down to the hands folded in the lap of her gauzy blue gown. Her shoulders were slumped in a posture of defeat. Dear God, at least she appeared physically unscathed.

But what had that man done to crush her spirit so swiftly?

Quietly, Julia shut the door and sank to her knees beside the chair. She took the woman's cold hands in hers and rubbed them. "Oh, Faith," she murmured. "What's happened? Will you tell me?"

At first, the art teacher seemed locked in a deep, impenetrable trance. Then she stirred slightly. Without lifting her head, she whispered, "Go away, my lady. Hurry. He mustn't find you here."

"I need to speak to you. Will you at least look at me?"

When she made only a small, choked response, Julia took gentle hold of the woman's chin and turned her face to the meager light.

A long, purplish bruise marked that pale cheek. Julia swallowed a gasp. "Oh, my darling. He struck you."

"He had to do it. I provoked him." Her eyes welling with misery, Faith lowered her chin to her chest. "I—I told him I'd only stay if he allowed me my art."

Julia's insides twisted with compassion and rage. Faith was a gentle, dreamy soul who deserved to be protected by her father, not abused. He should be encouraging her God-given talents rather than relegating her to the status of an unpaid servant. And a bullied one, at that.

"I won't let you stay here. Not for another instant."

Panic flared in those blue eyes. "But I *must* stay. It's my duty as a daughter. If I don't obey, he'll hurt me . . ."

"Shh. Leave him to me. Right now, I want you to think only about how very much you're needed at the school." Knowing that Faith treasured her students, Julia added, "The children will be lost without your guidance in the art room. Only think of all the wonderful lessons you've yet to teach them. Perhaps we could plan an art exhibit for later in the year."

Faith brightened a little. "In—in the corridor outside the art room?"

"Or in the ballroom or wherever you like. Now, come. We mustn't waste any time." Keeping her voice soft and soothing, she helped Faith to her feet. "We'll need to be very quiet in our departure. Can you manage that, dear?"

Faith shuddered, but slowly nodded her head. "I—I do wish to go back. But I'm afraid."

So was Julia. If they were caught . . .

She smiled encouragingly and slipped an arm around Faith's slim waist. "Then stay close to me. And don't utter a sound."

Julia opened the door to the dark, empty passageway. They went out, and for good measure, she turned the key in the lock so that nothing would appear amiss. With Faith at her side, she retraced her steps to the servants' staircase. They had gone only halfway down the corridor when a movement in the gloom ahead alerted Julia.

To her horror, the mastiff stood growling in their path.

Jack took one look through the rear window and immediately scrapped his plans for the rescue.

Hidden in the bushes of the garden, he studied the layout through a slit in the draperies. A blazing fire and a branch of candles lit a small library. Horace Rigby stood with his back to the curtained windows. Of above average height, he looked husky and fit, his skin baked dark by the tropical sun, his light brown hair neatly groomed. He strolled back and forth in front of the three women.

Each sat in a straight-backed chair with her hands bound behind her back. To the left, Miss Rigby kept her head bowed, her disheveled hair falling about her thin shoulders. In the middle, Elfrida Littlefield was the only one with a gag in her mouth—that figured. And finally, the third chair was occupied by Julia with her chin up and her eyes steady on Rigby.

He threatened to kill Lady Julia if ever he saw her again.

The horror of Margaret Pringle's words made Jack wild with rage. He wanted to beat that brute to a pulp. But he couldn't. Not while the women were guarded by an enormous mastiff.

The dog stood at attention, its teeth bared, as if awaiting the signal to attack.

Despite the chill of the evening, Jack broke out in a sweat. The situation was far graver than he'd anticipated. After surveying the place, he'd planned to knock on the front door, talk man-to-man with Rigby, and secure Faith's return to the school. If Rigby refused, Jack would use his fists as persuasion.

But the dog was a wild card that he hadn't expected. At a word from its master, the mastiff could tear out a man's throat—or a woman's.

Leaning against the stone wall, Jack tried to think. What the hell did Rigby intend? Was he trying to frighten Julia? Or did he mean to exact a more deadly revenge for his banishment to the West Indies?

He threatened to kill Lady Julia if ever he saw her again.

Jack's blood ran cold. Rigby had to be mad to think he could get away with harming three women—even if one was his daughter, one had no family at all, and the other had been renounced by her aristocratic parents these past eight years. But maybe he believed punishing Julia and reclaiming his daughter was well worth the risk of imprisonment.

Jack thrived on taking risks, too. He had a reputation for putting his neck in the guillotine, whether in a carriage race, a duel, or an all-or-nothing wager. But this time the stakes were too high.

Even with his small pocketknife, he couldn't take down both Rigby and the mastiff at once. Damn! He'd trade his estate near Wimbledon—his last and only resource—for a brace of pistols.

A key rattled in a lock at the other end of the house.

Jack crouched down into the shadows as a footman carrying a lantern hurried down the darkened path to the stable. Within moments, he led out a horse hitched to a small gig, secured the reins, and returned to the house.

Jack tensed. Rigby must be leaving. And he couldn't possibly take all three women with him, not in that gig. If the bastard came out alone, Jack could overpower him and then release the women.

Unless, before leaving the house, Rigby intended to commit murder.

"You can't possibly get away with this," Julia said for the tenth time. "If we don't return to the school at once, the other teachers will summon the watchman."

At least she hoped they would waste no time. How long would Margaret and Dorcas wait? And what of Jack? Had he returned to the school yet? Or had something delayed him?

Elfrida sat bound and gagged beside her, and Julia could see the truth in her grim eyes. They were on their own. They couldn't even appeal to the one servant, a footman named Smithers, for the nasty fellow had accompanied the dog upstairs, threatened to order the animal to attack if they didn't cooperate, and then had helped Rigby secure their bonds.

Rigby laughed at her threat. Smoke curled from the cigar between his fingers. "When will your friends come? Hours from now? We'll be long gone by then, my daughter and I."

The news frightened Julia. She glanced at Faith, but the artist appeared to have sunk into despair again. "Gone where?"

"Why, back to the West Indies, of course. With the money you so graciously gave me last time, I and another gentleman invested in a sugar-cane plantation." He flicked the stub of his cigar into the fireplace and turned to smirk at Julia. "Though perhaps I use the term *gentleman* too loosely. Buckland was clever enough to defraud a bank here in London. He escaped Newgate and made his way to Barbados with a considerable sum of money in hand."

"A criminal isn't fit company for your daughter."

"I'll be the judge of that." He strolled to Faith and stroked her tangled brown hair. "Englishwomen are scarce in the tropics. Buckland needs a wife, and he'll pay a pretty penny for this one."

Julia stiffened. He would sell his own daughter—to a felon?

Faith cringed from his touch. "Please, Papa. Leave me here. I don't wish to marry—"

"Silence!" he snapped. "It's your duty to do as I say."

"She's twenty-two and a grown woman," Julia said coldly. "You've no rights over her, especially since you've violated our agreement. You were never to return, never to bother her again."

Rigby swung toward her, raising his hand to strike, and Julia braced herself for the blow. "You forget, my lady, that *you* are the one without any rights—"

"Sir?" The footman with the sharp, shifty eyes of a squirrel stood in the doorway. "The gig is ready."

Rigby glowered at Julia, then lowered his arm. He walked around to untie Faith's hands. "Come, daughter," he said, his voice oily and coaxing. "We've a ship to board."

As the bonds fell free, she rubbed her reddened wrists. She straightened her shoulders and looked up at her father, who stepped in front of her chair. "I can't," she whispered. "I won't."

"You will," Rigby said in a steely tone. "Unless you wish me to set Lucifer upon your friends."

Hearing its name, the mastiff growled.

Faith shuddered, flashing Julia a look of wide-eyed desolation before grasping her father's proferred hand. He yanked her to her feet and led her to the footman.

"Take her out to the gig," he told the servant. "You may use that door over there." He pointed at the draperies that covered one wall, where Julia had come into the house.

In a whoosh of chilly air, the two of them vanished outside. Lucifer trotted after them, but Rigby commanded, "Come."

Instead of obeying, the mastiff whined and paced in front of the curtains, as if anxious over the loss of one of the prisoners. Rigby snapped his fingers, saying in a sharper tone, *"Lucifer!"*

The dog slunk back, its tail between its legs. Sinking down at Rigby's feet, the mastiff looked uneasy and agitated, its eyes sliding back toward the door.

Rigby's lip curled with amusement as he looked from the dog to the women. "The poor boy feels cheated with only the two of you left. If I gave the command, I wonder which one of you he would attack first . . . the sour old witch or the beautiful young lady."

Horror resonated in Julia. She had been straining at her bonds, but they were tied too securely. In Elfrida's eyes, she could see a mirror of her own fears. It was clear then why he had gagged Elfrida, but not her. He savored the prospect of Julia begging and pleading for her life.

"Let us go," she said with forced calm. "You'll only be in worse trouble if you leave us tied up."

"Rather, it's you who are in trouble. Your friends will come for you eventually. One can only imagine the shock they will feel on finding two bodies torn apart by a wild dog."

The gorge rose in Julia's throat. With effort, she kept her eyes firmly on Rigby. At a glance, he appeared to be a gentleman in his finely tailored garb. But she knew the cruelty behind the mask, and with cold certainty, she didn't doubt his ability to carry out his threat. "And you shall be hunted down and prosecuted. Do you wish to be tried for murder and sentenced to death?"

He laughed. "I won't be tried at all, my lady. I'll be long gone before then, leaving poor Lucifer to take the blame."

An odd scratching sound came from the garden door.

The mastiff leaped to its feet, barking and snarling, racing to the curtains. Rigby scowled, wheeling around to stride after the dog. "Blasted Smithers," he muttered.

He wrenched open the door, and the mastiff went tearing out into the darkness. "Lucifer!"

A frown creasing his tanned brow, Rigby glanced over his shoulder at the women, then returned his attention to the night, peering down toward the other end of the house, where presumably the mastiff had gone. Its distant barking blended with Rigby's frustrated calling.

Faith, Julia thought in dread. In frantic futility, she worked at the tight rope that secured her wrists. Faith was out there, waiting in the gig with the footman. What if the mastiff attacked her?

From the corner of her eye, Julia caught a furtive movement from the corridor. Turning her head, she started in shock.

A man entered the library. *Jack?*

Crouched low, he wore no coat or waistcoat, only a loose linen shirt and breeches. A distinct aura of danger surrounded him. With his rumpled dark hair and his fisted hands, he looked nothing like a mild-mannered mathematics teacher.

His gaze caught hers and he put his finger to his lips. Then, amazingly, he winked.

Her heart thrumming, she swallowed a cry of thankfulness—and a plea for him to save Faith.

He crept toward Rigby, who continued to snap orders, first at his dog, then at his absent servant. "Lucifer! Smithers, where the devil are you? Bring that dog back here—"

Jack lunged. Seizing Rigby by the scruff of his neck, Jack yanked him back and slammed the door shut in one lightning movement.

Rigby choked out a curse and swung up a fist. But Jack parried the blow and struck one of his own. Rigby's teeth clashed together and he staggered backward, crashing into a table. Jack dove after him, driving his fist into Rigby's abdomen.

The mastiff must have heard the commotion, for it jumped at the door, barking frantically and scrabbling at the glass. Julia could think only of Faith, outside without protection. "Jack," she cried out. "The dog. He'll go after Faith!"

Jack was too busy fighting Rigby to pay heed. The two men grappled on the floor, with Jack landing efficient, punishing blows that had Rigby fighting back in steadily weakening defense.

"My lady!" came a low voice from the doorway. "I'm safe."

To Julia's soul-bending relief, Faith scurried toward them, her frightened gaze flitting to the brawl. She knelt behind the chair and worked at Elfrida's bonds, saying in a low voice, "Mr. Jackman . . . he subdued the footman. He bade me wait in the back . . . but I—I couldn't leave you bound."

Elfrida's hands were freed, and as she reached up to undo her gag, Faith plucked with trembling fingers at the knot securing Julia's wrists. "This is all my fault," she moaned. "I—I'm so sorry . . ."

"Hush, darling. You're safe, and that's all that matters." As the rope gave way, blood tingled into Julia's numb fingers. She sprang out of the chair, looking for something heavy she could use to strike Rigby.

But it was over, she realized in a jolt of triumph. Jack had pinned the battered, bleeding man facedown on the carpet. A feral darkness in his eyes, he pressed a small gleaming blade to Rigby's throat.

"Call off your dog, Rigby. Or have your throat cut."

Chapter Nine

Upon their return home, Julia was acutely aware of Jack walking beside her. The shadowed entrance hall looked warm and familiar, its furnishings softened by an oil lamp resting on a table by the staircase. The tall casement clock showed the time to be only half past nine, but it seemed as if months had passed.

Years, for how else could her safe, comfortable world have been turned upside down in so short a span?

A pair of stout watchmen had carted both Horace Rigby and his servant off to jail. A dog catcher had been dispatched to collar the mastiff. After she and the teachers had given statements to the magistrate at Bow Street Station, Jack had escorted them back here to the school.

Now, Dorcas and Margaret clucked over Faith, exclaimed at the bruise on her cheek, and offered an outpouring of sympathy. "Come, dear, you must be exhausted," Margaret said. "We've tea waiting upstairs with apple cake and your favorite treacle tarts."

"In a moment." Leaving the others, Faith shyly approached Jack. "Bless you for saving me, Mr. Jackman . . . for saving all of us."

His mouth quirked. "Rather, bless *you* for enlivening a dreary Saturday."

"Your manner is entirely too cavalier," Elfrida snapped, though her stern regard lacked its usual malice. "However, if I may add, tonight you've proven yourself to be a worthy addition to our staff."

He swept her a lavish bow. "I'm happy to have been of service."

With the exception of Julia, the women ascended the staircase in a chattering group. She stood watching them, gripping the carved newel post, the wood solid and reassuring. The children were asleep, Theo included, and a part of her ached to kiss him good night, to stroke his brow and thank God for having been spared to love him another day.

But she also wished to speak to Jack in private. If truth be told, *he* was the source of her inner unrest.

She needed to reassess this man who had outwitted a villain, fought with cool precision, and afterward had taken charge with an innate air of command. Certainly, she was grateful beyond words and awed by his dashing heroism. But she was also shaken to discover the feral side to his nature.

And hers.

She turned to find him watching her. He stood in the shadows, enveloped by mystery, his expression unreadable. Until tonight, she had viewed him as merely an engaging charmer, a man who knew his effect on women and played it to the fullest. But there was more to Jack than met the eye. She sensed something about him that she was missing, something that defied her understanding. Her heightened awareness of him only served to emphasize how little she knew of his past.

Who was William Jackman? How could she have missed the hard imprint of experience that she now saw on his handsome features? The experience that had enabled him to come out of that deadly fight with nary a scratch?

The clock ticked softly into the silence. "Like the others," she murmured, "I don't know quite how to thank you for all you've done."

"It was my pleasure."

A slight grin awakened his dimples. But even as her body warmed to his smile, a disturbing realization lurched in her. He meant it. He had reveled in the grim thrill of danger. As perilous as the situation had been, Jack had enjoyed its stimulation.

And hadn't she herself enjoyed the aftermath? The world looked brighter and sharper, as if her senses had been honed by the sight of Horace Rigby thrashed and bloodied. It sickened her to remember how fiercely she had wanted Jack to punish him . . .

He ran his fingers through his dark hair, and she gasped. "Your hand," she said, taking hold of it and examining its raw, skinned knuckles. "You never said you were injured."

"It's nothing."

"It needs tending," she countered. "Come with me."

Picking up the lamp, she headed down the passageway to the back of the house, while Jack sauntered at her side. "May I ask where we're going?"

"To the kitchen. I keep a box of supplies there for when the children hurt themselves."

"Ah. Lead on, then."

From his indulgent smile, Julia knew that he had no

true interest in medical treatment. Nor did she. It was merely a pretense for them to be alone together.

So that she might question him, she told herself. As headmistress, she needed to know the background of each teacher. Clearly, this one had withheld certain vital details.

By the wavering light of the lantern, they descended a narrow flight of stairs to the kitchen. Night shadows shrouded the large, stone-walled room. The air held the lingering perfume of fresh bread and roasted meat and sweet confections. The staff had already retired to their beds; they would rise before dawn to light the fires and begin breakfast preparations. In the massive hearth, the banked coals gave off an orange glow that gleamed on the pots and pans hanging on the walls.

She waved Jack to the long, wood-planked table in the center of the kitchen. "Wait there."

The lantern in hand, Julia went into the large pantry and reached for the box of supplies kept in readiness for scraped knees and other minor injuries. When she turned around, hugging the small wooden container, Jack stood right behind her.

The assault of attraction took her breath away. But he was gazing at the shelves of foodstuffs. "We've missed our supper," he said, rummaging through the bounty. "What say you to a late meal?"

Her own stomach was too tied in knots to leave room for food. Rather, she craved the sustenance of his arms, the nourishment of his kisses. "Pray, take whatever you wish."

Their eyes held, and she blushed to realize the meaning he'd placed on her words. Seemingly oblivious to her inner turmoil, he brushed past her to fetch a wheel of cheese. "I shall, indeed."

Retreating, Julia sternly ordered her heart to stop racing. She dropped the box on the table, then took her time filling a bowl of water from the pump in the scullery.

Jack desired her; his manner told her as much. Would she allow him liberties? If she consorted with a teacher, she risked losing the self-respect that had sustained her these past eight years. Yet it grew increasingly difficult to think of herself as Jack's employer. By his actions tonight, he had made himself her equal—and as her equal he was all the more irresistible.

When she returned to the table, he had arranged a small feast: thick slices of Stilton, fresh bread and pats of butter, chunks of succulent ham, the outside encrusted with honey and cloves. He rubbed an apple on his shirt, sank his teeth into it, then held it out to her. "Care for a bite?"

The crook of his lips held an unmistakable challenge, the promise of shared intimacy, the fulfillment of all her longings. *Forbidden fruit*, said his devilish smile. *It's what you want, what you need, what you desire.*

"No, thank you," she said. "I'll see to your hand now."

Eating his apple, he meekly allowed her to administer to him. But his eyes were anything but meek. He watched her steadily, never wincing as she dipped his right hand into the bowl and used a cake of soap and a cloth to gently cleanse his wounds. The splash of water and the crunch of his apple frayed her heightened senses. His fingers were long and supple, and she refused to think of them gliding over her body.

"I was taken by surprise to learn about Miss Rigby's past," he said in between bites. "Tell me, what secrets should I know about the other teachers?"

"Secrets?"

"Does Mrs. Pringle have an estranged husband tucked away somewhere, waiting to kidnap her? Is Dorcas Snyder being stalked by a villain she wronged in her past?

Should I be expecting a disgruntled relative to attack Elfrida Littlefield during the night?"

The glimmer in those green eyes told her he was teasing . . . but not entirely. What should she tell him? Aside from Jack, she and her staff were all outcasts of one sort or another—a community of women brought together by their mutual need for a family. But she mustn't include herself, for that would only invite questions about topics she preferred to keep private.

"I suppose they've all had their share of trouble over the years," she said slowly. "Margaret has been shunned by her only grandson, Dorcas had a fiancé who perished on the battlefield, and Elfrida . . . well, she was born into the gentry, but circumstances forced her to work in a tavern for a number of years." In reality, it had been a brothel, but Jack didn't need to know that. "So you see, there is more misfortune than danger in their pasts."

"I wonder." He leaned closer, his forearm braced on the table. "What of the intruder who broke into the school last week? Could he have come to do harm to one of the teachers?"

"That's ridiculous."

"Then perhaps *you* were his target, my lady, for he was in your office."

Little did Jack know, she had lain awake nights worrying about that very possibility. What *if* someone had been looking for proof? "If he'd intended me harm, he'd have come upstairs."

"Quite true. He went through your papers instead. What do you suppose he was seeking?"

You cannot begin to imagine. "Money. Isn't that what all thieves want?"

"Not necessarily. Perhaps it was Rigby, looking for a contract you made him sign, barring him from returning to England."

"Such a contract would not have been enforceable in a court of law. Our agreement was verbal."

"Then maybe the intruder was seeking something else. Something known only to you."

With effort, she held his gaze. "Don't be absurd."

"Everyone has secrets, my lady."

"Then it is ungentlemanly of you to pry into them, sir."

Anxiety made Julia speak sharply, but she would not apologize. It was best he remembered who paid his salary. Affecting an air of cool aloofness, she lifted his hand out of the bowl and placed it in her lap, where by habit she had spread a towel, as she did while treating the children.

William Jackman was no child. His hand lay heavy and warm on her thigh, the sensation penetrating her gown and shift, making her breasts tighten. Irked by the betrayal of her body, she patted him dry and then applied ointment to the angry red weals that fanned over his knuckles.

"It's my turn to ask the questions," she said to defer any further probing into her past. "Tell me—"

"Wait," he said, holding up his uninjured hand. "Does this count as part of our game? Because you'll have to limit yourself to one question, then."

His eyes were twinkling again, making her relax. She resisted the impulse to smile back at him like a silly, lovestruck girl. "Under the circumstances, the game is suspended for the moment. Now answer me. Where did a vicar's son learn to fight so skillfully?"

"All boys engage in brawls while growing up." He grinned disarmingly. "It's in a man's nature."

"You showed an exceptional expertise in subduing Rigby, all without suffering undue harm to yourself. Such a high degree of accuracy can only be honed by practice."

He shrugged. "I took a few lessons at a boxing club

when I was younger. Besides, I had the advantage of surprise—and a dose of good luck."

Did humility prompt Jack to minimize his proficiency? Or did he hide certain truths about himself? "It seems to me you made your own luck. Not many men could have done as you did."

A dark gravity sobered his face. Setting down the apple core, he took hold of her hand and rubbed it soothingly. "I *was* lucky, my lady. Make no mistake about that. I don't know what I'd have done if Rigby hadn't sent Faith outside with the footman. From then on, it was a simple case of divide and conquer."

Simple? In the darkness of the garden, Jack had dispatched Smithers with a well-placed blow, then had ushered Faith back inside the house before returning to scratch on the door and attract the attention of the dog. His quick, decisive actions had not been learned while teaching mathematics. "How did you know that Rigby would let the mastiff out?"

"A calculated guess."

"And then you made a dash for the other door. What if it had been secured?"

"Smithers had unlocked it. And you forget, I knew it was still open since I'd just smuggled Miss Rigby back inside the house."

"What if you'd tripped and fallen in the darkness?"

A grin lifted one corner of his mouth. "Nary a chance, my lady. Not with a vicious dog on the loose, determined to rip me limb from limb."

Julia shuddered. The memory of the mastiff's bared teeth made her hands tremble as she groped for a length of folded cloth in the box of supplies. How could he be so blasé in the face of danger? Horror had held her so tightly, she still felt its imprint on her soul.

"Rigby threatened to set the dog on Elfrida and me. If you hadn't arrived when you did . . ."

When she made to bind his injured hand, Jack plucked the cloth from her and tossed it back into the box. He cupped her face in his hands, and she saw that all levity had vanished from his expression.

A cold, hard light burned in his eyes. "I did arrive in time," he said. "And Rigby is in prison. He will never again bother you or Faith."

She voiced her darkest fear. "What if he's released?"

"I'll see to it that he isn't. He'll be convicted of attempted kidnapping and transported to Australia for life."

"But how will you accomplish that? You're a teacher, a commoner, while he has connections to the nobility."

Jack's eyes narrowed. "He threatened a lady this time. *You*. No court will tolerate a crime inflicted upon innocent women. My only regret is that I didn't kill him."

"I wish you had." Julia stopped, shocked at her own vicious thoughts. She shook her head in a vain attempt to dislodge the bloodlust that would make her as foul as Rigby. She wouldn't have wanted Faith to witness the death of her father. "No, I don't mean that. I abhor violence."

"Yet you took great pleasure in Rigby's defeat."

Julia couldn't deny it. When she had paid Rigby an enormous sum to leave England for the West Indies all those years ago, she had not felt such a surge of joyful triumph as she had tonight. Tonight, it had been immensely satisfying to see his face torn and bleeding and bruised, a long overdue repayment for the years of abuse toward his daughter.

Perhaps in a way she had wanted Rigby to pay for the sins of all men who preyed on women. Including Theo's father.

"He deserved to be punished," she said. "Yet it cannot be right for us to revel in it."

"It *is* right. It's a natural response to overcoming a grave danger." Still holding her face, Jack rubbed his thumbs over her temples in soothing strokes. "What you're experiencing is the pleasure of being alive. It makes you aware of the blood pumping through your veins and the sweetness of each breath of air you draw."

No, she thought, *it's you who make me feel alive.*

His face had an uncompromising masculinity, its hard planes and angles tempered by the tiny laugh lines around his eyes. His lips were firm, the corners often lifted in humor, as if he derived great enjoyment from the world around him.

She wanted to share in that enjoyment.

He leaned a little closer. "A brush with death awakens the compulsion to savor life to the fullest. Wouldn't you agree, my lady?"

He was flirting, but she knew how to flirt, too. Unable to stop herself, she traced his lower lip, as he'd done to her the previous day. "I would very much like to hear you speak my name."

His eyes darkened. *"Julia."*

Gathering her close, he brought his mouth to hers. It was a light, tasting kiss designed to woo and entice, yet a wild yearning spread its siren call throughout her body. It made the empty places inside her crave the fulfillment of love.

She braced her hands on his broad shoulders lest she melt into a puddle at his feet. His lips held the flavor of apples and all the allure of that forbidden fruit. With his tongue, he coaxed for entry and she opened to him at once. He pressed his advantage, the sweetness of the kiss evolving into something deeper and richer. The increased hunger of his mouth created another surge of joy in her, this time a swell of greedy pleasure. She had kissed men before, but none in eight years, none so intimately, and none—*none*—had ever aroused such a riotous longing in her.

Somehow, she found herself sitting full on his lap, her breasts meeting the wall of his chest. His hands roved up and down her back as if to prevent her from escaping him. But of her own free will, she gave herself up to the bonds of passion. Her arms encircled his neck to hold him prisoner, too, while she learned the thickness of his hair, the muscled contours of his chest, the roughness of his cheeks. Their mouths were open, drinking of each other, and in some distant part of her mind, she was astonished by the scope of her wanton needs.

She must not allow herself to think of lying with Jack in bed. The cost would be too great, for if he learned one of her secrets he would want to know all of them. But surely, *surely,* she could allow herself the gift of this moment.

And dear heavens, nothing in her life had ever felt more right than the weight of his arms around her, the glory of his hands cupping her breasts. With increasingly frantic passion, he traced the edge of her bodice and reached inside the form-fitting fabric to caress the bareness of flesh. She gasped from the shock of pleasure that spread over her skin and into her depths.

He broke the kiss, but not their embrace. "Julia . . . darling . . . I want you. But this isn't the place."

She had a hazy awareness of the quiet shadows beyond the shining circle of their embrace. She didn't want to think of the world and its rules of proper behavior. "We're alone," she said, rubbing her cheek against his. "No one will come in here."

He laughed softly into her hair. "Perhaps one day we'll make use of a table, my dear, but not tonight."

Then, before her mystified mind could fathom his humor, his hands spanned her waist and he lifted her from him, rising to his feet and subjecting her to another deep kiss that sent all thought swirling away on a sea of desire.

"Come," he muttered. "We must go."

He was leaving. The bite of disappointment stung, even though she knew his departure was inevitable. Already, they had violated the code of conduct between teacher and employer. She wouldn't let herself speak, lest she entreat him to stay—and that would be utter madness.

Jealously guarding every last moment of his company, she let him propel her across the kitchen and into the darkened recess of the servants' staircase. They ascended the steps, pausing now and then to kiss and caress with bittersweet urgency. It was not until they emerged into the upstairs passageway and she saw the bedrooms that the cold fingers of reality invaded her glow.

"Jack—"

He nuzzled her hair, his teeth closing gently over the lobe of her ear and making her gasp. "Hush, darling. In a moment, we'll have comfort and privacy." His arm at her back, he guided Julia down the corridor toward her bedroom.

How does he know the location of my bedchamber?

The question vanished under a more alarming realization. Jack intended to have carnal relations with her. And it was her fault for letting him believe she was willing. How had she been so foolish as to encourage him?

How could *he* be so quick to take advantage?

She wrested herself from his seductive closeness. "No," she whispered forcefully. "I can't do this."

A tall shadow in the gloom, Jack reached out to her, his fingers brushing her face. "You can," he said softly, insistently. "You needn't fear discovery. We'll be very discreet—"

"You assume too much," she hissed, pushing his hand

away in a panic. She had the horrifying vision of one of the teachers walking out of the bedrooms. Or worse, *Theo.* "Now leave lest someone discover you here."

"I shan't go without you." Bending his head to her, he said in a compelling murmur, "Come to the carriage house with me. Please. I'm desperate for you, darling."

Julia drew a shaky breath. Under the veneer of common sense pulsed the reckless desire to invite him into her bed. If he knew how close she was to succumbing, he would seize the advantage. She made her voice low and harsh. "Go *now.* Else you'll find yourself out on the street without employment."

Jack slowly straightened, staring at her through the darkness. The quiet air seemed to throb with unfulfilled desires. Making a low sound in his throat, he raked his fingers through his hair. "My lady, you'll think me a cad. But I never intended to overstep my bounds. I was swept away by your beauty." In a tone of abject remorse, he added, "I pray you can find it in your heart to forgive me."

He bowed to her, then vanished through the staircase door without a backward glance. She stood in the gloom and reached up to touch lips that were swollen by his kisses. *I was swept away by your beauty.*

She knew better than to believe his honeyed words. Jack *was* a cad. He had just proven that to her. And yet . . . not even the cold, hard truth could extinguish the afterglow of raw desire. For the first time in many years, she felt alive and vibrant in every part of herself, aware of the keen ache to experience physical love with a man.

And therein lay a danger she must never, ever allow.

Certain vile men seek to misuse the women in their employ. Only last week, Lord T. attempted to seduce his younger sister's governess ...
　　—*The Rogue Report*

Chapter Ten

Sunday afternoon brought a festive atmosphere to the school. In the drawing room, the desks were pushed back against the walls and the benches arranged in groups. In the dining chamber, the maids scurried back and forth, loading the long table with a variety of dishes and filling a huge punchbowl on the sideboard. In the foyer, a slow but steady trickle of guests were admitted to the school, all of them women, all of them commoners clad in similar drab garments.

Jack deposited an armload of cloaks in a small antechamber. He had been assigned the role of footman while the other teachers kept the children in order and the hubbub to a dull roar. On his way out of the tiny room beneath the staircase, he nearly bumped into Margaret Pringle, who was leading Kitty into the entrance hall.

The tiny blond girl had regarded him with worshipful blue eyes ever since he'd written her name on her slate on his first day at the school. She was a pretty little creature, and he couldn't help grinning at her, especially now when she was fairly dancing with excitement.

"My mummy's come to visit me, Mr. Jackman." Glancing into the foyer, she pulled on Margaret's hand. "I see her, I see her! Hurry!"

Margaret laughed. "Run along, then."

The girl scampered away into the throng, heading straight into the arms of a thin woman who crouched down to hug her close. Her plain, careworn face lit up as bright as her daughter's. The sight brought a strange thickness to Jack's throat. It was ridiculous to feel so delighted that Kitty had someone in her life.

"Ah, it's lovely to see, is it not?" Margaret said.

He turned to find her looking up at him, her brown eyes wise in her wrinkled face. "*Surprising* is the word I would use," he said. "I was under the impression this was a school for orphans."

"Good heavens, no. But since most of the mothers of our students work as maidservants, they must live at their places of employment. Lady Julia has provided a safe home here for their children."

"I see." During his initial interview, Julia had emphasized that her pupils were the offspring of unwed mothers. It was he who had assumed the children had been abandoned to her care. "And the women are only permitted to visit on Sundays?"

"They are only *able* to visit on Sundays," Margaret clarified. She gave him a curious look. "Were the servants where you came from given more time off?"

"What? Oh, yes." Jack dredged up the name of his pseudoemployer. "The Ballingers were quite lenient in that regard."

"My goodness. Here in London, the aristocrats expect their servants to labor long hours for a pittance. Not all of the mothers could even be here today." Margaret clucked her tongue in disapproval. "Did you know, many noble households give their staff only half a day off a month?"

"I wasn't aware of that." How much free time were his servants allowed? Jack had no idea. Perhaps he'd check into the matter when he returned to his real life. "That certainly seems unfair."

"Exactly! While their servants rise before dawn and work without pause until past midnight, the gentry sleeps late and plays at frivolous amusements. They care for no one but themselves." Margaret stopped, smiling sheepishly. "Forgive me, Mr. Jackman. I didn't mean to lecture *you* on the injustices of the world."

"No offense taken."

She gave him a motherly pat on the arm. "You are indeed a dear man. I could see the goodness in you even before you rescued Faith. Lady Julia must be very thankful that she hired you."

Margaret trotted off to welcome another arrival, leaving Jack stunned in the alcove beneath the staircase. *Goodness?* Either the old woman must be in want of spectacles, or he was doing a superb job of fooling everyone. As for Julia being thankful . . . he thought it far more likely she was damning the day he'd walked into her office.

From his vantage point, he could see into the drawing room and the entrance hall, but Miss Vixen was nowhere among the children and mothers talking in groups, strolling down the corridors, and entering the dining chamber to partake of the food. He had glimpsed her from time to time, always busy, never alone where he might steal a private word with her. Julia had been treating him with polite disinterest all day, and he'd had enough of it.

After breakfast, she and Faith had taken charge of the

younger children while the entire student body had walked double-file to St. Swithin's for the nine o'clock service, with Dorcas and Elfrida in the middle, leaving Jack to shepherd the older pupils at the rear. Then, all during the party preparations, she had flitted in and out, scarcely giving him a glance. No one could have guessed that only the previous evening she and Jack had shared a series of torrid kisses, the likes of which he hadn't known in years . . . perhaps forever.

It must have been the aftereffects of danger that had set his world off its axis. Holding Julia at last, he had felt unbalanced by a fury of feelings, not the least of which was a fierce possessiveness. Julia had been wild for him, too, so responsive that he'd forgotten finesse, forgotten restraint, forgotten to heed the cues of her inexperience.

But now he remembered her tentativeness in touching him. Her gasp of shock when he'd touched her breasts. Her confusion at his reference to making love right there on the table in the kitchen.

Yes, now he could see there was an innocence about her that should have made him more careful of her sensibilities. She was a gently bred lady, not a seasoned courtesan. She likely hadn't lain with a man in eight years—and Jack had pushed her too hard, too fast.

The realization left him tense and frustrated and eager to make amends. This time, he would think with his brains and not his balls. He looked forward to sparring with her again, to wooing her so that he could gain access to her bedchamber. He must not lose sight of his mission to find out if she was behind *The Rogue Report*.

He strolled forward to glance into the drawing room, but Julia wasn't present. In one corner, Elfrida was reading a story aloud to a group of younger students whose mothers had been unable to visit. From the screeching of violins coming from down the corridor, Dorcas must be showing some of the guests the progress their children had made during the week. Even Faith was here, chatting with several of the visitors, the bruise on her cheek made less conspicuous by a liberal application of powder. That proof of her abuse at the hands of her father stirred the remnants of anger in Jack. If there hadn't been women present at Rigby's house, he'd have cheerfully slit that bastard's throat.

People strolled up and down the corridor, and in their midst, someone snared Jack's attention. A woman had just walked out of Julia's office, one of the mothers. The short, nondescript female turned back to nod, and he caught a glimpse of Julia standing just inside the doorway. Her dark, curly hair was caught up in a bun, her watch was pinned just above the well-shaped curve of her bosom, and her long-sleeved gown was a dull dark blue.

She was the headmistress again. Probably discussing some child's progress in school. Did she intend to conduct business for the rest of the afternoon, consulting with various mothers?

She must be, for the first woman left and another one took her place, stepping inside the office. Damn, it didn't bode well for his plan to charm Julia out of her high dudgeon. It would take time and effort to ease himself back into her good graces. Tomorrow started another school week, and his schedule would severely limit the opportunities to speak to her alone—

Feeling a tug on his coat, he looked down to see one of the younger girls regarding him with mournful brown eyes. Lucy Wilkerson was a solemn, unattractive nine-year-old with limp black hair, sallow skin, and plain features. "Help me," she whispered. "Please, Mr. Jackman."

Frowning, he looked around the busy corridor, but

couldn't see any of the other teachers. He bent down, the better to hear her. "What's wrong?"

"Those bad boys took Maggie. They're being mean to her."

Jack cudgeled his brain. "Maggie? I don't recall any student by that name."

"She's my *doll*. Mummy gave her to me for my birthday, but Theo and Clifford *stole* her."

Good God. Jack glanced down at Julia's office, shelved his own ambitions, and said in resignation, "Where are they?"

"In the library. And you must *hurry*." Her lower lip quivered. "They're . . . they're taking all of her clothes off!"

He didn't know whether to laugh or grimace. "I'll see to the matter."

He reached out, intending to guide Lucy by the shoulder through the congestion of students and guests. But she grasped his hand instead, her fingers small and trusting, like a little bird nesting within the safety of his palm. She clung tightly as they proceeded past the staircase to another corridor, this one blessedly free of people.

What an odd twist his life had taken, Jack thought with a glint of humor. He, who had prided himself on having no encumbrances, who had never given a second glance to children, now had the duty of supervising a vast brood of them. By all rights, he ought to be resenting every moment of it, but instead, he'd often found himself amused by the antics of the students.

Upon reaching the library, he bade Lucy wait outside in the corridor, then stepped through the open doorway. The spacious room would have suited a fine mansion in Mayfair. Tall windows intersected the long rows of bookshelves. On an oak table, a large atlas stood open to maps of China and Japan. Here, in between attending to administrative duties in her office, Julia taught her geography classes.

Now her son was engaged in less than academic activities.

Jack headed toward the sound of gleeful whispers emanating from behind a grouping of chairs. Quietly moving into position, he spied the two boys crouched on the floor in the corner, their backs to him. Brawny, dark-haired Clifford partially blocked Jack's view of Theo, who appeared absorbed in some mischief.

Jack inched closer. They had stripped the doll of its frilly white dress—not that there was anything remotely revealing about the beige fabric of the body with its floppy arms and legs. One of the boys had fashioned a noose out of a shoelace and tied it around the doll's neck. The china head with its profusion of blond curls lolled to the side as Theo attempted to hang the doll from the makeshift gallows of a ladderback chair.

"Hurry up," Clifford snapped. "If we're caught, I won't let you join my gang."

"I—I can't get this knotted."

"Bleedin' idiot," Clifford said, grabbing for the doll without giving Theo a chance to untangle the strings. "I'll show you how it's done."

"Wait—!"

But it was too late. Decapitated, the body thunked to the floor and the china head rolled under a nearby table.

Theo gasped. "Now look what you've done."

"Me?" Clifford gave the younger boy a push, causing him to fall back on his bum. "'Twas your fault, you clumsy sod. And you'd best not tattle on me."

"N-nay. I—I won't."

"Mind that you don't," Clifford said, raising his fist and making Theo cower. "Or I'll beat you bloody."

Jack loudly cleared his throat.

Both boys swiveled around and froze. Theo stared up from the floor, his eyes wide and his mouth forming an O in his freckled face. He looked small and scrawny beside the larger Clifford, whose rough features showed a blend of alarm and aggression.

In the next instant, Clifford scrambled to his feet and made a dash for the door. But Jack was quicker. He seized Clifford by the back of his collar and force-marched him to the nearest table, planting him in a chair. Finding pen, ink, and paper among Julia's class supplies, he thrust them in front of the boy.

"Start adding," Jack said grimly. "One plus one, two plus two, three plus three, and on up all the way to one hundred."

"But sir—"

"But nothing, or I'll make it one thousand."

From the aghast look on Clifford's face, Jack knew he'd lucked upon the perfect punishment for the thick-skulled troublemaker. Theo, however, was another matter. Such an assignment would be a joy for him.

Julia's son stood with his shoulders hunched in a pose of abject misery. "It—it was my fault, sir. I broke the doll."

"You're both in the wrong." And it was time Theo learned to defend himself from bullies. "For your punishment, you'll report to me in my classroom at the end of school tomorrow. Is that understood?"

"Yes, sir."

"Exellent. Now, find the pieces of the doll."

While Clifford's pen scratched laboriously across the paper, Theo scrambled to do Jack's bidding. He returned a moment later with a jumble of clothing and body parts which he dumped on the table. Jack examined the hollow china head with its pale, painted face—miraculously unchipped—retied the broken string that secured it to the body, and seated it into the neck. Then he handed the doll to Theo. "Dress it."

His face beet red, Theo set to working the doll's arms into the tight sleeves of the little pink gown. Tying the fluffy bow at the back took him even longer, and as he worked, he kept his tongue stuck in the corner of his mouth.

Standing over the two boys, Jack pondered the allure of a bully to an impressionable boy. Separating them would improve matters, and he hoped Julia had decided in favor of moving Theo to an upper-form mathematics class.

Then he wondered why it mattered to him. He'd be gone from this school as soon as he found his proof. Maybe he couldn't help remembering what it was like to be a little boy trying to make his place in the world. He'd been small for his age until he'd hit thirteen, when he'd filled out and grown five inches in one year.

Clifford lifted his head from his work and glowered at Theo. "Sir, shouldn't *he* be doing his numbers, too?"

"Mind your work," Jack snapped. "If it isn't finished properly, you'll answer to me."

As Clifford returned his sullen attention to the paper, Jack motioned to Theo. "Come along. You'll return the doll to Lucy and make your apologies."

His cheeks red, Theo gingerly picked up the frilly doll and held it stiffly in front of him.

Lucy sat waiting on a bench just outside the door. She sprang up and seized the doll, cradling it in her arms and checking it with eagle eyes. "Maggie! Oh, Maggie, did those bad boys hurt you?"

Jack gave Theo's shoulder a nudge.

Theo took the hint. "I—I'm sorry. For—for taking it."

"Her," Lucy corrected indignantly. "Maggie is a *girl,* and she doesn't like the way you've treated her."

"Oh." Theo scuffed the toe of his shoe on the marble floor, then added gamely, "I'm sorry for taking *her*. I shouldn't have done so."

"Well, then," Lucy said with ladylike manners, "I shall forgive you. But only if you join Maggie for a tea party."

"A tea party?"

"My mummy isn't here yet, and Maggie likes to have company."

Theo flashed a horrified glance up at Jack. "Shouldn't I write out my sums with Clifford?"

Jack subdued a grin. He wouldn't force the boy to play with dolls, but a little discomfort would make Theo think twice the next time Clifford tried to pull him into a scheme. "Rather, it would be kind of you to escort Lucy and Maggie to the dining chamber."

"Yes, sir."

His feet dragging, Theo walked alongside the taller Lucy, who marched like a virago-in-training. So much for her somber, timid nature.

Jack followed them, his mind leaping ahead to Julia. They would pass her office, and he'd see if she had a free moment. Given Clifford's slowness with numbers, he would be at his punishment for at least the next hour, giving Jack ample time to claim a few minutes in her presence.

As they reached the entrance hall, Lucy stopped abruptly and turned to Theo. "Never mind, my mummy is here."

Clutching the doll, she made haste to the front door, where Margaret Pringle was speaking to a new arrival, a short, dark-haired woman whose back was to them.

Once again, Jack felt that cursed sentimentality tighten his chest. He had been not much older than Lucy when he'd lost his own mother to lung fever. From out of nowhere, snippets of memory assailed him: the acrid stench of medicines, the shuttered darkness of the sick-room, his mother lying thin and pale in bed, smiling tenderly at him. And the very next day, being bidden by the vicar to kiss her cold, lifeless cheek . . .

Realizing he was gritting his teeth, Jack forced himself to relax. He hadn't thought about that in years and he wouldn't start now. *Never look back,* that was his motto. Once, when he'd asked his father why he and Jack's mother had lived apart, his father had refused to give an explanation. *What's done is done,* he'd said. *Forget the past and enjoy the present.*

Jack had lived his life by that rule.

He clasped Theo by the shoulder. "Saved from a doll's tea party. Now there's a stroke of luck you don't deserve."

Lucy's mother had turned slightly to greet the girl with an enveloping hug. Her broad, homely features looked strikingly familiar—especially that large, hairy mole marring her cheek.

Jack blinked. His maidservant?

Impossible.

But only yesterday he had bumped into the woman—*that* woman—at his town house. She had dropped an armload of linens, and he'd crouched down to help her pick them up.

Jolted, he retreated down the corridor and opened the first door on the left, stepping inside. What devilish misfortune! He would have to hide out until the cursed female left.

"Mr. Jackman."

He frowned down at Theo, only just realizing the boy had followed him. "What is it?"

"Why are you standing in a closet?"

Jack glanced around at the tiny, darkened enclosure filled with shelves of supplies, paper and textbooks, slates and chalk. The air smelled of lead pencils and ink. "I need a new quill," he said, taking one at random from a box.

"May I do my numbers now, sir?"

"Yes. Yes, go on."

Theo ran off toward the library before Jack realized the boy wasn't supposed to be joining Clifford. But that was the least of Jack's troubles.

Twirling the quill in his fingers, he puzzled over the situation. As a gambler, he was a firm believer in luck, both good and bad. But as a mathematician, he mistrusted coincidences. Lucy's mother worked in his house. In a city of one million people, what were the odds of *that*?

Considering it from another angle, what were the odds that Lady Julia Corwyn had a connection to his household?

A bolt of clarity held him riveted. No wonder she had spent the afternoon interviewing the maids in her office. They were spies, all of them.

That was how she obtained her gossip for *The Rogue Report*.

*The Earl of D. is in such dire straits from gambling that even the
usurers have refused him any more credit . . .*
—*The Rogue Report*

Chapter Eleven

If Julia hadn't overslept, she might have missed seeing
the small figure sneaking through the garden the next
morning.

She had been up into the wee hours, working at the
dainty white desk in her bedchamber, organizing her
notes into a new issue of *The Rogue Report*. A sufficient
number of scandalous behaviors had been relayed by the
mothers of her students, maidservants whom Julia had
placed in the houses of selected gentlemen of the *ton*.

One additional piece of information had pleased her
immensely. She had learned that the wealthy Miss Evelyn Gresham had called off her wedding to the most dissolute rake of them all, the Earl of Rutledge, scion of a
long line of ne'er-do-wells. According to the earl's maid,
the broken engagement was the direct result of the story
about his gambling that Julia had published in a previous
edition.

The news had bolstered her spirits. Although she'd had

other successes over the years, saving one more lady from being duped by a scoundrel made her efforts worthwhile. The latest issue of *The Rogue Report* now sat on her desk awaiting delivery to the printer.

But upon parting the curtains to peer out at the gray morning, Julia forgot all that. Below her bedroom window, a boy made a furtive dash across the graveled pathway. His thatch of russet hair and small form struck her with surprise.

What on earth was Theo doing in the garden at this early hour? The children were not allowed outside until later in the morning since the staff was too busy with breakfast preparations to keep an eye on them.

In the next moment, Theo's purpose became clear. He glanced around as if to make certain no one was watching, then vanished into the carriage house.

Julia stood stunned. So that was how Jack had managed to be on time for breakfast every day! He had persuaded her son to awaken him—without asking her permission.

Incensed, she wanted to throw on her clothes and march straight over there. But something stayed the impulse. Was it so wrong for Theo to have a man in his life?

Was it so wrong for *her*?

She went to the washstand and splashed cold water onto her face. The shock of it made her gasp, though it did little to dispel the heat that suffused her. In the aftermath of the danger, she had let down her guard and responded passionately to Jack's kiss. Now, no matter how hard she strove for indifference, her body had a life of its own. His taste, his touch, his scent had made an indelible imprint on her, as if he had woven himself into the fabric of her soul.

Drying her face on a soft linen towel, she recalled the roughness of his cheek on her skin. Shedding her nightdress, she shivered as if his hands once again caressed her bosom. Donning her shift, she ached to be held against the hard muscularity of his male form. She was furious at him for awakening those physical needs in her.

No, that wasn't it. She was furious—and hurt—because he had presumed her to be willing to have an affair. Like society, Jack had judged her. He believed her to be without morals because she had a son born out of wedlock. He had proven himself to be as despicable as those men who approached her from time to time, seeking a mistress.

Even more bitter was the knowledge that she'd fallen into the age-old trap that snared so many women. In her heart, she had hoped Jack would court her, that perhaps someday the attraction between them would grow into love and he might offer marriage.

Instead, he merely wanted to bed her.

And her body throbbed shamefully at the prospect.

Irked by her own foolishness, she pulled the bellrope to summon Agnes to fasten the back buttons of her gown. Then she went to the mirror and set to work taming her unruly curls into a respectable bun. She would have dismissed Jack on the spot had it not been for the problem of finding a qualified mathematics instructor to replace him.

Or perhaps the truth was, she couldn't bear to send him out of her life. Not even caution or common sense could quiet the yearning that he had aroused in her.

Yesterday, she had kept her distance, busying herself with the task of interviewing the maidservants. But now she needed to reassert her authority over Jack. She needed to prove to him—and to herself—that she would never engage in an illicit affair.

*   *   *

"Mr. Jackman," Elfrida said over breakfast, her brown eyes sharp and piercing. "You vanished during our Sunday social yesterday. Where did you go?"

Jack had anticipated the question, but he had a mouthful of delicious sausage and he didn't intend for the old battle-axe to spoil it. The noise of chatter and cutlery filled the dining chamber as the children ate their morning meal of toast, sausage, and boiled eggs.

Around the small table reserved for the staff, the other teachers sat listening. Dorcas Snyder stuffed a jam-slathered scone into her mouth, Faith Rigby used her spoon to swirl patterns in her half-finished bowl of oatmeal. Margaret Pringle sipped tea, her dainty, age-spotted hands wrapped around the white porcelain cup.

Across from him, Julia frowned slightly, and her gray-blue eyes flicked over him as if he were a rodent that had dared to creep onto the table to sample the crumbs. He felt a twist of cold amusement. She had no notion that he knew her secret—and in their high-stakes game of seduction that gave him the advantage.

"It isn't our place to pry," Margaret told Elfrida. "Perhaps Mr. Jackman felt ill."

Swallowing, Jack set down his fork and smiled at Margaret. "Actually, I needed to work on my lesson plans for the week," he lied. "Since I'm new here, I thought it best to review the instructions Miss Dewhurst left for me."

In truth, he had been forced to beat a swift retreat and stay out of sight of his maidservant. His maidservant! Encountering the woman here had been even more startling than the time he'd seen that jackass Ambrose Trotter sitting in Julia's office. Who would have thought that twice in the space of a few days he'd nearly run into someone he knew from his real life?

It wasn't in his nature to dwell on grievances against

others. He vastly preferred to laugh at the twists of life. But knowing that Julia had planted a spy in his house made his temper run hot.

Laying down her napkin, she rose to her feet. "Mr. Jackman, if you're finished, I'd like a word with you in my office."

The cool formality of her voice stirred the anticipation of a challenge in him. Did she mean to scold him for his disappearance? Good, for it allowed him an opportunity to romance her.

Springing up from his chair, he waved his arm. "After you, my lady."

She led the way down the wide marble corridor. In the distance, the bonging of the casement clock in the entrance hall announced the hour of eight. Fifteen minutes until classes began. He had fifteen minutes in which to chip away at the wall Julia had erected between them.

Her steps brisk, Miss Leglock marched ahead of him. Her hips swayed enticingly, though he doubted it was intentional. Her heels kicked up the back of her prim gray gown, giving him an occasional glimpse of trim ankles clad in thin white stockings and dainty black shoes. Little did she know, that schoolmistress demeanor only honed his desire to disrobe her, inch by slow inch.

Not that he would allow his balls to dictate his actions. He had bungled his seduction of her once by rushing matters. He wouldn't make the same mistake twice.

Especially now that he had every reason to crave his pound of flesh. He could think of no more fitting revenge than for Julia to be used by one of the scoundrels she'd exposed in *The Rogue Report*.

It was galling to the extreme to know that she had placed a spy in his house who earned wages for dusting his furniture and then turned around and betrayed his privacy. That maid—he didn't even know her name—undoubtedly had witnessed the party at his house, when he'd lost a large sum at cards. But he couldn't blame *her*.

Julia was the mastermind. She had recruited poor, unwed mothers who would have otherwise starved. Little wonder they had accepted her offer to provide their children with a home and an education in exchange for a wealth of titillating gossip. It was a clever, diabolical system, for the staff was privy to all the household secrets, yet who ever noticed the servants?

Following her into the office, Jack tightened his jaw. He only hoped none of the other women had recognized him, for surely some were employed by his friends.

Julia sat down behind her desk and waved him into the opposite chair. A dark ink spot marred the middle finger of her right hand. He had seen a lamp burning late in her bedroom window last night; no doubt she'd been working on a new issue of her scandal sheet.

Her last issue, though she didn't yet know it.

Those extraordinary eyes fixed on him. "This morning," she said without preamble, "I saw my son go into the carriage house."

Startled, he reorganized his thoughts. "So you've found me out."

"The children are not allowed outside before breakfast. You've encouraged my son to disobey the rules."

"Rather, I gave him permission to awaken me. I could think of no other means to be on time for classes." Leaning back in his chair, Jack gave her a smoldering smile. "Unless, of course, you know of someone else who might volunteer for the task."

To his satisfaction, a blush suffused her cheeks. But her voice remained crisp and sharp. "I've spoken to Theo about the matter. He admitted that you've bribed him by giving him number puzzles. He showed me a few of them."

Jack's mouth went dry. No wonder Theo had avoided his eyes at breakfast. "It's hardly bribery. Rather, it's a reward for his trouble in rousing me out of a sound sleep. You yourself know how difficult *that* can be."

Her eyes widened slightly, enough to tell him that she remembered him lying naked in bed. And enough to cause a heated tension in his loins. For the space of a moment, they stared at each other, and he actually considered the mad act of leaping over the desk and pulling her up into his arms for another drowning kiss.

"Where did you obtain those puzzles?" she asked.

"Pardon?"

"The number puzzles. Did you find them in a book? I should like to purchase a copy for Theo."

Jack scrambled for an explanation. Of course, she didn't know his true identity; it would be perfectly natural for a mathematics instructor to play with numbers. Nonetheless, the admission was difficult. "There is no book," he said stiffly. "I devise the problems myself."

Julia tilted her head, and her mouth unclamped into a soft smile of amazement. "You make them up? Just like that? But . . . how do you do it?"

"It's nothing. Just a pastime, that's all."

"Pray don't be modest, Jack. It's a marvelous skill. How many of these puzzles do you have?"

"Quite a few. I've never counted, but there's a stack in my satchel." At his house, the papers were everywhere, in the drawer of the bedside table, in the desk in the library, in the pockets of his coats. Marlon was forever complaining about having to collect the little scraps, for Jack had a habit of scrawling the problems as they occurred to him, whether on the back of a dun notice, on the margin of the morning newspaper, or even on a theater program.

Julia leaned forward, her eyes alight and her shapely bosom pressed to the desk. "Have you ever considered compiling them into a book yourself?"

"No." The notion of exposing his secret to the world appalled him. What a laughingstock he'd be among his friends! And yet . . . there was something exhilarating about the idea, too. Something so earth-shaking he wouldn't let himself even consider it. "They're for my own amusement. And for Theo and my classes."

"But there are many other children who might benefit from a fresh approach to mathematics." Her lips twisted wryly. "Heaven knows, *I* might have done better at the subject had it been presented in a more interesting manner."

The light of humor transformed Julia. It made her eyes bright beneath the dark curve of her brows, and her mouth soft and unguarded in the oval perfection of her face. He hungered for her to look at him that way more often. And she would, by God, once he'd ensnared her with physical pleasure.

"Then you can't object to my bargain with Theo," he said. "You'll permit him to earn his puzzles."

"You're changing the subject," she said shrewdly. "But perhaps you'll promise to think about that book. As you made *me* promise to consider moving Theo to another class."

He wasn't a man who made promises to women. And he wouldn't start now. "You've made your decision, then?"

Julia nodded. "I've arranged for my son to take his music lesson during first period. He'll join the nine- and ten-year-olds during your second class of the day."

Jack felt a surprising sense of satisfaction. He didn't stop to analyze it, instead changing the topic to his advantage. In a silken murmur, he said, "I'm glad to know that our kiss hasn't completely turned you against me."

Her lips parted, and she looked charmingly flustered. Then, to his regret, the softness faded, replaced by a businesslike demeanor. "That incident is best forgotten," she said. "We will not speak of it again."

Like hell. "Will you answer a question, at least?"

She gave him a wary look, then snapped open the gold watch that was pinned to her bodice. "I'm sorry, but it's eight-fourteen. You've less than a minute to reach your classroom."

Rising from her chair, Julia walked briskly around the desk, heading toward the large pewter handbell that sat on a shelf beside the door. Clearly, she believed the meeting to be finished. But he had no intention of being dismissed like a naughty pupil.

Not before he'd taken down a few more bricks from that wall.

Jumping up, he followed her, and when she reached for the bell, he placed his hand over hers. "Wait."

She cast a startled look over her shoulder. He stood directly behind her, close enough to see the dark blue rims around her irises, close enough to smell the faint fragrance of her skin. And close enough to lose the power to think if he wasn't careful.

Summoning all of his considerable charm, he said, "I've dreamed about you, Julia. And I wanted to ask, have you dreamed of me, too?" When her brows winged together in a frown, he swiftly added, "The truth now. Remember our bargain."

"*I* was to ask the next question, not you."

He grinned, for she hadn't denied the dreaming. "You've asked me a number of questions this morning. In fact, I'd say I've an outstanding debt to collect from you."

"That didn't count. We were discussing my son."

"And then you asked about my private pastimes."

"You didn't warn me we were playing the game."

A faintly coquettish quality to her eyes made Jack forget caution. He slid his fingers beneath the springy curls that had escaped the twist of her hair. "Then I'm warning you now," he murmured. "So answer me. Have you thought of me constantly—as I've thought of you?"

She stared at him, her lashes slightly lowered, lending her an aura of mystery that he ached to unveil. He took encouragement from her hesitation in replying. Julia wouldn't lie to him; she had too much integrity to break the cardinal rule of their game. Which meant he really *had* occupied a prime place in her mind.

The knowledge was an irresistible aphrodisiac. If ever he had met a woman in need of taming, she was Julia. Burned by need, he bent his head, hungry for another taste of her lips.

She swiveled, giving a hard shove to his chest. "Blast you, Jack. Go to your classroom. *Now*."

Seizing the bell, she stepped into the corridor and rang it. The loud clanging echoed off the marble walls and cleared his brain of the madness of lust. Blast him?

Blast her!

In the midst of frustration, Jack felt a niggling of humor. He enjoyed a good chase, and Julia certainly had a knack for keeping him off balance. If she thought he'd give up so easily, she would be forced to revise her thinking.

He paced to her side, waiting until she lowered the bell. "You do realize you've just used up your one veto," he said. "From here on out, you'll be obliged to answer all my questions."

She gave him a withering look. "From here on out, sir, you'll tend to your teaching. Good day."

Julia had arranged her schedule so that she taught no geography classes in the afternoons. The time after luncheon was spent completing paperwork and tending to other business related to the school. But today, she had gone to a small printing shop located near the Strand, left off the latest issue of *The Rogue Report*, and secured a promise from the owner—the same diligent, trustworthy man she always used—to deliver the newsletter to her in two days.

The long, brisk walk back to the school had helped to clear her head. She desperately needed to decide what to do about Jack. Especially since her emotions refused to obey the dictates of her mind.

Ever since their encounter that morning, concentration had eluded her. In class, she had asked one boy to identify China without noticing he'd pointed to Russia, and allowed another to mix up the Arctic Ocean with the Indian. At luncheon, she'd pretended to listen to Elfrida's and Dorcas's plans for a Christmas play, all the while shamelessly eavesdropping on Jack's conversation with Margaret about the mothers of the children. Julia had felt flushed and happy, adrift in a singing sea.

Have you thought of me constantly—as I've thought of you?

She had. Dear heaven, she had. It was gratifying to know that he shared her obsessive ardor. Like her, he was consumed by their budding attraction. A stern application of common sense could not erase the bond that connected them.

As a debutante, she'd had many men court her. While enjoying all the attention, she had never quite fathomed how anyone could make fervent declarations of love on short acquaintance. How could they fancy themselves besotted after a single dance or a simple conversation?

She knew now. For the first time in her life, Julia understood what it meant to be smitten. To hunger for a touch or a look or a crumb of affection. To awaken aching and restless during the night. To suffer the irresistible tug of temptation. Jack made her feel alive, excited, *radiant*.

She drew in a deep breath of tangy autumn air. Without noticing, she had left the bustling business district far behind and headed into her residential neighborhood with its streets of well-kept homes. Here and there, candles winked in windows. Dusk had come early, spreading chilly gray pools beneath bushes and trees.

Julia quickened her steps. A gust of wind tugged at her bonnet and snatched at her cloak. The overcast sky foretold rain, and she was anxious to reach the school. To see Jack again.

With him, she had the uncanny sense of being on a runaway carriage, racing toward disaster while savoring the wild exhilaration of the ride. Caution warned her to steer away from forbidden territory. But in heart and body, she wanted to go there. She wanted to explore all the wicked enticement that Jack offered to her.

What difference would it make? Her reputation was ruined, anyway.

She reined in the scandalous thought. He was her employee, that was why. By allowing him liberties, she would jeopardize her integrity and open her most private self to a man she had only just met. Worse, he might get her with child. That prospect above all others frightened her, for how could she explain such a situation to Theo? And the other children?

Turning the corner, she spied the white-pillared edifice of the Corwyn Academy toward the far end of the square. The glow of lamplight brightened the tall windows. The sight steadied her, and she felt a rush of pride in the school. In the darkest hours after Theo had been born and she had given up her place in society, she had dreamed of starting a new life. She had felt driven to help other women in her dire straits and, at the same time, to punish those scoundrels who would prey upon well-born young ladies like herself. She had succeeded in that twofold purpose, and nothing, not even the lure of the flesh, must be allowed to destroy what she had built here.

As she drew nearer, the faint shouts and laughter of children emanated from the garden behind the school. Those sounds of joyous innocence made her smile. If not for Theo, she might have wasted her life in marriage to an aristocrat, squandered her time in the pursuit of selfish pleasures, allowed her children to be raised in a nursery by maids and governesses—

A figure moved near the boxwoods alongside the school.

It was a man clad in a dark overcoat and hat. He crept toward the stone fence that bordered the garden, and his air of furtiveness set off an alarm in Julia.

She didn't pause to think. Grasping her skirts, she charged straight toward him. "You! Who are you?"

He pivoted in a crouch. The brim of a black cap shadowed his face. Seeing her, he took off at a run.

Julia raced in pursuit. But he wasn't hampered by skirts, and in the half a minute it took to reach the corner, he had vaulted onto a bay horse in the gloom of an oak tree.

As he galloped off into the dusk, she groped for a nearby lamppost and clung hard. She needed its support to hold herself upright. Her breath sawed in and out, more from fright than exertion.

Had he intended to break into the school? Perhaps he'd thought to take advantage of the noise from the children playing in order to sneak inside. He had been heading toward the window of her office . . .

Another thought shook her. Was he the intruder who had rifled through her desk a fortnight ago?

The very real possibility alarmed her, as did another observation. He had been no ordinary man of the streets. His clothing, his bearing, even his horse, marked him a gentleman.

Her veins turning to ice, Julia shivered. Dear God, had someone guessed her secret identity? Was he a disgruntled nobleman seeking proof that she published *The Rogue Report*?

Chapter Twelve

"Yes, Mrs. Angleton, I do understand that your rhododendrons were slightly trampled this morning." Although she wanted to slam the door, Julia kept her voice well modulated. "It was an accident, and the children are very sorry."

The middle-aged widow stood on the front porch, holding a pug with a squashed black face and tan body. Like the dog, Mrs. Angleton was short and squat, with prominent teeth and bug eyes. "Apologies, bah. I'll have you know, 'tis the third incident this month."

The most direct route to Hyde Park led past Mrs. Angleton's town house at the end of the street. The old biddy must have been spying out her front window to have noticed that a branch had been broken when a pair of skipping girls had collided and fallen. "If you'll send me a bill, I'll be happy to reimburse you for any damage."

"I want your little ruffians to stop running wild, that's what. This is a decent neighborhood, not a public zoo."

Julia stiffened. "I beg your pardon. My pupils are extremely well behaved—"

"To what do we owe this pleasure?" Jack said.

Startled, Julia turned to see him strolling across the entrance hall. He wore another of his ill-fitting coats, a dark green that matched his eyes, the sleeves a trifle short and the back too tight for his broad shoulders. Even so, an indefinable air about him commanded attention. His steps held the jaunty confidence of a man who viewed life as a challenge to be savored and enjoyed.

The dreary afternoon seemed to brighten, or perhaps it was the inner glow she always felt in his presence. Five days had passed since their explosive kiss. Since then, he had wooed her in small ways, leaving a late-blooming rose on her desk, winking at her during dinner, letting his hand brush hers at every opportunity. Beyond that, he had behaved himself, tending to his classes, befriending the other teachers, even giving Theo a private tutoring session after classes.

Yet still, she wouldn't—couldn't—allow herself to trust Jack.

She had not told him about the man she'd chased away from the school. To do so would entail confessing her authorship of *The Rogue Report*, and that was a secret too vital to share with someone she had known for less than a fortnight. Besides, her pride still stung from his assumption that her morals were lax. She could not expect him to understand her need to expose the blackguards of society.

Instead, she had discussed the situation with Elfrida, and the two of them had decided to take turns keeping watch downstairs at night. A locksmith had come the previous day to check all the doors and windows. Those precautions had eased her worries somewhat.

Now, irked that the mere sight of Jack made her ache, she spoke sternly. "Why are you not in your classroom?"

"I left my students with a list of conundrums to solve."
He swept a bow to their neighbor. "The truth is, I heard
your voice, Mrs. Angleton. May I say, you're looking exceptionally fine today."

Belatedly, Julia noticed that the haughty woman was
blushing like a girl straight out of the schoolroom.
"Why, thank you, Mr. Jackman. That's very kind of you
to say so."

Julia looked in bewilderment from him to Mrs. Angleton. "Have you two met, then?"

"He saved my Flossy from being run over in the
street." Mrs. Angleton turned her attention to the dog she
held nestled to her massive bosom. In a singsong voice,
she crooned, "You were a bad girl, dashing out in front of
that carriage. You might have been crushed, and Mummy
would be so sad without her precious little darling."

The dog wagged its stubby tail and licked Mrs. Angleton's double chin.

Julia arched an eyebrow at Jack. First Faith, and now
Flossy. "When did *this* rescue occur?"

"Yesterday," he said. "I took a quick jaunt to clear my
head during break. I trust that wasn't against your rules?"

The mischief in his eyes tickled her heart. She could
just see the indentation of his dimples amid the trace of
stubble on his cheeks. "Certainly not. You'll have Mrs.
Angleton thinking this is a prison."

"Rather, I'm sure she's pleased to have such a fine
school in the neighborhood." His mouth curving in an attractive smile, he reached out to scratch the dog's ears.
"Lady Julia is to be commended for the excellent behavior of her pupils. Wouldn't you agree, Mrs. Angleton?"

The older woman cleared her thoat. "Oh. Yes, of
course! It is only that—er—sometimes they do trample
my rhododendrons or screech rather loudly on their way
to the park. But not very often, mind."

Julia almost choked on an ironic laugh. The virago had come to complain at least once a week for the past five years. Did Jack know that? Had he heard the woman complaining and guessed the truth?

"Children can be rambunctious," he said in a commiserating tone. "But their high spirits can be rather enjoyable, too. May I ask, have you any children of your own?"

Cradling Flossy with beringed fingers, she looked sad for a moment. "Mr. Angleton and I were not so blessed."

"Then you must consider our students as your adopted family. Have you met any of them? Or perhaps visited the classrooms?"

"Why, no. I've never had the opportunity."

Julia raised an eyebrow at that. She had extended a polite invitation on several occasions, and the widow had adamantly refused to set foot inside what she had termed a charity home for street urchins.

"Then I'd be delighted to—" Jack paused, his smile disappearing as he stared past Mrs. Angleton. Returning his gaze to her, he went on rapidly, "I'd be delighted to take you on a tour sometime. If you'll accept my invitation, that is."

Mrs. Angleton simpered. "Why, thank you. How kind of you to take time out of your busy schedule."

"Speaking of which, I must return to my class. Good day." Rather abruptly, he turned on his heel and strode out of the entrance hall.

After voicing a remarkably civil farewell to Julia, Mrs. Angleton left, too. Julia didn't know whether to be irked or pleased by the woman's transformation. Then, as she started to close the door, she saw Mrs. Angleton slow down and stare.

A hansom cab was parked at the curbstone. A gentleman stood paying the driver.

Julia's heart sank as she recognized his ruddy features

and portly form, clad in dull brown. She wanted to duck out of sight, but it was too late.

Clutching a big bunch of chrysanthemums, Ambrose Trotter bounded past Mrs. Angleton and up the steps to the porch. He swept off his curl-brimmed hat and presented the bouquet to Julia. "My lady, it's a pleasure to find you at home."

It was far from a pleasure. She had piles of paperwork awaiting her, bills to pay, and no time in which to exchange banalities with a gentleman. But his puppy-dog eyes held an eagerness that made her feel guilty for her uncharitable thoughts.

She fashioned a gracious smile. "Mr. Trotter. Do come inside."

Leading him to her office, she found herself wondering at Jack's swift retreat. Had he seen Ambrose Trotter? He must have. But that made no sense. It would be more in character for Jack to amuse himself by flinging subtle barbs at her suitor.

Perhaps he was merely being conscientious in returning to his classroom. Her heart fluttered. Or perhaps . . . just perhaps . . . Jack was jealous.

Mr. Trotter settled himself on the chaise in her office and lingered for the better part of an hour, chattering about everything from the weather to his family to household economies. Julia had tried to give him signals that she had things to do. After ringing the bell at the end of the school day, she had gone to her desk. She had shuffled through a stack of papers. She had twirled her quill as if waiting to write.

Noticing his frown at the noise of the students streaming through the corridor, Julia had an idea of how to get rid of him. She would put a damper on his courtship by reminding him of the realities of her life.

"My son is finished with his classes, Mr. Trotter. Would you care to meet him?"

To her dismay, he beamed. "A right jolly idea, my lady."

Heaven help her. He'd taken the offer as encouragement for his suit. She could always pretend to look for Theo, then say that he was nowhere to be found. But she had promised herself to find a good stepfather for her son. Although Mr. Trotter lit no spark in her, he was loyal, decent, and honorable, all the qualities of an excellent family man.

And wasn't that better than pining for a man who muddled her thinking with wild yearnings? A man who wanted to bed her without the encumbrances of holy vows? Infatuation might be bright and glorious, but instinct told her it burned out fast. She and Theo needed roots, not ashes.

"Kindly wait here," she said. "I'll return in a moment."

Leaving the office, Julia headed down the corridor. Most of the children had gone outside to play; she could hear their faint voices from the garden. Escaping Mr. Trotter's company gave her a sense of guilty relief. And an exuberance that could only have to do with her destination.

Every day this week, Jack had given Theo private tutoring in mathematics, to help him catch up to the more advanced class. According to Jack, Theo had an aptitude for numbers. His willingness to nurture her son's gift caused a glow of warmth in her heart.

The door to Jack's classroom was closed. She turned the handle, stepped inside, and froze.

Her son wasn't working quietly at a desk. Nor was Jack lecturing him from the front of the room. They had both stripped off their coats and rolled up their sleeves. They faced each other in a cleared area near the windows.

Theo was attacking Jack. *Punching him.*

"Go for the face or the gut," Jack advised, dancing back and forth to parry the blows. "You won't knock a fellow down by hitting him in the ribs or arms. You have to be quick, too. Anticipate his next move, that's the way."

Julia surged forward. "Theo! Mr. Jackman! What on earth are you two doing?"

Theo guiltily dropped his hands to his sides. He hunched his shoulders, and his small face bore a look that said he wanted to shrink into the floor.

Jack, however, flashed her that famous smile, the one that displayed white teeth and deep dimples. Casually propping a hand on his hip, he said, "My lady, this is most unexpected."

"Quite." In the midst of her fury, she saw that he'd shed his cravat, affording her a glimpse of muscled chest. She despised herself for noticing. "There is no fighting permitted at this school."

"Then it's good we were merely play-acting."

"That's right," Theo piped up. "Mr. Jackman was teaching me what to do if we're ever attacked by pirates!"

"Or highwaymen," Jack added with a grin.

"Dragons, too."

"Don't forget the giants and the trolls."

Their camaraderie unexpectedly made her chest ache. "You know the rules, Theo," she said, trying not to let her heart soften at the sight of his suddenly woebegone face. "Go wait for me outside in the corridor. I should like to have a word with Mr. Jackman in private."

"Yes, Mummy." His feet dragging, Theo headed toward the door, snatching up his little blue coat on the way, one sleeve trailing on the floor.

Julia waited until the door closed before wheeling on Jack. He sauntered to his desk and perched on the edge. The coals on the grate had died, and despite the chill in the air, he did not unroll the sleeves of his shirt or don his coat. As her wayward attention strayed to his strong forearms, thorns of desire pricked her flesh.

Her cheeks warm, she forced her gaze to his face. "You are not to encourage my son to fight."

"He needs to know how to defend himself. All boys do."

"He can back away from confrontations, as I've taught him."

"If he runs like a coward from every altercation, the bullies will be after him in droves."

"Rather, as a peacemaker, he'll set a good example for the other children."

Jack raised a skeptical eyebrow. "There's an unfortunate flaw to your plan. Theo's solution to avoiding trouble is to fall into bad company himself."

Her knees turned to water, causing her to sink down at a student's desk. "He and Clifford . . ."

"Are thick as thieves."

Julia had noticed Theo's hero worship of the older boy. She bit her lip. "It's my fault. I encouraged him to befriend Clifford." Jack's eyebrow arched higher, so she added, "Clifford's mother abandoned him last year. She met a soldier and ran off to follow the drum. Unfortunately, Clifford has been sullen and difficult ever since."

"Be that as it may, it's no excuse for him to coerce Theo into doing his bidding."

"What have they done?"

"Just a few pranks here and there."

"Tell me."

Jack hesitated, then said, "They stole Lucy Wilkerson's doll on Sunday, that's all."

Julia sprang to her feet. "You ought to have informed me straightaway. I'll need to discipline them."

He took hold of her shoulders, stopping her from dashing out of the classroom. "Never mind, I took care of it. In fact, I'd be grateful if you didn't mention the incident to Theo at all. I won't have him thinking I'm tattling on him."

"I can't ignore something so serious."

"You can leave it to me for once," he countered, gently kneading her tense muscles. "He only needs confidence in his ability to oppose boys like Clifford."

Julia resented his implication that he knew her son's needs better than than she did. "Confidence comes from a sense of inner integrity, not from fighting."

"For a man, it comes from success in establishing one's place in the world."

She remembered his efficiency in thrashing Mr. Rigby; those same hands now massaged her shoulders and made her resistance dissolve. Jack certainly had confidence— far too much of it.

She stepped back and crossed her arms. "I abhor violence."

"Nevertheless, boys can—and will—be brutal to one another. Theo is small for his age. He should have the skills to stand up for himself."

Uncertainty wrenched her. Was Jack right? His argument made sense. She didn't want Theo to be the victim of bullies. She wanted him to grow up like Jack, strong, capable, sure of himself.

He closed the distance between them. Once again, his hands lightly rubbed her shoulders, his fingers moving to her neck to work their melting magic. "A man can't be soft, Julia. Not like a woman. You do see that, don't you?"

The air became fraught with tension, an urgency centered not in anger but in desire. Her breasts tingled, her insides ached, and her pulse throbbed. With every breath, she drew in his scent, something dark and wild. It gave her the shocking urge to put her mouth to his skin and taste him. Unable to resist flirting a little, she asked, "Does that count as one of your questions?"

He bent closer, his fingers playing with the fine hairs at the nape of her neck. His green eyes looked intense, mysterious. "No, but we'll start playing the game right now. Tell me about that chap who's been bringing you flowers. What are his intentions toward you?"

The romantic spell shattered.

Chagrined to have forgotten why she'd come, Julia stepped back. "His name is Ambrose Trotter. He's interested in marrying me." There, let Jack see that other men treated her with honor and respect. Never mind that Mr. Trotter hadn't asked her yet. "You'll have to excuse me now. He's waiting in my office to meet Theo."

The Honorable Mr. D.L. has purchased a new set of dueling pistols, and has been heard to profess an impatience to put them to use.
—*The Rogue Report*

Chapter Thirteen

"All's quiet, my lady," Elfrida said. "Not a thief to be found."

The oil lamp cast wavering shadows over the walls of Julia's bedchamber. Beneath the white nightcap that covered her gray hair, Elfrida's face looked drawn and weary. The deep circles under her eyes gave evidence to her long vigil. It was two in the morning, and she had kept watch downstairs since ten o'clock.

Now it was Julia's turn.

Tying the sash of her dressing gown, Julia battled a flare of guilt. "Perhaps we should hire a guard to patrol outside at night."

"And allow a stranger on the grounds?" Elfrida shook her head decisively. "I wouldn't trust a man, m'lady. I've known too many bad ones in my time."

"I'm costing you sleep."

"Never you mind that. I'm happy to help."

"But what if I'm wrong? What if that prowler has no intention of ever coming back?"

"Then we'll consider ourselves blessed. In the meantime, it never hurts to be careful."

Julia had told only Elfrida about the man she'd seen lurking alongside the school. Although all the female teachers on staff knew about *The Rogue Report,* she saw no need to alarm them. Dorcas would have fretted too much, Faith had not yet recovered from the blow of her father's treachery, and Margaret was too old and frail to keep watch.

As for Jack, she wouldn't allow herself to trust him. Not with so crucial a secret as *The Rogue Report.*

Julia embraced the older woman. "I don't know quite how to thank you."

Elfrida's brown eyes grew a little misty, but she gave her usual grumpy nod. "'Tis I should be doing the thanking, m'lady. You took me in when no one else would, and one good turn deserves another."

Five years ago, when Julia had advertised for a literature teacher, Elfrida had shown up on the doorstep of the school, her face bruised and one eye blackened. While employed as housekeeper at a brothel, she had been attacked by a drunken client. When she had dared to fight back, the owner of the place had dismissed her on the spot for bloodying the man's nose.

Julia had had her doubts about hiring a woman of such dubious background, but after questioning her further and learning she had had an educated upbringing, Julia had decided to give Elfrida a chance. Never once had she regretted doing so.

As Elfrida went off to bed, Julia took the lamp and headed downstairs. An eerie hush lay over the darkened school. Statues stared from shadowed niches in the corridors. She found herself hurrying past the black maws of doorways, the only sound the echo of her footsteps.

By welcome contrast, her office was warm and cheerful with a fire burning on the grate. She stirred the coals with the poker, tipped in a few more lumps from the bucket, and relished the radiant warmth on her cold, slippered feet.

Elfrida, bless her again, had left a fresh pot of tea and a plate of scones and jam on the desk. Julia poured a steaming cup, then went to the window and parted the curtains to peer out at the black, moonless night. From her perspective on the side of the mansion, she couldn't see the garden or the carriage house where Jack slept. If only he were here with her, she would feel safe.

Safe? She would merely exchange one peril for another. She had more faith in her ability to chase off a prowler than to resist Jack's charm. Scouring him from her mind, she pressed her nose to the window glass and studied the bushes. She could barely distinguish the mounds of rhododendrons from the rest of the side yard.

All lay still.

Yet a stranger might be out there, hiding, watching, waiting.

The thought raised the fine hairs at the nape of her neck. She drew the draperies closed and overlapped the edges. Determined not to succumb to fear, she went to her desk, unlocked the bottom drawer, and withdrew a thick pile of folded newsletters that had been delivered the previous afternoon.

Julia inhaled the scent of fresh ink. At any other time, she would have felt a thrill of accomplishment at seeing the fruits of her labor. She would have been comforted by the hope of saving another young lady from falling victim to a scoundrel.

Tonight, however, she worried that her secret work might have invited trouble to her own doorstep.

The man she had seen outside the school had to be the same one who had broken into her office a fortnight ago. Two such incidents within the month couldn't be mere coincidence. Besides, she'd had the fleeting impression that he was a gentleman.

Long ago, she had convinced herself that no one would ever connect her to *The Rogue Report*. She had left society eight years ago, and the first issue had come out three years later. It had taken that much patience and planning to place her network of maidservants in the houses of selected gentlemen of the *ton*.

Perhaps the prowler had heard the tale of her fall from grace and suspected her culpability. Gossip was the mainstay of ballrooms and drawing rooms. It would be simple for a determined man to compile a list of dishonored ladies to investigate.

What did he want from her? Did he seek revenge for exposing his foibles? Did he mean to do her bodily harm?

The possibility made her shiver, and she took solace in the fact that both times, he had run from her. Clearly, he wished to avoid a face-to-face confrontation.

Which meant he was merely looking for proof that she was responsible. Perhaps he intended to put an end to her newsletter by revealing its author to be a fallen woman.

Her stomach clenched. *The Rogue Report* was her one and only way to help other women avoid men like Theo's father. By the heavens, she wouldn't let anyone stop her!

Opening her address book, Julia stared down at the alphabetical list of names. They were all young, unmarried ladies who would never be allowed to associate with a woman of her reputation. Not for the first time, she wondered if, when mothers warned their daughters to remain chaste, they pointed to Lady Julia Corwyn as an example of hedonistic behavior.

The possibility tasted bitter in her mouth. It had been many years since she had felt rubbed raw by the past. Years in which she had built a good life for herself and Theo. Rather than deriving happiness from rank and riches, she had learned the value of hard work and the satisfaction of giving to others. But of late, a desire for respect had needled her.

Because of Jack.

Like society, he believed her to have loose morals. Never mind that she had encouraged him by responding passionately to his kiss—or that the desires he had awakened continued to plague her. Even now, the memory of their closeness sparked a vexing heat in her nether regions.

Curse all men! They were nothing but trouble.

Picking up her quill, Julia dipped the sharpened tip into the inkwell and penned the first address onto a folded newsletter.

Jack sat upright in his narrow cot and blinked into the darkness. The fire in the tiny hearth had died hours ago, leaving only an orange glow in the ashes. His bleary eyes scrutinized the black lumps of furniture, the washstand where he shaved every morning, the chest that held his too-tight, borrowed clothing, and the desk with its hard-backed chair.

He was usually a sound sleeper. What had awakened him?

Perhaps he'd had that nightmare again. The one where he was chained in a deep pit with a huge stone pressing down on him.

But he wasn't gasping for air. Besides, it didn't take a genius to figure out that debts inspired that particular dream, and he'd won two thousand pounds at his club the previous Saturday.

No, something else weighed on his mind. Something that made him feel restless, uneasy, angry. Something named Julia.

He's interested in marrying me . . . He's waiting in my office to meet Theo.

Combing his fingers through his hair, Jack scowled into the darkness. She couldn't be seriously considering Ambrose Trotter as a husband. He was a dull dog who wanted only to sink his teeth into her fortune. She had to be playing games, trying to make Jack jealous.

Much to his annoyance, the ploy was working.

He had never been one to brood about women. If his current love interest found richer pastures, there was always someone else to take her place. Despite his frequently empty pockets, he'd never had any difficulty in attracting female companionship. He kept his liaisons light and fun, and even when he'd charmed Evelyn into accepting his offer of marriage, he had not invested his emotions.

But now he found himself irritated beyond measure. He lusted for Julia, and no other woman would do. Given half a chance, he'd plant his fist in Trotter's face. Then he'd swing Julia up in his arms, quiet her protests with a kiss, and show her how wrong she was to resist him.

Jack flung back the covers and rolled out of bed. The floorboards felt icy against his bare feet as he went to peer out into the night. Or rather, to stare at the dark monolith of the school where Julia slept.

Much to his chagrin, she had called in a locksmith to fix the door to the music room. She kept the downstairs locked as tight as a spinster's underdrawers. But what about the upstairs?

Jack's gaze strayed to the massive oak tree in the garden. He gauged the strength of its branches and the proximity to her window. And he imagined Julia lying in bed, her dark hair spread over the pillow, her eyes closed in slumber. On the night of the storm, when she'd nearly brained him with the poker, she had been wearing a thin silk dressing gown over a lacy nightdress, the complete opposite of her prim daytime garb. He pictured the hem riding high on her slender thighs. And he thought about sliding his hands up the silky path of her skin.

Jack groped in the darkness for his breeches and shirt. Curse it, if he was going to lose sleep over a woman, he might as well be enjoying himself.

Julia had finished only half the pile of newsletters when her hand began to ache from wielding the pen. She pressed on through one more: *Miss Cornelia Lavinford, Number 18 Hanover Square*. Then she set down the quill and wriggled her fingers to ease their cramping.

The predawn chill had seeped into her bones. Her shoulders ached from weariness and her eyes felt gritty. Yawning, she rose from the desk and went to the hearth to add coals to the dying flames.

The night had been quiet, the only sounds the scratching of her pen, the hissing of the fire, and the distant bong of the casement clock marking every quarter hour. It was just past four, and while she'd worked at the tedious task of penning addresses, her mind had kept circling around to Jack.

Not even in her days as a debutante had she known any man quite like him. His appeal lay far deeper than a charming manner and a handsome countenance. Beneath that devilish smile, he had a true gallantry and a compassion for others. He had risked his life to rescue Faith from being abused by her father. He had dashed out into traffic to save Mrs. Angleton's dog. And he had befriended Theo.

In less than a fortnight, Jack had made a difference in her son's life, helping him to develop his intellect and to build his confidence—even if she didn't always agree with his methods.

Teaching him to fight, indeed!

Picking up the poker, she stirred the coals. The trouble was, there was a mystery to Jack that she couldn't quite fathom. During her interview of him, he'd claimed to be penniless, having lost his life's savings to thieves. Yet by pursuing her, he risked losing his livelihood. He had to know that engaging in an affair with the headmistress would result in his dismissal from the school. Yet he continued to flirt with her at every opportunity.

And Julia relished every minute of it. Oh, why not face the truth? Her heart fluttered whenever she heard his footsteps out in the corridor. Her insides contracted whenever she caught sight of his lean, tall form. Her lungs felt starved for air whenever he aimed that sinful smile at her.

Closing her eyes, she remembered the searing pressure of his mouth on hers and the exhilarating slide of his hands over her flesh. The experience had made her pine for more.

Who would be the wiser if she stole out to the carriage house and slipped into his bed? If she allowed him to show her all the ways a man could love a woman?

The narrow staircase lay shrouded in gloom. Keeping one hand on the wall, Jack descended to the main floor of the carriage house. The stygian darkness held a musty hint of old leather. He carefully made his way to the black outline of the door.

Emerging outside, he sucked in lungfuls of damp, chilly air. The cold restored a scrap of sense to his brain. The beast in his loins began to subside—until he glanced up at Julia's bedchamber again.

Never in his life had he been so obsessed with a woman. Ever since that one kiss, she had thwarted his every attempt to romance her. The constant presence of teachers and children further complicated his seduction of her.

But at the moment, she was alone, vulnerable, soft with sleep. With her defenses down, she would respond with unguarded passion—although he suspected she'd never forgive him for it afterward.

Nevertheless, it would be well worth the price. Who the devil cared if she dismissed him in the morning? He wanted his revenge. And he wanted it now.

Spurred by purpose, Jack started down the garden path. Only to stop cold in his tracks.

At the rear of the house, the dark figure of a man crept through the shadows.

Julia paced her office. The temptation to pay a middle-of-the-night visit to Jack held a shockingly strong attraction to her. Only a fortnight ago, she had been content with her lot. She had believed herself settled and satisfied, having outgrown the impetuous passions of youth.

Then Jack had turned her life upside down. He had forced her to acknowledge the needs of her body. Now, she craved the ultimate closeness with a man. She yearned to explore the richness of intimacy, to follow the lure of excitement that he had stirred in her.

But Jack didn't love her. He viewed her as a soiled dove, rather than a respectable woman. He had made insulting assumptions about her morals. Even if she *was* an unwed mother, he had no right to take her willingness for granted.

Wearing a path in the carpet, Julia reminded herself that she would be better off with a gentleman like Mr. Trotter. *He* regarded her with respect. Never once had he attempted to take liberties with her. If she found him rather dull, well, at least he would make her an honorable offer.

And what of Theo? His meeting with her suitor had been less than a success. Mr. Trotter had been far too jovial in his attempt to win over her son, and Theo had used monosyllables in answering questions about his schoolwork. She had been hoping for the easy rapport Theo shared with Jack, but perhaps in time—

Outside, in the distance, a man shouted.

Jack?

He had lost the element of surprise.

Believing the garden to be deserted, Jack had made no effort to move silently. The prowler spied him and scuttled toward the back wall of the garden.

Loosing a roar, Jack went after him at a run.

Gravel from the pathway spewed from beneath his feet. He leaped over a bed of scraggly rosebushes, the thorns tearing at his breeches. His legs pumping, he reached the stone wall at the same time as his quarry.

Through the darkness came the ominous sound of a pistol cocking. "Stop!" the man hissed. "I'll shoot!"

The bastard didn't know Jack's reputation for recklessness on the dueling field. "Pray do."

He lunged, aiming for the fellow's midsection and, at the same time, thrusting aside the arm that held the gun and pointing it away from the school. The trigger clicked, but the weapon failed to discharge. He squeezed the man's wrist and the pistol thunked to the ground.

For a brief, furious interlude they struggled in the darkness. Scratching and gouging, the intruder fought back with the desperation of the cornered. Jack had landed only two solid punches to the abdomen when his right foot met something slippery and he lost his balance.

He fell hard, jarring his shoulder and tasting dirt.

Cursing, he rolled to his feet. In those few seconds, the intruder had scrambled through the shrubbery and clambered to the top of the wall.

Jack grabbed for the man's leg. But the villain kicked out savagely, his heel striking Jack hard on his temple. Pain exploded in his head and his grip loosened. He staggered backward.

And the man vanished over the wall.

Stinking of cheap perfume, the Marquess of S. returned home at dawn after a night spent in a brothel.
  —The Rogue Report

Chapter Fourteen

The ring of keys jangled in Julia's fingers. The darkness of the music room made it difficult for her to find the right key and unlock the door. Successful at last, she dashed out onto the back porch and strained to see into the gloom of the garden.

An instant later, the clatter of hooves came from the mews.

Elfrida came hurrying out the door. She held up the oil lamp from Julia's office. The yellow light played over her gaunt features, framed by a white nightcap. "What is it?" she asked, her voice gruff with sleep. "I heard a man shout."

"So did I. It sounded like—" A thump came from the rear of the garden, followed by a muttered exclamation. Julia caught her breath. "Jack?"

For three beats of her heart, she feared someone else lurked out there. Someone who meant her harm. Someone who wanted revenge.

Then Jack's blessedly familiar voice floated through the night. "Bring the lamp here, will you? To the rear wall."

Relieved beyond measure, Julia motioned to Elfrida. Then she flew ahead down the darkened path, heedless of the gravel that poked into the thin soles of her slippers. She was scarcely aware of the chilly breeze that penetrated her dressing gown.

Jack walked along the wall, crouching down now and then as if searching for something in the bushes. He wore no coat, only breeches and a wrinkled linen shirt. He took the lantern from Elfrida and shone the light over the tangle of boxwoods.

"What happened?" Julia asked breathlessly. "Did you see someone trespassing?"

"Yes. Unfortunately, he escaped on horseback."

"It's the middle of the night," Elfrida said. "What were you doing outside at this early hour?"

Jack flashed an enigmatic glance over his shoulder. "I couldn't sleep. When I looked out, I saw a man in the shadows behind the house."

Shivering, Julia hugged herself. It wasn't so much the cold air, but icy fear that seeped into her bones. Dear God, the intruder had come back, after all. While she had been working at her desk, he had been lurking outside, looking for a way to get in.

What if he'd managed to break a window? Or to pick the lock on one of the doors?

He would have made noise, she told herself to calm the wild beating of her heart. She would have fended him off with the poker. And screamed for help.

Reaching down, Jack produced a long, flat wooden object. It was a bat used by the boys when playing cricket. "Here's why the villain got away."

For the first time, Julia noticed the reddened welt on

his temple. Horrified, she hastened to his side for a closer inspection. "He struck you with the bat!"

Jack grimaced. "Good God, no. I stepped on it and tripped. It gave him time to climb over the fence."

"One of the children must have left it here," Elfrida said, taking the bat from him. "I'll have a talk with them in the morning about putting away their playthings."

Julia found herself touching Jack's shirtsleeve, his arm hard and warm beneath her fingers. "I'm so sorry. Please come inside now. I'll need to have a look at your head."

"Never mind. It's merely a bruise." Turning his back on the women, Jack continued his scrutiny of the darkened shrubbery. He bent down and poked around beneath a bush, the leaves rustling. When he stood up, a long-barreled pistol gleamed in his hand. "Here's what I was looking for. Our prowler left it behind."

"Dear heavens," Julia whispered. Despite her lack of experience with firearms, she could tell this one belonged to a gentleman. "Is that a dueling pistol?"

"Yes." Jack handed her the lantern. With keen interest, he turned the gun from one side to the other and studied the sleek design. Then he gripped the ivory stock, aimed the pistol in the direction of the carriage house, and sighted down the barrel. "A fine one, too. It seems our trespasser has expensive tastes."

"He probably stole it from someone," Julia said. The last thing she needed was for Jack to figure out that the man wasn't a common thief.

"Perhaps. Nevertheless, it's a pity to break up a matched set."

"Matched?"

Jack flashed her a veiled look, unreadable in the darkness. "Such pistols always come in pairs. That way, the opponents in a duel can use identical weapons."

Elfrida regarded him with narrowed eyes. "How do you know so much about these pistols, Mr. Jackman?"

"From my previous employer. He had an excellent set that he showed me once." The ghost of a smile curved Jack's lips. "He never had cause to use them, but they were there all the same, just in case."

The older woman snorted. "Men! I'll never understand their need to resolve disputes with weapons."

"Men don't waste time talking as women do. We prefer things to be simple and straightforward."

"And fatal, I suppose," Julia said scathingly. "Well! At least we can be thankful you weren't shot tonight."

"Oh, he did try. But the gun jammed." With a manner that was entirely too casual, Jack disengaged the hammer. "The powder may have been damp."

Her legs turned to jelly. Jack could have been killed. He could have died defending her. In an instant, he could have become the victim of murder. She felt sick with horror at his life being cut short, all his strength and charisma and kindness gone in one pull of the trigger.

Another thought increased her queasiness. Had that bullet been meant for *her*?

"Give me the gun," she said, extending her hand and willing it not to shake. "I'll turn it in to the magistrate tomorrow—or rather, today."

When she did, she wouldn't reveal the reason for the prowler's presence. Yet if she concealed her connection to *The Rogue Report*, then what purpose would be served by contacting the law?

"I'll handle the matter," Jack said, tucking the pistol in the waistband of his breeches so that he resembled a pirate. "In the meantime, I'll keep the gun in my chamber. It shouldn't be anywhere near the students."

"Mr. Jackman does have a point," Elfrida said, surprising Julia by taking his side. "It's dangerous to have a weapon in the school."

"Then it's settled." Jack aimed a penetrating look at Julia, one that prickled her skin and delved deep inside her. "However, before I return to the carriage house, my lady, you and I need to talk."

A few minutes later, Julia found herself back in her office. Her teeth were chattering, and she headed straight to the fire to warm herself. On Julia's order, Elfrida had retired to bed, though not before giving Jack a suspicious glare and a warning to keep the door open.

He'd placated her with a smile and a promise. The moment Elfrida's footsteps died away, however, he closed the door.

As she picked up the poker and stirred the glowing coals, Julia could see him from the periphery of her vision. He placed the dueling pistol on the small table beside the chaise. Then he parted the draperies and peered out the window into the darkness. His strong, sure movements tightened the knot of tension inside her. Her entire body trembled as she thought of his narrow escape—and hers.

Jack had no inkling of her role in the situation. He didn't know about *The Rogue Report*. He believed her to be the innocent prey of a random thief.

How wrong he was!

Approaching her from behind, he gently pried the poker from her icy fingers. Then he adjusted her shawl so that it lay more securely around her shoulders. "You're shivering," he said. "You've suffered quite a shock."

The thick woolen folds wrapped her dressing gown, yet she felt chilled through and through. His solicitous manner only made Julia feel more guilty. "Jack, hold me. Please just . . . hold me."

Swiveling toward him, she burrowed against his body, tucking her head in the crook of his shoulder and wrapping her arms around his waist. He was like a furnace, giving forth heat that melted the ice of her fears. His hands stroked over her back as he mumured soothing nonsense into her hair. Gradually, the shudders quieted, leaving her with an intense awareness of him. He smelled deliciously spicy, and the hard wall of his chest made her breasts tingle. If she tilted her head up, her lips would brush his jaw and she could taste his skin . . .

He placed his hands on her shoulders and drew back. His face showed a gravity at odds with his usual smiling charm. "Tell me what's going on, Julia."

The statement brought her crashing back to earth. A fusion of attraction and alarm strangled her. The prowler. Dear God, he was referring to the prowler. "What do you mean?"

"The fire here was already lit. You were working just now. Why?" His gaze flitted over the tea tray on the table, then the desk, where a stack of folded newsletters was barely visible in the shadows.

The newsletters!

She curbed the impulse to race over to the desk and sweep them into a drawer. Such an action would only stir his suspicions. "Like you, I couldn't sleep."

"Is that the whole truth? Why do I have the feeling you're hiding something?"

Those sharp green eyes jangled her nerves. Stepping to the chaise, she busied herself with straightening the shawl around her shoulders. Somehow, she had known it would come to this. Jack was too perceptive not to probe deeper. She had to tell him *something*.

"All right, then," she admitted. "If you must know, I was keeping watch. I was afraid the intruder might return."

"The man who broke in here a fortnight ago?"

"Yes."

"I don't understand. What made you think he'd come back?"

Biting her lip, Julia fought a losing battle with her conscience. "There's something you don't know. A few evenings ago, I saw him again, lurking outside the school. When he spied me, he ran away."

A thunderous scowl lowered Jack's dark brows. As he strode forward to confront her, a muscle clenched in his jaw. "And you didn't tell me until now? My God, Julia! What were you thinking?"

Unaccustomed to being lectured, she fixed him with a glare. "I was thinking that it was none of your concern, that's what. Elfrida and I decided to stand guard. She offered to take the earlier shift, while I did the later one."

"So you would confide in Elfrida, but not me. I suppose the two of you intended to fend off an armed criminal with nothing but a damned poker."

Put that way, it *did* sound foolish. But his sarcasm only made her angry. "How was I to know he had a pistol? And if you intend to curse at me, you may return to your chambers at once."

Julia sat down on the chaise and arranged the folds of her dressing gown for maximum concealment. Blast the man! She didn't need to be harangued when she already carried a burden of guilt.

Pacing, Jack raked his fingers through his hair, causing a few dark strands to tumble onto his brow. Then he lowered himself beside her on the chaise. "Forgive me, my lady," he said, the words sounding forced. "But pray remember the circumstances. I've just discovered the dastard has come here for a *third* time. And tonight, he escaped over the wall and kicked me in the head in the process."

The news made Julia forget her wrath. She reached up

to examine the lump on his temple. The redness was beginning to fade. "I thought you said you'd slipped on the bat."

Jack drew her hand away, holding lightly onto her wrist. "Both events happened. Now, tell me about this second encounter. Can you describe the man?"

"It was dusk, and I didn't get a good look at him."

"You must have seen *something*. Was he tall or short? Stocky or thin? Dark or fair?"

"He was hunched over, and he wore a greatcoat and hat." Sensing Jack's frustration from his taut fingers, she added, "But I'd say he was average to tall in height. And he rode away on a bay horse."

He cocked an eyebrow. "A gentleman, then. I thought so from his voice."

"He spoke to you?"

"Only to command me to stop, or he'd shoot."

She sat up straight. "I certainly hope you obeyed."

Jack's mouth curled into a deadly half-smile that made him look far removed from an ordinary mathematics professor. "I don't take well to orders, my lady. You should know that. Besides, the pistol didn't fire, remember?"

"But it might have!"

He stroked the back of her hand. "We're straying from the subject." Lowering his voice to a musing tone, he gazed deeply into her eyes. "And I must confess that I'm puzzled. Why would a gentleman break into this school? You don't keep valuables lying about."

Her mouth went dry. "No . . ."

"Then what do you suppose he was looking for in your desk that time? It must have been something extremely important for him to try again. Twice."

"I—I can't imagine."

His thumb traced a soft path over her knuckles. "Tell me, Julia. There's something here that doesn't add up. Whatever trouble you're in, I want to help."

His touch soothed and aroused at the same time. Jack was inviting her to trust him. With all her heart, she longed to do so. He exuded strength and proficiency, and with the dreadful turn of events, she could use a powerful ally . . .

Her gaze strayed to the dueling pistol, the long barrel gleaming in the firelight. Jack could have been killed tonight. For that reason alone, she owed him the truth.

Subduing her apprehension, Julia rose from the chaise. "Wait here," she murmured. "There's something you need to see."

In a contest with his cronies, Mr. B.F. consumed an entire decanter of brandy. Shortly thereafter, he fell while attempting to mount his horse and landed in a row of boxwood outside his club.

—*The Rogue Report*

Chapter Fifteen

Jack watched her walk through the shadowed office to her desk. Despite the worrisome matter of the intruder, he found himself distracted by the sway of her hips. It was enough to make him forget all about the dull throbbing in his skull.

From the moment Julia had come running down the pathway of the garden, he had been aware that she was naked beneath that thin robe and nightgown. The ugly gray shawl couldn't hide the shapeliness of her figure. She wore her hair long and loosely braided, and fine brown curls had sprung free to frame the classic beauty of her face.

Damn, who the devil cared about unmasking the perpetrator? The only mystery he wanted to unravel was Julia herself. He should seduce her while he had the chance, press her down onto the chaise, and coax her into submission. Tonight was the perfect opportunity, with the house dark and everyone sleeping, and her defenses crumbled.

Yet the desire to wrest the truth from her also burned in him. By God, if it took him the rest of the night, he would make her admit she'd brought danger to her own doorstep by publishing that scandal rag. He would never have a better opportunity than now, when she was still horrified by that pistol-toting villain.

"I'd like you to look at this," she said.

Julia stood before him, holding out a folded paper. Her eyes were curiously intense in the flickering illumination of the fire. Intrigued by her serious manner, he took the sheet and opened it, catching a whiff of fresh ink. Only then did he look down at the paper.

The bold black title punched him in the gut. *The Rogue Report*.

He flashed a glance at her desk, where stacks of folded papers lay in the shadows. Newsletters, he realized. She must be preparing a new issue for mailing. The same one he held in his hands.

Good God. How had he not noticed before?

He scanned the lead article. It was a callous account of Viscount W.'s—that had to be Whistler's—huge loss at the gaming tables, and his need to find a wealthy bride. Below it was a story criticizing the Marquess of S.'s visit to a brothel, then a scornful description of a Mr. F.— Foxworthy, no doubt—falling into the shrubbery outside of White's after a night of drinking. Their actions were detailed with scathing spite, and Jack grew hot under the collar at the way his friends were portrayed as fools, rather than gentlemen seeking harmless amusements.

Well, perhaps Whistler's predicament wasn't harmless. He didn't have tuppence to rub together, and Jack could certainly understand the desperation that would drive a man to seek a leg shackle. It also reminded him of something George Gresham had mentioned.

Whistler was hoping to court Evelyn.

Jack's stomach churned sourly. Just like him, Whistler would lose his shot at the wealthy heiress because of an exposé in *The Rogue Report*. The realization brought a resurgence of his own humiliation at being snubbed by Evelyn. When he had gone to her house in the hopes of smoothing her ruffled feathers, Evelyn—lovely, blond, pretentious Evelyn—had looked straight past him as if he didn't exist.

Now, Jack wanted to crush the paper into a ball and hurl it into the fire. Instead, he gazed up at his nemesis and schooled his face into a look of polite bafflement.

"A scandal sheet, my lady? Why would you ask me to read such nonsense?"

"It isn't nonsense, it's quite serious." Julia sank down beside him and laced her fingers in her lap, so tightly that her knuckles turned white. "You see, the purpose of *The Rogue Report* is to reveal the misdeeds committed by the scoundrels of society. It's been delivered twice a month for the past five years to all the young ladies who might otherwise be ruined by such men." She bit her lip, eyed him warily, then added in a low tone, "And I am the author."

Jack sat unmoving. At last he had a confession of guilt straight from Julia's exquisite mouth. So why didn't he feel a surge of triumph? Why did he feel frustrated beyond measure?

Perhaps because he had not expected to fall so completely in lust with her.

For nearly a fortnight, he had endured being awakened each morning by Theo jumping up and down on the bed. He had worn coats that were too tight and old breeches more suited to a commoner. He had adhered to a rigid schedule and spent long hours teaching mathematics to hordes of children. All the while, he had waited patiently for the moment when he could put an end to Julia's scandalmongering. He'd intended to announce his true identity and savor the shock on her face when she realized how thoroughly she had been duped.

But he couldn't do so now. She would throw him out on his arse, and he wasn't ready to leave the school. Not yet. Not when he craved more of Julia.

His gaze lingered on the creamy flesh revealed by a gap in her dressing gown. Much more, indeed.

Seeing her frown, he dragged his mind back to the conversation. "Your name isn't on the masthead."

Her cheeks pink, she drew the lapels of her robe together. "*The Rogue Report* is published anonymously. Only the teachers on staff here know about it. No one else."

"Except for one gentleman." *Make that two*, Jack added to himself. He had thought himself clever in tracking her down, but apparently he wasn't alone in his quest to punish Lady Julia Corwyn. "Doubtless, our prowler is one of the men you named in a previous issue. And he's seeking proof that you're responsible."

Julia gave a small nod. "I'm afraid so. Oh, Jack, I can only think he wants to reveal my identity to the world."

"That would certainly prove awkward for you."

"It's far more than that. My newspaper will lose all credibility if the *ton* discovers it's been written by a fallen woman. No one will pay heed to it anymore. They'll toss it straight into the rubbish."

"I see."

She looked so distraught, Jack felt a trace of discomfort. But it wasn't as if she profited from the venture, so he wouldn't be harming her livelihood. In fact, without the newsletter, she would have more time to devote to her school. Educating young minds was a far more worthy endeavor.

Realizing she would expect more questions from him, he said, "You're no longer a member of society. How do you come by all your information?" He snapped his fingers. "No, let me guess. The mothers of the students are maidservants in the houses of the wealthy. They provide you with the gossip to put in your paper. It's very clever of you."

"It isn't gossip," she corrected. "Everything I write is completely factual. I make certain that my informants have firsthand knowledge of every incident."

Jack feigned amazement. "Surely a maid didn't follow the Marquess of . . . whatever his name . . . to a brothel."

"He's Lord Singleton, and Daisy Peabody overheard him telling his valet about his indecent activities."

Amused in spite of himself, Jack hid a grin. Singleton was a braggart who reveled in dramatic descriptions of his prowess with women. He wondered if the maid had repeated that conversation to Julia verbatim. "And what about . . . what was his name? Mr. F., the man who fell into the bushes outside his club?"

"Mr. Foxworthy returned home full of scratches and bruises, with twigs in his hair. Nora Spratt said he reeked of spirits."

"So that explains why you poured brandy over me on my first morning here. You've a vendetta against drunkards and other ne'er-do-wells."

"It isn't a vendetta. Rather, I'm dedicated to helping young women make good choices as to their future husbands."

Jack couldn't resist a little jab. "Yet the fellows you've portrayed here are likely to view it as a personal affront and an invasion of their privacy."

Julia regarded him coldly. "Are you defending these men?"

Hell, yes. Giving her a crooked smile designed to allay suspicion, Jack lightly ran the backs of his fingers over her peach-soft cheek. "Pray don't be offended, my lady.

I'm merely trying to give you the male perspective. It's important to understand the mind of the enemy."

"I don't care what they think. If men behave badly, then the young ladies of society have a right to know about it."

He subdued the temptation to set her straight on the matter. Dammit, a man was entitled to conduct his life as he chose. Without having spies reporting on his every activity.

Maybe it was time to give her a taste of her own medicine by probing into *her* secrets.

"I find myself curious as to what inspired you to start this newsletter," he said. "Was Theo's father a rogue?"

Her cheeks blanched, and she stared wide-eyed as if he'd punched her in the stomach. "That has naught to do with the matter at hand," she said stiffly.

"Are you so certain? What if *he's* the prowler?" Jack didn't really believe that, but he wanted an excuse to question her about the man.

"That's a ridiculous supposition."

"Is it? If he's been vilified in *The Rogue Report,* he might very well look to you as the source. Tell me, have you ever published an article about him?"

Her lashes were lowered, her eyes hazy, as if she were looking far into the past. She gave a firm shake of her head. "No, and I won't discuss him."

"I've one more question, and I hope you'll favor me with an honest answer. Was he violent toward you?"

Julia sat absolutely still. In the silence of the office, the fire hissed and spat. Seeking clues in her inscrutable expression, Jack kept his hard eyes trained on her. If she had been raped, he would find the man and beat him to a bloody pulp.

"No," she said. "I was not forced. Now, the subject is closed."

Relief filled Jack, yet he also felt a twist of frustration. For a person who claimed to want the truth laid bare between men and women, Lady Julia Corwyn was far too tight-lipped about herself.

Why was she so unwilling to speak of her former lover? Did she still harbor feelings for him? The thought nagged like a sore tooth. He wondered if the fellow was a servant or a commoner, someone unworthy of mention in *The Rogue Report*.

He shifted his mind to her stalker. If the man didn't have a personal connection to Julia, then who the devil was he? Had Jack played cards or attended parties with the same villain who had kicked him in the head tonight?

By God, he'd give away his last remaining possession— Willowford Hall—for the chance to wring the bastard's neck!

The irony of the situation didn't escape Jack. He too wanted to shut down Julia's newsletter. But at least he would conduct his revenge through the pleasures of love-making, not by sneaking around in the dark and threatening her with a gun.

His gaze flashed to the weapon lying on the side table. He was familiar with the dueling pistols owned by his friends, but not this one. The design didn't appear to be the work of one of the English gunsmiths frequented by the nobility. The fleur-de-lis pattern on the stock suggested a French origin, a fact that would make the piece more difficult to trace. The minute he could get away from the school, he'd show the pistol around, see if anyone could identify its owner.

"If we've nothing more to discuss tonight," Julia said, rising to her feet, "I've addresses to finish."

He had no intention of being dismissed. "Do you have copies of your other newsletters? I'd like to make a list of all the gentlemen you've denounced over the years."

"I keep the files in the supply closet. Follow me." She picked up the lamp and led the way out the door.

The darkness of the corridor enclosed them in a small circle of light. He caught a whiff of her perfume, something light and flowery and far more sensual than the image she cultivated of the prim headmistress. From the kiss they'd shared, he knew Julia had hidden depths of passion. She had been wild for him, and his heart picked up speed at the memory.

No, the lust he felt now came from her nearness. She was soft and feminine, with just enough thorns to make his conquest of her a challenge. He had a fantasy of her naked and moaning beneath him . . .

"Here we are." Moving briskly, she opened a small door and revealed stacks of paper and slates, containers of chalk, and a score of other necessities. She pointed to a wooden crate on the top shelf. Clearly anxious to get rid of him, she added, "You may take the box back to your chambers. But pray, don't feel obliged to examine the papers right now. It's too early for you to be up."

He was up, all right. She had only to look down at his breeches to see the proof of that. He reached for the box and stepped back. "I'll have a look at them later."

Julia shut the door with a soft click, then turned toward him, clutching the shawl over her bosom. "You'll show me the list when you're done?"

"Of course. Perhaps you'll describe each fellow to me. Did you know all these men when you were in society?"

She glanced away into the shadows. "Only a few. I wasn't allowed to associate with gamblers and rakehells."

Then who had seduced her, dammit? *Who?*

Her parents were the Earl and Countess of Brookville, and Jack had a vague memory of being introduced to them at a ball a long time ago. They had been a typical aristocratic couple, Lord Brookville discussing politics with the men, and Lady Brookville exchanging gossip with the ladies. Now, their daughter was the subject of gossip, and apparently they had never overcome the disgrace. They had cut her out of their lives and retired from society.

Jack wondered if they'd ever even met Theo, their one and only grandchild, for Julia had said she had no siblings. It was on the tip of his tongue to ask her, but he deemed it wise not to introduce such a volatile topic.

The distant, hollow bonging of the clock in the entrance hall announced the half hour. Julia started in surprise. "It's four-thirty. Well, good night, Jack. I'll see you at breakfast."

As she headed toward her office, he fell into step beside her. "I'll escort you."

She frowned up at him. "That's very kind, but it isn't necessary."

"I left the pistol in your office."

"Oh! Yes, I nearly forgot."

Little did she know, the gun was merely an excuse. They had at least another hour before the servants rose to begin their duties . . .

In her office, he placed the box on a chair, then collected the pistol and laid it inside, atop the neat stack of old scandal sheets. Julia put the lamp on the desk so that it shone over the piles of her soon-to-be mailed newsletter. The glances she aimed in his direction betrayed a keen awareness of him.

He was every bit as keenly aware of her. The perfect symmetry of her face. The womanly curves of her body. The shawl she clutched like a shield over her skimpy dressing gown.

Reining in his impatience, he walked to the door and closed it quietly. When he turned, the headmistress was standing behind her desk and glowering at him.

"You said you were leaving."

Rounding the desk, he caught her by the arm just as she pulled out the chair. "I'm not sleepy," he said in a beguiling tone. "It's pointless to go back to bed for only an hour or two." He let his eyes communicate the rest: *Unless you agree to come with me.*

Much to his satisfaction, her gaze dipped to his mouth. Then she met his eyes straight-on and said rather breathlessly, "I've work to do. These newsletters must go out in the morning mail."

"Is that wise? Given the situation, perhaps you should wait rather than stir up more trouble for yourself." And he'd save a few of his friends from humiliation.

"I won't be frightened off. If that's all you have to say . . ." She lifted her hand up as if to check her watch, but of course it wasn't pinned to her bodice. The sign of discomposure encouraged him.

"It isn't all. I've a matter to discuss with you." Giving her no opportunity to object, he drew Julia back to the chaise, urged her to sit down, and seated himself beside her.

Instantly, she scooted back against the armrest, as far from him as possible. "We've nothing more to discuss."

Jack draped his arm over the back of the chaise. His fingertips barely brushed her shawl, and already she was as skittish as a wild filly. "Perhaps *discuss* is the wrong term. Rather, I'd like to know something. Did Theo approve of your beau?"

"My beau? Oh, Mr. Trotter. They got on reasonably well for their first visit."

She looked defensive, and that told Jack all he needed to know. With a flash of satisfaction, he said, "So Theo didn't like him."

"I didn't say that! Well, perhaps the meeting *was* a bit strained. But in time, he'll grow fond of Mr. Trotter. I know he will." She gave Jack a challenging look. "Not that it's any of *your* concern."

Smiling, he feathered his fingers over her soft cheek. "It is my concern. Trotter is encroaching on my territory. He's trying to take my woman, and I won't allow it."

Her eyes widened to a fathomless smoky blue, fringed by sooty lashes. "He's not . . . ! You're not . . . !" She drew a flustered breath. "May I remind you, Mr. Jackman, you're my employee."

"Mr. Jackman, is it?" He noted the subtle cues of desire, from her flushed cheeks to her softened lips. "It's time to tell the truth, Julia. I suggest we play our game of questions."

The charming scoundrel is the most dangerous one. A prime example is the Earl of R., renowned for his ability to tempt ladies into sin.
—*The Rogue Report*

Chapter Sixteen

Julia knew she was in trouble. Not because she feared Jack might overpower her, but because whatever wicked intentions he had in mind, she doubted her ability to resist him.

Sweet heaven, he was handsome. His smile created deep dimples on either side of his mouth. He had high cheekbones, dark brows, and forest-green eyes with a hint of mischief. *Come closer*, they seemed to say. *I know all sorts of fascinating secrets.*

The romantic setting only enhanced her awareness of him. On the hearth, the fire whispered its encouragement. Beyond the glow of the lamp, the house lay dark and quiet. It fostered the illusion that they were the only two people in the world. If she gave in to her desires, no one would be the wiser.

"I'm too busy to play games with you," she said with a semblance of calm. "Besides, it's my turn and I haven't any questions for you."

"Then may I suggest you ask me why I couldn't sleep tonight."

Julia pursed her lips. It was dangerous for her to remember Jack lying in bed, the sheets riding low on his hips and revealing his broad chest. Dangerous to let him stay here a moment longer. But an imp of curiosity freed her tongue. "Why did you awaken?"

"Because I was aching for you." His voice grew low and honeyed. "I was dreaming about you, darling, thinking about how much I wanted you in my arms again."

Ever so slowly, he bent his head closer, and a wild excitement rushed through her veins. Jack meant to kiss her. She could see the desire in his eyes, could feel it in the tenderness of his hands cupping her cheeks.

Turn away, her mind ordered. *Deny him the chance to beguile you. He wants to use you for his own pleasure.*

But the pleasure would be hers, too. She craved the weight of his chest against her bosom, the press of his lips, the stroking of his hands. With every breath, she could smell his spicy masculine scent. She didn't want to battle her longing for Jack anymore, nor did she wish to heed the voice of prudence.

She wreathed her arms around his neck. "Oh, Jack. Kiss me."

Before he could react, she sealed their lips together. For an instant, he seemed surprised by her forwardness; then he took control. Shifting his hands to her shoulders, he held her close while his mouth worked its magic. He teased her with light, smooth movements before parting her lips to penetrate her with his tongue.

Her limbs melted. The melding of their mouths awakened other parts of her body, secret places that ached for his attention. The proximity of his hard form aroused in her the temptation to explore.

She threaded her fingers into his hair and tested its

silken thickness. Then she turned her attention to his shoulders and chest, learning the contours of muscle and sinew through the fabric of his shirt. Her zeal seemed to transmit to him, for his restraint crumbled and he kissed her with increasingly frantic need.

In the long-ago past, she had known the stirrings of physical attraction. She had enjoyed the attentions of many adoring gentlemen. But none of those men had been Jack. None of them had made her burn. None of them had provoked this reckless desire to join herself with him in every way humanly possible.

And certainly none of them had risked his life to protect her.

She drew back to run her fingers over the dark stubble of his cheek. "You could have died tonight."

"Or you," he added gruffly. "As long as I'm around, no one will hurt you, Julia. I swear it."

As long as I'm around. Would Jack himself be the one to cause her pain? The possibility was daunting. But at least he needed his position here as mathematics instructor. He wouldn't leave the school anytime soon. They had many months in which to sort out their feelings for one another. And perhaps . . . just perhaps he was the dream she had given up long ago, the one man who could make her happy.

The warmth of the shawl left her shoulders as he consigned the garment to the floor. He worked at the knot of her belt, parted her dressing gown and pushed it off her shoulders. Then his hands encircled her waist over her nightdress.

Her heart pounded so hard she felt on the verge of swooning. She wore nothing beneath the fine silk, and the heat of his palms penetrated her skin. Like her, he appeared caught up in the moment, his eyes dark and intent, his cheeks flushed.

His actions were leading them into forbidden territory. She knew too well the dangers of succumbing to passion outside the bounds of holy wedlock. There would be consequences, and as a woman, she would bear the brunt of them.

And surrender was tantamount to proving herself unworthy of his respect. *She* didn't view it that way, but a man would. Jack was bound to think less of her, and that was something she couldn't bear.

She pulled back. "No, you mustn't . . . *oh!*"

He was cupping her breasts in his palms, his thumbs rubbing lightly over the tips. In a throaty tone, he said, "Yes, my lady?"

Starved for air, she grabbed hold of his wrists. "That's enough. If I allow you any more liberties, you'll think badly of me."

"Badly? I assure you, darling, I'm far more likely to adore you."

His clever fingers commenced stroking again, and she clutched them firmly. "Do listen. I'm not in the habit of letting men touch me like this."

For many years she had not allowed herself to become close to any man. She had kept to herself for a reason known only to a handful of people. But tonight, she had confided one of her secrets to Jack. Dared she entrust him with another?

Perhaps—just perhaps—it wouldn't be necessary.

"I'm glad. Because I want you all for myself." All teasing gone, Jack's expression showed a wealth of tender understanding. And a glorious heat inspired by her. He turned up her palms and planted a skin-tingling kiss in each of them. "Darling Julia, I can give you great pleasure. Will you allow me?"

Her insides melted. Oh, Lord, he did know how to

charm her. He gazed intently at her, a powerful man awaiting her choice.

And she did face a choice. She could go on with her life, denying the temptations of her body and settling for a bore like Mr. Trotter. Or she could throw off the restrictions of a society that had condemned her anyway. She could seize her chance at happiness.

With Jack.

A torrent of emotion drowned her doubts. Taking his face in her hands, she brushed her lips over his. "Make love to me, Jack. Here, now."

Forever. The unspoken word shone in her mind. Her defenses in shambles, Julia realized the truth. She loved Jack, loved him with the fullness of her heart. She loved his smile, his kindness, his courage. He was a kindred spirit who had brought a wealth of joy and laughter into her life. Whatever the future held, she would have no regrets about giving herself to him.

His hands sought her breasts again, and to her startled delight, he bent his head to suckle her through the silk of her gown. Cords of fire spiraled downward, deep into her belly. For a long moment, she couldn't think, couldn't breathe, couldn't move.

With deft fingers, he undid the tiny buttons at the front of her nightdress and exposed her breasts. His eyes dark, he gazed down at her. "Beautiful. No, you're magnificent."

His praise made her blush, and she brought her hands up to cover herself. She whispered, "Must you stare?"

"How can I not? Pray, look at yourself." Taking hold of her chin, he tilted her head downward so that she had a reluctant view of her rounded flesh. "Your skin is white and soft as silk. Here's how it feels to me." Taking her hand, he guided it over the twin hills of her bosom.

It was shocking to touch herself, directed by his large

palm. Shocking to feel a deep throb of desire between her legs. Yet she craved the sensation and pressed her thighs together to sustain it.

"Your breasts are full and perfectly formed," he went on in a rough tone. "The peak is very sensitive, is it not?"

He brushed their entwined fingers over one, and it contracted into a tight bud. Weak and trembling, she rested her head in the crook of his neck. He aroused a hunger in her that she knew not how to satisfy. "Oh, Jack, I want . . ."

"This?" He helped her massage the tip of her other breast. "Here, you're the color of honey. I wonder if you taste as sweet."

Lowering his head, he drew her nipple into his mouth.

Julia moaned at the slide of his tongue, the gentle nipping of his teeth, the stimulating suction of his lips. She found herself moving involuntarily, clutching at him for support, unsure how much more she could bear, yet needing him to continue. Never had she imagined that a physical act could make her ache so deliciously.

Until he slipped his hand beneath the hem of her nightgown. His fingers inched up her bare leg, leaving a trail of fire over her skin. As he progressed to her thigh, she waited, feared, anticipated. But the twisting of the silk proved a barrier to his exploration.

Uttering a low growl of frustration, he sat back and whipped his shirt over his head, tossing it aside. The sight of him, half-naked in the firelight, enthralled Julia. He was even more powerfully built than she remembered. His shoulders were wide and roped with muscle, his waist narrow and tapered, his chest brawny beneath a dusting of black hair.

She skimmed her fingers over him. His skin was hot, and it was remarkable to realize she had made him so fevered. She murmured, "*You're* magnificent."

His mouth quirked, as if he wanted to smile but was too distracted. "If you're pleased, that's all that matters."

"I'm more than pleased." She continued to touch him, tracing the ridges of his ribs and the circles of his flat brown nipples. "I'm awestruck. You'd put the finest statue to shame."

As she lightly caressed his stomach, he sucked in a breath. "Be glad I'm not made of cold marble. Now, if you don't mind . . ."

He reached for her nightgown, tugging it upward before she realized his intention. Julia gasped as cool air rushed over her nakedness. She grabbed for the garment, but Jack dropped it behind the chaise, out of her reach. All she had was her hands, and they did a less than adequate job of concealing her privates. "Oh!"

A quizzical tenderness softened his face, and he stroked her cheek. "You really do have little experience, don't you?"

Julia didn't intend to discuss her past—at least not now. Whenever she had allowed herself to fantasize about being with a man—a faceless, anonymous husband—the scene had always taken place in bed under the covers. With her gown still on and merely adjusted to permit certain activities. "Perhaps you should put out the lamp."

"Rather, bring it closer. You're lovely, and I wouldn't deny myself the pleasure of looking at you."

His gaze descended to her curves, and she blushed under his scrutiny. Her nudity felt discomfiting, nay, downright wicked. Yet there was something liberating about it, too, and in an act of daring, she shifted her hands to his thighs and let him view everything. The hot appreciation in his eyes imbued her with a sense of feminine power.

Nuzzling his lips, she flirted with him. "And what of you, Jack? You're still wearing your breeches."

"Oh. Yes. So I am." He gave her a bemused look. "Perhaps you'll help me remove them."

Two rows of buttons marched down either side of the front placket. In between, a telltale bulge showed against the plain brown cloth. The sight made her heart stutter and her fingers clumsy. When at last the flap came open, she discovered he wore no underclothes and his male member jutted in full glory.

A dark, shivery desire swept through her. She stared, closed her eyes briefly, then stared again.

He had his hands clamped around her waist. "Touch me," he said hoarsely.

It wasn't an order, but a plea. Anxious, craving, and curious, she indulged him—and herself. She brushed her fingers from the base of the shaft all the way up to the purplish cap. He was hot and velvety, and a fierce ache seized her loins. What would it be like to take him into herself? She burned to know.

He sat watching her, his expression taut, his lashes at half-mast. She sensed he was holding back, waiting for a cue from her. "Jack?"

His chest expanded. His eyes were dark and intense, his fingers taut around her upper arms. "I won't force you, darling. You need never fear that from me."

His restraint only made her desire him all the more, and she rubbed her cheek against his. "You're an honorable man."

"Honorable?" His voice was harsh, raspy. "If only you knew the things I'd like to be doing right now . . ."

Tension and euphoria tangled her insides. Placing her hands on his shoulders, she gave him a lingering kiss. "Then do them," she whispered. "Seduce me, Jack."

"With pleasure."

Those were their last coherent words for a long while. Holding her close, he slid his hand between her legs for the most intimate caress of all. The blaze within her gained strength in a windstorm of sensations. The feelings built until she became a mindless creature of passion, utterly without defenses, crying out for surcease. She achieved it at last in an explosion of pure, shocking joy.

Caught up in the glorious throes, she had a vague perception of Jack stripping off his breeches, then laying her down on the chaise and positioning himself between her parted legs. The pressure of his entry caused a flash of discomfort followed by another amazing pulse of ecstasy.

He kissed her again, long and deep, his tongue mimicking the rhythmic thrusts of his hips. She held tightly to him and savored the phenomenon of their joined bodies. As his movements grew more frantic, he groaned low in his chest, stiffening under the force of his own release. Moments later, he melted down over her, breathing hard, to bury his face in her hair.

The quiet bliss of the aftermath held her in thrall. Julia relished the weight of him, the closeness of their coupled forms. Nothing in her experience had prepared her for the perfect contentment of lying naked with Jack. It was as if they were one person, one heart, one soul.

She threaded her fingers through his damp hair. A languid happiness filled her from head to toe. Surely Jack must have strong feelings for her, too, for he had loved her with such exquisite tenderness. Together, they had found heaven on earth, and she had absolutely no regrets.

He stirred. His chest expanded in a deep breath as if to savor her scent. Then he lifted his head and stared down at her.

Something in his expression struck a knell of alarm in her. Those dark green eyes looked almost . . . horror-struck.

She smiled uncertainly. "Jack? What is it?"

But she thought she knew. She feared it.

He scrambled off her and stood up. Superb in his nudity, he gazed intently at her privates in a way that made the warm glow of pleasure dissipate. In its absence, Julia suffered a return of awkwardness. She shifted uneasily and closed her legs, but he reached down to part them again.

His face was stark with disbelief and budding anger. "What the devil— By damn, Julia. You were a virgin!"

The best way to predict a man's conduct after marriage is to scrutinize his actions before it. The Duke of W. was a drunken scoundrel in his youth as he is now in his dotage . . .
—*The Rogue Report*

Chapter Seventeen

Jack felt as if someone had yanked the rug out from under his feet. As if he'd fallen into stone-cold reality.

Only a moment ago, he had been basking in perfect satisfaction. Making love to Julia had been an amazing experience that had wrung every last drop of strength from him. But in the midst of his reverie, he had remembered meeting a barrier inside her. In a frenzy, he had breached it, too caught up in pleasure to question its significance.

But now the proof lay before him. His discarded breeches had somehow become tangled beneath them, and he was staring down at a telltale rusty stain on the brown fabric.

The sight left him shaken. Even the most irredeemable rogue avoided seducing aristocratic maidens. The ramifications were far too costly.

Julia propped herself on her elbow. She gazed up at him with enormous gray-blue eyes. Their wild coupling had caused corkscrews of dark hair to spring loose and drape her shoulders. Several strands straggled down over her perfect breasts. An untimely lurch of attraction assailed him, and he despised himself for it.

No, he despised *her* for tricking him.

"So?" he snapped. "Have you nothing to say for yourself?"

She lowered her lashes slightly, hiding her thoughts. "I'm sorry. I'd hoped you wouldn't guess."

"Not guess?" Jack struggled to find a thread of sense in her deception. "A man is bound to notice if he has to break through his lover's maidenhead."

"You needn't be crude."

"The truth is crude." Dammit, she was inexperienced, and she wouldn't even know . . . "Do you have a handkerchief?"

Warily, she pointed to her desk. "In the middle drawer."

As he padded across the office, the sight of the newsletters fed the panic and ire that twisted inside him. By damn, this seduction was supposed to be *his* revenge, not hers!

Returning to her side, he made a move to cleanse her, but she went scarlet and snatched the handkerchief from him. "I can manage."

"No doubt you can." He turned his back to give her a moment's privacy. Those all-too-frequent blushes of hers should have alerted him. Maybe if he hadn't been so blinded by lust, he would have heeded the clues to her innocence.

But who would have imagined that any young lady would willingly relinquish her place in society by posing as a ruined woman? And what the hell had induced her to do so, anyway?

When she offered no explanation, he paced back and

forth to vent his wild emotions. "You lied to me, Julia. You played me for a fool. And unless it was the second miraculous birth in the history of the world, you aren't Theo's mother."

Indignant, she sat up and groped for his shirt, using it to cover her midsection. "I *am* his mother. In all the ways that matter."

Jack grabbed his breeches and stepped into them. "I'll tell you what matters. You didn't trust me with the truth. You led me astray." Good God. He sounded more the outraged maiden than she did. Nevertheless, he forged on. "You deceived me into believing you were experienced."

"What difference does it make? I gave myself freely. I knew the risk I was taking, and I certainly *don't* hold you to blame."

He held himself to blame. Inadvertent though it had been, her deflowering had been his doing. There were certain obligations required of a gentleman in such a circumstance, the chief of which was . . .

His palms felt sweaty. No, he wouldn't let himself even consider marriage. Lady Julia Corwyn was his enemy. He had no intention of spending the rest of his life shackled to the woman who had vilified him in *The Rogue Report*.

Besides, her situation was vastly different from that of a pea-brained debutante who flirted with the wrong man. In the eyes of society, Julia had already fallen from grace. She was right; he didn't owe her any damn-fool noble gesture.

And hadn't it always been his motto to take his pleasure with no strings attached? It was every man's dream to bed a woman as beautiful and responsive as Julia and then suffer no recriminations afterward. So why did her nonchalance make him want to shout at her?

Because—*oh, God*—she'd been a virgin.

He watched as she went behind the chaise to retrieve her nightgown. She didn't have any siblings, so perhaps Theo's mother was a cousin or a friend. Possibly that woman—Eliza—though he didn't dare mention her by name. Julia didn't know that he had opened her mail, when he'd been trying to figure out how she obtained her information for the newsletter.

Her back to him, she pulled the virginal white garment over her head. But not before he saw the firelight shining on that curvaceous form and remembered the intense joy he had felt at her climax.

It was too soon, he was too angry, yet he felt the unmistakable pulse of lust. The primitive instincts she aroused in him had only been strengthened by their union. By God, he'd been her first, her only.

Blast her for saying it didn't matter!

"Who is Theo's mother?"

She looked up from buttoning her gown. Their gazes clashed across the shadowed office. "Don't ask. I won't answer."

Her cool reticence enraged him. "Like hell. We're playing questions, and it's my turn. I want to know why you gave up everything for a child who isn't even yours."

"Theo *is* mine." As fierce as a she-wolf protecting her pup, she stepped toward him, his shirt fisted in her hands. "You'll stop saying he isn't."

He caught hold of her wrist. Her delicacy of form belied her stubbornness of character. "I want an honest reply, Julia. You owe me that much."

"I owe you nothing."

"Answer me."

"I veto the question."

"You already used your one veto. Remember?"

Goaded by her caginess, he lowered his voice to a husky murmur. "A few days ago, you refused to admit that you spend your nights dreaming of me."

Julia gazed up at him. The evidence of their lovemaking showed in her reddened lips and tousled hair. Desire coiled in him like a snake, striking hard in his gut. By damn, he wanted to throw her over his shoulder and carry her off to his town house where they could make love for hours on end. It would take days, weeks perhaps, to rid himself of this powerful hunger.

She wrenched her hand free and stepped back. "This isn't a game, Jack. It has to end here and now."

"End? We've just begun, darling."

Julia shook her head decisively. "What happened tonight cannot be repeated. I will not engage in an affair with one of my employees. I have Theo to consider. Now take your shirt"—she hurled it at him and it caught him in the face—"and leave here at once. Before you're seen by one of the servants."

Then she marched to the door and held it open for him.

Jack fancied himself an expert on breaking off affairs with women. Whenever he wished to dispose of his current mistress, he employed a wealth of charm to soothe her injured pride. But now *he* was the one being dismissed.

And his devil-may-care humor had deserted him completely. He was speechless, chagrined, and itching to put his fist through the nearest wall.

Now was his chance to tell her his true identity. To announce that he too had been duping her. Since she was tossing him out, he might as well take his revenge, leave the school, and be done with her.

Instead, he strode out into the darkened passageway and pivoted on his heel. "It isn't over, my lady. I promise you that."

She arched a disdainful eyebrow. And shut the door in his face.

Late the following afternoon, a light rapping on the door disturbed Julia as she sat at the dainty desk in her bedchamber. She had given orders that no one disturb her except in an emergency. Since that tentative knock didn't sound like a crisis, she decided to ignore it.

Ordinarily at this hour, she was downstairs in her office, tending to business and solving the inevitable problems that cropped up every day. But she had felt too dispirited to face the other teachers—one in particular. Pleading a headache, she had retreated here, ostensibly to work on upcoming lessons for her geography class, but in reality to dwell on the wonderful tryst she had shared with Jack.

And its agonizing aftermath.

Julia twirled the feathered quill between her fingers. This room with its rosewood furniture and pale blue brocaded draperies was a pleasant haven that usually enhanced her productiveness. But not today. Today, whenever she tried to write, she found herself doodling *William Jackman*. And worse, *Mrs. William Jackman*.

Jack had no intention of asking for her hand in marriage. If there had been any hope at all of winning his heart, she had crushed it by her own actions. He was furious at her for withholding the truth.

The dreadful truth was, she deserved his censure. She had misled him on purpose. Blindly in love, she had convinced herself that her inexperience could be concealed. That he would never have cause to question Theo's birth.

But he had. And when she had refused to answer his questions, Jack had been hurt by her lack of trust. He had given her a look that cut her so deeply she would ache from it forever. If only he knew she'd had no choice.

It isn't over, my lady. I promise you that.

Despite that thrilling, romantic declaration, he'd scarcely paid her a glance at breakfast and luncheon. Apparently, he had reconsidered the statement made in the heat of anger. He had given up on her, and she tried to be glad. All day, she had forced herself to behave as if nothing had happened between them. She had smiled and chatted, although now she couldn't recall a word of any conversation during the meals. Dorcas, Margaret, and Elfrida had had to repeat questions to her. Even Faith, who often drifted in her own world, had given Julia a curious look.

What if Jack decided to leave the school for good? Surely his financial state would require him to stay at his post. But what if her refusal to confide in him drove him away?

The tapping sounded again. A familiarity to it caught her attention. Setting down the quill, she called out, "Come in."

Theo poked his head inside. In typical fashion, his thatch of reddish-brown hair was rumpled and his shirttail hung out of his dark pants. "Hullo."

With her emotions so raw, the sight of his small, freckled face brought a lump to her throat. She wanted to wrap him in her arms and never let go. But he was at an age when overly zealous mothering was beginning to cause him embarrassment.

Smiling warmly, she rose to her feet. "Hullo, yourself. Come and talk to me. Agnes brought tea and a plate of gingerbread and I can't possibly eat it all."

The truth was, she'd hardly touched anything on the tray by the fireplace. Her stomach had been tied in knots all day. The hunger in her had nothing to do with food.

Concentrating on her son, Julia sat down in one of the

pair of pale blue chairs by the hearth and refilled her teacup. Theo walked to the tray and gazed down at it without taking anything. It was unlike him not to tuck into a plate of sweets.

It also was unlike him not to chatter nonstop.

Frowning, she asked, "Are you ill, darling? Let me feel your forehead."

"I'm fine, Mummy." But he reluctantly trudged forward and allowed her to touch his cool brow.

She straightened the collar of his shirt. He had something on his mind, and she tried to root it out. "How is your new mathematics class? It isn't too difficult, is it?"

His brown eyes brightened. "Oh, it's great fun! Mr. Jackman gives us lots of puzzles to work out."

"I'm glad you like him." *No!* Jack was *not* a topic she wanted to discuss. "What about your other lessons? Miss Littlefield will be giving another spelling examination next week. Would you like me to help you study?"

Theo looked indignant. "I can memorize by myself. Just like everybody else."

A pang struck her. Her son was growing up so fast. It seemed only yesterday that he had been an infant in swaddling clothes. From the moment Julia had first held him in her arms, she had known she would raise him as her own. As difficult as it had been to relinquish her place in society, she had no regrets. For seven years, she had guarded the circumstances of his birth. Now Jack knew the truth—or at least a portion of it.

Should she tell him the rest? Should she betray the vow of silence she had made to her parents? Distraught and uncertain, she sipped her lukewarm tea.

Theo wandered around the bedchamber as if he were trying to work up the courage to tell her something. The muffled laughter of children drifted from the garden below her window. He paused only to touch the glass paperweight on her desk, the one he liked to hold up to the window because it distorted his view.

He didn't do so now.

"Theo, is something wrong?" she prompted. "Did you come here to talk to me about it?"

He stole a glance at her, kicked at the patterned rose carpet with the toe of one brown shoe, then blurted out, "Do I have a papa?"

Julia's heart gave a mighty thump. She froze with the teacup halfway to her lips. She had known he would ask about his father someday. She had given careful thought to an explanation that would be suitable for his age. But now she could only think, *Please, not today*.

Setting down her cup so that he wouldn't see her hand shaking, she rallied a smile. "Of course you do. Everyone has a father. Unfortunately, not all fathers are able to stay with their families."

"Why doesn't my papa live with us? Doesn't he like me?"

Oh, no. Her son looked so young and vulnerable that Julia suffered a deep stab of pain. Leaving the chair, she knelt down and drew him into her arms. He must be very distressed, she thought, because he didn't object when she held him tightly and brushed back a lock of his hair.

"He wasn't lucky enough to know you," she said softly. "But I'm certain that if he did, he would love you every bit as much as I do."

Theo squirmed out of her arms. "But where is he, then? Clifford said he didn't want me."

Ah, so Clifford was behind this sudden interest. Like all the children here at the Corwyn Academy, Clifford's mother had been used and abandoned by a man. And finally Julia could understand the passion that could compel a woman to risk bearing a child out of wedlock.

A thought that had flirted at the back of her mind crept forward. Perhaps she had conceived Jack's baby. The possibility was shocking, frightening—and breathtaking, too.

She focused on Theo. "I'm afraid your papa lives somewhere far away. I don't know how to find him."

In truth, she had no idea where the scoundrel lived—or even who he was. It was just as well. She didn't know what she would do if she ever came face-to-face with him.

Theo mulled over the information for a moment. "Can Mr. Jackman be my papa, then?"

She struggled to hide her dismay. "The only way that a man can become your father is for me to marry him. But that isn't likely to happen, not with Mr. Jackman."

"Why not?"

"Because . . . because it just isn't, I'm afraid." She ruffled his hair. "Now, go on out to the garden and play. You need some fresh air after being cooped up in class all day."

On his way out, Theo paused by the tea tray to grab a piece of gingerbread. Julia was so glad to see him behaving normally again that she didn't scold him for eating with his fingers and dropping crumbs on the carpet. Following him to the door, she leaned against the frame and smiled as he trotted down the passageway and disappeared around the corner.

Her smile slowly faded. Theo wanted Jack as his father. Heaven help her, what a tangled web!

She was turning to go back inside when Agnes emerged from the servants' staircase and waved. "M'lady!"

The young maidservant had pretty features and stylishly arranged blond hair beneath a white mobcap. With

every step, her trim ankles kicked up the drab gray skirt
with its long apron. She handed Julia a small parcel
wrapped in brown paper. "The postman brung this in the
late mail."

"Thank you."

It was from Eliza; Julia recognized the perfect penmanship and neatly knotted string. Her spirits lightened.
Bella must have made another figurine to add to Julia's
collection.

Bella.

What would Jack say if he knew about her? If he were
to meet her? The daring thought jumped into Julia's mind
and refused to be banished. It was foolish even to consider trusting a man she had known for so short a time.
Very foolish, indeed . . .

Lifting her gaze from the parcel, she realized that
Agnes was still standing in the corridor. The animation in
her expression put Julia on alert. It couldn't be the pack-
age; the maid didn't know about Bella. No one on the
staff did, not even the other teachers.

"Was there something else?"

"Aye, m'lady. I know ye said ye was busy, but 'e insisted and . . . well, 'e's waitin' in yer office."

Excitement flashed heat throughout her body. *It isn't
over, my lady. I promise you that.*

Julia smoothed her hair, tucking in several irksome,
springy curls. Breathily, she asked, "Is it Mr. Jackman?"

Agnes cocked her head quizzically. "Mr. Jackman's
gone out, m'lady."

"Gone out? Where?" Instantly, a fear wormed its way
into her mind. What if he intended to visit an employment
agency to look for job openings? What if she had driven
him away?

"Dunno. But 'e said not t' wait dinner fer 'im." The
maid leaned closer in a confiding manner. " 'Tis yer Mr.

Trotter downstairs. 'E's brung flowers, m'lady. Lots and lots o' 'em. 'E must've bought out all o' Covent Garden market."

Julia swallowed a groan. Would this day never end?

When choosing a husband, a lady should seek a gentleman who is dependable, honorable, and faithful. The antithesis of this paragon is Lord S., who has been known to gamble without pause for three days and nights . . .
—The Rogue Report

Chapter Eighteen

The brass-fitted door to the shop was locked, but the lamps glowed inside, so Jack rapped hard on the glass. It was dusk, he'd rushed here after his last class, and if it had been for naught . . .

To his relief, a tall, thin man emerged from a back room and paused a moment to peer at him. Then he stripped off his long white apron and hastened forward. A key rattled in the lock and the door swung open.

Seymour Ledger bowed respectfully. "Lord Rutledge, it is indeed a pleasure. But I'm afraid it's after hours and—"

"I'm not here to make a purchase. Only to ask your advice. It shouldn't take more than a few minutes of your time."

"As you wish, then."

Jack went inside, drew the dueling pistol from inside his coat, and handed it to the gunsmith. "I found this abandoned beneath a bush," he said glibly. "I'd like to return it to its proper owner, and I was hoping perhaps you might recognize it."

Ledger frowned down at the gun. "It isn't immediately familiar, my lord. But I'll certainly take a look at it in the light."

With the care a priest might give to the Holy Grail, Ledger laid the long-barreled pistol on a square of dark blue velvet beneath one of the hanging brass lamps. He was a graying, aesthetic man clad in a white linen shirt and trim black breeches. Bending down, he fitted a monocle over his right eye and examined the weapon.

Jack curbed his impatience. Located just off Bond Street, the gunshop was a popular haunt for the gentlemen of the *ton*. Glass cases held a variety of firearms, including flintlocks for hunting, pistols of all types, and even old-fashioned fowling pieces. Despite the fine cabinetry and gilded trim, the odors of oil and metal tainted the air.

For the umpteenth time, Jack questioned his intelligence in seeking out the villain. He owed nothing to Julia; she had made that fact extremely clear. By seducing her, he had achieved his purpose of revenge. He should tell her the truth, leave the school, and return to society. A few words in the ears of the right gossips, and within a day, all the *ton* would be buzzing with the news that Lady Julia Corwyn was the author of *The Rogue Report*.

But he couldn't leave her in danger. He had to know she was safe. Even if it meant being tortured by lust in the meantime.

Seymour Ledger straightened. "I'm afraid I've no recollection of seeing this pistol before now. But the gunsmith is Gaston Vallois. I recognize his hallmark."

The name was vaguely familiar. "Is he here in London?"

The gunsmith shook his head. "He owns a small shop

in Paris. He makes specialty weapons for wealthy clients."

Damn. There wasn't time for a jaunt across the Channel. "With the war over just last year," Jack said, taking the pistol and tucking it into his waistband, "it must be fairly new."

"Rather, it's somewhat dated, perhaps fifteen or twenty years old."

"Indeed? Any ideas as to who might own such a piece?"

"I would have no way of knowing." Ledger discreetly eyed Jack's ill-fitting coat, as if assessing the current state of his credit. "You might do better to ask your acquaintances, my lord. Perhaps another gentleman will recognize it."

That was exactly what Jack was reluctant to do. If he started showing the pistol to his friends, its owner might connect him to Julia and the Corwyn Academy. Because how else would he have gotten his hands on it?

Unless he could invent a story about picking it up in a pawn shop. Trick the fellow into thinking Julia or a servant on her staff had found it and sold it. If the man recognized Jack's voice and called his bluff, then so much the better. Jack was itching for a good bout of fisticuffs—or maybe a duel.

"Thank you for your advice."

"I'm happy to be of service." Ledger turned an oily, salesman's smile on Jack. "How is that set of pistols I sold you last year? Have you found much use for them?"

"Not yet." Jack smiled grimly. "But you can be certain that I will quite soon."

Julia stared down in dismay at Mr. Trotter's receding hairline.

A few minutes ago, she had entered her office to find

the desk and table awash in gold chrysanthemums, yellow daisies, and pink snapdragons. Mr. Trotter had been pacing nervously, and he had done the extraordinary act of falling to his knees before her.

God save her. The day was going from bad to worse. "Do have a seat on the chaise," she said in an effort to forestall what she feared. "You're making me very uncomfortable."

"Forgive me, but I must speak." Mr. Trotter clapped one hand over the breast of his brown tweed coat. His puppy-dog eyes gazed up at her with concentrated purpose. "Pray know that I view you in the very highest esteem. You are an angel of grace, a goddess of beauty."

Julia took a step backward. "That's very kind of you to say—"

"You must hear me out. Please, I beg you." Hobbling forward on his knees, he grasped her hand, his palm hot and moist. "Although we've had but a short time in which to cultivate our acquaintance, my respect and admiration for you have grown enormously. The warmth you inspire in me has become too powerful to be borne in silence."

"Thank you, but—"

"Thusly, I must confess the ardent sentiments I hold in my heart. I vow, I cannot live without you. Lady Julia Corwyn, will you do me the great honor of accepting my offer of holy matrimony?"

Oh, drat. As a debutante, she had fielded many a proposal. But she was out of practice and had more compassion now than in her callous youth. Especially knowing that he'd done the extravagant, romantic, useless gesture of bringing her masses of flowers.

Extricating her fingers, she made a concentrated effort not to wipe them on her skirt. What was she to say? Certainly not that she was in love with another man, a man who had made exquisite love to her in this very room only hours ago. A man who hadn't offered her marriage.

"This is most unexpected, Mr. Trotter. As you said, we scarcely know one another."

"Those few hours have been long enough for me to determine the truth. You, my dear, are the only woman in the world who can make me happy!"

He made another grab for her hand.

Julia stepped back, and lest he lunge toward her on his knees, she moved behind her desk, where a heap of blooms half hid him from view. "Please stand up," she said. "It's difficult to hold a rational conversation like this."

"As you wish." Mr. Trotter lumbered to his feet and advanced on her. "I vow, you'll find me the most agreeable of husbands. Whatever pleases you, you've only to say it and it's done."

His overblown declarations stirred only pity—and guilt for having led him on. His stealthy approach also filled her with alarm.

She edged backward. "That's very thoughtful, Mr. Trotter, but I don't think—"

"Ambrose," he interrupted. "Please, let me hear the music of my name upon your beautiful lips while I hold you in my arms."

"No, Mr. Trotter. I fear you've misinterpreted my—oh!"

He pounced, and she fled around the desk in a hurry, dislodging a few blossoms that scattered to the floor. She and Mr. Trotter did a madcap dance, with him on one side of the desk and her on the other.

"Come closer, my darling, you needn't be so timid. It's quite acceptable for a betrothed couple to share an embrace."

"We are *not* betrothed. And I'm certainly not timid."

"You are sweet and lovely, and I ask only a kiss to seal

our pact. One kiss, and we shall both be transported to heaven."

He feinted to the left, then rushed her from other side. With a yelp, she dashed to the fireplace and seized the poker, spinning around to brandish it in his face. "Kindly keep your distance, sir!"

His brown eyes widened. He froze with his hands splayed in the air. A flush turned his cheeks ruddy. "My lady! Are you angry?"

Good Lord, was the man so obtuse? "I'm merely trying to make you listen. I will not accept your proposal, not now, not ever."

Voicing the statement gave her an instant lifting of relief. Enduring his visits had been a trial, and she had done so only in an effort to find a father for Theo. But now Julia could see how wrong she had been. Marrying Mr. Trotter would have meant cheating both her and her son of happiness. Theo preferred Jack—and so did she. Even with the almost certain knowledge that she would never have the man of her dreams, she wasn't willing to settle for less.

"Well!" Mr. Trotter said in indignation. "Surely you must see the value of my proposal, for you're unlikely to receive a better one. Not many decent men would be willing to take on the role of father to young Theodore."

He had struck in her most vulnerable spot, and she hid her pain behind the scorn of a lady. "That's quite enough. I must ask that you leave and never return."

His nostrils flared as he drew in a breath. Resentment twisted his features as he looked her up and down. "A pretty penny I spent on you, and this is the thanks I receive!"

Before she could frame a suitable reply, he wheeled around and stalked to the desk, where he scooped up a portion of the flowers on his way to the door. There, he swung toward her, his chin bordered by masses of orange and yellow chrysanthemums. "You'll lament your ill-treatment of me," he declared. "By Jupiter, you will!"

Mr. Trotter vanished out the door and, as the tapping of his angry footsteps faded into silence, Julia lowered the poker and leaned on it. The jellied consistency of her legs made it difficult to stand without support.

A chill prickled the nape of her neck. His expression had been uncharacteristically malicious. Had he merely been stating his belief that she would regret rejecting his marriage proposal?

Or had bland, innocuous Mr. Trotter just issued a real threat?

Darkness had fallen by the time Jack returned to the school. Aided by the light of a few stars, he walked through the gloom of the mews and entered the carriage house by the rear door. He needed to talk to Julia, but the matter could wait until the morning. He was chilled, weary, and frustrated, and the last thing he wanted was to invite another tongue-lashing.

As he made his way up the darkened staircase, he was startled by a sliver of light beneath the door to his chamber. He had a visitor.

Julia?

All the blood in his head descended to his loins. She must have changed her mind about their affair. He had a vision of her lying on his narrow bedstead, wearing only a come-hither smile and an abundance of loose, curly hair. They'd spend all night making love, and this time, he would take it slow and introduce her to an infinite variety of pleasures.

Jack cudgeled sense into his empty brain. His caller was far more likely to be Theo. The boy had probably sneaked out of the dormitory after curfew to strike a bargain for more number puzzles. He reminded Jack of himself at that age, his curiosity always landing him in trouble.

Jack grinned. But as he opened the door, all humor died. He'd been right the first time.

Except for the fantasy part.

Beneath the slanted ceiling of the attic bedchamber, Julia sat in the straight-backed chair by the window. An oil lamp glowed on the desk behind her, and a book lay open in her lap. And damn his ill luck, she was the headmistress again. That long-sleeved gray gown with its lacy fichu concealed any hint of bare bosom. Her lips were thinned, her chin high, her eyebrows drawn in a frown.

If she didn't have another session of vigorous coupling in mind, then why the devil had she come here? To dismiss him for seducing her?

Like bloody hell.

He swept a bow that strained the back of his too-tight coat. "My lady, what an unexpected pleasure."

Rising from the chair, she flicked open the gold watch that was pinned to her bosom. "It's five minutes past nine, Jack. Where in heaven's name have you been?"

He sauntered closer. "I wasn't aware of the need to account for my free time. Is that a rule here at the Corwyn Academy?"

"No, it's simple courtesy." She took a deep breath and released it, then said in a less strident tone, "I've been worried. I thought perhaps—"

"Perhaps?"

Her gaze dipped, then met his again, softer and more anxious. "After what happened between us, I was afraid that you might have gone out to seek another position."

What? He had read her completely wrong. And the vulnerability in those big, blue-gray eyes scored a direct hit to his heart. Not that he intended to give her more ammunition by admitting so.

Determined to widen the chink in *her* armor, he caressed her baby-soft cheek. "Rest assured, my lady. I've no intention of finding work elsewhere."

It was a mistake to touch her. She flinched, stepping aside and gripping the book like a shield to her bosom. "Then where *did* you go? To turn in that dueling pistol to the magistrate?"

"Not exactly," Jack hedged. "I thought it might be better to show it to a gunsmith first. You know, one that caters to the Quality."

"And?"

"And it took a while, but I located a shop off Bond Street. However, the gunsmith didn't recognize the pistol. He could only confirm that it's of French origin."

"French! Then it must be fairly new."

Jack drew the pistol from his waistband and admired its sleek design in the lamplight. "Rather, it's something of an antique. Fifteen or more years old, by the gunsmith's reckoning. A collector's piece."

Julia eyed the pistol with revulsion. "Most gentlemen own a variety of firearms. I can't imagine how we'll determine who dropped it."

Jack had a few thoughts on the matter, but he didn't intend to share them with her. Nor did he care to think about the prowler at this particular moment in time.

Not while he breathed in her light, intoxicating scent. Not while they stood alone in his bedchamber with the entire night ahead of them. Not while he had this golden opportunity to pursue his seduction of her.

But his cursed brain kept remembering her distressed words of that morning. *This isn't a game, Jack. It has to end here and now . . . I have Theo to consider.*

Theo, for whom she had thrown away a life of privilege. Why?

He'd never know because she wouldn't trust him with her secret. And he had no right to feel rubbed raw by that. Because hell, she *shouldn't* trust him. She ought to run screaming in the opposite direction.

Except, of course, she didn't realize that he was duping her.

Walking away, Jack yanked open a drawer and buried the pistol beneath a pile of cravats. "I'll find the owner somehow," he said, his voice rusty with the strain of self-control. "You can depend upon it."

"But how? Unless you're a member of society, there's no way to do so discreetly."

If only she knew. "For a start, we can show it to those maidservants, the mothers who show up on Sundays. Perhaps one of them might recognize it."

"What a clever idea! Why didn't I think of it?"

Her face glowing, Julia touched his arm. The warmth of her hand on his sleeve made him feel as if he'd gone up in flames.

Then she blinked, retreated to the desk, and eyed him warily as if she were afraid of giving him the wrong idea. "I'm glad you're still willing to help me, Jack. I wouldn't like to think that . . . that my behavior this morning had driven you away."

Once again, Jack puzzled over her purpose here. Did her flushed cheeks indicate discomfort . . . or lust? She seemed to want him to keep his distance, and yet she showed no eagerness to depart, either.

Dammit, he'd had little experience with virgins—or rather, newly initiated former virgins. But he wanted her to remember just how good it had been between them.

"Your behavior?" he asked, strolling to the narrow cot with its brown blanket and single pillow. "Do you mean your wildness while in the throes of passion? Let me assure you, it's perfectly normal for lovers to lose all their inhibitions."

Her blush deepened, and she clutched the book tighter. "I was referring to our quarrel afterward. You were angry and . . . what are you doing?"

Turning down the covers, he looked over his shoulder. "Preparing for bed."

"I didn't come here for that purpose, Jack. Nothing has changed. Given the circumstances, having an affair with you is impossible."

"Given the circumstances?" He pivoted to face her. "Then you're saying you *would* consider it if we were away from the school?"

Her lips parted for three heartbeats before she said, "No! I didn't mean to imply that. I seldom leave here, anyway. I've too many duties and responsibilities."

Her rapid speech betrayed her nervousness. It took all of his strength to keep from pulling her close and soothing her fears, convincing her that no one need ever find out about their tryst.

But for once, acting on his base instincts seemed all wrong. He wanted their next assignation to seem like *her* idea.

"You're right," he said. "An affair is impossible, and we shouldn't even be speaking of it. We were both carried away this morning."

"We weren't thinking rationally."

"Yes, and I won't have you believing me a knave who takes advantage of women. I know how you abhor such men."

She took a step closer. "Oh, Jack. I never meant to suggest you're like the scoundrels I write about in *The Rogue Report*. You're not."

"I seduced you."

"I let you believe I was experienced. And you would have stopped if I'd asked."

"You can't be certain of that. You're quite the irresistible woman, you know." It was no performance for him to gaze longingly at her, especially when he had intimate knowledge of the curvaceous body that lay hidden beneath that drab gown.

"I *am* certain." Tilting her head to the side, Julia regarded him with discomfiting directness. "In fact, I rather suspect your charm is merely a mask."

What the devil?

He chuckled. "A mask."

"Yes. You use flattery and bantering as a means of turning attention away from yourself. If you keep things light, then no one will look beneath the surface. No one will notice that you're a caring, considerate man." Julia frowned meaningfully at the narrow bed. "Even if you do seem to think you can tempt me from my decision."

She had his character all wrong. Nevertheless, Jack felt an odd thickness in his throat. He half wished he really was worthy of her respect, that he could be the man she believed him to be. If it meant having Julia in his bed, he wouldn't even mind staying here for the foreseeable future.

And wouldn't his friends hoot with laughter if he told them? Jack Mansfield, the infamous Earl of Rutledge, so moonstruck by a bluestocking that he would teach mathematics at her charity school.

Swinging back to the cot, he gathered up the blankets, along with his pillow. "Then allow me to clarify my actions. I wasn't suggesting you join me in my bed tonight."

"No?" She stared pointedly at the bed.

"I'm merely collecting my things because I intend to sleep in your office tonight. To watch for the prowler."

Her eyes widened, smoky blue and rimmed by dark lashes. Clearly, she didn't like the idea of him spending the night on the chaise where they had made love. "Surely that isn't necessary."

"The man will return. Make no mistake about it."

"All the doors and windows are kept locked."

"And that's why you and Elfrida have been taking turns sitting up all night." He shook his head. "It's settled, so you needn't bother trying to talk me out of it. Now, will you kindly fetch the lamp?"

She moistened her lips with the tip of her tongue, and Jack almost died of deprivation. Thank God, she had the sense to turn and to do his bidding.

As they started down the narrow staircase, Jack with his armload of blankets, he cursed the need to sacrifice this night together. He could have coaxed her into bed. A series of long, sultry kisses would have melted her resistance—and filled the hollow ache inside him, at least for the moment.

But her innocence had changed everything. She wasn't like the other women in his past, women he could walk away from after a night of mutual pleasure. And she didn't yet realize that one encounter couldn't possibly douse the sparks generated by the two of them.

No, they shared flames of white-hot intensity. The mere thought of her made him ready to explode.

Emerging into the gloom of the garden, he slowed his steps to let Julia walk at his side. The odor of damp humus hung in the chilly air. He scanned the shadows for any sign of movement. If that bastard came back, Jack would be ready for him.

"You can't sleep in the school every night," she said, her expression genuinely concerned in the light of the lamp. "It won't be comfortable. You're tall, and your feet will hang off the end of the chaise."

Then invite me up to your bedchamber.

"It won't be necessary after tonight," he said.

Her steps faltered on the graveled path. "What do you mean?"

"I'll tell you in a moment," he said, inclining his head toward the house. "This isn't a conversation we should hold outside."

He doubted there were any listening ears. It was highly unlikely the prowler would return so soon; he'd wait a few days before making another attempt. However, Jack wasn't taking any chances.

Julia gave him a mystified frown, but at least she didn't nag as many women would have done. Upon reaching the darkened loggia, she extracted a key from a pocket hidden in her skirt and opened the door, taking care to relock it once they were inside.

The school was quiet except for the hollow echo of their footfalls in the passageway. The lamp enclosed them in a small circle of light, creating the illusion that they were all alone. He tried not to think about the fact that the children were asleep upstairs and the other teachers were settled into their rooms.

As they walked into her office, Jack detected an odor in the air. Something faintly earthy . . . flowers?

"Now," she said, "tell me what's going on."

He dropped the blanket and pillow on the chaise. With the lamp in her hand, he had a clear view of her face. High cheekbones, dainty nose, kissable lips. But unlike the conventional lady who appreciated a man's help, she was stubborn and independent, which was why he braced himself for trouble.

"On my way back this evening," he said, "I also visited Bow Street Station. I took the liberty of securing the services of a Runner to patrol the grounds."

Predictably, she stiffened. "No. Absolutely not. I won't allow a strange man to mingle with the children."

She looked so distraught, Jack went and put his hands on her shoulders, rubbing them soothingly. "It's only at night, he'll stay outside, and he won't be a stranger. His name is Hannibal Jones. He's promised to come by tomorrow afternoon so that you can meet him—and discuss his fee."

"I know nothing whatsoever about his character."

"He came highly recommended by the magistrate. Apparently Jones has a reputation for cracking difficult cases."

"Did you tell him about my connection to *The Rogue Report*?"

"I merely said we've had a problem with prowlers. I left it to you to reveal whatever you like."

Julia shook her head. "I don't like the idea, Jack. I can't trust a man so easily—"

She stopped, her eyes widening with the realization of what she'd said. Jack held her gaze. Instinct told him not to hammer home the point. And oddly, he could almost sympathize with her. She had fashioned a life here exclusive of men. Something in her past had induced her to do so, something, he suspected, that involved the mystery woman who had given birth to Theo.

Julia broke eye contact first. Oddly nervous, she stepped away to set the lamp on the desk. "I'll meet this Hannibal Jones," she conceded. "Then we'll see."

"Fair enough." Jack spied something lying on the carpet beside the desk, almost invisible in the shadows. A single, short-stemmed chrysanthemum.

Picking it up, he inquired, "Is this yours?"

"Oh!" Julia hurried toward him. "I thought I'd collected all of them."

She tried to take the bloom, but Jack held it out of her reach. Every muscle in his body felt suddenly tight.

"Trotter's been here. Today. It must have been while I was gone."

When Julia avoided his gaze, a hot sensation burned in his gut. Jealousy. He was jealous of her namby-pamby suitor.

Those beautiful eyes focused on him again. Cool and sincere, they challenged him. "As a matter of fact, he did come to call. He brought me an impressive array of flowers. And he asked me to marry him."

The news caught Jack like a punch. He fought to conceal his shock, his *fury*, that another man had tried to poach his woman.

Tried? Hell, maybe Trotter had succeeded. All women wanted marriage, the chance to put a ring through a man's nose and lead him around like a trained monkey. And it wasn't as if Jack had made her an honorable offer himself.

His beleaguered brain grasped at something she'd said. "You removed the flowers. I presume that means you refused him."

At least he hoped so. Maybe she'd taken the bouquet upstairs to her chamber so she could see it from her bed and dream about being Mrs. Ambrose Humdrum Trotter.

Twirling the stem between her fingers, she watched him through narrowed eyes. "As it happens, you're right. It would have been wrong for me to lead him on."

Jack restrained himself from dancing a jig. Seizing the advantage, he cupped his hand around the side of her neck, tracing the delicacy of her jaw. "Because you prefer me."

"Yes." Julia took firm hold of his arm, pulled his hand away. And gripped his fingers as if trying to work up her courage. "I have to ask you something, Jack. Something very important."

"The answer is yes."

She stared at him, laughed, then sobered, and a heart-breaking softness shone in her eyes. "On Saturday, I'm going out of town for the day. Will you accompany me?"

Lord A.Q. has lost so much at the gaming tables that he has been forced to sell his horse and carriage and make his way about town on foot.
　　—*The Rogue Report*

Chapter Nineteen

A day later, they departed the city before dawn. Jack's ease in handling the sleek gray gelding came as a surprise to Julia. He'd surprised her as well by securing a well-sprung curricle for the journey, one that didn't jolt her bones or rattle her teeth like the vehicles she'd rented in the past. "I found a stable near Mayfair," he'd explained. "It's used by aristocrats who can't afford to keep equipage of their own."

Allowing someone else to do the driving was a novelty for Julia. She made this trip once or twice a month with Elfrida, although when they reached their destination, Elfrida would wait at a nearby inn. Not even her most trusted friend was privy to the secret.

The secret Julia soon would divulge to Jack. He had no inkling . . .

The gentle sway of the carriage failed to lull her nerves. For the past four hours, she had sat beside him, pretending to be calm even though her insides were knotted so tightly she could scarcely breathe. Would he offer compassion—or would he shun her? And would the truth affect his friendship with Theo?

Surely not. Jack was a kind, thoughtful man, or she wouldn't even consider taking such a risk.

She forced her gloved fingers to relax in her lap. The die was cast. She would abide by her decision. For now, she must bury her doubts and wait.

It was a glorious morning in late September, one of those balmy autumn days that carried the memory of summer. Fluffy white clouds drifted in an impossibly blue sky. Flocks of migrating geese gathered in stubbled fields that had been harvested weeks ago. Occasionally, Julia spied a rabbit hopping through a meadow or a fox slinking past a hedgerow.

But mostly, she looked at Jack. Surreptitiously, of course, so he wouldn't realize how much he fascinated her.

Today, he wore a deep green coat that accentuated the rich color of his eyes. It was a bit worn at the cuffs, but with his white cravat and his black hair tousled by the brisk breeze, he looked like the idealized image of a gentleman. More than high cheekbones or chiseled handsomeness defined him; he exuded an abundance of confidence and character, as well. If he were to stroll into a ballroom, dressed in high fashion and displaying that dimpled smile, he would stir a noticeable flutter of interest from all the ladies.

Thank heavens he was *not* a nobleman. She'd had her fill of aristocrats who looked disdainfully at the rest of the world, who idled away their time in worthless pursuits. Besides, she had developed a decided possessiveness toward Jack. She wouldn't want to share him with a throng of fluttering ladies.

Nothing in her life had prepared her for the intense pleasure of intimacy or the burning desire to experience it again. Once would have to be enough, though. Not only because of the risks, but because Jack was her employee. It would be unconscionable to carry on an affair at her school. Impossible!

Yet there was no going back, either. Their relationship had changed forever. She was so smitten, she could almost believe they were a courting couple out on an ordinary excursion.

Almost.

As he guided the curricle to the top of a hill, she spied familiar landmarks far in the distance, the hazy blue ribbon of the river, the dark smudge of the village nestled on its banks, the steeple of the ancient Norman church.

Anxiously, she groped for a distraction. "Where did you learn to drive so well?"

"My father taught me. He was an excellent whip, known for his—" Jack paused, giving a shrug. "But never mind. It isn't important."

"Are you saying he *raced* carriages?" Julia asked in some confusion. "I thought he was a vicar."

"Quite so. I merely meant that he was known for his ability to handle even the frisky mare that pulled his dogcart." Jack smiled, dazzling her with his white teeth. "Now, we've been journeying for quite some time. You have me very intrigued. When do you intend to tell me where we're heading?"

If only he knew, their destination lay in the woodlands of the next valley. Julia swallowed hard. "Soon. Half an hour, perhaps less."

His eyes softened, and he ran his gloved fingertip along her cheek. "So, my mysterious lady, would you prefer we speak of the gentlemen on our list?"

"Yes," she said gratefully. They had spent the morning discussing the names he had compiled from combing through old issues of *The Rogue Report,* and trying to determine which man might have dropped that dueling pistol. "Where did we leave off?"

"I believe the next one is the infamous Earl of R." Jack gave her a hooded stare. "He seems a singularly wicked character, given to wild parties and gambling. Yet he wasn't featured in the newsletter until quite recently."

"The Earl of Rutledge," Julia said in disgust. "You're right, he *is* one of the worst of the lot. He escaped mention earlier because I was able to place a maid in his house only a few months ago."

"Who is she?"

The edge to his voice made Julia wonder if he *was* annoyed by her evasiveness about their trip. But it was better this way. Surely he would love Bella, too, if he didn't have the chance to form preconceptions.

Aware of him watching, Julia dragged her mind back to the conversation. "The maid's name is Ellen Wilkerson."

"Ellen." Jack turned his eyes back to the road. "I believe I saw her last Sunday. She's Lucy Wilkerson's mother. She's rather short and has a mole on her cheek."

"Yes," Julia said, pleased that he'd paid attention to the mothers of his students. "May I add, she's a very brave woman, as are all the maidservants who report to me. They've volunteered to work in the houses of knaves who view their underlings as fair game."

A thunderous frown descended over Jack's face. "Are you saying that Ellen Wilkerson has accused Rutledge of seducing her?"

"Certainly not," Julia hastened to clarify. "Though he did bump into her last week and knock a pile of linens out of her arms. She said the glare he gave her was quite fearsome."

"Hmm. If he's such a depraved villain, it seems he would have ravished her on the spot."

"Perhaps he was in a hurry to ravish someone else."

Jack chuckled. "Perhaps. I hope *you* never encountered this paragon of wickedness while you were in society."

"No, I didn't. Rumor had it, he'd fled the country for a time after nearly killing a man in a duel."

"Which means he owns dueling pistols. But I suppose all these scoundrels do. There's no reason to think Rutledge is our man—"

"Wait." A thought had popped into Julia's mind, and she caught hold of Jack's sleeve. "How could I have forgotten?"

"Forgotten?"

"There's something else Ellen told me. The Earl of Rutledge was engaged to marry Miss Evelyn Gresham, the wealthiest heiress in London. He was counting on her dowry to pay off his gambling debts. But when Miss Gresham read the exposé about him in *The Rogue Report,* she called off the wedding." A dreadful conviction took hold of Julia. "Which means the earl has more reason than the other men on the list to hold a grudge against me."

Jack raised an eyebrow, but kept his attention fixed on the road. "Surely that's happened before, a gentleman losing a marital prospect because of your newsletter."

"Not as often as one might hope. And there's another important fact. It was shortly after that particular issue was mailed that the intruder made his first appearance."

"That does seem odd. But we mustn't leap to conclusions, either."

"Rutledge is the most likely suspect we've come up with thus far." Since Jack wasn't well versed in the wastrel ways of society, she strove to clarify her point. "He's more than capable of using a gun to threaten a woman. You see, ne'er-do-wells like the earl are weak, foolish, immoral men who fritter away their own fortunes at the gaming tables, then seek to acquire another through marriage. They're no better than thieves."

In the shadow of the carriage, Jack's face looked carved from stone. "Thieves, my lady? Permit me to play the devil's advocate. Perhaps Miss Gresham was purchasing his title, to have the privilege of calling herself Countess Rutledge."

"Then she should consider herself lucky to have realized she was paying too steep a price. The earl would have squandered all of her money, too. Men like him don't ever change."

His mouth formed a faint smile that didn't quite reach his eyes. "You've a harsh view of my gender."

Julia touched his arm in contrition. "Not you, Jack, only those privileged men who would take the gifts of their birth and throw them away on a turn of the card. You may labor for a living, but you're far more noble than any of them."

Jack stared at her with concentrated intensity, and for a moment there was only the clopping of hooves, the jingle of harness, the rattle of wheels. Then he looked away and said slowly, "So Rutledge is in debt."

"According to Ellen, he's in desperate straits. And rather than accept the responsibility for choosing to gamble, he would blame *The Rogue Report* for his problems and seek revenge."

A muscle worked in Jack's jaw. "This is all speculation, and the law will require evidence. You should show that dueling pistol to Ellen. Perhaps if she takes a look at the earl's guns, she'll see the other one of the set."

"I will. But even if she doesn't find it, I intend to ask Hannibal Jones to investigate Rutledge."

Jack must have momentarily tightened his grip on the reins, for the gray gelding snorted and sidled before resuming its trot down the country lane. "With all due respect, my lady, if Jones has no proof, the earl will simply toss him out on his ear."

"I have to do *something*." Frustration welled in Julia. "The villain could break into the school and harm one of the teachers—or possibly even a child. And it would be all my fault."

His expression softened, and he placed his gloved hand over hers. "You didn't ask to be stalked by a gunman, Julia. And you mustn't worry. Hannibal Jones will be conducting his nightly patrols. He'll nab the fellow the moment he sets foot on the property."

Julia had been impressed by the tall, gangly Bow Street Runner. He had asked intelligent questions, listened closely to her answers, and in general, exuded an aura of strength and competence. "I hope you're right. I'll try not to think about it."

"That's the spirit." Jack gave her a heart-melting smile. "Now, we're approaching a village. Would you care to stop for refreshment?"

He pointed ahead with his whip, and the knot in her stomach did a somersault. All thought of the prowler fled her mind.

"That's Camberley, and we'll turn off before we reach it," she said, willing her voice to remain steady. "Look for a stone fence on the right, and a gate with an engraving of a swan."

Jack gave her another curious look, but she lowered her gaze while searching through her reticule for the key. In part, her anxiety stemmed from the prospect of breaking a sworn confidence. In greater part, she worried about Jack's reaction to it all. She had kept the secret of Theo's birth for eight years, and a related secret for even longer.

Then the familiar sight came into view, the sharp bend in the road, the dry stone fence that meandered down past the wooden bridge over the stream, the grilled iron gate barely wide enough to admit a vehicle.

"If you'll unlock the gate," she said, handing him the key, "I'll drive inside."

Jack complied, leaping down from the high perch to do her bidding. That he didn't question the reason for such high security in a rural area showed his courtesy in waiting for her explanation. As the gate swung open, she guided the gray gelding through the narrow opening and reined to a stop. He closed the gate, then clambered up beside her again.

When he made to take the reins, Julia forestalled him. "Before we proceed, it's time I enlightened you." She paused to watch him peel off his gloves, then continued in a low voice, "Very few people know what I'm about to say. But first, I need your solemn vow that you'll never breathe a word about this to another living soul."

He laced his fingers with hers. "You have it, of course."

His expression was serious, his green eyes focused on her. The heat of his hand penetrated the thin kidskin of her glove. She wanted so badly for him to understand. To share the burden she had carried for so long. "The other day, you asked me about Theo's mother, and I vetoed the question. Today, I'd like for you to meet her."

"Ah, so that's the reason for the secrecy."

She gave a shaky nod. "Jack, I have to confess that I've lied to you about something. Please understand it was not by choice. Years ago, I made a vow to my parents never to reveal that I've a twin sister. Her name is Isabella—or rather, Bella."

He gave a start of surprise. "A twin? Identical?

"No, we don't look alike, not precisely, anyway. She's fairer than I am, and her eyes are bluer."

"What of this vow? Why is she kept hidden?"

"Bella is . . . different. You'll understand when you see her. She lives here at Swan House, under the care of my former governess, Eliza Harrison, and her husband, Ned."

"Because she's disfigured in some way?" Jack said rather grimly.

"Not in a physical sense. Rather, it's her mind that's affected." The relief of admitting the truth was eclipsed by the fierce desire to protect her sister, especially when she saw the stunned look on Jack's face. "Please, you mustn't recoil from her like the rest of the world. She's simply a child in the body of a woman. If you accept Bella as God made her, you'll find she has a beautiful, warm, loving spirit."

"I see."

He was frowning, and Julia couldn't tell if he was horrified and repelled, or merely taking it all in. There was only one way to find out.

Her throat taut, she snapped the reins, and the gelding took off smartly down the lane that meandered through the woodland. Jack must be shocked, for he didn't object to her taking over the driving. She was only glad he hadn't asked questions about the circumstances of Theo's conception. She didn't want to tell him just yet.

Not until after he had met Bella.

The most vile of scoundrels indulges a taste for illicit liaisons. Last week, Mr. H.M. was forced to bolt from the bed of his lover and escape out the window when her husband returned home early from his club.

—The Rogue Report

Chapter Twenty

The woman standing on the front step wasn't quite what Jack had expected. Nor was the house.

He had pictured a large, two-story residence as befitting the daughter of the Earl and Countess of Brookville. Not this simple stone cottage with its thatched roof and the smoke puffing lazily from the single chimney, nor the little garden that brimmed with pinks and marigolds.

He had also expected Eliza Harrison to be a dour, forbidding female like the governesses he remembered from his youth. Instead, she was short and round, with a pudgy face, graying brown hair, and a merry smile.

She trotted forward to greet them, her apron white and spotless over an indigo dress. "Welcome, my lady. A fine day for a drive, was it not? And are we to have another visitor, as well? How lovely!"

Her blue eyes, bright with curiosity, fixed on Jack as he helped Julia down from the high seat.

Today, Julia had abandoned her headmistress rags for a fashionable gown of dark bronze silk topped by a gold pelisse. A straw bonnet framed her delicate face, and he could see a hint of strain in the set of her mouth. As if she already regretted breaking that blasted vow.

Apparently, he hadn't given her the reassurance she'd been seeking. But words had failed him—still failed him. He had been bowled over by her disclosure of a simple-minded sister.

Julia turned to Eliza. "Forgive me for not warning you I was bringing a guest. This is Mr. William Jackman, the new mathematics instructor."

"Oh, yes! You've mentioned him in your letters, my lady, but you didn't say how handsome he was. Welcome to Swan House, Mr. Jackman. I'm most happy to make your acquaintance."

"The pleasure is mine, Mrs. Harrison."

As he bowed over the woman's careworn hand, he sensed her amazement and delight. This must be the first time Julia had brought a man to visit—or anyone, for that matter.

He felt dizzied by the enormity of her trust.

Truth be told, it wasn't so much the nature of Julia's secret that had shaken him. It was the depth of her faith in him. She had given him a confidence that, if disclosed, could rip apart her family and send the London gossips into a frenzy.

Did she feel she owed him an explanation for lying about her innocence? For that, he deserved to be flogged, not rewarded. If she knew he was the very scoundrel she had denounced so soundly . . .

Ne'er-do-wells like the earl are weak, foolish, immoral men who fritter away their own fortunes at the gaming tables, then seek to acquire another through marriage. They're no better than thieves.

His chest hurt from the scourge of her words. He would have laughed had anyone else described him in such despicable terms. After all, didn't most gentlemen seek to profit by a marriage? Didn't they live a life of leisure as ordained by birth? But from Julia's lips, the denunciation had cut deeply.

"I've made a nice picnic basket for you and Bella," Mrs. Harrison was saying. "It won't be the least trouble to add a bit more for Mr. Jackman."

"Thank you so much," Julia said. She removed her gloves and bonnet, handing them to the older woman. "Where is Ned?"

"Gone into Camberley to fetch new hinges for the door. I declare, the man isn't content unless he's fixing something. Today, I bade him take a little holiday since you'd be here to help watch your sister."

"How is Bella doing? Is she well?"

"She's having a marvelous day. She's in the back garden, busy with her painting. And making a fine mess." Mrs. Harrison laughed, but not in a way that Jack judged to be mockery. Her face was too open and honest for derision.

"Wouldn't she have heard us drive up?" he asked.

"Not when she's concentrating," Julia said. Her smile faded into a soft look of vulnerability that he found utterly disarming. She extended her hand to him. "Will you come with me to see her?"

As he matched his palm to hers, he was only peripherally aware of Mrs. Harrison gawking at them before bustling toward the house.

Fingers entwined, he and Julia walked down the flagstone path alongside the cottage. He hadn't held hands with a woman since . . . well, in so long he couldn't remember. There was something infinitely sweet about it, something that answered a need in him he hadn't been aware of until this moment.

Nonsense. The extraordinary situation had stripped him of savoir-faire, that was all. Never before had he been required to meet the half-witted sister of his lover. In fact, when it came to females, he avoided family connections altogether.

So how the devil had he fallen into this predicament?

As they came around to the rear of the cottage, he spied a young woman sitting on a stool in the sunlight. A crown of wildflowers rested atop the reddish-blond hair that hung down the back of her blue gown, and her skirt was hiked up to her knees, revealing slender calves. He could see only a portion of her fine-boned profile, and had he not known, he would have thought her a lady, albeit an unconventional one.

Julia's sister. Theo's mother.

There was no easel with a stretched canvas. Instead, she was bending over a table, paintbrush in hand, her attention focused on the small object lying before her.

His brain made an instant connection. "The figurines in your office," he murmured.

Julia nodded. "We look for odd-shaped stones along the bank of the stream, and Bella paints them as creatures of fantasy." She gave him another of those heartfelt, beseeching looks. "Will you wait here a moment?"

She walked toward her sister, spoke her name, touched her shoulder. Glancing up, Bella reacted with a burst of exuberance, throwing her arms around Julia and dropping her paintbrush into the grass. Then Julia drew back to speak, stroking her sister's hair and straightening her clothing.

Bella stole a glance at Jack. Putting her head down, she hunched her shoulders while Julia continued to talk in a tone too soft for Jack to make out the words.

He swallowed, recalling the purloined letter he'd read,

the one written by Eliza Harrison. He had believed Bella to be a child. *Bella wept when she found a butterfly lying dead beneath the yew hedge; we had to stop and give the poor little creature a proper burial.*

Ill at ease, he crossed his arms. She must be a complete simpleton for Lord Brookville to go to such elaborate lengths to hide her from the world. Was she unbalanced, as well? Although he had acquaintances who found it a lark to visit Bedlam Hospital and view the raving lunatics, he had never been able to bring himself to do so.

Julia could have told him about her sister without bringing him here to meet her. Or he could have politely declined the rendezvous—if only she hadn't waited until the last moment to tell him, granting him no time to conquer his shock and invent an excuse.

Then Julia turned her head and beckoned to him.

He forced himself to walk forward. Good God, the girl had rainbow smears of paint all over her smock and also on her face, where she must have pushed back tendrils of hair. Her skin was sun-browned, the bridge of her nose slightly burned. Sitting on the stool, she clutched Julia's arm and looked up at him like a shy child hiding behind her mother's skirts.

In spite of his own wariness, Jack was intrigued. Her delicate bone structure betrayed more than a passing resemblance to Julia. But Bella looked far younger than her six-and-twenty years. Perhaps it was the absolute lack of guile in her expression that made him think of her as only a girl.

Julia placed a hand on Bella's shoulder. "Jack," she said, her voice soft, "this is my sister, Bella."

He put out his hand. "Hello, Bella. It's a pleasure to meet you."

He glanced questioningly at Julia, who gave him a slight shake of her head.

So much for that. Now what?

After a moment's hesitation, Jack crouched down on the grass so he could look her in the face. The sunlight fell on her fair hair with its crown fashioned of daisies and pinks and tiny blue flowers. Despite the paint streaks marring her skin, she was astonishingly beautiful. She had luminous blue eyes and an exquisite figure that would draw considerable attention from any man she encountered.

An inkling of understanding gripped him. Most men who met Bella would want to lie with her. And if that fellow was a villain who contrived to catch her alone . . .

Hiding his horror, Jack looked down at her artwork, a fantastical creature with green scales. "What are you painting?"

"A dragon."

She had a soft, musical voice, and praise God, at least she wasn't a babbling idiot. "It's lovely. I like the colors you chose, the green and gold."

She graced him with a smile. "I've been working for hours and hours. I'm almost finished."

"So I see."

There, he'd completed the required social niceties. He could rise to his feet, end this awkward conversation. But for some reason, he found himself compelled to add, "My mother was a painter, too. She painted a picture of me once, a long time ago. It still hangs in the house where I grew up."

Bella stared at him a moment, then leaned closer to pat his hand. "Would you like to have my dragon? You can put it in your house, too."

The offer took him aback. "Don't you want to keep it for yourself?"

She shook her head so vigorously a shower of petals fell from her crown. "I always give away the pretty ones."

His throat felt unusually thick. "Then I'd like the dragon very much. Thank you."

"Perhaps while it dries," Julia suggested, "we could go for a walk down by the stream. Eliza has promised to prepare a picnic."

"Oh, yes!"

Bella sprang up, taking Julia by one hand and Jack by the other, dragging them toward the cottage, where Jack collected the heavy basket. Then she skipped ahead of them down the narrow path that wended through the trees.

"I'm surprised at how easily she accepted me," he murmured. "Is she always so trusting with strangers?"

Julia gave him a haunted look that spoke volumes. "She seldom meets new people, but after an initial shyness, she sees only the good in them."

Jack again reflected grimly on the probable circumstances of Theo's conception. If a trespasser were to encounter Bella, it would be easy for him to coax her into following him deep into the forest. There, he could force himself upon her, muffling her screams . . .

With effort, he pushed the terrible thought to the back of his mind. It wouldn't do any good to speculate. He would ask Julia later.

Spreading a blanket near the bank of the stream, they shared a meal of cheese, bread, and roasted chicken, followed by a pie made with preserved blackberries that Bella and Julia picked a few weeks earlier. Afterward, Jack was surprised to find himself enjoying their hunt for rocks. Bella expressed delight at one lumpy specimen he plucked out of the stream bed, for it resembled a fat troll.

He and Julia relaxed on the blanket while Bella danced

with the brown-speckled butterflies in the dappled sunlight. After a time, she plopped down in the grass to examine a cluster of mushrooms while Julia spun stories about the sprites and fairies who made their homes inside toadstools. Jack offered a few plot twists of his own, and relished the intent fascination on Bella's face. He had never before met any adult who believed in mythical creatures.

But she wasn't an adult. How had Julia described her? *A child in the body of a woman.*

Unlike the clever, sophisticated ladies of society, Bella was sweet, naïve . . . refreshing. It was impossible *not* to like her. And he understood Julia's desire to protect her sister because he felt the same way himself. Odd that, for in the space of a few short hours, he had developed a genuine fondness for the girl, to a degree greater than what he felt for friends that he'd known for years.

All too soon, it was time to depart. Bella wept piteously, cheering up only when Julia whispered something in her ear. The girl dashed off behind the cottage and returned bearing Jack's dragon. He took it, feeling strangely humbled to have met someone who took true joy in giving.

As they drove away, the little artifact tucked safely in a leather pouch attached to the carriage, Jack inquired, "How often are you able to come here?"

"Once a month, twice if I can manage it." Her eyes watery, Julia bit her lip as if fighting tears. "Usually I stay overnight."

He put his hand over hers. "If it's so important, then do so. I can stay at an inn."

She shook her head. "The teachers will wonder where we are. How would I explain it?"

It wouldn't matter if you were my wife.

The thought made everything inside him go still, except for the rapid thud of his heartbeat. He couldn't marry the woman who had condemned him in *The Rogue Report*. That was *not* his plan.

But he could no longer seek the ruination of her, either. He felt a powerful need to hold Julia in his arms and never let go. Somehow, this day caused a radical shift in his thinking. He had been drawn deeply into her life, yet he didn't even know the whole of it.

And he was curious beyond belief.

He drew the carriage to a stop just inside the iron gate at the entry to the property. Now he understood why the gate was kept locked—not to imprison Bella, but to discourage outsiders from intruding upon her garden of Eden.

Julia was looking in her reticule for the key. He took hold of her hands, searched those gray-blue eyes and saw beyond her beauty to the generous, loving woman who would raise her sister's bastard child. "Before we go on," he said, "it's time you told me about Theo's father."

In the dappled afternoon light, Jack's face held a gravity that demanded answers. His thumb traced soothing patterns across the back of her hand. Although the last thing Julia wanted was to revisit that terrible time, he deserved to hear the story. The trouble was, there were parts of it that she had never admitted to another living soul.

But Jack had been extraordinarily kind to Bella, so why should she be afraid?

She swallowed the lump in her throat. "First, you should know about Bella's childhood. She didn't always live here at Swan House. She grew up on my father's estate some twenty miles distant."

"How long has she been this way?"

"She was always different, even at birth." Her eyes burned, and to stop the tears from falling, Julia looked past him. The sylvan landscape was peaceful, and brilliant autumn colors were beginning to appear in the leafy green canopies of the beech trees. "I was born first, but there was trouble with Bella, a knot in her cord, Eliza said. She was blue all over, and by some miracle the midwife managed to revive her. As a baby, she developed more slowly, walking and talking much later than I did. Nevertheless, we were inseparable."

Odd snippets of memory inundated Julia. Bella falling down in the dirt and gamely pulling herself up again. Bella laboring over her alphabet while Julia recited her spelling words. Bella listening raptly while Julia read from a book of fairy tales.

"She was a beautiful child, all golden curls and bright smile. But adults were always whispering to each other about her. By the time we were seven, my parents decided . . ."

Her breath caught and she closed her eyes tightly. Nevertheless, the warm wetness of tears spilled down her cheeks. Jack put his arms around her, drawing her close to the comfort of his body. He pressed a folded handkerchief into her fingers, and she used it to wipe her eyes.

"What did they decide?" he asked.

She took a breath and released it slowly. "That they couldn't allow her to be seen in public any longer. So they separated the two of us. Bella was moved to an unused wing of house, in the care of Eliza. Claverton Court, you see, has more than sixty rooms, so it was a simple matter to shut my sister away and pretend she didn't exist."

His mouth tightened. "Did you know?"

She nodded. "My mother summoned me to her chambers. She said Bella was too fragile to live in the nursery with me, and the doctors thought it best she be kept isolated. It was . . . difficult for me to accept." Julia had wept and pleaded and raged. She could still remember being shaken to realize that her mother was crying, too.

"Where was your father?"

"Most likely in his library. Papa never could abide emotional scenes." She attempted a weak smile, which Jack didn't return. He looked disapproving, though he kept silent and allowed her to continue. "Mama said she would allow me to visit Bella from time to time, so long as I vowed never to speak her name to anyone outside the family ever again. It was only later that I found out they'd let everyone believe she'd fallen ill and died."

"Good God." His fingers pressed into her shoulders. "You were only seven, Theo's age. What sort of parents would ask a young child to keep such a secret?"

Long ago, Julia had decided not to let herself wallow in bitterness. "They aren't dreadful people, Jack. Narrow-minded, perhaps, and misdirected, but not wicked. I've come to realize it was their way of protecting Bella from the cruelties of the world."

"Then why was she moved here?" he asked in a hard tone. "Did it become inconvenient for them to care for her?"

The knot swelled in Julia's throat again. "No, it was my idea. At Claverton Court, she wasn't allowed outdoors for fear someone would ask her identity. Oh, Jack, she hated being confined to her suite of rooms. She tried to escape at every opportunity. On one of those occasions . . ."

When she paused, too choked up to speak, he finished the sentence for her. "She conceived Theo."

"I have to tell you . . . how it happened." Julia struggled for composure, fought to ward off the guilt that had weighed on her for so long. "When I was eighteen, my parents took me to London for the season. We were gone for more than three months, and I had a glorious time. I became caught up in the social whirl and scarcely gave a thought to Bella, who had been left back at home."

Unable to meet his eyes, she gazed past him, seeing not the gray gelding but herself, dancing in ballrooms with a succession of adoring swains, making assignations in darkened gardens, parrying offers of marriage. It had all been a wonderful game . . .

"You were young," Jack began, but she placed her finger over his lips.

"Wait, there's more. When it was time to return to Claverton Court, I couldn't bear to be parted from all the excitement. So I convinced my parents to invite a large party to our estate for a week. They were reluctant because of Bella, but in the end, I had my way. So I enjoyed my flirtations for another week, and on the last night, there was a masquerade ball. Somehow, Bella stole out of her rooms when she was supposed to be asleep and met one of the male guests."

Jack's gaze was narrowed. "You've no idea who?"

"No, and at first we didn't realize what had happened. The next day, Bella had a terrible crying spell, as she did sometimes, from frustration at being kept indoors. It wasn't until much later . . ."

"You or Eliza realized Bella had conceived a child," he said in that strange, hard voice. "And by then, her violator had escaped without punishment."

Julia felt trapped in a black hole of despair. "It was my fault, Jack. I should never have held that party. Why couldn't I have been content to let the season be over? Why did I want more?"

He cupped her face in his hands. "For God's sake, you were eighteeen. You'd had your first taste of freedom. Of course you wanted more. And how could you have predicted the consequences?"

"I know that. But in my heart . . ."

It was too much to be borne. She lapsed into great, noisy sobs while Jack held her close and murmured gruff words of solace. He didn't seem to mind that her tears were soaking the front of his coat, or that she couldn't seem to stop. When at last she did, she felt drained, as if every last drop of emotion had been wrung from her body. And lighter somehow, as if relating the story had cleansed away the darkness.

He tipped up her chin, swiped his thumbs over her wet cheeks, catching a few stray tears. "It wasn't your fault, Julia. You've enough burdens without blaming yourself, too."

She straightened her spine. "Theo isn't a burden," she objected. "He's a blessing."

A ghost of a smile touched his lips. "There's the spirit. So tell me about him. You moved Bella here for the duration of her pregnancy?"

"No, not until afterward." It had been a confusing, disruptive time for everyone. Bella had been bewildered by the kicking of the baby inside her, and during the birth, she had cried from the pain. Afterward, she'd curled up in a ball and refused even to look at Theo.

Jack sat watching her pensively. "What did your parents have to say? They must have objected to you taking Theo."

"Strenuously. Before he was born, they spoke of giving him away for adoption, and I . . . I supported them." Even now, the thought left her aghast. She had clung selfishly to her illusions of a grand life. "They didn't want me to be present at her confinement, but Bella was frightened, and I had to be there. The moment I held Theo in my arms, I knew that I would give up my life for him."

"So you let the world believe he was yours."

She threw back her head to stare at Jack. "Yes. Without a single regret. And I began *The Rogue Report* as a means to stop other ladies from being abused by scoundrels."

He sat silent a moment, staring past her into the forest. "Did your father never attempt to find out who violated her?"

She shook her head. "He was furious, of course. But what could he have done? It would have meant admitting to the world that Bella existed."

Jack's mouth twisted. "*I* would have tracked the lecher down. In fact, if you'll give me the names of all the men at that party, I will."

His declaration gave a thrilling boost to her spirits. She hadn't realized it, but she had craved that kind of staunch support for a long, long time. She had needed to know that she wasn't alone. That someone cared for Bella as much as she did.

She tenderly touched his cheek. "Thank you, Jack. But it's better to leave things be. I've already done my best to vilify them in *The Rogue Report*. And besides, Bella is happy, and that's all that matters to me."

He pressed a lingering kiss to her palm. "And what of me, my lady? Does not my happiness matter to you, too?"

He cocked one of his eyebrows, and the mischief in those green eyes caused an instant reaction inside her, a twist of attraction, the breathlessness of longing. Just like that, the atmosphere between them became charged with heat and excitement.

"Yes," she whispered. "It matters to me very much."

Julia didn't know who moved first, but in an instant they were kissing, their arms wrapped around each other. Desire burned so hotly inside her that she felt on the verge of swooning. His taste, his touch, his scent, all conspired to seduce her senses so completely that her world consisted only of Jack, his strength, his integrity, his allure.

He drew back slightly, his breath deliciously warm, his lips brushing her cheek. "I know a place where we can be alone for the night. Will you allow me to take you there?"

Chapter Twenty-one

Julia turned around slowly, absorbing the beauty of the entrance hall with its rose-veined marble floor and soaring staircase. The soft light of sunset poured through the fan window over the door to illuminate a room decorated with exquisite taste.

"Jack, I'm astonished! I had no idea your family was wealthy."

"My mother was a gentlewoman. She grew up here at Willowford Hall." A faint smile tilted one corner of his mouth. "According to some, she married beneath herself."

"Because your father was a vicar? Surely there can be no more admirable vocation."

"Quite true." Frowning, Jack glanced away. He had seemed preoccupied on the ride here, and she had assumed he was reflecting on the situation with Bella. But now, he was giving Julia the distinct impression of secretiveness. Was he uneasy about bringing her to this house?

She touched his arm. "Perhaps we shouldn't have

come here. If your grandfather finds out that you've used his house for . . . for a tryst, he'll surely be angry."

"Rather, he'd tell me that life is short, and we should seize happiness whenever we can." Cupping her cheeks, Jack brushed his mouth over hers. "He's visiting friends in Cornwall until the end of the month, so we'll have the place to ourselves."

A dark thrill of anticipation simmered inside her. A week ago, she could never have imagined herself abandoning her moral code and engaging in an illicit affair. It was exactly the sort of behavior she decried in her newsletter. Yet she craved this night with Jack as much as she needed air to breathe.

Sliding her hands inside his coat, she reveled in the solidity of his muscled form. "Then I'm glad we're here," she murmured. "I can't think of anywhere else I'd rather be right now than with you."

He gave her a quick smile and an even quicker kiss. "The drawing room is behind you," he said. "If you'll wait there, I'll find Mrs. Davies and tell her we're here."

"Mrs. Davies?"

"The housekeeper. Ah, there she is now. I'll be back in a few moments."

"I'd be happy—" *To go with you.*

The words died on her tongue. Jack was already striding down a long corridor, heading toward a stout, gray-haired woman who hurried forward, a pleased smile on her plain features. Jack glanced back over his shoulder as if to assure himself Julia wasn't following, then took the servant by the arm and drew her out of sight.

Had the woman known Jack for a long time? Perhaps since he was a little boy, visiting his grandfather?

Julia found herself walking a few steps in hopes of having a better look at the old retainer. But the passageway was empty now. Considering their purpose here, he likely meant to spare her the embarrassment of facing the servants.

Strangely, she didn't feel shame at all. Perhaps because the emotional turmoil of the day had allowed her to see Jack more clearly. He was a fine man, a man who had demonstrated kindness to her sister and unflinching support to Julia. It had been a catharsis to reveal the secret that had weighed on her for so many years. And she couldn't have asked for a better champion of her cause than Jack.

Absently untying the ribbons beneath her chin, she drew off her bonnet. She was curious about everyone and everything in his life. Judging by this stately stone manor house, he had withheld a great deal about his background. By the heavens, she had believed him to be a pauper, without any prospects at all!

Had she not asked him the right questions? Or was he just a modest man, not prone to boasting about his connections?

Whatever the reason, she welcomed this opportunity to find out more about his life. Going into the drawing room, she admired the cheerful décor done in yellows and blues. The furnishings were made of richly polished oak, and cozy groupings of chairs and settees gave the room an inviting aura of comfort. The tall windows looked out over the vast green lawn and the long, curving drive that was lined with willows.

Her mind teemed with questions. Had Jack played out there as a boy? Had he raced down these corridors? Had he sat in this very room with his mother and grandfather?

Julia's gaze alighted on the portrait that hung over the marble hearth, and her heart melted. It was the painting he had mentioned to Bella, the one done by his mother. Bonnet in hand, she walked closer to get a better view.

A young boy, no older than Theo, sat in a rosewood

chair, his elbow resting on the arm while he gazed long-ingly out the window. He wore a brocaded blue coat, short breeches, and buckled shoes in an old-fashioned style. His dark hair was tousled, and she could just see the green of his eyes . . .

Footsteps sounded behind her. Before she could tear her gaze away and turn around, the subject of the painting slid his arms around her waist, drawing her back against his chest. "So you've found the portrait," Jack said. "I was quite a little rascal, wasn't I?"

"You were a darling boy who couldn't wait to escape outdoors."

"Precisely. There were tadpoles to be caught, lambs to chase, woods to explore. I can remember sitting in that chair for what seemed like hours, wishing and hoping my mother would hurry."

His hands were splayed over her midsection. Relishing the warmth of his body, she spoke over her shoulder to him. "She had tremendous talent, Jack. Did she ever sell her work?"

He chuckled. "Certainly not. She didn't need to. Other than a few pieces she gave to friends, everything she ever painted is hanging right here in this house."

"You don't own any of them yourself?"

"They'll be mine someday when I inherit this house."

Julia ached to discover all the mysteries of Jack's past. "Will you show me all your mother's paintings? Along with the rest of the house?"

She attempted to turn to face him, but Jack held her in place. His hands moved upward to cradle her breasts, while his lips nuzzled the back of her neck. "All in good time," he said in a low, silken timbre. "For now, we've a bedchamber awaiting us upstairs."

Heat pulsed deep inside her. "But it isn't even dark yet."

"So much the better." Taking the bonnet from her, he

tossed it onto a chair. "Come, we'll occupy ourselves with something far more enjoyable than tours."

His arm around her waist, he steered her out the door and up the grand staircase. The moment they reached the top, he pulled her close for a kiss that went on and on, until her world consisted only of the taste and touch and scent of Jack. Unbuttoning her pelisse, he peeled it off and slung it over the oak balustrade. His eyes held an ardent intention that caused her insides to clench.

Realizing that they stood in full view of the entrance hall below, she murmured, "The housekeeper—"

"Has orders to stay belowstairs unless I ring for her." His thumb rubbed slowly along the silk of her bodice, over the crest of her breast, causing spirals of warmth to flash down to her depths. "No one will see us or hear us." He bent closer to whisper in her ear, "Not even if we were to make love right here."

The scandalous notion gripped Julia. A long corridor stretched in either direction, empty save for the dainty chairs set at intervals against the pale blue walls. Beneath their feet lay a soft Turkish carpet . . .

"Jack," she breathed. "We daren't."

"No?" His lips brushed hers, and his mouth curled into the smile of a rogue. "Are you quite, quite sure?"

They kissed again, and within moments, the fire of unleashed passion swept them into a maelstrom. They were both gasping, both tearing open garments, both intent on becoming one. Backing her against the wall, Jack pushed up her skirts to stroke her intimately. And she was too far gone to care where they stood.

"Now," she begged. *"Now."*

It was heaven she craved, heaven she strained to reach. And heaven she found when he lifted her onto himself. Instinctively wrapping her legs around his waist, she cried out from the bliss of his entry, cried out again as his rhythmic thrusts sent her over the edge into paradise. She felt him tumble there with her, quite literally, for when she came back to herself, they were lying in a conjoined tangle on the floor of the passageway.

The house was quiet, save for their panting breaths. His chest heaved beneath the shirt he hadn't bothered to remove. In his arms, Julia lolled in brazen satisfaction. And amazement, too, for she'd never dreamed that coupling could be so wonderfully reckless.

After a moment, Jack pushed up on one elbow to regard her with a look of stunned pleasure.

"Well!" Running a finger down the bridge of her nose, he chuckled softly, his dimples giving him the mischievous look of the boy in the portrait. "It seems the headmistress has hidden depths."

Her heart full, she teased back, "Or perhaps you've had a corrupting influence on her."

His smile died a little, his eyes growing more intense. For a moment, he gazed at her in a manner she could only describe as . . . mystifying. It shook her to realize she had absolutely no notion of what he was thinking.

A throat-tightening wistfulness caught her unawares. She wanted their closeness to matter to him. She wanted to know they shared more than bodily attraction. She wanted Jack to love her as much as she loved him.

Julia had swallowed his story about the house. He had convinced her of every falsehood. She had no idea that he, not his grandfather, owned Willowford Hall.

A few hours later, as he finally escorted her on a tour of the upstairs, Jack told himself not to be bothered by the deception. It was just that she had confided her secrets today, which enhanced his awareness of his own deceit. The pretense made him feel unclean, and he felt a compulsion to be as honest with her as she'd been with him.

But revealing the truth would be disastrous. Julia would be horrified to discover she'd been seduced by one of the rogues from her newsletter, a man she had denounced in no uncertain terms. He would lose her, and the very prospect caused a wrench of panic in his chest.

Blissfully unaware of his dark thoughts, she strolled beside him, her arm around his waist, her head on his shoulder. The silver branch of candles in his hand cast a shimmery light over the walls of the corridor. They had peeked into all fourteen of the bedchambers, pausing in theirs to enjoy another bout of lovemaking—much slower this time, yet equally as riveting as that wild encounter at the top of the staircase.

He'd never walk past that spot again without becoming aroused.

Now Jack had a craving to create another memory, this one in his own chamber, the one she believed belonged to his grandfather.

He threw open the door at the end of the passageway. "And here we have the master's suite," he announced, ushering her inside.

Her eyes sparkled. "Oh, Jack, we shouldn't be in here. I feel as if we're trespassing."

"Nonsense. My grandfather won't mind."

He wouldn't mind because he had occupied a plot in the graveyard at St. George's Church since before Jack had been born. Jack's sole remaining grandparent, the Duke of Wycliffe, seldom set foot outside of London.

Julia took the branch of candles and roamed around the darkened bedchamber. She studied his collection of snuffboxes on a table, admired a landscape painted by his mother, even peeked into the shadowy dressing room.

Content to watch her, Jack leaned against the mahogany bedpost and folded his arms. A waterfall of dark, curly hair cascaded down her back. She wore only a shift, so thin he could glimpse the lush curves that moved sinuously with her every step. A fortnight ago, he'd have wagered a thousand guineas that Lady Julia Corwyn would never prance around his house in a state of near nudity. He had deemed her the sort who would only undress under the covers. But she had astonished him by becoming a creature of sensuality.

Perhaps you've had a corrupting influence on her . . .

His stomach tightened. When she had spoken those words to him, he'd been overcome by . . . remorse? No, that was absurd. Rakes like him didn't suffer regrets over the women they'd bedded. Especially when the female in question had reaped great pleasure by giving herself freely.

But Julia was different. His feelings for her had grown into something deeper and richer, something far beyond the realm of his experience. And his purpose in seducing her had undergone a radical change, as well. He no longer wished to ruin her, he wanted to make her happy, to see her smile. He wanted to fight her battles and protect her from harm.

The colossal irony was, now that he had met her sister, he could understand why Julia published her scandal sheet. He had completely lost his appetite for exposing her identity to society—

"Your grandfather must be interested in mathematics, too," Julia said. "He has quite a lot of books on the subject."

Snapping out of his reverie, Jack saw her standing by the bed with one of his books in her hands. Having placed the candelabrum on the nightstand, she tilted the volume to the light and started to open it.

No! She'd see the inscription on the frontspiece: *Jack William Mansfield, Earl of Rutledge.*

His heart pounding, he sprinted to her side, took the

book, and set it back in its place on the bedside table. As a distraction, he drew her into his arms. "Surely you've no interest in such dry reading matter."

"I suppose not." Her smile pensive, she reached up to straighten the collar of his shirt. "But I *am* interested in learning more about your grandfather. You've mentioned him on only one other occasion."

"The morning you gave me a rude awakening by emptying a flask of brandy over my head."

She dipped her chin and looked up at him through the screen of her lashes. "I'm sorry to have been so judgmental. But at the time I didn't know that your grandfather—"

"Drinks too much." Even as Jack acknowledged that painful fact, he ached for Julia to see beyond Wycliffe's failing. Rubbing his hands up and down the supple curve of her spine, he went on, "You mustn't think ill of him for that. He has a keen wit, a strong sense of loyalty, and a true devotion to me."

"I like him already."

"He's always been robust until recently. But he's becoming forgetful in his old age." Jack's throat tightened. Did his grandfather even remember that Jack had said he was leaving? "I haven't seen him in a fortnight, and I do miss him sorely."

"Surely you'll visit him here upon his return."

Yes, but in London. He held her tightly. "I want you to know him, Julia. I want you to meet him."

Eventually, he would have to confess his true identity—and if she could find it in her heart to forgive him, he would introduce her to Wycliffe. By God, he'd make her see that his grandfather deserved better than to be portrayed as a dissolute drunkard in *The Rogue Report*.

"Thank you, I'd like that." She leaned up on tiptoe to kiss him in a way that was unbearably sweet. "Oh, Jack, I love you. So very much."

His world tilted on its axis. Never in his adult life had anyone said those words to him. A rush of sentiment filled him, so pure and intense he couldn't think, couldn't breathe, couldn't stand. His legs gave way, and he sank onto the edge of the bed, bringing Julia with him. He tangled his fingers in her hair and turned up her face to nuzzle her lips.

"Marry me, then," he whispered urgently. "Be my wife."

The words were out before he had thought them through. But they had originated from somewhere deep inside himself. And he knew that nothing, absolutely nothing he had ever said in his life had been more sincerely spoken.

Julia caught her breath. A smile lit her eyes with joy, and her hands tightened on his shoulders. "Yes. Oh, *yes*."

They melted together in a kiss that ignited the burn of desire. Absorbed in each other, they lay down on the bed, stroking and caressing, savoring the delight of being together. This time, their passion was so rich and boundless, he wanted it to continue for an eternity.

When at last he entered her, he gave his heart into her keeping. "I love you, Julia. I'll always love you."

Stars shone in her eyes, and the world dissolved into the bliss of being one with her. Yet in the quiet aftermath, as she lay spent and trusting in his arms, a single troubling thought wormed its way into his drowsy mind.

She loves an illusion.

Nestled against him, Julia hardly stirred as he drew the covers over them. In the candlelight, her eyes were closed, her lips soft and sweet. His betrothed, the woman who loved him with all her heart.

But he wasn't the man she believed him to be. He wasn't honorable or worthy. He had duped her in the worst possible manner, charmed her into loving a mere mask. How was he to get her to the altar? He couldn't use a false name; the marriage wouldn't be valid.

Which meant he would have to tell her the truth. Very soon.

Fear burned raw in his throat. When she found out he was Rutledge, she would be livid. Worse, she would be devastated by his treachery. Julia would despise him with more ferocity than she showed the men she had crucified in *The Rogue Report*.

But perhaps in a few weeks, if he could make himself a vital part of her life, he would improve his chances of talking his way out of the web of lies. Otherwise . . . he was doomed.

It is said that Mr. G.G. recently has been disowned by his father for his dissolute ways.
—*The Rogue Report*

Chapter Twenty-two

Julia awakened to the brightness of sunlight. For a moment, she didn't recognize her surroundings. The huge four-poster bed had dark blue hangings, and the mahogany furnishings were decidedly masculine. The sheets held a faintly spicy aroma.

Memory flooded her with delicious happiness. Rolling over, she found Jack's side of the bed empty. The other pillow showed the indentation left by his head.

Oh, heavens. They had fallen asleep in his grandfather's bed. What would the housekeeper think? In the darkness of night, Julia had been too swept away by passion to consider where they made love, but now she blushed to realize they had used two different beds.

Then a surge of euphoria tempered her embarrassment. Jack loved her. He had proposed marriage, and she had accepted. Soon, she would be Mrs. William Jackman.

And just in time, for with the frequency of their lovemaking, she faced the real possibility of becoming pregnant. She might already have conceived his baby.

Smiling dreamily, she rested her hand over her flat belly. Nothing would make her happier than to give birth to a little boy or girl who had Jack's dark brown hair and lively green eyes. A brother or sister for Theo.

And wouldn't Theo be thrilled to find out that his adored Mr. Jackman was to be his father!

Rejuvenated, Julia threw off the covers and slid out of bed. Her shift lay in a crumpled heap on the plush blue and gold carpet. As she drew it on, the silk slithered over places that glowed from Jack's touch. A pleasant ache lingered between her legs. Would they have time to make love again before they left here? Surely she could entice him into bed once more. Eager for his company, she wondered where he had gone.

Then she noticed something odd. The silver branch of candles still sat on the nightstand, the tapers burnt down to stubs. But the pile of books had vanished. Had Jack taken them?

Curious, she glanced around the bedchamber and spied the neat row of books sitting on a shelf over the mahogany chest of drawers. Or at least she thought they were the same volumes.

She went over to look, scanning the spines until she spotted the one on geometry that Jack had taken from her the previous night. Odd, that he would have moved the books. They certainly hadn't been in anyone's way.

She picked one at random and ran her fingertip over the gilt lettering on the maroon leather cover. As she leafed through the pages, several scraps of paper fell out and fluttered to the floor.

Stooping down to gather them up, she saw numbers scribbled on each one. The top one read, *How can 6 + 24 = 1? A: Six days plus twenty-four hours equals one week.*

Julia laughed. Did Jack's grandfather like to create number puzzles, too?

She resolved to ask Jack. And to suggest again that he compile a book of riddles for children. Perhaps Theo could even help with the project by testing the difficulty of the problems. Her heart melted at the notion of them working together, father and son.

She opened the front of the book to replace the notes. Her gaze fastened on the bold black inscription on the first page.

And her smile died a slow death.

Jack sat in the dining chamber, delving into a hearty breakfast of sausage and eggs. The vigorous activities of the previous night had left him ravenous. That, and the fact that he hadn't eaten since the picnic luncheon with Bella and Julia on the riverbank yesterday. Upon their arrival here, he and Julia had been so deeply involved in each other that he hadn't even thought about food. Now, a keen sense of well-being made him feel more relaxed than he'd been in ages.

"You certainly look refreshed this morning," Mrs. Davies said, bustling over to fill his coffee cup from the silver carafe. Her brown eyes twinkled from a plain, round face. Country bred, the widowed housekeeper had a practical nature with regard to intimate topics—and a free tongue, for she had known Jack since babyhood. "You and your woman must've had a powerful itch to scratch last night since you didn't ring for that tray you requested."

Buttering a piece of toast, Jack grinned wryly. "I'm sorry. I hope I didn't keep you up waiting."

"I dozed by the fire, so never you mind." The aging housekeeper spooned more scrambled eggs onto his white china plate. "Will she be coming down to breakfast? Or is she one of those high-and-mighty London ladies who'll want it brung up to her on a silver tray?"

"She's an absolute darling who wouldn't dream of putting you to trouble on her behalf. And if she doesn't make an appearance soon, I'll awaken her."

His loins stirred at the prospect. Julia had been sleeping soundly this morning, her body curled into his, looking so soft and sweet that he'd had to fight a powerful temptation to make love to her again. But a newfound tenderness had obliged him to set aside his own needs and let her sleep. He added, "We'll be leaving soon, anyway."

"Hmph." The housekeeper offered him a pot of plum jam. "The first time you bring a woman here, and you whisk her away before I've a chance to take a gander at her."

"You'll be seeing quite a lot of her in the future," Jack said with studied casualness. "Her name is Lady Julia Corwyn, and she's accepted my offer of marriage."

The spoon Mrs. Davies had been holding clattered to the linen-draped table. "My word! 'Tis less than a month since Miss Gresham threw you over."

The mention of Evelyn struck him with a vast sense of relief. By now, he'd have been wed to that cold, condescending blonde. If not for *The Rogue Report,* he would never have met Julia. What an incredibly ironic turn his life had taken!

"That was merely a business arrangement. But this time . . ." Unable to contain himself any longer, Jack jumped up from his chair and waltzed Mrs. Davies around the dining table. "This time, I'm madly, completely, wildly in love."

The housekeeper chuckled, her cheeks rosy with reflected happiness. "Now, I *do* have to see her, m'lord."

"Curb your impatience. You'll meet her if you like." He stepped back to shake a stern finger at her. "So long as you cease addressing me as *m'lord*."

Mrs. Davies shook her finger right back at him. "I can't approve of this game you're playin'. Pretendin' you're a poor scholar, that your grandfather owns this house. 'Tisn't right."

Jack agreed. He would have to tell Julia the truth. But not yet. Not until he had charmed her so completely that she would forgive him anything. And his chances would greatly improve if she conceived his child.

Yes. Although he'd always had a horror of fatherhood, now he felt a lurch of tenderness to imagine Julia cradling their infant in her arms. When they returned to the school, he'd see to it that they made love frequently, even if he had to climb the oak tree outside her window in the middle of the night. He would lean over her bed, awaken her with a kiss, and she would open her sleepy eyes and say—

"Lord Rutledge."

Julia's voice yanked him out of the fantasy. No, that icy tone must have come from Mrs. Davies.

But the housekeeper was staring past him.

He wheeled around. And froze.

Julia stood in the doorway of the dining chamber. She was dressed in the same bronze silk gown that she had worn the previous day, now somewhat crumpled. The severe upsweep of her hair left not a single curl to soften her stark expression.

Realization slammed into him. She knew.

God help him, she knew.

Julia searched desperately for denial on that impossibly handsome face. She wanted Jack to laugh and assure her

it was all a jest, that he had signed the name of a
scoundrel in each one of those books as an elaborate, if
misguided, prank.

But the shock in those green eyes confirmed the truth.
His unmoving posture conveyed guilt. And the horror of
his treachery seized her anew. He was *not* her beloved
Jack, *not* an unpretentious, hardworking mathematics instructor.

He was the notorious Earl of Rutledge.

A man who had squandered his fortune at gambling. A
man who threw hedonistic parties and consorted with
lightskirts. A man whose name had featured prominently
in her newsletter.

A man who had insinuated himself into her life on purpose to avenge his loss of Miss Gresham. Because he
wanted to acquire Julia's fortune as retribution.

By tricking her into marriage.

She fought off a dizzying sickness. She would *not*
swoon. Nor would she slump against the doorframe and
give him the satisfaction of seeing her lapse into weeping.

Concentrating on placing one foot in front of the other,
she walked with dignity to the stout, elderly woman who
stood beside Jack. "You must be Mrs. Davies. It's a pleasure to meet you."

The housekeeper bobbed a curtsy and studied her with
great interest. "May I serve you breakfast?"

The odors of sausage and eggs nauseated Julia. "No,
thank you. Lord Rutledge and I need a few moments
alone."

Twisting her age-spotted hands in her apron, Mrs.
Davies glanced worriedly at Jack before addressing Julia.
"It isn't my place to speak, but I've known the master
since he was a tyke in leading strings. He's done you

wrong, m'lady, there's no doubtin' that. But he does have a good heart."

The servant's loyalty failed to sway Julia. Clearly, Jack had charmed her, too, for she didn't realize the extent of his sins. "If you wouldn't mind, close the door on your way out."

Thankfully, Mrs. Davies took the hint this time and left the chamber. Julia waited in rigid silence until she heard the click of the latch behind her.

Jack stood watching her. The morning light flowed through the long windows to play over his vigilant features. He wore no coat, and a linen serviette was tucked into the collar of his shirt. The remains of his breakfast sat on the table, a white china plate, silver fork and knife, a cup of coffee. While sitting there, he'd probably been gloating over her gullibility.

I love you, Julia. I'll always love you.

A storm of wild emotions threatened, and she focused on fury. "Have you nothing to say, then? This is your moment of triumph, my lord. You must have planned for it for quite a long while."

He stepped toward her, his hands spread in supplication. "Julia, believe me, I did want to tell you. So many times."

"Oh? I saw no such attempts. In fact, you tried to hide the truth from me this very morning by moving those books."

"So you didn't overhear me talking to Davies?" He closed the distance between them and gently rubbed her shoulders. In a husky tone, he added, "If you had, you'd have heard me avow that I'm madly in love with you."

The warmth of his hands penetrated her cold body. In spite of everything, she felt a softening of desire. She wanted him to kiss her, to hold her close, to make her forget that he was the Earl of Rutledge.

She wrenched out of his grip. "The pretense is over, Jack. I won't heed your lies any longer. If you had any genuine feelings for me, you would have confessed the truth before asking me to marry you."

"It wasn't the right time. You wouldn't have understood. But believe me, I intended to tell you eventually."

"When? At the altar? Or would you have lied even then, tricked me into a sham marriage?" She crossed her arms in an effort to hold in the pain. "But no, of course not. You needed this marriage to be real. So that you could use my fortune to pay off your gambling debts."

"No! My purpose was to put an end to your newsletter, nothing more. I swear it." He made as if to touch her, then raked his fingers through his hair instead. "God help me, I'm sorry, Julia. I know that's inadequate, but I made a mistake—"

"A mistake." She paced the dining room and listed his sins, ticking them off on her fingers. "You came to my school under false pretenses, convinced me you were destitute, lied about your credentials—"

"I *am* skilled at mathematics."

"—and gave me a forged letter recommending you as a tutor. I trusted you to instruct my students." Aghast, she took a shuddery breath. "Instead, I allowed them to be exposed to a man of your vile character. I should have guessed the truth when I discovered you teaching them to play cards."

"I'll agree my methods have been unconventional, but—" He paused to snatch off the napkin and throw it onto the table. "My God. You can't possibly believe I'd ever do harm to any one of those children."

He looked genuinely appalled. But when it came to him, she no longer trusted her own judgment.

"You *did* do harm, Jack. By posing as a qualified teacher, you used them to further your plot of vengeance. Theo, in particular." Julia's throat caught on a choking sob. "Did you ever consider how disappointed he'll be when you abandon your position at the school? For hurting my son, I can never forgive you."

She braced herself for a slew of silver-tongued excuses, but Jack didn't speak. He absently rubbed his chest as if his heart ached. *His* heart!

Julia spun away and walked to the window to stare out at a thicket of trees. Her vision blurred, and she battled the tears. This had all happened because she had played right into Jack's hands. Like so many other foolish women, she had fallen under his spell.

William Jackman. Jack William Mansfield. Even his false name had been a clue. Other signs had been there, too, but she had been too captivated to see them. His initial difficulty in adjusting to the early schedule. His casual manner in addressing her. His seduction of the headmistress.

Of course he could risk being dismissed! He'd never had any intention to stay at the school.

Incensed, she swung toward him. "You own this house, don't you?"

He nodded slowly. "Yes, I inherited it upon my mother's death when I was ten."

"So we didn't spend the night in your grandfather's bed. The drunkard was another invention, a bid for my sympathies."

He gave her a stony stare. "I was referring to my paternal grandfather. The Duke of Wycliffe."

"I see." She spoke coldly, chiding herself for not remembering the connection. How had Jack described him? *Keen wit . . . strong sense of loyalty . . . true devo-*

tion to me. By contrast, her spy had portrayed Wycliffe as an inebriated old rake who took delight in pinching the bottoms of his maidservants.

For all she knew, Jack did the same.

Dear God, how could he be such a stranger to her? How could he have fooled her so completely? Especially yesterday, when his behavior toward Bella had shown such sincere kindness . . .

In dry-mouthed panic, Julia crossed to the table, groped for a knife, and brandished it at him. "I confided in you. And if you dare to breathe a word about my sister to anyone, I'll slit your traitorous throat."

Jack raised an eyebrow. "Not with a butter knife."

His attempt at levity enraged her, and she threw down the dull weapon. "You don't care whose life you ruin. This is all a jest to you."

"No, no it isn't. I simply . . ." He passed his hand over his haggard face. Then he came forward to lean on the table and look her deeply in the eyes. "If you believe nothing else I say, please know that I would never betray Bella—or you. I give you my word as a gentleman."

"Your word means nothing to me."

"Then let me add that if ever I betray you, I will hand you one of my dueling pistols and invite you to shoot me."

Did he offer another of his glib lies because he rightfully presumed she was incapable of murder? Or did he for once mean what he said?

She was frustrated by her inability to find her way through the maze of his falsehoods. All this time, Jack had hidden a secret as explosive as hers. He had been searching for proof that she published *The Rogue Report*. That was why he had been in the school on the night of the storm. And it was why he had been so quick to offer his help after the prowler had appeared for the third time. Like a trusting simpleton, she herself had handed the newsletter to him—and then given him her body as well. How he must have relished his success!

Another thought grabbed her by the throat. "It was you the first time, wasn't it?"

"What?"

"The prowler. And when I chased you away, you decided to walk boldly into my school and live under my roof."

Jack gave a start of surprise. "Absolutely not. That theory doesn't even make sense. The man came back twice, and it wasn't me."

"Perhaps he's a crony of yours, acting on your instructions, to keep me on edge and give you an excuse to offer me comfort. You must admit, it's rather a coincidence to have *two* gentlemen seeking my downfall, considering there's been no one for five years."

"I admit no such thing." He walked around the dining table and grasped her shoulders again. "Julia, I swear on my mother's grave, I've no notion of who's been prowling around your school. But I intend to find out."

She struck his hands away. "Don't trouble yourself. It's no longer your concern."

"I want it to be my concern. You can't imagine how much." Stepping closer, he lowered his voice to a rapid, coaxing murmur. "I needn't disappoint Theo. If you'll allow me, I'll continue teaching at the Corwyn Academy. My work there matters a great deal to me. And more than that, *you* matter to me, Julia. So very much. Never in my life did I dream I could feel such love for a woman. I want to devote myself to you. Forever."

She stood transfixed as he bent his head nearer. As he touched her face with tender fingers, as he traced her mouth. God help her, she craved his kiss. His dark, tumbled hair and fine masculine features had become so familiar and dear to her. His scent intoxicated her, as did the radiant heat of his body. It brought back vivid memories of their coupling, the joy and the ecstasy of being one with Jack.

But he wasn't Jack, he was the infamous Earl of Rutledge. How many other women had heard sweet words of love from his lips? How many other women had he cozened?

With a furious cry, she slapped him. So hard that her whole arm tingled. "Liar. You care nothing for me. It's my fortune you covet."

Jack staggered back, his hand to his reddened cheek. A muscle worked in his jaw. Breathing heavily, he stared at her in stunned silence. Then he said gruffly, "I'll admit that I came to the school with vengeance on my mind. I never meant to fall in love with you, Julia. But it happened nonetheless."

Though her heart was breaking, she kept her expression cold. "Then that's your misfortune."

A short while later, she absconded with the rented curricle.

She refused to suffer Jack's company for the journey back to London. But it was Sunday, and no public transportation existed until the mail coach on the morrow. So when a groom brought the carriage around, she sent Jack back into the house to fetch the bonnet she had deliberately left behind.

Then she drove off and left him. Glancing behind, she saw him come tearing out of the house at a run, shouting at her to stop. Her sense of triumph lasted only as far as the main road.

For the remainder of the ride, utter desolation shrouded her spirits. She ached to be home. She wanted to hug

Theo, to retire to her bedchamber, and to cry her eyes out, in that order. She wanted to be surrounded by all the familiar trappings of the life she had built for herself before Jack had strode in to charm her with his dimpled smile and laughing green eyes.

Jack. He didn't exist. The man she loved with all her heart was merely a fantasy, an illusion. And although she deeply mourned his loss, Julia kept reiterating in her mind all the ways he had duped her. She wanted to stay angry so that she wouldn't burst into tears and attract the attention of the passersby.

Bone-weary from anguish, she wended her way through the traffic of the city. The sun was directly overhead when she turned down her street at last. Seeing the tall white pillars and stately stone façade of the Corwyn Academy cheered her somewhat.

Then she noticed the small cluster of people standing on the front porch. Several teachers, along with a few neighbors, including portly Captain Perkins and nosy Mrs. Angleton carrying her pug, Flossy. They all turned to stare at her approach while talking excitedly to one another.

Julia's heart sank. Surely it wasn't a search party, raising a hue and cry over her and Jack's absence. When they'd left yesterday morning, she had promised to return the same day. The last thing she needed was a barrage of questions.

Margaret Pringle came running down the steps, a knitted lilac shawl draping her elfin slenderness. "Thank heavens you're back. But where is Mr. Jackman?"

Julia clambered down from the high perch. "It's a long story. Oh, Margaret, I do apologize for worrying you. I was delayed unavoidably."

"It isn't that." Her blue eyes overflowed with tears. "It's Theo."

Terror struck Julia's breast. She groped for Margaret's hand. "What's wrong? Tell me!"

"He's gone. Oh, my lady. He's been abducted!"

Heartache awaits the lady who chooses a rogue as her husband. Ne'er-do-wells like Viscount W. will never change their wicked ways.
—The Rogue Report

Chapter Twenty-three

It felt odd to be back in his own sumptuous dressing room, enduring Marlon's fussing. The valet smoothed the lapel of Jack's dark brown coat, then plucked a piece of lint from the sleeve.

"There now, ye looks like the earl again. 'Tis only fittin' ye return t' yer rightful place." As Marlon limped to the chest of drawers and fetched a handkerchief, his rough-hewn features wore an expression of self-righteousness. "'Tis fittin', too, fer ye t' get yer comeuppance from the lady. I never did like yer plan t' trick 'er."

His movements mechanical, Jack took the folded square of linen and tucked it inside his coat. He glanced in the pier glass, seeing a stranger in the tailored coat, perfectly tied cravat, and butter-soft buckskins. He was no longer the man who had taken pride in outfitting himself in the latest fashion. Instead of his usual zest for life, he felt only an aching knot in his chest.

Marlon continued to rant as he gathered up Jack's discarded clothing, the disguise of William Jackman, mathematics instructor. "Ye've spent yer life lovin' the ladies an' leavin' them. Now one o' 'em's given ye a taste o' yer own medicine. 'Tis about time ye was knocked off yer high horse."

Jack fastened a gold stickpin in his stock. Nothing Marlon said could equal the drubbing he had given himself all the way back to London, riding in the dogcart that belonged to Mrs. Davies and glaring at the hind end of a plodding, swaybacked nag.

Julia's ploy had caught him by surprise. If he hadn't been so desperate to please her, to find some way to erase the coldness from her beautiful face, he wouldn't have been gulled into fetching her bonnet.

The trauma of losing her assailed him anew. Was she so furious that she would ignore the dangers of a woman alone on the road? Yes, she despised him that much—and more. She had enumerated all of his sins in stark detail. She had regarded him with horror and loathing, as if he had sprouted horns and a forked tail.

You care nothing for me. It's my fortune you covet.

She was wrong. Wrong!

Yet Jack couldn't fault her for drawing the erroneous conclusion. He had considered that very notion at one time, just as he had plotted her downfall. But that had been before he'd met Bella and realized the impetus behind Julia's actions. Before he'd fallen in love with the woman who would sacrifice everything to raise her sister's child. The woman who had filled his heart with joy.

Your word means nothing to me.

He had deceived Julia in the worst possible way. He had set out to seduce her as revenge, tricked her into believing him to be a humble scholar. Little wonder she mistrusted everything he said. If he'd talked until he was blue in the face, he wouldn't have convinced her of his sincerity.

And maybe she was right. He *was* a rogue and a gambler, in debt and short of funds. What had he ever done in his misbegotten life to deserve a woman like Julia?

"Nothin' t' say?" Marlon asked, peering closely at Jack. "By yer hangdog look, methinks the lady might mean somethin' t' ye."

"I love her, Marlon. More than anyone or anything. And now she won't have anything to do with me." Jack's mouth twisted. "Ironic, isn't it?"

Leaving the valet speechless for once, he fetched his mount from the stable and paid a call on his grandfather. Unfortunately, Wycliffe was having one of his befuddled days, addressing Jack by his father's name and inquiring for news about people long dead.

After his grandfather fell asleep in his chair, Jack departed and rode aimlessly around the city. The rosy brilliance of sunset gave way to the blue-gray shadows of early evening. Nothing appealed to him. Not his friends. Not his club. Not his usual amusements, the brothels and the gaming dens. Everything paled beside the memory of Julia.

Nevertheless, he stopped at White's for a time, half hoping to run into Viscount Whistler or George Gresham. A dose of male camaraderie might distract him. But neither were present, and Jack found himself out riding the streets again, his way lit by the occasional gas lamp.

A keen nostalgia for the Corwyn Academy gripped him. At this hour, everyone would be finishing dinner, laughing and talking. He ached to look across the table and wink at Julia, to watch her blush, to see her smile. If not for his own stupidity in moving those books this morning, he'd be there right now, cooking up a scheme to get her alone.

His throat tightened. Had she already told Theo that Mr. Jackman had quit his post? Would Theo miss waking up Jack each morning by bouncing on his bed? Would he feel deprived of collecting his number puzzles as payment? Yes, yes, and yes. Jack mourned the loss of that friendship almost as much as he mourned the loss of Julia.

For hurting my son, I can never forgive you.

The truth was, he couldn't forgive himself. Until Julia had pointed it out, he hadn't considered how many lives had been affected by his deception. All of his pupils had been depending upon him for proper instruction. Who would she find to replace him on such short notice?

He would never have believed it possible, but he had enjoyed teaching. He liked seeing the faces of his students light up when they understood a concept. He liked developing their minds, and he liked viewing the world through their innocent eyes.

I allowed them to be exposed to a man of your vile character.

Julia's horror cut him to the quick. She believed him to be the most wicked of villains. God! He was locked in a prison cell of his own making, forever parted from the woman he loved. Their separation had caused a visceral wound inside him. It felt as if his heart had been ripped out of his chest.

He found himself listing all the reasons he needed to go to the school again. To collect his things from the carriage house. To fetch the dueling pistol so that he could track down its owner. To get Bella's dragon, which had been left in the curricle. Most of all, he wanted to know that Julia had arrived home safely.

And that she wasn't in danger from the prowler.

He wanted to be there to protect her. At the very least, he could have a word with the Bow Street Runner, make certain the fellow was doing his job properly.

Hell, maybe Jack should offer his assistance. Two pairs of eyes were better than one. Julia needn't know he was nearby, watching.

Energized by the plan, he spurred his mount to a canter. By God, if he did nothing else in his sorry life, he'd punish the bastard who was stalking her.

Theo sat huddled on the bed, his knees tucked up under his chin and his gaze fixed on the shadows. The little room had grown steadily darker. Were those black lumps the chair and table—or dragons?

Dragons lived near castles, and Theo knew he was in a dungeon. A real dungeon like the ones in the stories Mummy read to him. He had been captured this morning when he'd gone to wake up Mr. Jackman, and the next thing he'd known, he was in this cold room with the stone walls.

He hadn't been afraid to leave the bed then, not when sunlight came through the skinny windows that were too high for him to reach. The door looked like a dungeon door, too, thick and sturdy. It was locked, so he had pounded on it until the Bad Man had come stomping down the steps to tell him to hush.

Theo hated the Bad Man. Hated, hated, hated him. The Bad Man had called Theo mean names when he wouldn't do as he was told.

But now Theo would almost prefer the Bad Man to the dragons.

He didn't mind the dark when he slept in the dormitory. He could always hear the other boys, breathing softly or turning over in their sleep. Mrs. Pringle or Miss Rigby took turns sleeping on a cot near the door. Mummy, too, sometimes.

But *this* darkness didn't feel cozy and safe. It felt alive, as if another dragon lurked beneath the bed, waiting to roast his legs with fire if he dared to climb down.

Shivering, he pulled the blanket around himself. Mr. Jackman would know how to kill the dragons. Mr. Jackman wasn't frightened at all of dragons, because he had laughed when he'd talked about them. He had showed Theo how to use his fists to trounce the enemy.

Trounce, Theo repeated to himself. He liked the word that Mr. Jackman had used. *Pow, pow! Trounce the enemy!*

But Mr. Jackman wasn't here. He and Mummy had gone away in the carriage, and the Bad Man said they were never coming back. The Bad Man had said *he* was Theo's papa now.

"You might as well practice saying it. Papa. Go on, I want to hear you."

"You aren't my papa. Mr. Jackman is." Or at least Theo prayed every night for him to be.

"I'll give you sweets if you say you're my son," the Bad Man coaxed. *"I'm going to take you to visit your grandpapa, and while we're there, you're to call me papa and give me a kiss on the cheek."*

"No, I won't!"

"Blasted little devil. I'll leave you to ponder the matter, then. I'll come back later and see if you've changed your mind."

He had returned two more times, pretending to be nice and then yelling when Theo refused to cooperate, the second time calling Theo a "mulish bastard." Theo didn't know what a bastard was, but it sounded nasty, so he had kicked the Bad Man hard in the shin.

The Bad Man had howled, chasing him around the room, only to trip over the chair and crash to the floor. Cursing and snarling, he had limped out and locked the door.

That had been hours and hours ago.

Theo blinked back tears. He wanted to feel Mummy's soft arms around him. But he wouldn't bawl. Once, when he had wept after skinning his knee, Clifford had told him that only babies cried.

He scrubbed at his eyes with his sleeve. He wasn't a baby. He was growing big and strong; Mr. Jackman had said so. Mr. Jackman had warned him to watch out for bullies because besides hitting, they liked to tell lies.

The Bad Man was a bully. That meant he had lied about Mummy. She wouldn't leave him forever, Theo knew she wouldn't. On Friday night, she had given him a kiss and promised to return, and she never broke her promises. Maybe . . . maybe she didn't know he was imprisoned in the dungeon of a castle.

But Mr. Jackman would guess. He would find clues that would lead him to Theo. Then he would use his fists to teach the Bad Man a lesson. And Theo would help him.

Pow, pow! Trounce the enemy!

Heading up the steps to the darkened porch, Jack had second thoughts about coming to the school. The only lights shone from the upper-story windows. Surely it wasn't *that* late, was it? Perhaps eight o'clock, which meant the children would be preparing for bed.

He ought to go home, return in the morning—or not at all.

Nevertheless, he rapped on the door, so hard the sound echoed through the entrance hall. He was painfully aware that he no longer had the right to walk in unannounced. He was an outsider. And an unwelcome one at that.

Julia would have told the other teachers about his duplicity. Whoever answered the door would have been warned not to admit him. So he braced himself to be charming, persuasive. It would take a hell of an effort since he felt only the bleakness of despair. If it was Julia herself, he'd have to act fast to keep the door from slamming in his face.

On edge, he kept an eye peeled for Hannibal Jones. It was full dark, and the Bow Street Runner had orders to commence his nightly shift at dusk. Perhaps he was patrolling the back garden or the mews.

Then Jack spied the approach of a light through the window. The door opened a crack, and the plump face of Dorcas Snyder peered out.

Praise God, he stood a chance of gaining entry. He gave the music teacher a warm smile, hoping she could see it in the meager light. "Good evening, Miss Snyder. I trust I'm not calling too late."

Dorcas Snyder flung open the door. In one hand, she held a candlestick, and in the other, a lacy handkerchief which she used to dab at her reddened eyes. "Mr. Jackman! My word, I thought you'd left us. Thank heavens you've returned!"

Jack frowned. She had always seemed high-strung to him, but he hadn't expected her—or any of the other teachers—to be overly distressed by his dismissal. "I'm afraid I'm merely here to collect my belongings."

"Come in, come in. 'Tis been the most horrid day! We've just been putting the children to bed. It's very important for them to follow a routine so they don't fret too much over that terrible event."

Miss Snyder's agitated manner took on a sinister aspect. Fear clamped so tightly around his chest he could barely catch his breath. "Has something happened to Julia? Was she waylaid by brigands on her way home?"

Miss Snyder shook her head, her graying sausage curls in disarray. "'Tis Theo . . . he's gone, Mr. Jackman. Gone!"

"What the devil do you mean, *gone*?" Jack struggled to wrap his mind around the news. "Where would he go?"

"This morning, he didn't appear at breakfast. Nor did he come when we assembled to go to church. Clifford told us that Theo sneaks outside every morning to wake you up." Miss Snyder's voice caught in a sob. "Theo must have thought you'd come home last night, as you'd promised. Because when I went out to the carriage house to check on him, I found . . ."

Visions of gory accidents flashed in Jack's mind. Wild-eyed, he gripped the teacher by the arms. "What? Is Theo—" He couldn't say it, he couldn't force his numb lips to form the word *dead*.

"I found a note lying on the doorstep. Oh, Mr. Jackman, the poor little lad's been abducted." She lapsed into a fresh bout of weeping.

Abducted? By whom? And why? For a ransom?

In no mood for histrionics, Jack gave the woman a hard shake. "For God's sake, tell me what the note said."

"Just that we're not to search for Theo . . . lest he come to harm. Oh, Mr. Jackman, what a trying day this has been. It's Sunday, so the mothers were here, and in all that chaos, the second note was delivered." Miss Snyder clutched at Jack's arm. "This one bade her ladyship go alone to a rendezvous this evening."

"The devil you say. I'll accompany her." Jack stalked

across the darkened hall to the staircase. "Where is she? Upstairs?"

Miss Snyder trotted after him. "Oh, but you're too late. Lady Julia's already gone to meet Theo's kidnapper. And she wouldn't tell any of us where she was going!"

A vast number of gaming dens open their doors at the noon hour, at which time the noble bloods flock to the tables to risk their fortunes at the turn of a card. In this manner, Lord Y. lost ten thousand pounds in the course of a single afternoon.
—*The Rogue Report*

Chapter Twenty-four

Julia had obeyed all the instructions. She had dressed in dark colors and worn a veiled hat. She had made the journey alone. Having located the address in a row of town houses on the outskirts of Mayfair, she had driven the rented curricle back to the mews, then picked her way through a tiny dark garden and entered the house through an unlocked rear door.

Now, as she hurried into the morning room where the note had bade her to go, she yanked back the concealing veil and scanned her surroundings. To her anguish, the room was empty. She had been praying to find Theo here, anticipating him running into her arms, had pictured it so vividly that his absence was a knife to her breast.

By the light of the fire, she consulted the watch pinned to her bosom. Two minutes until eight o'clock. She was early.

Going back to the door, she peered down the empty,

darkened corridor. Was Theo somewhere in this house? Was he frightened? Had he been harmed?

Please, God, no. She gripped the doorframe to keep herself from rushing in search of him. The message left in the carriage house had been chillingly specific.

If you fail to heed my directives, you will never again see the boy.

She had been ordered to wait in this room, and here she must stay. Lit by a branch of candles and a coal fire, the austerely stylish décor hinted at a bachelor household. There were no vases of flowers or baskets of embroidery threads, no porcelain figurines or arrangements of knick-knacks to indicate a feminine presence.

Not that she had expected any. The man who had been audacious enough to hide in the carriage house and seize her son was one of the scoundrels she had maligned in *The Rogue Report*. He had to be.

She peeled off her kidskin gloves and dropped them on a table. Fury and bafflement tangled her insides. How had the devil known which child was Theo? Had he been watching the school?

The thought chilled her. If he had been spotted on three separate occasions, it only made sense that there had been other times. For all she knew, he might have seen her and Theo taking a walk together. And he certainly had observed that Theo had a habit of going out to the carriage house each morning.

Too agitated to sit, she paced the small room. She couldn't help thinking the horrific situation was her punishment for not returning home last evening, for indulging in an affair with Jack. She felt the certainty of that in her soul, even though logic reminded her that she often stayed overnight when visiting Bella.

Tonight, logic had no calming effect on the whirlpool of her guilt.

She had promised Theo she would return yesterday evening. On that mistaken belief, he had gone out early this morning to awaken Jack for church. The prowler had chosen a time when Hannibal Jones had left for the day. He must have been hiding just inside the door. Waiting for her son.

Julia pressed her hand to her mouth to stifle a cry of agony. Oh, God, she had exchanged the safety of her son for a night of pleasure with Jack. Jack, who had revealed his true colors as the wicked Lord Rutledge. Jack, who had fooled her so completely she had been overjoyed by his offer of marriage. *I love you, Julia. I'll always love you.*

Blast him!

No, blast herself for being so gullible. If she hadn't had such stars in her eyes, she would have questioned how a lowly mathematics professor had acquired such a suave manner. If he hadn't awakened in her the need for love and companionship, she would have realized he was too good to be true. Foolishly, she'd thought she'd found the perfect husband, devoted, strong, faithful.

But it had all been an act designed to bamboozle her. And though his betrayal cut deeply, it was nothing compared to her torment over Theo. Nothing mattered but Theo, her sweet, vulnerable little boy . . .

The squeak of approaching footsteps alerted her. Heart pounding, Julia spun around toward the doorway. And braced herself to outwit her son's abductor.

"You won't find it," Elfrida said from the doorway.

Jack glanced up from his frantic search of Julia's office. He'd been looking for the note. Dorcas Snyder had reported that Julia had been in her office when the second letter from the kidnapper had arrived. Shortly thereafter, Julia had summoned the teachers for a meeting, told them she was going to meet Theo's kidnapper, and that her son's life depended upon her complying with the instructions not to reveal her destination.

Jack had confiscated Miss Snyder's candle and come straight here. He had hunted through the drawers of the desk to no avail.

"She took the note with her, didn't she?" Jack said, stalking toward Elfrida. Her haggard face looked carved from stone. Dressed in a severe black gown, the older woman hovered like a vengeful witch against the gloom of the corridor.

"Rather, she burned it right there in the hearth. I saw her myself, and tried to stop her." When he veered in that direction, the woman added, "Don't bother. I've already combed through the ashes. And might I add, *your lordship,* Dorcas should never have let you inside."

The frostiness of Elfrida's manner didn't daunt Jack. "Julia confides in you. She must have told you where she was going."

"Do you truly believe I'd be standing here if I knew?" For a moment, anguish flashed in Elfrida's eyes; then she gave him another flinty stare. "Now leave at once. We don't need the help of a conniving scoundrel."

"You must know *something*. Did she give you any hint at all of the man's identity?"

"The letter contained only an address which she didn't share with me—with any of us."

Cursing under his breath, Jack strode back and forth through the shadows. "If I could have seen the penmanship, I might have been able to identify the author." He spun toward her. "What about the earlier note? What happened to that one?"

"I don't know." As if wrestling with an inner dilemma, Elfrida gazed searchingly at him. "It might be upstairs in her chamber. I'll fetch it for you."

Jack snatched up the candle. "I'm going with you."

For once, the older woman didn't argue. Like him, she must realize there wasn't a moment to spare.

As they headed toward the entrance hall, a plump, dark-haired woman in apron and drab gray gown came hurrying toward them. She bobbed a curtsy, saying to Elfrida, "Bless you fer allowin' me t' stay, mum. 'Tis a rare treat t' say good night t' me boy."

Elfrida gave her a distracted smile. "Indeed."

Jack didn't know what induced him to inquire, but the moment the stranger vanished down the corridor, he asked, "Who was that?"

"Clive Spratt's mother. She was given the night off unexpectedly, so she came here to sleep."

"All night? Isn't that unusual?" Struck by a thought, Jack stopped, staring down the shadowed passage. "Who employs her?"

He and Elfrida exchanged a wide-eyed glance. As if the same suspicion dawned on both of them at once. And when she named the man, Jack knew with chilling certainty exactly where Julia had gone.

"I'm glad to see you're so prompt, my lady. You must be very interested in getting your little brat back."

Julia curled her fingers to keep from clawing his refined face. Cloaked in shadow, he stood in the doorway, and his identity hit her with a shock. His build was broader than she remembered. His sandy-brown hair was styled in a fashionable tousle, and he was stylishly dressed in dark blue coat and cravat. He had been one of her suitors once, and she choked to remember how she had flirted with him.

"Mr. Gresham," she said coldly. "I wish to see my son at once."

"All in good time." Limping slightly, George Gresham

came into the morning room. "I'm delighted to know you
haven't forgotten me, my lady. Considering the number
of your suitors, I thought for certain I'd have been lost in
the crowd."

"My son, Mr. Gresham. Where is he?"

"In a moment, we'll talk about the conditions of his release. But first, would you care for a sherry?" Gresham
went to a walnut cabinet and opened it to reveal a row of
crystal decanters. "I myself intend to have one."

"This isn't a social call. And I won't agree to anything until I see Theo for myself and determine that he's
unharmed."

He poured himself a generous dose of sherry and sam-
pled it, smacking his lips. "You always were an impetuous chit. But this time, the game is being played by my
rules."

In a state of extreme frustration, she stepped toward
him. "What do you want? A printed acknowledgment that
you aren't a hardened gambler? Consider it done!"

Gresham frowned, the glass halfway to his mouth.
"What are you babbling about? What do you know of my
losses?"

Julia froze. Wasn't that what this was all about? The
scathing denunciations of him in *The Rogue Report*? Or
was there something else going on here, something she
couldn't fathom?

She decided to counterattack. "You've been prowling
around the grounds of my school," she said. "What were
you seeking? Money to steal? Are you holding Theo for
ransom?"

"In a manner of speaking."

"Then name your price. Name it!"

One corner of his mouth lifted in a smirk. "You're a
clever girl to guess my gaming losses are involved. You'll

need to hear the rest. My father is dying. And on his deathbed, he's changed his will, cut me out completely." Gresham walked back and forth, favoring his right leg. "It's no small amount, either. Half a million pounds will go to my cousin Evelyn unless I can convince the old miser that I've changed my ways."

"I fail to see how that involves me—or Theo."

He pointed his glass at her. "What I want from you is quite simple. You're to make your little bastard call me 'papa.' He won't listen to me."

"Papa?" Julia felt as if she'd had the rug pulled out from under her. "I don't understand."

"I'm taking the boy with me to see my father tonight. I'm telling him that your brat is my son. And the scheme won't work if he keeps kicking and hitting me."

Confused, she watched him rub his leg. "Why would your father believe you? Why would he not say that Theo is just a random boy you recruited to play a role?"

Gresham narrowed his eyes. "He closely resembles my younger brother who died as a child. My father always had a soft spot for Henry. So do your part and instruct your little bastard."

As he went to refill his glass, Julia stared at him. She was transfixed by a horrifying suspicion that wormed its way into her mind. Woodenly, she whispered, "You were present for the masquerade ball at Claverton Court."

"Masquerade ball?" His chuckle sounded strained, and he avoided her eyes. "Oh, you must be referring to that party a long time ago. I'd almost forgotten."

Nausea roiled in her stomach. She felt hot and cold all over. "You," she whispered. "It was *you* who raped Bella."

Jack stole through the darkened town house and headed toward the glow of light halfway down the corridor. The morning room, he knew from his visits here. The wild parties he had attended at Gresham's home had been too numerous to count.

On the way here, his thoughts had raced as hard as his mount. George Gresham had abducted Theo. Gresham, who had laughed over the reports of his exploits in *The Rogue Report*. It didn't make sense that he was the prowler. Why would he want Julia's son?

The answer had come to Jack in a blinding flash. An answer so chilling he had nearly gagged on it. Gresham . . . and Bella.

Was it possible?

Jack didn't want to believe it. But by God, he'd wrest the truth from Gresham. And he'd make certain the slimy toad never bothered another woman so long as he lived.

If he lived.

Hearing no voices, he risked a glance inside the room. It was empty, but someone had been here recently. Hastening inside, he found the remains of a glass of sherry. And a lady's fine kidskin gloves. When he picked them up and brought them to his nose, he caught a trace of Julia's scent.

Anxiety kicked him in the chest. She had to be somewhere in this house. When he found her, he'd find Theo.

And Gresham, who had better start saying his prayers.

After lighting a candle at the hearth, Jack conducted a swift search of the entire house, top to bottom. There was nothing out of the ordinary upstairs. But down in the cellar, he discovered a stone-walled room outfitted as a spartan bedchamber. The door stood wide open, and the blankets on the small cot were mussed.

As if a little boy had huddled there.

A tight band of terror robbed Jack of breath. What had happened to Theo and Julia?

Where the hell would Gresham have taken them?

Chapter Twenty-five

In the semidarkness of the coach, Julia and Theo sat across from George Gresham. He held a pistol, the match for the one he had dropped behind the school. When she had accused him of Bella's rape, he had drawn the gun from inside his coat. And he had sworn to kill Julia if she pursued the issue.

Considering the nervous grip Gresham had on the long-barreled weapon, she had no intention of angering him. Not yet, anyway. Not so long as Theo might be hurt.

Tensely, she kept a protective arm around her son's small form. The joy of seeing him again had been sweet and sharp. Gresham had taken her down into the cellar, where he had unlocked a door to a dark room. She would never forget the moment when Theo had run into her arms, clinging to her neck, and babbling about dragons.

And then he had asked about Mr. Jackman. She had been forced to admit that Jack had gone away.

"Mummy." Theo tugged on her sleeve now. In the

shadows, his small face looked troubled, and she bent her head to hear him over the rattle of the wheels and the clatter of hooves. "I don't want that bad man to be my papa."

Her heart aching, she brushed back his tumbled hair. "It's only pretend, darling. Just this once." Putting her lips to his ear, she murmured, "I'll be right there with you. And if I tell you to do something, promise to obey me without question."

He nodded solemnly, and she hoped he understood. Whatever chance arose for escape, they must not hesitate to seize it.

"Speak up," Gresham snapped. "I won't have you two muttering to each other."

Julia regarded him with cold revulsion. Raising her voice, she said, "I've taught my son not to tell falsehoods. I was explaining to him that what he must do is merely playacting."

"Quite," Gresham said. "And he had jolly well better be convincing, or I'll make him sorry."

Theo glared at him. "*You'll* be sorry when Mr. Jackman comes to rescue us."

Julia's heart twisted, the pain so sharp she had to blink back tears. "Darling, you mustn't get your hopes up. Mr. Jackman has no way of finding us."

"Mr. Jackman," Gresham said testily. "Who the devil is this fellow you two keep prattling about?"

Struck by a disquieting insight, Julia frowned. Wasn't Gresham one of Jack's—or rather, Rutledge's—cronies? She knew from her network of spies that the two men were often in each other's company.

"You've been watching the school," she said. "That's how you knew Theo went out to the carriage house every morning. And that's where Mr. Jackman slept. Surely you saw him."

"I only came to have a look at the boy. Why would I care about some riffraff who works for you?"

"Mr. Jackman isn't a riffraff," Theo said huffily. "He's my maths teacher, and when he finds us, he's going to trounce you." He mimicked a fistfight. "Pow, pow!"

"Trounce me, eh? Let him try. I've had plenty of practice in the boxing ring." Gresham pointed the pistol. "Now cease your chattering. If you don't do as you're told, I'll shoot your mother. You don't want that, do you?"

Theo's fists dropped to his lap, and he mutely shook his head.

Julia clenched her teeth and forced back her rage. "Frightening him will only make him uncooperative."

"I'll do worse than that if he fails to persuade my father to loosen his pursestrings." As the coach slowed, Gresham lifted the shade and peered outside. "We're here. From this point on, brat, you're to call me 'papa.' Is that clear?"

At an encouraging nod from Julia, Theo said in a subdued voice, "Yes . . . Papa."

"Excellent. Make sure you say it often in front of your new grandpapa."

Gresham threw open the door and clambered out of the coach. He glanced quickly around while Julia and Theo emerged onto a darkened street alongside a huge monolith of a house. A gust of cold wind whipped at the veil on her hat, dragging it across her face and obscuring her vision. She drew the gauzy material back and took a closer look at their surroundings.

Recognition jolted her. During her one season, she had attended a ball here. The image of Gresham's father flashed in her mind, a stern-faced gentleman with the keen brown eyes of a fox. She remembered him because he had chastised his son in front of a company of guests.

Was he still sharp? Would he be so easily convinced to sign over his fortune to his profligate son? Or would he agree only to put it in trust for his newfound grandson?

The very real possibility chilled her. In such a circumstance, Gresham would want to keep Theo under his thumb for a long time. She could never allow her son to be controlled by the man who had committed violence against Bella.

Gresham motioned with the gun for them to proceed up the walk. She glanced desperately at the coachman. He stared impassively ahead, as he had done back at Gresham's town house when she had appealed for his help. If not for the pistol, she might have grabbed her son and made a dash for it down the street.

But it was better to comply, better to swallow her distaste, better not to risk endangering Theo until she found a safer way to escape.

Yet the fraud grated on Julia. She hated being a party to deceiving a dying man. She especially hated Theo's involvement, and not just because of the danger. She regretted the loss of his innocence, as well. He was too young to suffer the schemes of a wicked man.

Theo's father. That staggering truth ignited a firestorm of fury in her. But she mustn't think about the brutality this man had committed against her sister. She mustn't let herself be distracted from her primary goal of keeping Theo safe.

Gresham pushed open the door, and they went inside the house. Wax lights burned in wall sconces, illuminating an entrance hall of grand proportions and excessive gilding. A footman in white wig and crimson livery trotted forward from an alcove to greet them.

He bowed to Gresham, who had hastily tucked the pistol inside his coat. "Good evening, sir. Your father is ex-

pecting you." The man turned to Julia. "May I take your
cloak?"

On impulse, she stepped to him. "My son has need of
a chamber pot. Will you show us to one?"

She squeezed Theo's shoulder, and bless him, he did an
unmistakable wiggle. "Please, sir, I need to go right *now*."

The young footman looked nonplussed. "This way—"

"I'll take him," Gresham said, seizing Theo's arm and
marching him toward the broad marble steps of the staircase. "We're heading upstairs, anyway. Come along, my
lady. I'm sure you wouldn't want to be left behind."

Julia hastened after them. The ruse was the only way
she'd been able to think of to separate him from Theo.
Had Gresham swallowed it?

At the top of the stairs, he took a sharp right turn.
"I'll go with you while your mother waits right here," he
said, gesturing at a gilded chair in the corridor. "You
wouldn't want a lady watching you do your business,
would you?"

"I don't need to go anymore," Theo said, breaking
away to grab Julia's hand.

Gresham chuckled nastily. "Called your bluff, did I?
Did you really think I'd let you make a break for freedom?"

"Leave him be," Julia said, stepping in front of Theo.
"Can't you see you're upsetting him? That doesn't bode
well for your scheme."

"He ought to be cowed. Children should be seen and
not heard, and your brat is far too cheeky—"

His voice broke off as a door down the passageway
opened and a fair-haired young woman emerged. She was
wearing a pale green gown that accentuated her white
shoulders and swanlike neck. Spying them, she stared,
then glided forward at a brisk pace.

"Damn and blast," Gresham hissed under his breath.
He opened the nearest door and gave Theo and Julia a

push inside. In a harsh whisper, he said, "Stay in there and don't come out until I say so."

Holding Theo's hand, Julia scurried thankfully into a bedchamber that was sumptuous in dark blue and gold, and illuminated by a lamp on the bedside table. Was there another way out? Spying a closed door, she hastened toward it, only to discover a dressing room with no handy connection to the neighboring chamber.

Theo abandoned her and went to the window to push aside the draperies. "Let's jump!" he said with entirely too much relish. "We'll land in the bushes and escape!"

Julia went to his side. Her stomach turned as she peered down at the distant ground. "No, darling. We'd break all our bones."

"Mr. Jackman would do it. He'd go first and then he'd catch us both."

His hero-worship of Jack broke her heart. Little did Theo realize that the golden object of his adoration had feet of clay. But perhaps he needed his illusions at the moment, so she didn't correct him.

She looked around the bedchamber for something to use as a weapon. Going to a casket of jewelry on a table, she rifled through it and picked up an emerald brooch.

Raised voices sounded in the corridor, and hearing the rattle of the knob, Julia shut the jewel case and sprang away from it. Just in time, for the door was flung open and the blond woman marched inside to glare at Julia. "Who are you?"

"Who are you?" Julia countered coolly, while keeping Theo behind her.

The woman looked taken aback, though she recovered quickly. "I am Miss Evelyn Gresham. My uncle is extremely ill, and I won't have George bringing his lightskirts into this house."

"It's no concern of yours what I do," Gresham snarled from the doorway.

"It became my concern when you sent your little tart into *my* bedchamber. I'm spending the night here so that I can sit with your father—something *you* should be doing, too."

A wave of dizziness swept over Julia. Evelyn Gresham. Jack's former fiancée. The rich heiress who had left him because of the story about his gambling in *The Rogue Report*.

Julia found herself avidly examining Miss Gresham. So this was the type of wife Jack would choose from his own world. A porcelain, blue-eyed beauty with a brittle, snobbish air and absolutely no trace of warmth. Julia had known women like her. Haughty ladies who believed themselves superior to the rest of humankind by virtue of their wealth.

She didn't care for that intimidating stare. So she countered with one of her own. "I'm Lady Julia Corwyn, and my son and I have been brought here against our will."

"She's jesting," Gresham said, scowling at Julia from behind his cousin. He slid a hand inside his blue coat in a clear reminder of his hidden pistol. "Hush now, or Evie will think you're serious."

But Evelyn wasn't paying any attention to him. She was staring at Julia. "I've heard your name . . ." Then her lip curled with distaste and she went on. "You're Lord Brookville's daughter, the one who bore a child out of wedlock." She cast a scornful glance at Theo. "Leave this house at once. Both of you."

"Gladly." Julia grasped Theo's hand and started briskly toward the door. Gresham wouldn't dare murder them in front of his cousin.

"Oh, no you don't," he said, darting to block her path.

"The boy is mine, and I'm taking him to see my father."

"Yours?" Her expression aghast, Evelyn regarded Theo, who peeked around the edge of Julia's skirts. "I don't believe it."

"Then you don't know his true character," Julia said, hoping to recruit Evelyn's help. "He's a vile man, and he wouldn't hesitate to use force on an unwilling woman, if you understand my meaning."

Ignoring Julia, Evelyn walked around her to study Theo closely. "He *does* resemble the portrait of Henry in Uncle's chamber, now that you point it out. In fact, the likeness is quite startling."

"There now, you see?" Gresham said. "I thought it only fitting that Father should see his only grandson before he dies."

Evelyn's lovely face twisted with anger. "So that's what this is all about. You're hoping Uncle will change his will back into your favor. You want the money he's promised to me."

Gresham attempted a cajoling smile. "Don't look at me like that, Evie. You've millions of your own. Why would you want to claim my rightful inheritance, too?"

"Better it should go to me than to the owner of some gaming hell." She waved her fingers dismissively. "But go on, take your bastard in there. Uncle will suffer a heart spasm. He'll die on the spot, and then it will be too late to change the legal papers, anyway."

While they quarreled, Julia manipulated the brooch in her palm, keeping her hand hidden in the side of her skirt. Theo stood listening with rapt attention, and she pulled him close, nudging him toward the doorway, where Gresham stood.

She might never have a better chance.

Gresham's attention remained focused on his cousin. "Then for good measure, I'll tell Father that Lady Julia and I are getting married. She ran off eight years ago, and I've searched for her ever since. Now that I've found her, we'll be a happy family—*argh*!"

He yowled as Julia plunged the long pin of the brooch deep into his thigh. While he staggered backward, doubled over and clutching his leg, she pushed Theo out the door. "Run, Theo! Run ahead!"

Her son stared wide-eyed for a heartbeat. Then he scampered in the direction of the staircase, with Julia right behind him.

But Gresham recovered enough to lunge at her. He caught hold of her cloak, yanking backward, choking her. She stumbled, lost momentum, and staggered sideways. The iron bar of his arm closed around her waist, and she felt his hot, panting breath on her neck.

Along with the cold muzzle of the pistol.

On a misty dawn a week ago, Lord B. and Col. J.D. met in a secluded area of Hyde Park, to fight a duel with pistols, after Lord B. accused the colonel of cheating at cards . . .
—*The Rogue Report*

Chapter Twenty-six

"Have you gone completely mad?" Evelyn asked her cousin, as he dragged Julia back into the bedchamber. "What do you think you're doing?"

Julia didn't resist, didn't dare to make a false move lest the pistol discharge. But at least Theo had obeyed her and escaped. Theo! Would he run outside—or ask a servant in the house for help? What if she'd sent him into worse danger?

"I've every right to seize the chit." Gresham spoke gutturally, through clenched teeth. "Did you see how she attacked me? God Almighty, I'm bleeding."

Julia caught a glimpse of Evelyn's blond head as she bent down to inspect the wound.

"Only a bit," she pronounced. "Well, it serves you right for trying to maneuver her and the boy—and my uncle. Now put down that pistol and release her at once."

Julia was beginning to like Jack's ex-fiancée.

"I'll do no such thing," he growled. "Fetch me a sash

from one of your dressing gowns. I'm tying her up. Then I'll see about finding the brat."

Instead of heeding his directive, Evelyn walked across the bedchamber to the mantelpiece, where a long velvet rope dangled. "I believe *this* cord will work better." Then she gave it a hard yank.

Gresham's arm tightened convulsively around Julia's middle. "Blast you, Evie! Why'd you summon a servant?"

"Someone needs to put an end to your folly. I'll send my maid for a pair of stout footmen. And another to Bow Street to fetch the constable."

"You'll be arrested for kidnapping Theo," Julia added. "As proof, I have the notes you left at the school." He needn't know she'd burned the second one according to his instructions.

"I'll kill your son first," Gresham hissed. "And then I'll see *you* in hell—"

"Well, well," said an amused male voice from the doorway. "What have we here?"

At that familiar deep tone, Julia's heart did a flip. Heedless of the gun, she turned her head to see Jack leaning against the doorframe, his arms folded and his tousled dark hair giving him a rakish air.

No, not Jack. The Earl of Rutledge. In his tailored brown coat, form-fitting buckskins, and knee-high boots, he looked every inch the nobleman. And he was smiling, the two-faced toad. Smiling at the sight of her being held captive!

"Jack?" Gresham said in obvious astonishment. "What the devil are you doing here?"

"Better I should ask the questions." As if he were inspecting a curiosity in a museum, Jack strolled into the bedchamber. "Are you having to hold women at gunpoint these days, Gresham? It doesn't say much for your ability to charm the fairer sex."

"I caught the chit trying to steal my cousin's emerald brooch. She stabbed me with it. Tell him, Evie."

Her lips thinned, Evelyn glared at the man she had spurned. "How dare you enter my bedchamber. You and George probably planned this scheme together!"

His dimples deepened. "I assure you, my dear, I've haven't seen your cousin but once this past fortnight. I've been very busy, and Lady Julia can corroborate that fact."

Evelyn raised an eyebrow at Julia. "You two know each other?"

"I operate a school for impoverished children," Julia said stiffly, suspicious of Jack's motive for revealing their association. "Lord Rutledge recently took a post there as a mathematics instructor under the false name of William Jackman."

Despite the gun at her neck, she cast a challenging glare at Jack. Now he would show his true colors. He would tell these two about her authorship of *The Rogue Report*. He would expose her to society and ruin her newsletter.

Gresham gave a start of surprise. "Jackman? *You're* Mr. Jackman? I don't believe it. You'd never soil your hands with common labor."

"What humbug," Evelyn said with an unladylike snort. "The two of you must have been off on a tryst somewhere."

"You're wrong," Jack stated, his gaze on Julia—or perhaps on the pistol. "I'll admit, I began my work at the Corwyn Academy merely as a whim. You see, I've always enjoyed inventing numerical puzzles—"

"Nonsense," Gresham said on an incredulous laugh. "You've never cracked a book since you left Eton in disgrace."

"Rather, I've taken great pains to hide my interest in intellectual pursuits. But over the past few weeks, I've discovered that I have an aptitude for teaching children. And something else happened during the course of my work. I fell madly in love with the headmistress."

Julia experienced a jolt of pain that had nothing to do with Gresham's tight hold on her. Why was Jack continuing the charade? Or was he for once telling the truth?

Even if he was, it didn't matter. The enormity of his deception couldn't be dismissed at the snap of a finger. Nor could a public declaration of love change who he was, a debt-ridden scoundrel with a taste for loose women and a compulsion to gamble.

"Do you mean *her?*" Evelyn said with such scorn that Julia instantly reverted to disliking her again.

"Indeed I do." Jack sauntered closer. "Julia is the love of my life. Which is why I take exception to anyone putting a gun to her head."

Now that he was near, Julia could see how mistaken she was about his nonchalance. A dangerous fury burned in his green eyes. He radiated menace from the hard line of his jaw to his aggressive stance.

Gresham must have realized it, too, for his breathing grew harsh. He lowered the gun and released his hold on Julia. "I—I didn't mean anything by it, old chap. I had no idea she was your woman."

Julia spun around to face him. The sweet relief of freedom poured through her, yet perversely, she was irked that he would heed Jack, and not her. "I'm not his woman," she snapped. "Now, hand me the pistol."

"I'm keeping it." His wild gaze darting from one person to another, Gresham looked as if he didn't know where to point the weapon. Not at her, not at his cousin, and certainly not at Jack.

"Rather, you'll give it to me," Jack commanded, holding out his hand.

Gresham hesitated, his manner distinctly jittery. His

fear of Jack was palpable, and clearly he didn't want to antagonize him.

"Go on," Jack drawled. "*I* would never shoot an unarmed man—or woman. It isn't sporting. Besides, you've never showed that pistol to me, and I confess to having an interest in it."

"It belongs to my father," Gresham admitted, giving Jack the gun with a show of reluctance. "I had to pawn my own set of pistols in order to pay an installment on my debt to Sefton."

Jack turned the dueling pistol over in his hands. "How very odd. I recently found an identical one. You wouldn't happen to have lost its mate, would you?"

Gresham froze. In the lamplight, his high brow shone with sweat. "What? That night . . . my God, Rutledge. It was *you* in the garden."

"Indeed so," Julia said. "And I'm taking this pistol as evidence for the magistrate."

She marched to Jack, prepared to wrest it from him, but he gave her the weapon without a murmur. He kept his gaze trained on Gresham while speaking to her. "Go to Theo, Julia. He's waiting downstairs on my orders. You, too, Evelyn. I'll handle this matter."

"Handle?" Gresham said in obvious alarm. "Everything's settled, no one's been harmed."

"I'm staying," Evelyn said waspishly. "You've no right to evict me from my own bedchamber."

At that moment, a young serving maid stepped into the doorway. "M'lady, ye rung?"

"Yes," Evelyn said, sailing toward the girl. "I need a footman to eject Lord Rutledge from this house. And tell another one to bring a length of stout rope here to tie up my cousin."

"M-m'lady?"

"Don't stand there gawking." When the maid remained

paralyzed, Evelyn seized her by the collar. "Oh, for pity's sake, I'll give the order myself!"

As they headed out into the corridor, Jack called out, "Don't worry, Evelyn. Your cousin and I are merely going to discuss what happened at a certain masquerade ball a few years ago." He lowered his voice to an ominous murmur. "Aren't we, Gresham?"

Gresham, who had been examining the seeping bloodstain on his breeches, straightened up and turned chalk white. "What—what do you mean? If Lady Julia has made accusations, they're lies. I swear it!"

Pistol in hand, Julia had been about to go and assure herself of Theo's safety, but she turned back in a fury. "You forced yourself on Bella. At least have the decency to admit your crime!"

"I'll do no such thing. She gave herself freely!"

Jack removed his coat and tossed it onto the bed. "Did I hear you correctly? Are you calling Lady Julia a liar?"

"No! That girl—*she* lied. She claimed to be Lady Julia's sister. I—I didn't even know she *had* a younger sister." His faintly puzzled gaze darted to Julia, who didn't correct his mistaken notion about Bella's age. "She wanted to play a game. Catch the princess, she said. She teased me, led me on a merry chase."

Julia groped for the back of a chair to steady herself. Now she remembered Gresham's costume that night. He had outfitted himself as a prince, complete with gold crown and rich medieval garb. When Bella had escaped Eliza's watchful eyes and encountered him in the corridor, she must have believed him part of a fairy tale come true.

Oh, Bella! She was too naïve to knowingly entice a man.

To protect her sister, Julia told a lie of her own. "She died giving birth to your son. Was *that* part of your game?"

Jack stepped toward Gresham. "Answer the lady."

Limping badly, Gresham retreated from Jack's advance. "Hold right there, Rutledge. You know how it is when a female leads you on. I couldn't stop myself."

"Certainly. I can't stop myself right now, either."

Jack's fist flashed out and caught Gresham squarely in the jaw. The crack echoed through the bedchamber. The man staggered backward, knocking over a small rosewood table and sending a vase crashing to the floor.

"That was for Bella," Jack said. "But it wasn't nearly enough."

In swift succession, he landed several more solid blows. Gresham struck back viciously, but Jack parried the worst of the attack. Within moments, Gresham slumped to the floor, his nose streaming blood and his mouth swelling. "I'm sorry," he mumbled on a groan. "Is that what you want? An apology?"

"There's also the matter of your breaking into Julia's school," Jack said, looming over him. "What were you looking for? Proof of Theo's birth, I'll wager. So you could see if he'd been born nine months after you raped Bella."

"The boy resembles Henry . . . all I want is for my father to see him . . . have pity, you know how badly I need to secure my inheritance."

"So you abducted a seven-year-old boy and locked him up in your cellar while you tried to force him to do your bidding." Jack hauled Gresham to his feet. "This is for Theo."

Lightning swift, he bashed him hard in one ear, then the other, causing Gresham to throw up his arms in a vain effort to protect himself. He stumbled against a chair and sagged down into it.

"Come now, at least fight back," Jack taunted. "When Theo wouldn't cooperate, you decided to capture Julia as well. I haven't yet had the satisfaction of punishing you for *that*."

He proceeded to pummel Gresham with a series of blows to the abdomen that had him doubled over and moaning, babbling for surcease. "Didn't know," Gresham muttered, panting. "I shwear it. Didn't know Lady Julia belonged to you."

I don't belong to him, she wanted to shout. But there was no point in speaking. Neither man would heed her, anyway. Especially not Jack, who clearly believed he still had the right to claim her as his.

Jack was going to win. Of course he would win. He was bigger and stronger, more skilled with his fists. She should walk away now, find Theo, leave this house.

Nevertheless, Julia stayed and watched in fascinated revulsion. She rejoiced to see Gresham bloodied and beaten, exulted in the sight of Jack committing raw violence on her behalf.

Then a movement from the doorway shattered the spell.

Theo was peeking into the bedchamber. His eyes were huge and brown in his freckled face, his attention fixed on the fighting men.

She hastened to his side, calling over her shoulder, "That's enough, Jack. I won't have his death on my hands."

"Then let it be on mine," Jack said gratingly, and landed another well-aimed blow. "He isn't through suffering for what he did to you."

Julia caught Theo and shielded his view. "This is *my* fight, not yours. And *I* say it's finished!"

Jack hauled off with one more mighty clout that sent Gresham crashing to the floor, where he lay unmoving and unconscious on the plush blue carpet.

"There," Jack said, flexing his skinned knuckles and

planting one booted foot on the fallen man's back. "*Now* I'm done."

Theo broke free and ran to him. "Mr. Jackman, you trounced him. Pow, pow! I saw it!"

"I thought I told you to wait downstairs." Jack gave him a stern look, then relented with a grin, ruffling Theo's hair. "But never mind. It's all over now. The rascal won't hurt you or your mother ever again."

Jack sent her a concentrated stare that conveyed an unmistakable possessiveness. It awakened all the wild longing that had persisted despite his trickery. She wanted to cleanse the angry welt on his cheek, to wipe the blood that trickled from a corner of his mouth. At the same time, she despised his aura of the conquering hero. Did he expect her to cast herself adoringly into his arms and announce that all was forgiven?

It wouldn't happen. Nothing had changed. Jack was still a gambler, still a miscreant, still an indolent nobleman. And she could never allow her son to grow up under the influence of a scoundrel. The very thought horrified her.

"Theo, come with me. We're going home now."

He dawdled, his head tilted back to regard Jack with hope. "Are you going with us, Mr. Jackman? Please?"

"It may be impossible. Wait out in the corridor. I need to speak to your mother alone."

As Theo trudged out into the passageway, Jack kept his gaze on her. He was asking her with his eyes. Begging her to reconsider. And for a moment, Julia felt so heartsore she considered tossing aside all her scruples.

Blast his charm!

"I'm grateful for your help tonight," she said coolly. "But there's really no need for further discussion between us."

When she walked past him, he caught hold of her wrist. "I meant what I said about teaching, Julia. I want to return to the school. If you'll let me back into your life, I'll give up all my vices. I'll try to be a better man for you. I swear it to you."

"And you expect me to take you at your word?" Shaking off his hand, she drew a quivery breath. "I'm sorry, Jack, it would never work. I fell in love with a fantasy. I don't even know who you are."

Then she turned her back on him and walked away.

Having no funds with which to pay off the dun collectors, Mr. G.G. has been sent to debtors' prison for a period of six years.
—*The Rogue Report*

Chapter Twenty-seven

The Duke of Wycliffe was enjoying a rare, lucid day. In his pale green brocaded coat and old-fashioned white wig, he appeared robust and hale, exactly as Jack remembered him from childhood. They sat in the library at Wycliffe House, sipping brandy, listening to the rain sluice down the windows, and talking about Julia.

Or rather, Jack was talking about Julia. His tongue loosened by drink, he had poured out the whole story, beginning with the article in *The Rogue Report* and his plot to expose her as the author, moving on to his stint as a schoolteacher, and ending with Gresham seizing Theo. The only detail Jack had left out was Bella. That was one secret too vital to tell another living soul.

When he reached the part about Julia refusing to give him a second chance, his vision blurred. He fumbled for the decanter on the table. At last he understood why people craved drink. Brandy, he had discovered these past four days, helped to dull the pain of heartbreak.

His grandfather moved the decanter out of his reach. "No more for you. You've had enough."

Jack struggled to focus. "What the devil? Afraid I'll clean out your supply? I'll buy you some more."

"No, you young fool. I don't want you to end up like me, that's all." Wycliffe's hazel eyes turned watery, and he leaned over to grasp Jack's hand in his bony fist. "Don't do it, my boy. Don't turn into a lonely old drunkard. Fight to get her back."

Jack slouched in his chair and gazed at his empty glass. "How can I? She won't even speak to me."

"So write her a letter."

"A letter?"

"Hell, why not?" Wycliffe looked out at the gray, rain-soaked garden. "Same thing happened with your mother, she refused to talk to Charles. So I told'm to write, but he refused. Your sire had too blasted much pride to make amends with her."

Wycliffe had never spoken of the trouble between Jack's parents, and Jack found himself immensely curious. "I never saw them together as a child. Why did they quarrel?"

"She caught him with his mistress right after you were born. A man has a right to do as he pleases, he said, and I'm shamed to admit he'd learned that at my knee. So she packed her bags and took you to Willowford Hall. And Charles said 'twould be a cold day in hell before he went begging to his wife." The duke snorted. "'Tis why you've no brothers or sisters."

Jack understood pride. "A letter won't help matters," he said, setting down his empty glass before he hurled it at the wall. "Julia will simply burn it."

"Then write her another and another. B'gad, she should see my grandson for the fine man he is."

For once, Jack couldn't be cheered by Wycliffe's assessment. He kept remembering her final words.

I don't even know who you are.

Little wonder she mistrusted his promises. Julia had no way of separating fact from fiction. But if she refused to see him, how was she ever to know him as the Earl of Rutledge? How was she to realize that the rogue portrayed in her scandal sheet was merely a mask, too? How was she to understand that he had shown her his true character already—with Theo, with Bella, and most of all with Julia herself?

The notion of revealing every wretched detail of his life scared the bejesus out of him. He would only be reinforcing her ill opinion of him. But he had sunk to the bottom of a dark pit without a glimmer of light.

What the hell did he have to lose by trying?

The first letter arrived five days after Theo's abduction.

Julia had stopped in the ballroom to observe a rehearsal of the play the students would be performing in a few weeks. The rain had kept everyone inside for the past few days. As she watched Theo strut across the makeshift stage, playing the part of a street urchin with a swagger reminiscent of Jack's, she wished she could blame her low mood on the gloomy weather.

At least her son had suffered no ill effects; he'd reveled in his newfound stature as hero of the school. Even Clifford had been in awe that Theo had been held at gunpoint, that he'd seen Mr. Jackman trounce Theo's abductor. And they'd all been abuzz to learn the mathematics teacher was really the Earl of Rutledge.

It wasn't Rutledge she mourned, but William Jackman. No matter how much she despised his deception, his absence had left an aching hole in her life. She missed his smiles, his quick wit, and oh, heaven, his kisses . . .

Someone tugged on her skirt. She looked down to see one of the younger students, golden-haired Kitty, clad in the white costume of an angel. She was so timid, her approach had surprised Julia.

Crouching down, she asked, "Yes, darling?"

Kitty tiptoed closer to whisper in Julia's ear. "Will Mr. Jackman come to see me in the play?"

Oh, no. Hiding her anguish, Julia stroked Kitty's silken cheek. "I'm afraid he's gone away for good."

Her blue eyes filled with tears. "But I want to tell him that I can write my name now. K-i-t-t-y." She traced the letters in the air.

"I'm very proud of you," Julia said, giving her a hug. "Your mama will be, too. She'll be here for the play. And she'll think you're the prettiest angel on stage."

Looking cheered, Kitty ran back to the other children.

Julia straightened up, wishing it were so easy to distract herself. Lately, everything conspired to remind her of Jack. Seeing the carriage house from her bedroom window. Entering her office and remembering their first time together. Walking past his old classroom and half expecting to glimpse his roguish smile.

Would she ever accustom herself to his replacement, stout Miss Dickenson with her doughy face and pinched mouth?

"The post, m'lady."

Agnes was handing her a letter. As the maid walked away and Julia glanced down at the distinctive black penmanship, time seemed to freeze. The laughter and chatter of the children died away into nothingness. Feverishly turning the missive over, she ran her fingertip over the red seal with its distinctive *R*.

Rutledge.

Somehow, she managed to walk out of the ballroom. Her legs had all the consistency of melted butter. Why would Jack write to her? To ask for another chance? To tell her more lies in hopes of working his wiles on her?

She would never allow it. Although he had worked here for a fortnight, he had been driven by the purpose of discovering her secrets. But a scoundrel couldn't survive as a maths teacher. Not for years to come. He would miss his freewheeling life, grow weary of the routine. It was too absurd to think otherwise.

Nor would she ever return to his world.

Nevertheless, she did believe Jack loved her in his own way. The intensity of feeling in his eyes had not been a pretense. And when he'd had the opportunity to betray her secrets to Gresham, he hadn't done so. He had kept the confidences that she had entrusted to him.

But he also had gaming debts up to his gorgeous dimples. He went to wild parties and consorted with light-skirts. Men like him never changed—only look at his reprobate grandfather, the Duke of Wycliffe.

Angered by his presumption in writing to her, she tightened her fingers around the letter. By the heavens, she ought to burn it unread!

The short, ugly, black-haired man scurried out of the shrubbery, where he had been lying in wait outside Jack's town house. Avid fortitude on his badgerlike face, he thrust a paper at Jack as he returned from a visit to his banker.

"M'lord, a moment of your time, if you will. My employer begs payment on this invoice. 'Tis six months in arrears."

The old Jack would have fobbed off the man with a careless promise. But today, he examined the sum and deplored his former extravagance at the bootmaker's. "I'll settle it now. Follow me."

"Aye, m'lord!"

Striding up the steps and into the house, Jack reflected on the grim state of his finances. He had spent the past few days tallying all of his bills and searching for ways to cover the payments. The amount he still owed was staggering. He received a tidy quarterly income from Willowford Hall, but even so, it would take years to settle all the debts.

Years!

In his office, he counted out the gold, gave it the badger, and deducted another sum from the ledger. When the man had gone, Jack sat at his desk and pinched the bridge of his nose. That was it, the last of the two thousand he had won shortly after he'd begun his stint at the Corwyn Academy.

You could do it again, temptation whispered. *You could win it all in one night of lucky play.*

The allure of the cards was so strong he could almost taste it. He could feel himself sweating with the effort to resist. So he closed his eyes and pictured Julia's horror that he would use her fortune to finance his gaming habit.

Somehow, he had to climb out of this hole alone, without risking further losses. The trouble was, he had no more resources at his disposal.

Except for one.

Julia curled up in a comfortable chair in her bedchamber to read Jack's latest letter. She lifted it to her face and caught a trace of his spicy scent. She was exceedingly foolish to torture herself.

Again and again.

Each day for the past fortnight, he had written her a long letter. He had told her about his childhood, how he and his mother had lived together at Willowford Hall. She had been a civilizing influence in his young life. She had taught him proper manners, required him to study hard, and made him treat the servants with respect.

In another, he had related how, after his mother's death when he'd been ten, he had gone to live with his father and grandfather. They had allowed him to do exactly as he pleased, eating sweets for breakfast, ignoring his schoolbooks, going to bed at midnight. And as he'd grown older, he'd adopted their profligate ways.

In yet another, he had recounted his experiences as a gambler, what the cards meant to him, how he craved the sense of excitement, the thrill of turning over a card to find a winner. He had depicted a life spent in idle pursuits, where people were revered according to their pedigree and their bank account, a life she remembered too well.

In subsequent letters, he had written about his stint here at the Corwyn Academy. He had described the shock of having to adhere to a schedule, of facing a classroom full of students and having no notion how to teach. He had related comical tales about the children, and had asked about all of them, especially Theo.

In persuasive prose, he had conveyed his feelings for Julia, too, his gradual change from plotting her downfall to desiring her love. That letter had come yesterday, and although Julia knew better than to let him get under her skin, afterward she had indulged in a good, long cry.

Jack claimed to have changed his ways, but how could she believe him? He was a silver-tongued devil. He knew exactly how to charm women, how to wear down their defenses. And he was doing it to her, letter by letter.

She wanted him desperately. She thought about him every moment of every day and dreamed about him at night. But although it had been wonderful to love Jack, loving the Earl of Rutledge was impossible. How could he possibly give up his world for hers? How could a man like him truly alter the habits of a lifetime?

Nevertheless, she broke the seal on the new letter and scanned the text. Today, he had written at length about meeting Bella, the protectiveness he'd felt for her, and his realization of Julia's purpose in publishing *The Rogue*

Report. Then he explained why he'd taken her to Willowford Hall afterward, that he had been keen to reveal at
least one true portion of his life, to show her where he'd
grown up. And he was glad he had done so because. . . .

Julia blinked in shock. The letter slipped from her
nerveless fingers and fell to her lap.

Oh, dear God, he had sold Willowford Hall.

On rare occasions, there are those rogues who are willing to reform their wicked ways. For a shining example, one has only to look at the Earl of Rutledge . . .

—*The Rogue Report*

Chapter Twenty-eight

His jaw set, Jack drove up the long drive with its border of willows. Returning here had not been in his plans for the day.

But when he had visited the Wimbledon office of his estate agent to sign the final papers, Hathaway had been gone. His secretary, a nervous man who had shuffled papers convulsively, had informed Jack that the meeting would take place at Willowford Hall. Apparently, the wealthy young couple who had purchased the furnished house and its surrounding farmland had forgotten to check the condition of the attic.

The attic! What the devil difference did *that* make?

Jack didn't want to see the house again. He had already made his peace with selling the place. He had come here a few days ago to make arrangements for shipping the few pieces that held sentimental value. He had bade goodbye to Mrs. Davies.

Now he'd have to face her tears again, and God knew,

he didn't look forward to consoling another weeping woman.

The house came into view. Built of honey-colored stone, it stood on a hill surrounded by a sweeping green lawn and thickets of trees, their leaves bright with the reds and oranges of autumn. He saw the tall, mullioned windows where he had peered out longingly on rainy days, and the porch where he had played jacks as a child.

But today he replaced his pride of ownership with stony indifference. He rode straight to the front portico, dismounted from his bay horse, and tied the reins to the iron post, next to an unfamiliar black phaeton that must belong to the Dudleys.

Jack wondered briefly if he should knock, then decided against it. Since the papers weren't signed yet, he still had the right to open the door this one last time.

Afternoon sunlight flooded the entrance hall. Hearing the murmur of voices from the drawing room, he strode across the rose-veined marble, his boot heels clicking with his determination to complete the transfer of the deed.

He wouldn't let himself dwell on the memory of bringing Julia here. He had made his decision. Now he wanted it over with and done.

The first item in his line of vision was the boyhood portrait of himself still in place over the fireplace. Dammit, he'd instructed the agent to remove all his mother's paintings. They should already have been shipped to his London town house.

A little figurine sat on the mantelpiece. Bella's dragon? It couldn't be. He'd left it in the curricle all those weeks ago . . .

Then he noticed the woman sitting beside the balding agent on the yellow striped settee. And he froze in mid-step.

"Lord Rutledge." Rising, Julia came toward him, smiling warmly as if greeting an acquaintance at a ball. She offered her kid-gloved hand. "What a pleasure to see you again."

Jack took her hand, held it to assure himself she was real. He had dreamed of those smoky blue eyes and the dark upswept hair, the riotous curls framing the perfect oval of her face. But he couldn't get his mind around the shock of her presence. "Why are you here? Where are the Dudleys?"

"Lady Julia has topped their price," Mr. Hathaway said, bouncing up from his seat, a gray-haired man of well-fed proportions. "By a tidy sum, I might add. She wanted to surprise you."

Jack was speechless. His jaw dropped. Was this some sort of elaborate hoax to pay him back for duping her?

But revenge wasn't her style. *He* was the trickster, not she.

Her hand felt small and delicate, yet she gripped his fingers with the firmness of strength. And still, he couldn't figure out her purpose.

"Why?" he asked hoarsely. "Why are you buying my house?"

"It's a wedding gift." She gazed at him steadily. "From me to you."

What? Now he *was* dreaming!

Mr. Hathaway stepped forward. "Why, my lord, you could have knocked me over with a feather when I heard the news! You never mentioned you were engaged to be wed. And to such a lovely lady."

Julia turned her head toward him. "Perhaps you'd better give us a few moments alone."

"Certainly." The agent rubbed his rotund belly, which strained against the brass buttons on his waistcoat. "I'll just toddle off to the kitchen to see what Mrs. Davies has prepared for tea."

He left the drawing room. His footsteps died away into silence.

Her heart in her throat, Julia watched the play of emotions on Jack's handsome face. She saw strength of character there now, not just the charm of a scoundrel. He looked alternately incredulous and delighted and chagrined, and she waited for him to absorb the shock.

Then he frowned and strode to the window, his manner agitated. But she had expected as much. He was a man, after all, and men had their pride.

He swung to face her, and a muscle worked in his jaw. "I want to marry you, Julia. More than anything in the world. But dammit, I was going to call on you tomorrow. To tell you that I'd cleared my debts, that I had enough left over to invest, and that I wasn't coming to you empty-handed." He raked his fingers through his hair, giving himself a rumpled look. "But now it's *your* money. It's *you* who'll be paying off my debts. I won't have it."

She went to him, took his hand again, rubbed her fingers across his hard knuckles. "After reading your letters, I understand what this house means to you. You shouldn't have to give it up for me."

"I want to give it up. To stand on my own two feet and not live off your bequest. It's important to me, Julia. It wasn't before, but it is now."

She lifted his hand and kissed it, the hand that had landed blows in her defense and had stroked her with great tenderness. "Compromise is important in a marriage. So is trust and devotion, and when I heard you were selling the house, I knew just how determined you were to change for my sake. That's all that matters to me."

Jack continued to scowl. "It's for my own sake, too. I was on the wrong path, and you showed me the right way. Which is why I don't approve of what you've done."

Stubborn man! But she could be stubborn, too. And she knew exactly how to ease him into acceptance.

She stepped back, peeled off her kid gloves. "When I'm here, I'm much closer to Bella. I'll be able to visit her more often."

"I won't be swayed, Julia."

"Think of it as an investment for the school, then. Our students deserve the occasional holiday, the chance to leave the city for a few weeks. This place seems perfect, wouldn't you agree?"

"Don't try to get around me by using the children, either."

Hiding a smile, she walked to the doorway of the drawing room. "Of course, we would have to make a few changes. An office for me. Extra tables and benches in the dining chamber. And more beds upstairs, of course."

Much to her pleasure, he stalked after her. "You can't write *The Rogue Report* from here."

"On the contrary. Elfrida has offered to collect the information from the maids and send it to me." Giving him a come-hither look over her shoulder, Julia started toward the stairway. "We'll also need to inspect the nursery. It won't be long before Theo has a brother or sister."

Jack stood absolutely still. Then he raced after her, placed his hands on her shoulders, and gave her the dazed stare of a man just informed of impending fatherhood. "You can't mean—"

"I do." Smiling tremulously, she took his hand, nesting it between hers and her womb. "Are you as happy as I am?"

"My God, Julia. Must you ask? I want very much to have a family with you." He wrapped her in his arms, kissing her with such great tenderness that she felt the joy of coming home after a long journey. They were one heart, one body, one soul.

When at last he drew back, she said breathlessly, "So will you marry me or not, Jack? Because if the answer is no, I'll need to find myself another rake to reform."

He grinned. "Like hell I'll let you consort with scoundrels. No scoundrel but me, that is. We're getting married as soon as I can secure a special license."

"You aren't a scoundrel, not anymore." She traced his beloved features, the indentations on either side of that beautiful mouth. "You're the finest man I know, Jack. I can't imagine myself loving anyone else."

"And I intend to spend the rest of my life making you proud of me. I'm going to keep teaching, and I'll publish that book of number puzzles for Theo. In fact, I've just thought of another." Those gorgeous green eyes smiled into hers. "When does two plus two equal one?"

She thought about it. The answer came to her in a flash. "Two parents plus two children equal one family. Oh, Jack, that's so clever."

"You inspire me," he said, giving her that smoldering look she knew so well. "Shall we inspect the bedchambers, then?"

As they started up the staircase, their arms around each other, Julia reflected that marriage to a rogue would suit her very well, indeed.